EXPERTUS

THE GENEX SERIES

BOOK TWO

HOLLY LAUREN

EXPERTUS: THE GENEX SAGA (BOOK TWO)

by
Holly Lauren

Published by Howling Wolf
(An Imprint of Ravenswood Publishing)

HOWLING WOLF

1275 Baptist Chapel Rd.
Autryville, NC 28318
http://www.ravenswoodpublishing.com
Email: RavenswoodPublishing@gmail.com

Paperback orders can be made through Createspace
http://www.createspace.com

Printed in the United States of American
Second Edition
10 9 8 7 6 5 4 3 2 1

ISBN-13: 978-0692273005
ISBN-10: 069227300X

The GenEx Saga by Holly Lauren

(Book One) *Tempus*
(Book Two) *Expertus*
(Book Three) *Veritas*

Dedicated to the one and only Henry Watson—a man I am proud to call Dad and blessed to call Friend.

You took copies of my first book to all your poker games and golf tournaments and gave them out to your buddies.

Your love is boundless, and I am better because of it.

I love you!

EXPERTUS

Expertus - Test

"Si vis pacem, para bellum."
If you want peace, prepare for war.
(-Vegetius)

CHAPTER ONE

Zay's eyes skated along the perimeter of the crowded restaurant before he returned his attention to his dinner guests.

He was habitually vigilant.

Chapel liked that about him. Liked how his tall frame hummed with energy, even when he was sitting, like now. Chapel knew he could be on his feet in a breath, incapacitating any threat before half a minute brushed off the clock.

She watched Zay's reflection in a mirror over the bar as he brought a cup to his mouth and took a long, indulgent drink, laughing at something Rush or Marielle just said.

Running a hand down the back of her auburn bob—a wig—Chapel stood. She left a cash tip and slipped from her stool.

Cigar smoke hung in the air like a fog. It stung her eyes and throat, but she breathed slowly, almost relishing in the ache. She enjoyed this part more than she cared to admit—stalking the prey.

The men in the room had loosened the knots on their ties, and the women were languishing in their chairs. It was late, but Chapel's mind was alert, her muscles taut.

A set of bookcases divided the bar area from the dining room, and Chapel dipped behind the one adjacent to Zay's table.

It was loud, but as long as she leaned her head their direction, she could hear most of what was said.

"I think a Seer would round out our team," Marielle was saying. "I heard Gabriel Luxe is training a new recruit who never misses."

"We don't need a Seer," Rush said, sounding more aggressive than normal. "We need Peaches."

Marielle made a gagging sound. "You're worse than Zay."

Chapel shifted so she could see them. Through the crevice between two thick books, she had a partially obscured view of the three of them.

"All I know is," Rush said, "that girl has trained more in the last eight weeks than you've trained in the last eight months."

Marielle's full lips tugged downward in a pout. "I don't like to sweat."

Zay finished his drink and leaned forward. "Neither does Chapel. But she doesn't like to lose more."

Marielle's dark hair swayed with the slow shake of her head. "I can't decide if she's really *that* good or if you're really *that* whipped."

Rush moaned. "Dang, Marielle. Aren't you tired of these entry-level missions? Spying on potential recruits? The *occasional* fist fight?"

Zay rubbed a hand down the side of his jaw. He'd shaved. "I am. I'm ready for our team to move to the next level." His eyes touched Rush's, then Marielle's. "With Chapel as an asset, Jackson will have us upgraded to a Field Team before the end of the year."

Marielle twirled her straw in her drink, around and around. "If she weren't your girlfriend, would you be campaigning so hard to have her join us?"

Rush smacked a hand on Zay's back and laughed. "Of course he would. Have you seen the legs on that girl?"

"Watch yourself, Lopez," Zay said.

"And if I don't?"

Zay touched the cufflinks at his wrists. "We'll go outside and settle it like gentlemen."

Rush's mouth twisted in amusement. "My boy, you ain't never settled *anything* like a gentleman."

Their server came by and Rush ordered several desserts. He gave a big yawn, settling back into his seat and nodding at Marielle.

"What's your problem with Peaches, anyway?" he asked once they were alone again. "I thought the two of you had come to some sort of an agreement."

Marielle speared a piece of rare steak and bit into it with her front teeth. Chapel grimaced. They had been sitting so long it had to be frigid.

"You know, I ask myself that question a lot." She chewed thoughtfully. "I think it has to do with how she comes off— all concerned and wide-eyed. She's like bubble gum. Sweet at first, then it loses its flavor."

"On that happy note." Zay stood and headed in the direction of the bathroom.

It was time.

Chapel closed her eyes and let their conversation melt into the innumerable ambient noises around her: the sound of glass connecting with glass, the undertones of hushed voices, the burn of cigar paper.

Goose bumps swept across her body and she sucked in a breath.

Easing around the bookshelf, Chapel approached the table on Marielle's side. She wasn't worried about being seen—she had watched Marielle train.

Marielle spent so much time worrying about what was behind her that she rarely registered anything in front of her face. That was true for all areas of Marielle's life.

Walking while preparing to use Tempus was a lot like walking and needing to pee. It made Chapel jittery and stiff. That was why, when a server dashed out in front of her with a tray full of drinks, Chapel was thrown off balance.

Or maybe it was the fact that she was an amateur at four-inch heels.

"Excuse me," she said, using the shelf to keep herself upright.

She needed to hurry. She had altered Zay's drink before it left the bar, and its result would be fast acting.

It would prompt a visit to the restroom, induce nausea, and—depending on how much he'd eaten—knock him out for five to ten minutes.

She only needed three.

Anticipation and anxiety clashed inside of her. She couldn't suppress the growing pool of energy any longer.

Chapel blinked for a breath longer than normal, and when her green eyes fluttered opened, everything around her was still and quiet.

She had done it—*Tempus.*

Chapel knew now that she wasn't actually *freezing* time. As Rush had explained to her on more than one occasion (and once with a crude drawing), the explosion of energy her body released during an episode had a paralytic effect on most objects around her.

Leaning her neck from side to side, Chapel focused on pushing through the burn in her thighs. It was getting easier to take immediate action after Tempus, but Chapel's body still resisted.

Jackson said it was because her muscles were convulsing after the exhaustion of her own energy, and that eventually they would grow accustomed to the phenomenon and relent.

Rush said she was just out of shape.

Chapel crossed to their table and reached inside the pocket of Rush's suit jacket. Easily, she found what she needed—a silver chain attached to a tarnished watch. It had been his grandfather's, and inside it was a faded photograph of his parents. She unhooked it from its clip and slipped it into her purse.

Marielle was simple. She had a Japanese butterfly comb holding up one side of her black satin hair. The wings were encrusted with tiny diamonds and pearls, and its antennae were sapphires the same gray blue as Zay's eyes.

Appropriate, since he had given it to her for her birthday.

Chapel tugged the piece from Marielle's hair and tossed it beside Rush's pocket watch.

"Bubble gum," Chapel mumbled. She unwrapped a piece that she had in her purse.

She chewed it until it was good and slobbery before taking it out and sticking the wad inside Marielle's half-open mouth. "I've got your bubble gum," she said, clamping Marielle's jaw shut with a finger.

Chapel was turning to leave when two hands slipped around her waist.

"Hello, Sweet Girl," Zay said directly into her ear. She shivered. "That was an awfully mean thing you just did."

Chapel choked back her gasp and swallowed. "She kind of asked for it." She wiggled against him, but he tightened his grip.

"Maybe," he said. "But you provoke her. If you ignored her, she'd stop."

"You're probably right." Chapel bared her chin into her chest and jerked. His hold was secure. "But where's the fun in that?"

Zay's laugh tickled her neck. "I'm crazy about you. Did you know that?"

With a restrained arm, she motioned to the table. His attention needed to be divided. "What's the story tonight? I thought you were working."

"We just finished and thought we'd have dinner."

"Tracking a potential recruit? Or Rogues?"

He shook his head. "Classified."

Chapel tried not to let that sting. "More insider info I can't know?"

"Pledge Thanatos, and I promise to brief you within an inch of your life."

She swallowed. "I'm working on it."

Then she jumped in the air and let her weight drag her to the ground, breaking his hold on her.

She scrambled up and spun around, the fringe on the edge of her dress getting caught between her thighs. She laid her purse on the table to smooth her hemline.

"Maybe next time," she said, "I'll think through my mission wardrobe a little better."

Zay's eyes sparked like flint striking steel. "Nah," he said. "I'm into it."

She fought a smile. "So, tell me. How is it that you're still awake?"

Zay ran a hand down his tie. His suit contained exactly zero wrinkles.

"Chloral hydrate as a sedative is not a terrible choice." He started orbiting her as he spoke. "But sometimes, when made by someone of—How should I say it?—*limited* experience, it can taste salty."

Chapel gritted her teeth. She *knew* she'd used too much salt.

She retrieved the purse from the table and matched his movements, not letting her guard down. They circled each other like they had so many other times in the training ring.

"But I watched you drink it all," she argued.

"Did I?"

Chapel chanced a glance at the table. There were so many dishes and glasses, it was difficult to tell whose was whose.

"You switched glasses," she said. "But with whom?"

"Let's just say Rush is going to sleep well tonight. Really, really well."

In a movement so fast she didn't even flinch, Zay stepped toward Chapel and snatched the purse.

Chapel stopped moving and stamped her foot. "Give that back."

He raised a single, dark eyebrow. "Seriously?" He motioned to Marielle's fallen hair. "I remember this challenge. Jackson loves it. The favorite things one, right?"

She was in the middle of a Genex practice test, and Zay was about to ruin it.

Chapel backed up against Zay's vacated chair. "Yes."

"Then what were you going to take from me?" he asked, sticking her purse in the back band of his pants. "What's my favorite thing?"

She pushed her lips together. "Well, I thought about your pride. But Jackson said I have to return with tangible items."

He moved her direction and she skittered back. Grabbing his suit coat, she rolled it into a ball and threw it at him.

He swatted it away and laughed. "You've resorted to throwing things?"

"No," she said. "I've resorted to taking things." She held up the Shelby's keys that she'd just lifted from his jacket. "Thanks for the ride home." Then she popped the scoop of a spoon on the table and let it fly his direction, dinging him on the side of the head.

"Hey," he said, "that hurt."

She laughed. Using her slight build to her advantage, Chapel slipped between Rush's chair and the wall.

But Zay was blisteringly quick, and he met her as she was passing on the other side. She laughed as his fingers skimmed her shoulder.

"I knew you were going to be trouble," he yelled at her back. "But I had no idea."

Chapel laughed harder.

It took Zay several long strides to bring himself within arm's reach of her. Chapel felt the pads of his fingers brush her arm just as she slid between the legs of a frozen server.

Zay had to go around him and the table he was leaning over, costing him precious seconds.

Chapel circled and headed back the way she came—toward the exit.

But Zay anticipated her movements and met her there, backing her into the row of shelves she'd just hidden behind.

A tug inside her gut let her know that the window Tempus created was coming to a close.

Just over her left shoulder was a stacked-stone fireplace. The flames inside were immobile orange spikes, though she still felt their warmth licking at her back.

Chapel took the Shelby's one and only key and dangled it in the air. "I want to offer a trade," she said. "Give me the purse and I won't throw these into the fire."

Zay stared at her hand. "You wouldn't."

"I know Jackson thinks I'll fail," she said. "But I need him to believe in me. I need him to fight for me to be Thanatos." She licked her lips. "So, you tell me. How desperate am I? To get out of this deal with Bellum?"

Zay hesitated. "Nah," he said. "I don't think you'll do it."

"No?" To highlight her point, Chapel took a step back and draped her arm near the flames. "How much do I hate to lose?"

When Zay flinched, she knew she had him.

"But then you won't have my keys," he said, eyeing her warily. "You won't have my favorite thing."

After two months of being his girlfriend, she knew one thing for certain.

"Won't I?" She lifted her other hand to her waist.

A slow smile broke across his face. "You're bad."

"The baddest good girl Thanatos will have the pleasure of hiring. Now, I'm going to count to three." If she waited too long, Zay would find a way to outsmart her. "One, two . . ."

"Wait." Zay reached behind him and removed the purse. "I'll give it back. But we'll make the trade at the exact same time."

Chapel refrained from showing her excitement. For the first time since she'd entered the restaurant, she thought she might actually accomplish her goal.

"I'm serious," she said, drawing out her threat. "I'll do it."

Zay put her purse on the floor and placed a foot on top of it. "Throw me my key, and I'll kick you your purse."

"Zay." She waited until his gray eyes locked with hers. He was so handsome it made her throat burn.

"Yes, Chapel?"

She let her head tilt to the side as she assessed his expression carefully. His thick, dark eyebrows were lifted slightly as if in question. His lips were gently pursed, drawing attention to the silver pucker of a small scar indenting the top crescent. His gaze was steady, revealing nothing.

Typical Zay.

"Zay," she repeated. "Do you promise?"

"Of course," he said.

"Okay." Chapel shifted, her heels pinching against her sweaty feet. "Let's make the trade."

Zay nodded. "Ready? One, two, *three.*"

Chapel tossed the key and let it fly, silver body, end over end, spinning in time with her quickly beating heart. Zay stretched a hand up and snatched it from its arc in the air.

As for the purse, the purse he kicked high in the air right in front of him. It landed in his other hand.

Disappointment flooded her chest. He had tricked her. And it hurt. A lot more than she thought it would.

"You *jerk,*" she said. She meant to sound angry; instead her voice was thick with tears.

Zay made a frustrated sound. "Why did you trust me?"

Chapel cleared her throat before answering. She would *not* cry. "You gave me your word."

He pointed to himself. *"I* am the enemy."

She jerked the wig off her head, loosing strawberry blonde hair down her back. She scratched at her itchy scalp.

"Our deal was mutually beneficial," she said. "We didn't *have* to be enemies. You just chose to be."

Zay put both hands on his hips and looked down at her. "Anyone who has something you want is the enemy, Chapel."

"Well," she said, "that's a terrible way to live."

"That's the way you have to live now," he snapped.

Chapel's eye widened at his tone.

"I'm sorry." He opened his mouth, shut it, then opened it again. "I just want you to be safe. I just want you to understand the dangers of this way of life."

Her gut contracted and she almost fell to her knees. Her energy was depleted—it was time to close this thing down.

Behind her was a gap in the bookcases just wide enough for her petite frame. She stepped through it just as Zay lunged after her. His fingertips brushed down her elbow, but he couldn't reach far enough to stop her.

"I want to trust *you,*" she told him. "Even when you have something that I want."

He moved a stack of books out of the way. His eyes looked sad. "Don't mistake Zay your boyfriend for Isaiah the Reader," he said. "When it comes to war, you *can't* be suspicious enough."

"You're so dramatic." She reached inside the sleeve of her dress and pulled out a purse—her purse. "And yet, so right."

Zay's face froze while he put the pieces together. "When you were messing with your dress," he said. "You switched your purse with Marielle's."

"Confuse the enemy," she repeated the words he had told her so often. "One of the best methods in defeating someone physically superior to you."

"Babe." He was grinning at her now. "That was hot."

11

Chapel tried to push a smile to her face, too, but it felt plastic. "Thanks." Her body shook with a heave, and she walked backward to the door. "Enjoy the rest of your date."

"I'm working, Chapel."

She glanced over her shoulder just as she left. "With you, Zay, is there ever a difference?"

CHAPTER TWO

Chapel's eyes were the color of pale sea glass in the amber light of the setting sun. She stretched in front of her bathroom mirror, feeling Zay's training session on every inch of her body.

He pushed her hard—harder than she had ever been pushed. He trained her as if her life depended on it.

Because it did.

They hadn't spoken about last night's encounter during the three-hour Martial Arts class. He mentioned it once, but she had put her hand to his lips and said, "Later."

They both knew *later* would never come.

She had a bruise on her ribs where Marielle had landed a kick beneath her pads when Zay wasn't watching. Payback, she imagined, for the gum incident.

Chapel ran her fingers along it and thought, *Definitely worth it.*

Her bathroom at Taylor Manor was gray and white marble—perpetually cold and unyielding at all hours of the day, all days of the year.

Especially so on that frigid evening in late February.

She shivered as she finished undressing, waiting for the shower to warm up.

Around her the house was quiet. Todd was in session in D.C., and Valerie was in Virginia overseeing the renovations to an apartment Todd had bought so he could be close to her and the twins.

Chapel surveyed the contours of her body. A gymnast for years, she'd always had an athletic build. But after two months of workouts and running, some of her baby fat had hardened, and the curves of her hips looked more pronounced.

She looked like a woman.

Her fingers traveled to her neck and dipped just below the hollow of her throat.

The burn that Hunter had left on her was fading in some places, but the outline of a hand still remained. She brushed over the raised, leathery skin, squeezing her jaw together. It wasn't the physical scars Chapel lay awake at night thinking about.

She traced the silhouette of the hand that had held the back of her bike as she learned to ride it for the first time and was struck by an intense mixture of shame and sadness.

Because she actually missed Hunter—missed his empathy, missed his chocolate brown eyes, and the way he flipped his sandy hair across his forehead.

How could she not have seen the warning signs that Hunter was dangerous? That he led the Rogue Genex group who had ravaged Bennett Park to fund his corrupt idea of unity?

How could she have missed that he was a killer?

I did it for you, he had said.

What had he been thinking? Did he know her father was actually alive? That he'd been communicating with Valerie by letters at his own headstone? Would Chapel ever know the truth?

She stepped away from the mirror and closed the bathroom door to conserve what little heat the steam was creating. As she did, she caught a glimpse of her food journal laid open on her bed.

14

Needless to say, it was blank. Chary had brought it to their last meeting. Another one of her *brilliant* ideas to help Chapel prepare for her Bellum entry exam in May.

But Chapel wouldn't be joining Bellum, the faction who had manipulated her at her weakest moment. She had no idea how, but she had to rescue herself. Rescue her future.

The shower had grown cold by the time she got in it. Chapel barely noticed.

CHAPTER THREE

Chapel woke up before the sun on Monday morning. Her knuckles fisted the sheets she slept on, wrinkled and damp beneath her.

Another nightmare. Only this one she'd never had before.

Erica had been lying on her stomach in a pool of her own blood. She had gurgled and coughed, clearly dying. And Chapel had been unable to stop it.

The dream had cut to another scene. A funeral. Zay stood behind her, a hand on her shoulder. When the casket lid thudded shut, she turned, pressing her face into his navy shirt.

Chapel never fell back asleep.

She finally rolled out of bed just before her alarm went off. She was standing in front of her closet wishing that an outfit would put itself on her when Erica called.

Usually she would ignore it until she got in the car, but after that dream . . . She stretched for the phone.

"Hello?"

Chapel was greeted by a loud sob, snotty and long. Her first thought was Rogues—Genexes without allegiance. Her spine tingled.

"What's wrong?" She started stepping into a pair of jeans with the phone smashed against her cheek. "Where are you?"

There was a hideous-sounding sniff, then a cough. "It's . . . ." *Sniff, sniff.* "An emergency. I'm at home." Then she wailed again.

"Erica, stay calm. I'm coming. Can you get to your dad's gun?"

Erica cleared her throat. "Yes. And I'll use it if I have to."

Chapel shuffled into her boots and flew down the steps. "Can you see how many there are?"

"How many what?"

"How many—" Chapel broke off. She couldn't really call them *Rogues*, could she? "How many people are trying to hurt you?"

The line went silent on the other end.

"Chapel, what are you talking about?"

"Wait. What are *you* talking about?"

Erica started crying again. "It's too terrible to say out loud. Just—just get here as fast as you can." Then she hung up.

A little less hurried than before, Chapel still broke a handful of traffic laws getting to Erica's house on Lighthouse Way.

She passed by the small yellow cottage that she'd once shared with her mom. It seemed like a thousand years ago—several lifetimes, at least.

Someone had finally bought it.

"Jersey?" Chapel called into Erica's house. It wasn't often that one found the Monroe house empty. It was creepy. "Erica?"

"Up here," came a muffled voice.

Chapel took the stairs to the only full bathroom on the second floor. The door was ajar, and from inside came the smell of ammonium and bleach.

It wasn't Rogues that had gotten to Erica. Though, maybe something just as alarming.

"How bad is it?" Chapel asked.

"Bad."

"On a scale of one to Britney Spears circa meltdown?"

A small, tiny voice squeaked, "An eight?"

Chapel sucked in a breath through her teeth. With a finger, she widened the door.

Erica was curled in the fetal position on avocado green tile, hugging a stained towel to her chest.

Her gorgeous, shiny, corkscrew curls had once been the ideal shade of chestnut brown. Now, they were closer to orange. Bright orange. Highlighter orange.

Chapel coached her face into a non-reactive expression. "We can fix this."

Erica sat up and rubbed her arm across her snotty nose. "No. We can't."

"We can't?"

Erica ran a hand through her matted hair and produced a fistful of damp strands. "It's already falling out. If I put color on it any time soon, I'll go bald."

Erica leaned back down to the floor and cried for a few moments, her tears running sideways down her nose.

"Come on," Chapel said after a brief pause. "Up and at 'em."

With an outstretched arm, Chapel tugged Erica to her feet. Placing a hand on either shoulder, she turned her friend to face the mirror. "Look at yourself, Jersey."

Erica peeked at herself through a squinted eye, then squealed. "I look like—. I look like a bag of cheesy puffs exploded on my head."

"Well." Chapel pressed her lips together briefly. "Charlotte and Shae *love* cheesy puffs."

She and Erica made eye contact in the mirror, and after a breath of restraint, they both burst into laughter.

They laughed so hard that Erica slid back down to the floor and dragged Chapel with her.

"Cheesy puffs," Chapel gasped. "That's exactly what they look like."

"I know. Your sisters are going to try to eat me."

Their somber expressions broke into giggles again.

Once they regained control, Erica stared at herself in the mirror.

"You know you're like, model pretty, right?" Chapel said, picking at the scuffed toe of her boot. "You're tall. You've got perfect skin and teeth. No one is going to look at your hair. They'll just look at *you.*"

Erica sniffed a few times. Then she pressed her elbow into Chapel's sore rib. "That might be the nicest thing you've ever said to me, Steel."

Chapel shrugged. "Maybe I'm going soft in my old age."

Erica gave her a brief smile. "My Steel Magnolia? Soft? No way."

Chapel squeezed Erica's hand. "You're probably right. Here. Let's see what it looks like in a high bun."

Erica allowed Chapel to sit her down on the closed toilet seat and pick through her chartreuse curls with a wide-tooth comb.

"I'm going to be a terrible cosmetologist," Erica sighed. "I can't even do a bleach job right."

"Why were you trying to go blonde anyway? Doesn't seem like your style."

Erica picked up an empty squirt bottle and fiddled with the nozzle. "I don't know. Just needed a change, I guess."

Chapel put a few bobby pins in her mouth and gathered Erica's hair at the crown of her head. "This is about Timmy Valentine, isn't it?"

Erica slammed the water bottle on the counter, knocking over a soda can, toothbrush holder, and contacts case in a resounding *WHACK.*

"No," Erica said. "This isn't about Timmy Valentine."

"Oh. Right." Chapel finished pinning and held up a mirror so Erica could see. "Look."

Erica turned her head to the left and to the right. The hair was still orange, but at least it wasn't poking out of her head at weird angles.

Actually, it almost looked auburn underneath, so the bun was a vast improvement. That's why Chapel flinched when Erica's mouth twisted and she crumbled into a heap of sobs.

"It is about Timmy," she wailed. "I— I— I think I *love* him!"

Love. That was a word neither Chapel nor Erica used often—outside of references to Dairy Queen and ankle boots.

Chapel squatted down in front of her and handed her a wad of toilet paper.

"Have you told him yet?"

Erica shook her head. "No. I don't want him to know."

"Because of Thanksgiving?"

Erica shrugged. "I know he's lying to me about what happened that night. I don't think he was like, meeting another girl, but he definitely is leaving out a part of his story." Erica bit down on the center of her thumb. "It doesn't make sense."

Chapel swallowed the bitter taste that burned in the back of her throat.

Erica was right. Timmy had been with her, held hostage by their former teacher Hunter Carter, a Genex who was determined to make Chapel the star in his plan to unite Rogues, Thanatos, and Bellum under one supreme order.

"But that's not the only reason," Erica said. "I don't want Timmy to know because I'm not sure how he feels about me. I *might* have said some pretty crazy stuff to him. Like, I may have called him a few names."

"You don't say?" Chapel looked at Erica sideways. "Do you want me to talk to him?"

Erica gasped. "No. No way. You can't. Chapel, promise me you won't."

"Okay, okay. I promise I won't say anything."

Erica grabbed her wrist. "Wait. Will you really? Will you talk to him for me?"

Chapel laughed out loud. "You know you sound insane, right?"

Erica clutched at her own chest. "This is what love does to a person. It makes them act like a freaking lunatic." Erica paused to swallow. "I know you don't understand. You're always so . . . *controlled*. You've never let your heart get away from you."

Immediately, Chapel thought of Zay—thought of Friday night, and the sinking, sucker-punched way his double-cross had made her feel.

She just shook her head, not bothering to correct Erica as her friend burst into another wave of uncontrollable sobs.

CHAPTER FOUR

"Okay, okay," Chapel said, arms raised in surrender. "Calm down." She leaned over to Zay and whispered, "This is getting out of hand."

He looked up at her with eyes the color of a cloudy morning. "Can you blame them?"

Chapel sighed. "No. I really can't."

Chapel's Sunday school class was begging for Zay to tell the Bible story. Again.

"No the fence, Miss Chapel," Katie Monroe said, "but Mr. Isaiah has cuter voices."

Chapel nodded seriously. "No *offense* taken, Katie. His voices *are* pretty good." She gave the stapled sheets of paper to Zay. "Mr. Isaiah. The floor is yours."

Zay squeezed her hand before walking to the front of the room. He lifted the top sheet, scanning the script he was supposed to read from.

He shrugged, tossing it to the side. "Alright kids, raise your hand if you know what *improvise* means."

Chapel let her forehead fall into her hands. He was adorable. He was silly. He let kids crawl on him like he was a jungle gym. He was perfect.

Then she remembered Friday night.

She must have been making a sour face, because Zay paused in the middle of his story—a highly exaggerated version of Paul being struck blind on the road to Damascus—to tilt his head at her in question.

Chapel lifted her shoulders and smiled. She didn't feel like talking about it today.

Or tomorrow.

Or the next day.

Tiny hands clapped excitedly when Zay finished. Class ended, and parents began to pick up their children. The influx of mothers who lingered by the door, sliding their eyes over Zay did not go unnoticed by Chapel.

When the room was empty, Zay started stacking chairs while Chapel double-checked the attendance sheets.

"I don't know how I did this for so long without you," she murmured. "You make things so much easier."

The pen was tugged lightly from her hands. She looked up to find Zay standing right in front of her.

"I wish you really thought that," he said softly. "About every part of your life."

"Zay." Heat burned at the back of her neck. "What are you talking about?"

He stooped so their eyes were level. "Babe, I've been reading you for almost a year now." He touched a hand to her temple. "I can see those wheels spinning. And listen, you don't *have* to tell me, but sometimes, you *can* tell me."

She reached up and caught his fingers, pressing them against her cheek. She shook her head at him. *Great,* she thought, *then he goes and says something like that.*

She took a breath. "Remember the other night, when you told me not to mistake Zay the boyfriend for Isaiah the Reader?"

"Yeah."

"I guess I have a hard time doing that. Everything is so black and white to you. In work, in life. But for me, sometimes it's just gray."

Zay nodded. "So, basically, I'm a boring robot?"

That made her laugh. She realized, when he didn't smile, that he wasn't joking.

"No, Zay. Sorry—gosh. That's why I don't bring these things up. I'm terrible at talking about stuff like this."

A crease appeared on Zay's forehead. "Do I look like *I* know anything about functional relationships?" He twirled a piece of her hair around his thumb and forefinger. "Just tell me how you feel. Spit it out."

"Okay." She rubbed her palms down the sides of her navy dress. "Sometimes I wonder if you're living your own life. Or, if you're living *Jackson's* version of your life. You're on the road more than you're at home. And when you're home, you're always in meetings or running errands for Jackson." She touched a button on his shirt. "I want you to make your *own* choices."

"Make my own, choices," Zay said flatly. He stepped away from her. "Make my own choices."

She didn't answer. His tone was not pleasant. He began pacing in front of her.

"Do you know what happened," he asked, "the last time I made a series of my *own* choices?"

"I know about your past—"

"No, you don't," Zay said, shaking his head. "You know the delicate version of my past." He pointed to the script he'd set aside. "I was like Saul—a *terrible* human being. Then, when Jackson came to me, literally saving my life, he showed me a better way." He pointed at his shirt, right over the Theta tattoo on his chest. "He showed me *this* way. And it was like scales falling from my eyes. And now that I can see again, you want me to pretend that I'm still blind?"

Instead of saying anything else, Chapel closed the distance between the two of them and put her hands around his waist, pressing her face into his chest.

"Don't be mad at me," she whispered. "That's the last thing I want."

He was stiff for a few heavy moments. Then, slowly, his arm came around her back, resting along the curve of her spine. He pressed her to him.

"Then stop doubting me," he said into her hair. "That's the last thing *I* want."

CHAPTER FIVE

It was Monday afternoon, and instead of driving straight home from Back Porch, Chapel was driving by Timmy's house for the third time.

I'm an idiot, she chanted in her head. *I-D-I-O-T. Idiot.*

Why had she offered to get in the middle of his and Erica's relationship?

She turned around in the cul-de-sac and headed back up Timmy's street. As she approached his house, she saw a hunched over figure standing at the end of his driveway. It was Timmy. She rolled to a stop as he walked to the passenger side and slid in.

"Stalk much?" he asked, rubbing his hands in front of her heat vents. "My mom thought you were a Jehovah's Witness. She made the little kids hide under her bed so they'd think no one was home."

Chapel snickered. "My bad."

"It was actually kind of funny. And, bonus, Mikey found my favorite sweatshirt under there." Timmy pointed to what he wore. It had a human brain on the front with the words *Zombie Food* beneath it.

"We really need to discuss your fashion choices."

"What?" Timmy asked. "Zombies are trendy."

Chapel leaned to turn on Timmy's heated seats. "Actually, you're kind of right."

"Hey." Timmy pointed to her neck. "Where'd you get that necklace? I've never seen it before."

Chapel touched the thin chain. "Oh, this? It's, um. My dad. He actually left it to me." Along with a fat bank account that she had no explanation for.

"May I?" Timmy reached out to touch the silver pendant, turning it over. "Chap, this thing is sick."

Chapel sat back in her seat, darting a look at Timmy. "Are you feeling okay?"

Timmy slid his black-rimmed glasses up his nose. "Yeah, why?"

"It's just . . . " Chapel centered the necklace's clasp at the back of her neck. "It's a pretty gaudy display of gemstones, don't you think?"

"Take it off," Timmy said. "Let me show you something."

Chapel fumbled with the hook before dropping it in his hands.

Timmy held it up, the late afternoon sun throwing glittery streaks across the Jetta's console. "This isn't just a cluster of stones," he said. "See this blue one in the middle?" Timmy touched the large sapphire outlined in diamonds. "That's an eyeball. And these—" He pointed to the two lines of dark stones that curved around either side of the sapphire. "These are the eyelids. It's the Eye of Horus."

He handed the necklace back to her.

"The Eye of Horus?" Chapel squinted at it. "Should that sound familiar to me?"

Timmy shrugged. "Not really. I think I learned about it in AP History."

"What does it mean?"

"It's an ancient Egyptian symbol. Hold on. Let me look it up to be sure." Timmy typed something into his phone, then shifted to look at her. "Here we go. Yeah, I was right. Here's what it says: 'The Eye of Horus was often used to symbolize sacrifice, healing, restoration, and protection.'" Timmy showed her the photo on his phone. He was right—it was a match.

"It's really cool," Timmy said. "I bet your dad was super legit. I mean, this basically proves it."

With all this talk of Michael Ryan, Chapel's chest felt hot and cold at the same time. Her hands trembled slightly as she put the necklace back on.

The silence that followed buzzed between them. Finally, Timmy took off his glasses and rubbed the back of his hands over his eyes.

"Okay," he said, "what's up? Why were you canvasing my house?"

Grateful for a change in subject, Chapel rolled her head along the headrest to look at Timmy. "Um. You're not going to like this."

"Is it about Erica?"

She pressed her lips into a line. "Maybe?"

"It's cool." Timmy sighed. "I knew this conversation would happen."

"In that case . . . " Chapel twisted to face him. "Put me out of my misery and just give me the scoop."

Timmy tugged at his sweatshirt and pulled it over his head. He shook out his copper curls and stared at his hands. "I like Erica."

"Like?" Chapel asked. "Like, how *like* are we talking?"

"I guess more than a little."

"Okay. Then why don't you date her?"

Timmy pressed out a deep breath. "She's a lot to handle."

Chapel laughed. "Well, you knew that before you started making out with her on the regular. Come up with something better."

Timmy wiped his hands down his jeans. "Look. I saw what dating each other did to you and Logan's friendship. It ruined it. It took Erica getting mad at me about Thanksgiving to remember how quickly relationships can go from great to crap."

Chapel thought about Timmy's words. Of course, he was right; Logan had a new girlfriend now, and even though he and Chapel had patched up their friendship months ago, it would never be the same between them again.

"And, Chap?"

"Yeah?"

Timmy looked her right in the eye. "As much as I like Erica, I would never in a million years want to make my friendship with you hard or weird."

"What do you mean?"

He tilted his head at her. "I mean, you driving by my house three times. I mean this conversation we're having right now." He pointed between the two of them. "In the beginning, it was just you and I. We've only got a few months left together. I don't want to ruin it."

Chapel's mouth swung open. *Dang.* In the meantime, all her friends were growing up and getting sentimental.

Timmy, probably knowing she wouldn't know how to respond, reached over his shoulder and buckled his seatbelt. "Roosters for dinner?"

Chapel smiled at him. "Duh."

She left the topic of Erica untouched the remainder of the night. Mostly, she let Timmy talk. He had gotten in to his number one school, MIT, and he could think of little else.

"They have their own language there," he said, wing sauce dribbling down his chin. "Like a math major, for example, me. I'd be called a six dash three." He paused to gulp down some soda. "They even offer pirate certification."

"Pirates? As in Captain Hook?"

Timmy nodded. "Sick, right? You just have to complete certain phys ed classes."

Chapel gave him a dubious look.

"Hey, I didn't say *I'd* be taking them," he said, "I'm just saying that it's possible."

"I'm happy for you. Like, *really* happy for you, Timmy."

He smiled at her. "Thanks. So, how about you? Heard back from any schools?"

College was one of the many variables in Chapel's life. If she wasn't forced to pledge Bellum after graduation, she still wasn't sure how higher education would fit in to her being Thanatos.

"Not yet," she said. "I applied pretty late, so . . . we'll see."

Timmy shook his head. "It's so weird to me how unstressed you seem about college. It's not like you."

Chapel shoved a wing in her mouth and shrugged, hoping he'd change the subject. He didn't. Timmy just stared at her intently; then he did his hacking thing—the cough sound he made when he was about to say something difficult.

"I had a dream the other night."

The hairs on Chapel's arm went stiff. "A dream?" she asked.

His hazel eyes seemed to be measuring her. "You were in it."

Chapel reminded herself to breathe, but her lungs felt sticky. "Hopefully, wearing something cute," she said, trying to make a joke.

But Timmy just shook his head. "No, it was . . . weird. You were . . . strapped to a bed. But the weirdest thing of all?"

Chapel was frozen. She couldn't even blink as she watched Timmy's lips form ideas that he shouldn't even have.

"Hunter *Carter,*" Timmy said. "He was there, too."

Chapel shot sweet tea out of her mouth and nose. She started choking, tears springing to her eyes. Timmy leaned over and clapped her on the back.

"You okay?" he asked once she could swallow. "You going to live?"

29

"Yes," she said, hoarse. She pressed a napkin beneath her eyes, heart galloping in her chest. "Though, death-by-sweet-tea wouldn't be the worst way to go."

Timmy laughed, but there was a tightness around his eyes that Chapel knew all too well. *Curiosity.* Her reaction had made him extremely and dangerously curious.

They made small talk on the drive home, but Chapel wasn't present in the conversation. With Timmy's words about his dream, she had been transported to a cinderblock room and a cold, stiff cot.

Ice seemed to coat her veins, and she couldn't get warm—not even after the scalding bath she took to try and soak away her anxiety.

Timmy Valentine hadn't had a bad dream. He'd had a bad *memory* resurface. One that he had been hypnotized into forgetting by people who would stop at nothing to make sure Timmy never voiced the memory again.

CHAPTER SIX

The next day dawned with clouded skies the color of bone. Craving the burn of cool air in her lungs, Chapel was making plans to walk the few blocks from school to work.

Chapel's spring semester was a senior's dream. For first block she had Theater, which basically amounted to some poor-quality videos, students making out in dressing rooms, and Chapel spending a great deal of time on various social media outlets.

Then, for second block, Chapel helped out in the front office for a class called Office Aid. Mostly, she wrote tardy slips for students late to class and eavesdropped on the receptionist's gossip. The remaining idle time gave Chapel the opportunity to study the texts Jackson gave her about the Genex community.

After that, Chapel left for Work-Study at Back Porch.

The bell that signaled the end of second block rang and Chapel shrugged her book bag over her shoulder and pushed through the cramped hallways and out of the school.

She stepped outside and turned her face down to the senior parking lot. Timmy's bug sat in its usual spot, the driver's side door a slightly different shade of navy than the rest of the body.

Because the original door had been melted off by the man who had kidnapped him. The man Timmy was starting to remember.

A cold breeze whipped through her hair, and Chapel tucked her chin into her jacket.

Timmy's dream had kept her awake all night long. She wasn't sure what to do. She wasn't sure if she *should* do anything. Yet.

Chapel pulled out her phone and texted Zay.

CHAPEL: *Would it make me codependent to say that school isn't the same without you?*

Zay, Marielle, and Rush had gotten so busy that Jackson allowed Zay to withdraw from high school. He already had enough credits to graduate, and would be walking at the ceremony come May.

Until then, his primary job was to help find the final two members of their cell. Once completed, Jackson promised to promote them to a Field Team. Instead of recruiting, they'd be chasing bad guys.

Chapel thought that idea should probably scare her for Zay, but really, she thought it was kind of hot.

Instead of texting back, Zay called her.

"Hey you," she answered.

"Was that text your way of saying you missed me today?"

"Yes." She smiled into her phone. "Am I lame?"

He laughed quietly. "If you are, I am. I've been watching the clock for the last twenty-six minutes, waiting to call you."

They chatted while Chapel walked her way up Main Street.

"I'm at work," she told Zay, stopping at the corner. "Where are we training today?"

Zay's sigh pushed through the receiver. "Actually, I have to go out of town tonight."

"Oh." She knew better than to ask for details. He couldn't tell her. "That sucks. You've been working so much lately..."

"I know." He paused. "But that's not all the bad news. Jackson wanted me to see if you could meet tomorrow night. Dr. Battacharya wants to speak with you."

Another gust of air pulled at the edges of her clothes. Chapel shivered. "Okay. But I just saw her last week. What does she want?"

"I imagine she's just keeping close tabs on her number one recruit."

"Cool." Chapel pinched the bridge of her nose. "I think I'll go barf now."

"I won't let them take you, Chapel." Zay's voice was quiet, but sure. "We'll find a way. I promise."

They never discussed the vision Gabe had last fall. The one where Chapel was Bellum, Zay was Rogue, and Gabe loved her. The one where Chapel was on a mission to find and eliminate Zay.

And though they never said it out loud, she knew part of her desperation in getting out from under Bellum was to make sure *that* vision never fabricated into reality.

They got off the phone and Chapel leaned her forehead against the green stop sign post. Life was weird. And it kept getting weirder.

Her shift at Back Porch was uneventful; Erica had to make up a test at school, so Chapel worked alongside the owner, Thomas, to serve the handful of customers who came out in the dreary weather.

Without her permission, Chapel's eyes kept traveling to the booth Hunter Carter used to sit in. His presence in her life had been so constant that she didn't realize how big of a gap his absence would leave. He had been like white noise, and now, the moments she thought about him were deafening with silence.

Thomas let her off early, so she had some time to kill before meeting Rush for training. As it often did now, she pointed her car toward Bennett Park Memorial Gardens.

When she got out, it was raining. Not a good, solid rain, but the wispy, non-stop drizzle that made everything gray and sticky.

Chapel walked through the cemetery with her head down, the wind whipping her hair into ropes like a blonde Medusa.

She bent in front of Michael Ryan's headstone, letting her fingers slip over the date of his death: *September 28, 1997.*

It had been a closed-casket funeral. At the time, Chapel hadn't known why. Now, she did.

Michael Ryan wasn't dead.

Chapel had watched the video Timmy's hidden camera had captured a thousand times. Zay had watched it, too. There was no denying the resemblance of the man exchanging notes with her mother—her father was very much alive.

"You can't tell Jackson," she had begged Zay. *"Please."*

Zay hadn't understood why she wouldn't want to turn the video over to his uncle Jackson, a man who had infinite resources, infinite connections. But Chapel wasn't sure she trusted Jackson. There was something about him that she couldn't point out—something *off.*

Maybe he'd changed since his days on Project Exception, but Chapel wasn't sure she forgave him. Not completely. Not yet.

In the end, Zay had agreed to let her talk to her mother about it first. Only, she hadn't had the chance. And she didn't plan on having the chance, either. She had her own plan.

Chapel slipped the folded square from her sleeve.

It had taken her several trips to different craft stores to find the exact shade of green she wanted, but the paper she casually dropped into the metal planter attached to her father's headstone was a perfect match to the slim leaves of the Calendulas that had been freshly planted last week.

I know the truth, the note read. *I have a clean phone.* Then she'd added the number of the cell phone she'd purchased at the drug store.

She'd left variations of the same message six times. Each time she returned, her notes were gone.

Chapel sat back on her heels and titled her head to the sky in a silent prayer. The breeze whined over her, kicking up leaves and pine straw.

Finally, the clouds gave in, splattering fat drops of rain down her face.

CHAPTER SEVEN

Chapel showered under pelting water that was so hot the droplets stung her skin numb.

Her meetings with Chary were tricky. She had to appear to want to pledge Bellum even though the thought made her dizzy with rage. She had to appear to be less smart, less trained, and less *good* at Tempus.

Chapel hated it because it felt like losing. But she also realized it was a game she had to play.

She dried her wavy hair smooth, applied a little makeup, and put on nice jeans and a cream cardigan. Chary liked her to look nice.

Chapel wanted to gag on the thought.

Barnabus, Jackson's assistant, answered his door. "Ah, Miss Ryan. Do come in." He pulled a small black notebook from inside his jacket pocket. It was attached to a chain. "Yes, your meeting is scheduled to begin in six minutes. Do you know your way into the basement?"

"Uh. Sure. Yeah." Chapel's attention was piqued—she'd never been invited downstairs before. It was where the team prepped for missions.

Chapel took the stairs two at a time. When she came around the landing, she walked into a large wood-paneled room with a slick conference table in its center. Jackson stood over it, tentatively pressing buttons on a thin device.

"Hey, Jackson," she said.

"Chapel, hello." He glanced over his shoulder, giving her a quick smile. "Forgive my rudeness, but this technology is giving me fits. Isaiah usually works it."

"I would offer to look at it," Chapel said, "but I would probably destroy it."

Jackson made a humming sound. "Oh, I doubt you could do much worse than me. I think Barnabus is familiar with it. Would you excuse me?"

"No problem," Chapel said. "Is Chary here, yet?"

Jackson's eyes widened, and Chapel thought that was probably his version of an eye roll. "Hardly," he said. "You know that Chary's time table is quite her own."

Chapel sat at the table and wasted time on her phone until she heard feet on the stairs. She stood up, ready for Jackson to enter the room.

But it wasn't Jackson.

The man rounding the corner was tall, dressed in a gray three-piece suit, and had a head that was almost shaved, save for a tuft of short, light hair cropped close on the top.

A wide smile stretched across his face. His very tan, very different-looking face.

She hadn't seen Gabriel Luxe since the day he'd told her of the horrible vision he'd had. And when she'd asked Chary about him, she had told Chapel that Gabe took a new job. But here he was.

Gabe walked slowly toward her until he reached the table. He paused, squeezing the back of the leather chair he came to rest behind. "Hello, Chapel," he said with a breath.

If possible, his Australian accent was thicker. Gabe stuck his hands in his pockets, darting his light eyes to the ground and smiling.

"Gabe? Is that really you?" Chapel grinned. "You look so . . . proper."

His eyes found hers at last, and he laughed. "Yes, well. I took a little vacation."

"To where? GQ headquarters? Ryan Gosling's closet?"

Gabe rolled his eyes, but he was smiling at her. "I went home," he said. "To Australia."

"Wow. How long did you stay?"

"Six weeks."

That explained the accent. Chapel suddenly didn't know what to say. So she just stared at him, holding his gaze.

"You look good," they both said at the same time, then laughed. The silence after was pulled taut.

Chapel rubbed a finger across the bridge of her nose. "So, did you find a long-lost razor at home, or something?"

Gabe shook his head. "It was time to grow up a bit, I guess." He rubbed his face. "Though, this cold weather has me missing my long hair and beard." He tilted his head briefly. "Amongst other things."

"And here we are," Jackson said grandly.

Over Gabe's shoulder, Chapel watched as Jackson escorted Chary into the room. When her honey-colored eyes fell on Gabe, Chary's entire body froze. But by the time Gabe turned around, Chary's face had opened into a bright smile.

She spread her arms for a hug, her pale blue sari swishing about her like a glittering waterfall. "I didn't realize you were going to be here," Chary said. *"Mr. Luxe."*

Gabe crossed the room. "Gabe." He kissed her caramel skin on either cheek. "It will always be Gabe."

"Yes," Jackson said with a small bow. "Congratulations on your promotion, Mr. Luxe. Success suits you."

Gabe shook Jackson's hand. "Thank you, Jackson."

Jackson motioned to the table. "Shall we, then?"

Chapel tried to get Gabe's attention with her eyes. *Promotion?* But he wouldn't look at her. And the twitch at the corner of his mouth told her it was on purpose.

They all sat down, Jackson by Chapel, Gabe by Chary. Jackson slid his finger across the tablet on the table and entered a series of numbers. "I had to get the password from Barnabus," he explained. "Otherwise, I would have had this pulled up already."

A projector overhead clicked on, and a screen rotated down from a compartment in the ceiling. The image on it looked like a spreadsheet of Chapel's tests over the last eight weeks.

"Gabriel, these are Chapel's most recent statistics," Jackson said. He flipped to the next page of numbers. "Chary gets updates daily, and meets with Chapel at least every other week." He highlighted her improved times. "As you can see, she is getting more than adequate development with us, here."

Chary hummed to herself, clicking her long nails against the slick table's surface. She looked at Chapel. "Fifteen minutes of Tempus?" she asked.

"That was the day after our last meeting," Chapel said, her face feeling warm. "My next best time is only eleven minutes."

Lies, lies, lies. She could Tempus for almost twenty-five minutes.

"Still. Not bad," Chary said, looking at Gabriel. "Actually, it's unbelievably good."

Gabe said nothing, but Chapel could feel his eyes on her face. "And you are working out every day?" he asked.

"Almost every day, yes."

"Who does the training?"

"I work with her Tempus," Jackson answered. "And the team takes care of the rest."

Chary clicked her tongue. "Isaiah Halstead does most of it. Your *nephew,*" she added, turning to Jackson. "How lovely to have family so close."

Jackson shifted his shoulders forward. Chapel thought he might be shrugging. "Yes," he said. "It is."

Then Chary's eyes flitted to Chapel. "Are you and he still romantically involved?"

All eyes in the room were on Chapel. She tugged at the neck of her sweater, unsure of how that question was pertinent to the conversation. "Yes. We are dating."

"Ah." Chary smiled widely. "He's a handsome one. Is it serious?"

Chapel sucked in a breath too quickly and it caught in her dry throat. She coughed, saving her from answering.

"He's very protective of Chapel," Gabe murmured when she was quiet. "Chapel is safe with him."

They spent more time looking over her schedule, running times, weight lifting numbers, and Tempus control. All fabricated.

Chapel said very little, and wondered why she had to be there at all.

Finally, Chary sat back in her chair, twisting it slightly from side to side.

"Typically," she said, "I would insist she train with us at a Bellum facility. But, this one is special."

"I agree," Jackson said. "We are committed to keeping her identity as anonymous as possible. If too many people find out what she can do—"

That got Chapel's attention. "What? What would happen?"

Jackson and Chary exchanged a look.

Jackson cleared his throat. "When we say Tempus is rare, Chapel," he said, "we mean that you're currently the only known case."

Chary leaned across the table. "There are many who will fear your power." She trailed her nails along its lacquered finish. "And fear can make people unpredictable."

Chapel's pulse tapped against her wrist rapidly. "What are you saying?"

No one answered immediately.

Then Jackson touched the center of his lips with his forefinger. "Since we are a recruiting cell and not a Field Team, our activities are not closely monitored."

"We're working on a long-term plan," Chary said, directing her comment to Gabe. "But, in the meantime, we are prepared to allow her to stay here. The fewer people who know about her, the better."

Gabe tugged at his vest. His eyes were still on her numbers. "I agree. For now."

"It's settled, then." Jackson turned off the tablet and clasped his hands. "I appreciate your trust, and you have my word, I will guard Chapel with every resource in my arsenal."

Chary's giggle was like a bell tinkling. "I'm sure that you will."

Everyone started standing, but Chapel. She raised her hand. "Um, hi. Yes. Question."

The three of them froze, looking down at her.

"Yes, Chapel?" Chary asked. Her smile was friendly, but confused. As if she were genuinely perplexed as to what Chapel could possibly be curious about.

Chapel stood, too, so she wouldn't be the only one sitting. "What about college? I should find out any day now if I got into Georgia, my first choice. But I also applied to a few other schools. And where will I live? Who will I live with? And what if I really, *really* want to be Thanatos? Surely people change their minds. Zay did."

Chary glanced at Gabe before responding. "College is not out of the question," she began. "Especially if you plan on studying foreign policy, political science, or maybe even another language—Eastern languages, that is. As for being Thanatos." She shook her head. "I'm sorry, Chapel. But you made a verbal agreement with Mr. Luxe. If he safely returned your friend, you swore an oath of intent to Bellum. We have it on video."

Chapel's nostrils flared with anger. "I'm sure *Mr. Luxe* can explain to you that he only physically removed Timmy from the warehouse Hunter had us in. It was Zay who saved us all."

She looked hard at Gabe who merely stared back at her rather vacantly.

Something flashed behind Chary's honey-colored eyes and she flattened her lips. "It's not up for discussion," she said. "An oath is an oath."

"Isaiah was merely training with Bellum," Jackson added softly. "He had not yet sworn an oath."

"It's the law," Gabe spoke up. He was still staring at her intently. "Defectors stir up dissention between factions. Once you swear yourself to one, you must follow through. Especially you. Bellum isn't likely to make an exception for the most valuable Genex currently in play."

Chapel pointed to herself, her eyes growing wide. "That's me?"

They all nodded.

Chapel fell back into her chair. "That sucks."

Chary clicked her tongue again. "Yes, well. Welcome to being an adult."

They all walked back upstairs. Gabe and Chary excused themselves to leave. Chapel couldn't catch Gabe's eye, but she wanted to speak with him. She wanted to know why he went home for six weeks. She wanted to know why he hadn't reached out to her. She wanted to know if he was still going to help her get out of her oath to Bellum.

She watched through the dining room window as Gabe tucked Chary inside her car. She cranked it up and rolled down the window. With a glance back at the house, they began talking with their heads closely together.

Chapel couldn't fit words around the change in Gabe, but it was there. And it was something that ran deeper than his new tan and haircut.

"Chapel, may I speak with you for a moment?" Jackson's voice behind her made her jump. "I'm sorry, did I startle you?"

Chapel pressed a hand to her chest. "It's fine. I guess . . . I guess I'm just a little freaked out right now."

He dipped his head. "Well. That's understandable. "

Chapel turned away from the window and gave Jackson her attention. He stood in slacks and a sweater vest, impeccably pressed and stiff-looking. He was an attractive older man, but rarely smiled to where it touched his light eyes. She wondered, briefly, why he never married.

"What's up?" Chapel asked.

Jackson's mouth pressed into a firm line as he hesitated. It was the first time she had seen him indicate any emotion outside of complete confidence and control.

"Excuse me," he said. "This isn't easy for me."

Immediately, she tensed. "Jackson, is Zay—?"

"He's fine. No, no. He's okay. Isaiah is always okay." Jackson clasped his hands behind his back and began to pace. "It's just—I have been thinking about your rendezvous—however incidental it was—with Gabriel Luxe in Washington, D.C., last November."

Chapel's mouth slid open and stayed that way. She didn't say anything.

"I am aware of Gabriel's former assignment," Jackson went on. "To seek out the families of those whom were involved with Project Exception. And if I were Gabriel, and I were trying to win you to my side, I would be tempted to stoop to very low levels." Jackson stopped pacing and looked at her. "You avoid me," he said quietly. "Even in our training sessions, you are distant."

Chapel's heart was thumping hollowly in her chest now. "Yes," she whispered. "I do."

"He has told you things," Jackson said. "Or, probably more likely, shown you things, that have changed your opinion of me."

Chapel didn't even try to lie. "Made me question my opinion of you," she said. "Yes."

Jackson's eyes held wrinkles around the edges. He was concerned. "I should have told you about your father, Chapel. There is no excuse for it. Nor is there any excuse for my allowing his abuse—*any* abuse." His voice trembled slightly. "It was my darkest hour," he said. "From which I had no way out."

Chapel remembered; Doctor Sevawn, the baseless mastermind behind Project Exception, didn't allow any of the scientists to leave with their life.

"After Jacques was killed," Jackson continued, "I sank into a depression so deep, I feared there was no climbing out. And there wouldn't have been—if I hadn't come across Isaiah." He had been pacing. Now he came to a standstill and looked at her. "You and I both know Isaiah's capacity for care is far deeper than he pretends. He's been a son to me these last years."

Jackson turned toward the wall behind them, and Chapel thought it was to hide how much his words were affecting him.

"Zay would do anything for you," she said after a long silence. "So, I think it's safe to say that the feeling is mutual."

Jackson cleared his throat. "Am I right, then, in my assumption that you have not told him? About my mistreatment of your father?"

Chapel's spine straightened. "Yes, you are. I . . . couldn't."

She watched as the back of his head titled. He was sighing. He was relieved.

"I don't even feel worthy to ask for your forgiveness," he said. "If it's any consolation, I am so very sorry. And I—It haunts me, what we did. I should have left and not cared about my life. I should have—"

He stopped speaking. Jackson was quiet for so long that Chapel walked up to his back, touching his shoulder lightly. When he turned to her, his light eyes were pooled with unshed tears.

Chapel flinched at the sight—foreign and strange on his austere expression.

"Tell me the price of your continued grace," he said. "Name it, and it's yours."

Chapel hesitated. Instead of answering, she walked to the dining room table and picked up a linen napkin from its golden coil and shook it free. She handed it to him.

Giving her an almost-smile, Jackson used it to dab at his eyes. Then he folded it into a perfect square and put it in his back pocket. He looked at her expectantly.

"Wait. Was that a serious question?" she asked. "You really think you have to give me something for not telling Zay?"

"You have every right to tell him," Jackson said. "I am obviously very ashamed of myself. If I were you, I wouldn't even be having this conversation with me."

"Jackson, I don't keep it from Zay for my sake. I keep it from Zay for *his* sake."

His eyes softened. "You remind me of a different time, Chapel. A time when kindness was free."

Chapel shook her head slowly. "If it's not free, it's not kindness."

Jackson clenched his jaw tightly. "Thank you for your time this evening. If there's nothing else . . . "

Then he left her in the dining room.

Moments later, Chapel heard a bedroom door shut. The sound of bedsprings giving beneath the weight of someone sitting down. And his quiet sobs, playing through the empty house like a dirge.

* * * *

Chapel checked her pockets before she walked back home. Her phone was missing.

"Ah. The basement," she muttered to herself, figuring she had left it on the table during their meeting. She found it right where she thought she would, then turned to go. She paused mid-stride, however, as an exterior door down the hallway drew her attention.

The door gave her an idea.

Easing herself outside, Chapel aligned herself with a low row of hedges that encircled the far side of Jackson's house. From her position, she could see Gabe was still leaning inside Chary's car, motioning with his hands.

She made a decision—if they weren't talking about her, she would walk away. But if they were, she could see if Gabe were someone she could still trust.

Chapel's conversation with Jackson had her emotions sizzling like embers, so Tempus came fast and easy. It took her several minutes to jog down Jackson's driveway, then back up hers on the other side of the iron security fence.

A line of Cypress trees grew tall and skinny along the boundary that separated Taylor Manor from Jackson's, and Chapel stood behind the thickest one.

Then, like Jackson had taught her, Chapel imagined her energy like it was the oxygen around her. She sucked in calm, cooling breaths, pulling, pulling, pulling it all inside of her.

"Hard for you to believe," Gabe was saying, "imagine how *I* feel."

Chary laughed, her fondness for Gabe clear in its softness. "It's a marvelous turn for you," she said. "I am so proud."

Chapel's ears burned. They were just two friends, catching up on Gabe's promotion, and *she* was the rat in the bushes eavesdropping. She turned to go.

"Tell me the truth," Chary continued, "why are you here tonight, Gabriel? Checking in on recruits is below your pay grade now."

Chapel froze.

She couldn't see Gabe, but she heard the wariness in his voice. "Chapel Ryan isn't just any recruit; she's *the* recruit. Locking her in to Bellum is priority."

"And she *will* be locked into Bellum," Chary said. "In time. She resists because of Isaiah, you know this. But that will work itself out in time. His trajectory is just as high as hers. Only, in the opposite direction."

Chapel started cracking her knuckles, one by brittle one.

"I'm not so sure," Gabe said. "They seem more serious than kids their age—especially him. They're not kids their age, I guess. They're different."

Chary made a humming sound. "Young love. It does color things very black and white, doesn't it?"

Gabe sighed. "Very much so."

"I'm sorry, Gabriel," Chary said quickly. "That was insensitive of me."

There was silence for a few beats before Gabe spoke again. "No, it's fine. It's been, what, two years now? I'm moving forward."

Chary didn't speak for so long that Chapel had to peek around the bristles of the Cyprus to make sure she hadn't left without her somehow knowing it. Chary's golden eyes were looking out over the steering wheel, not quite focused.

"I've known you since you were just a boy," Chary said at last. Her voice was stiff—so un-Charylike. "You are like family to me."

"I know," Gabe started. "You—"

"Let me finish," Chary interrupted, and Gabe's voice fell off. "You are like family to me," she continued, "and I would hate to see you get sidetracked by a needless distraction."

Chapel tilted her head. *Wait.* Was *she* the needless distraction?

"Focus on your new role," Chary said, voice buttery again. "Let me take care of things here."

Gabe cleared his throat. Chapel wanted to look at his expression, but didn't dare show her face again.

Chary laughed. "Oh, Gabriel. I give you my word, I can handle Chapel Ryan. Yes?"

He chuckled, but Chapel thought it sounded unsure.

"What? You don't think I can?" Chary asked, tone teasing.

Gabe groaned, and Chapel heard shoes shuffling back and forth on the pavement. "I'm not here because I doubt your capabilities, Chary."

"Oh, I know why you're here," Chary said. "You missed her. It's okay to admit it."

Gabe was quiet for a long stretch until he spoke again. "You haven't seen it," he said quietly. "That moment she decides she's all in. It's a tornado of . . . of carelessness, and passion, and naivety, and yet—you want to throw yourself into it. She's more than the sum of her skill, Chary. She could *change* things."

Chapel heard the sharp clicks of Chary's tongue. "Be careful, Gabriel. You can speak like that with me, but others who don't know better will think you a Unifist. Regardless of how high your throne sits."

Unifist? Chapel turned that word around and around, the repetition of it bringing little clarity.

She heard his hand tap the top of Chary's car. "We should go. Knowing Jackson, he has eyes and ears very close by."

"Will I see you soon?" she asked. "Or will you head back to D.C.?"

"Actually, I'm staying."

"You . . . are?" Chary sounded confused.

"Chapel was my case," Gabe said. "I want to finish her."

CHAPTER EIGHT

Chapel checked her phone one last time. Nothing. No texts, no voicemails, no missed calls. Zay had been off the grid for two days now.

Chapel slipped the phone into the cup holder of her car and left Back Porch. It had been another slow lunch shift. The cold was keeping people indoors—which was exactly where Chapel wanted to be. Instead, she was meeting Marielle at the park to run.

She'd rather chug bleach.

When she got there, Marielle was stretching.

"I'll just go to the bathroom to change," Chapel said.

Marielle didn't even look up at her. "I'm running in five minutes with or without you."

It literally hurt Chapel to hurry up for Marielle's benefit, but she didn't want to be left behind. She needed to be trained, to be pushed, to be challenged. The only thing worse than failing her pledge exams would be for Marielle to be better than her.

Now, *that*, she would not have.

Chapel sprinted from the bathroom, dropping her clothes in a pile by her car as she raced to the track. Marielle was already there doing high knees in hundred meter intervals. Chapel joined beside her.

"You smell like grease," Marielle said.

"And you smell like regret."

Marielle grunted—her version of a laugh.

They did sprints, resistance training with parachutes, stair runs, and lunges with weights. Chapel's legs felt like brittle twigs by the end of it.

They trudged up the final hill to their cars.

"Have you heard from Zay?" Chapel asked—hating herself for having to do so.

Marielle dabbed at her face with a towel. "Yes."

It was on the tip of her tongue to ask when, to ask if Zay were okay. But Chapel knew Marielle was baiting her. Technically, Chapel wasn't privileged to mission related intel—a fact that Marielle basked in.

Instead, Chapel went a different route. "What happens if they need someone slated and you're not there?"

"What do you mean?"

"Well, I'm assuming Zay and Rush are scouting a potential recruit. What if someone sees or hears something they shouldn't?"

"Zay doesn't get caught. Jackson, though, once or twice. And Rush, too. The only times I've had to make an emergency slate, I've been transferred by a private plane. Let's do our cool down here." Marielle pointed to an empty practice field. Chapel sat across from her, mimicking her movements.

"That sounds like a lot of pressure," she said. "Slating on demand like that."

Marielle slid to the ground and stretched into a perfect split. She leaned her torso over, touching her nose to the ground. "I like pressure."

Chapel tried to bend her body like Marielle's, but even after years of gymnastics and cheerleading, her pesky spine wouldn't allow her to contort like a pretzel.

"Does it always work? Slating?"

Marielle moved from the center and bent her body over her left leg, flexing and pointing her toes in intervals. "My slating does. Yes."

50

"I heard you were very good," Chapel said. She watched as Marielle's breathing stopped, probably waiting for the jab that Chapel might add to the end of the compliment. But it never came.

Marielle switched legs. "I am one of the best. But that's because I take what I do very seriously."

"I would, too. It could probably mess things up for real if someone weren't slated properly."

Marielle gave a rigid laugh. "You have no idea. Back at Trinity, there was this idiot Slater, Micha Dankewich. She had the IQ of a doornail with the body and forehead to match. She tried to slate our history professor into forgetting our Civil War exam."

"What happened?"

Marielle crossed her legs in front of her and pulled an elbow over her head. "She screwed that man up so badly that he still thinks he's Stonewall Jackson."

"Did she get into trouble?"

"She was slated to forget she could slate. So, yes. I'd say that's the worst kind of trouble."

Chapel blinked several times. "Wow. Seems harsh."

"Yes, well, slating is *the* most fragile arena in this world. Think about it—we have the ability to remove memories. To remove thoughts, in some cases. And, if you're very, very good, Slaters can plant memories, too. Vague ones—nuances of real ones, but still. It's a dangerous amount of power."

"I've never thought about it that way," Chapel said. Which was true. She lounged back on her palms, desperately hoping to look casual. "Do you remember that story you told me? About the boys who remembered you had slated them?"

Marielle's chin jerked Chapel's direction. She narrowed her almond-shaped eyes. "Of course I remember the story."

The back of Chapel's neck flushed hot, but she had to press. For Timmy. "I know you're one of the best Slaters around. If not, the best. So, what happened?"

Marielle changed arms and pulled on her elbow, then stretched both of them across her chest. Chapel thought she wasn't going to answer until she stood.

"When you slate in a hurry, the effects aren't as solid. The memories, the information—they're all still there. They're just buried. And I didn't dig deep enough."

Chapel stood, too, and tugged the sleeves of her sweatshirt over her fists.

"Has that happened since?" she asked. "Not with you, I mean. But with other people?"

Marielle's eyebrows were thin, harsh lines. They pushed together in the center of her high forehead. "Are you going somewhere with this?"

Chapel's face burned. She had pushed too hard. To hide her embarrassment, she leaned all the way back on the grass and huffed an exasperated sigh. "Nobody ever tells me anything," she muttered, throwing her arm over her face.

She figured blaming her curiosity on her thirst for knowledge would at least muddle any theories Marielle was forming.

Chapel heard the other girl snort. "You're such a child."

They walked in silence to their respective cars. Chapel's mind was racing.

She had been hoping it had been a Genex quality that prompted the boys' memories of Marielle's betrayal. She had been hoping that Timmy's dream had been a strange, terrible coincidence. She had been hoping she was wrong.

But she wasn't—Timmy's memories of being kidnapped by a gang of Rogue Genexes were coming back. Chapel needed to talk to someone immediately—someone she could trust.

They came to Marielle's car first. Chapel fumbled with the hem of her sweatshirt as Marielle took off her running shoes and replaced them with tall black boots.

The inside of Chapel's mouth tasted like pennies. "Hey, before you go," she said, then balked. She knew her guilt was a weakness, but still felt like a tool for using Marielle's most painful memory to get information. Moreover, she knew doing so made her more like Marielle than she ever wanted to be. "I shouldn't have brought that up back there. It was stupid."

Marielle's eyes flitted to the side. Her skin, flawless and pale, looked like porcelain in the gray daylight.

"It has happened before," she murmured. "People remembering. It's been happening more lately, in fact." Marielle used two fingers to rub her forehead. "They're getting sloppy. Putting Slaters on Field Teams before they've had adequate training."

Chapel suddenly became very aware of every breath she was taking. "Why?"

Marielle huffed. "This stupid interfaction crap. It's screwing up everything."

"What do you mean?"

"Bellum against Thanatos. Thanatos against Bellum." Marielle pointed to Chapel. "You should know just as well as anybody what I'm talking about. Both sides are desperate for the best of the best. And if that means effing up a few minds here and there, they don't care anymore."

"What happens to the people who remember?" Chapel asked. "Do they just slate them again?"

Marielle looked down at her as if seeing her there for the first time. Suspicion tightened her features. "No. They're taken into custody," she said quietly.

"By who?"

"Whoever slated them. What are we talking about here, Chapel?"

The truth filled up her mouth, terrifying her. She swallowed. "I—"

A song started playing in Marielle's bag. *Strangers in the Night*, by Frank Sinatra. She held up a finger, a sly smile creeping across her face.

"Sorry," she said, tilting the screen just long enough for Chapel to see Zay's name flashing. "Gotta take this one in private."

CHAPTER NINE

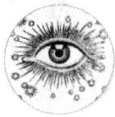

"Um, Chap?" Timmy asked. He glanced over at her, then back to the road he drove them down.

"Huh?"

"You're, um, sort of staring at me."

Chapel flinched, darting her eyes out the window in front of her.

She had just been trying to figure out how to ask Timmy if he'd had any more dreams that were actually memories. She thought she had been discreet.

Apparently, not.

"Oh," she said. "Right. Sorry."

Timmy took off his glasses and rubbed his eyes. "What's up?" A yawn swallowed the space between his sentences. "You've been looking at me like that all night long."

Chapel shifted in her seat, scrambling for something to say. "I was just, you know, thinking."

"About what?"

"About—Well. I was thinking about your . . . neck."

Timmy made a face. "My what? My . . . my *neck*?"

"Absolutely, your neck." She gestured to it grandly. "And its size. It seems a little above average. Actually, way above average. What would you say?"

Timmy's hand came up to the collar of his T-shirt. "Nah. This shirt's from seventh grade. It just makes me looks buffer than I really am."

He made quick eye contact with her—held it—and they both cracked up.

Chapel turned up the music and sat back in her seat. She'd been caught, of course. But Timmy wouldn't call her on it. He let her off the hook. He always did.

"So, what big plans do you have this weekend?" Timmy asked, pulling into her driveway to drop her off. "You and Zay hanging out?"

It had been twenty-four hours since Zay had called Marielle. And not a word from him to her. She knew she should reach out to him about Timmy—had picked up her phone and stared at it until it became nothing but a heavy, black rectangle, and not a tool of communication.

But she didn't.

"I'm not sure," she said. She dipped her mouth into her Styrofoam cup of coffee and slugged it down. "What are you up to?"

Timmy put his Beetle into park. "There's a thing, but it's later on tonight."

Chapel turned to look at him. "Is it a thing with a girl?"

He lifted his shoulders in a shrug.

"Don't be lame," she told him.

He made a face at her. "Okay, maybe there's a girl involved. But you can't tell Erica."

"Timmy."

"What? She's crazy. She'll burn someone's house down. And by someone's, I mean mine."

Chapel didn't respond, but she silently agreed.

"If she asks me," Chapel said, "I can't lie to her. But I won't offer information."

"Fair enough." Timmy started beating out a rhythm on his steering wheel. "Oh, and thanks for dinner tonight. Next time, I'm buying."

Chapel didn't answer. There were more zeroes at the end of her bank account balance than she could find the time to spend.

"No sweat, Valentine."

"Who is that?" Timmy asked, adjusting his rearview mirror. "Is that Zay?"

The shaky beams of headlights danced as a car pulled in the driveway behind them. Chapel gripped Timmy's wrist. She wasn't expecting company.

"Timmy. Stay calm."

Chapel was drawing herself up to Tempus when the car cut its ignition. In the dark, she could see the insignia of a Porsche on the hood of the white SUV.

And behind the wheel sat Gabriel Luxe.

Chapel released a heavy breath. "Oh, it's okay. I know him. He's a friend."

Timmy rubbed his wrist, staring at Chapel with a look of perplexity and worry. "You really have to stop living alone," he said. "It's making you paranoid."

"Says the boy who sleeps with nunchucks under his bed."

"Whatever." Timmy rolled his eyes. "When the zombies are having your brains for breakfast, you'll be wishing you had weaponry, too."

She tilted her chin down and looked at him. "How will I be wishing anything if they're eating my brains?"

"Because you're just stubborn enough to stay alive until the very last bite."

"Sick." Chapel laughed, pushing against Timmy's shoulder. "I'm going to see what he wants. He's probably looking for Zay." The lie rolled off her tongue with ease, burning it.

"Who is this 'friend,' anyway?" Timmy said, twisting in his seat. "I don't really feel good leaving you with . . . "

Gabe had gotten out of his car and was looking down at his phone, a cool blue light illuminating his face.

"Hey . . . wait a minute," Timmy said. "I think I know him."

Chapel's heart sank to her knees. "Hey, call me when—"

"No, I know him. I've *seen* him." Timmy squinted. "Where do I know him from?"

"You've probably seen him around. He works with Zay sometimes."

"Maybe," Timmy said slowly. He closed his eyes. "But for some reason, I picture him sitting across from me. In your house? Did I meet him over here?"

"I don't really remember." Chapel gathered her jacket and shoved it down into her purse.

"Greg. No, Abe . . . Baaay . . . Gabe." Timmy looked at her. "His name is Gabe."

The urge to scream crawled up Chapel's gut. She pressed it down and opened the door to get out. "Call me tomorrow, okay?" She ignored him. "Let me know how your *not*-date goes."

Timmy nodded, but his smile was half-hearted. "If you're sure you're okay," he said, flicking his eyes back at Gabe.

She reached to close the door. "Yes, I'm fine. Go on, now. Shine up those nunchucks before bed."

Chapel almost collapsed in a puddle of relief when his Beetle finally rolled down the driveway.

What if Timmy had gotten out and questioned Gabe? What if he had strung the truth together—right there in her driveway?

Gabe was still on the To Be Determined list in terms of trust, especially with the way he was staring at her—as if she were one of those hologram puzzles, and the 3D image he was trying to draw out of her wouldn't come.

The night air pushed her hair back, whipping the tail of her cream dress behind her. She had worn it hoping Zay would come home today and see her in it.

"Everything okay?" she asked warily. One day the answer to that question was going to be *no*.

He lifted his chin slightly. *Yes.* "I want to show you something."

Zay would lock her up for a month if he found out she went somewhere with Gabriel Luxe. In fact, she was supposed to check in with Jackson in half an hour to let him know she was okay before turning in. She was always checking in. Always obeying orders. Always being a good girl. They told her it was to protect her. They told her to trust them.

Chapel walked toward Gabe as if her body wasn't quaking with the realization that Timmy had just remembered him. In his hands was a set of keys. She plucked them from him. She needed an answer she could hold on to.

"I'm driving."

She expected him to put up a fight—Zay never let her drive. Even if they were in her car, he preferred to be the one behind the wheel.

Gabe followed her wordlessly.

"If you try to kidnap or murder me," she said, "I will use Tempus and give you a thousand tiny paper cuts along the tips of your fingers."

She thought there was a shadow of a smile along his mouth before he touched the corner of it with his tongue. "Deal."

Chapel didn't know a lot about cars, but she knew what it felt like to hold power in the palm of her hand. The engine growled with the promise of what she needed—control.

"Atlanta," he said.

Chapel pushed the Porsche as hard as she dared.

"Was that Timmy?" he asked once they were out of Bennett Park.

Chapel nodded. He knew it was—knew Timmy's car, knew Timmy's face. And probably a plethora of other things about Timmy. As part of his former mission, Gabe had followed Chapel for months and months without her ever knowing it.

Chapel had no idea what he knew.

"How is he doing?"

Chapel resisted a sigh. She didn't feel like talking. "He's good."

When she said nothing else, Gabe must have taken a hint. He reached over and turned up the music.

"Oh, you're in my veins and I cannot get you out."

She lifted her face without looking at him. "Another song."

He pressed a button. A heavy thud bumped beneath her, making her seat vibrate. She recognized it from Erica's rotation.

She raised a single eyebrow at him. "Jay Z? Really?"

Gabe's mouth twitched. "You're not the only one capable of surprising people."

She didn't know what that meant, and she didn't care to. "No," she said, "but you are a skinny white boy from the sticks of Australia. I think it's safe to say you're not his target audience."

Gabe's mouth popped open briefly, then he shut it. He looked stunned—she'd sounded harsh.

She turned the music down. "That was a stupid thing to say."

"It's okay." His eyes swept over the side of her face. "For the record, though, I'm not *that* skinny."

He was right. His broad torso stretched wide across the tan leather of his seat. He had traded his suit for jeans and a starched button-up shirt. It was the same color as the aquamarine eyes that held hers steadily. They were deep-set eyes with short, dark lashes. They looked clear and curious, yet somber.

Again, Chapel was struck by the thought that there was something very different about this Gabe. The one who had gone home to Broken Hill, Australia for six weeks and returned to *finish her.*

Suddenly the car felt much, much smaller.

A horn beeped behind her. She cleared her throat and resumed driving.

They didn't speak much after that.

Once inside the city, Gabe pointed to an exit. "There."

She pulled into a large complex that was half glass and half white brick.

"Where are we?" she asked.

"It's called The O."

"What are we doing here?"

He opened his door, tilting his neck toward the building. "Having dinner."

Chapel didn't move. "I thought you wanted to show me something."

"I do. You'll have to be patient, though."

She made a face. She hated patience because she had very little.

Chapel reached for her purse, but realized that she didn't have it. No purse. No phone. No jacket. She had left it all in Timmy's floorboard. She couldn't check in with Jackson, couldn't answer the phone if Zay called.

Essentially, she was at the mercy of a man whom she suspected was teetering on the edge. Of what—she was planning to find out.

They walked inside. The restaurant was all warm-colored wood and dark iron. The music was up and the lights were down.

There were two floors, and they were upstairs. She couldn't see what the first story held, but the one she looked at was packed to capacity with bodies and tables.

Gabe leaned toward the hostess whose nametag read *Kacie* and whispered something in her ear. The girl giggled and put her hand on Gabe's chest. She was tall and thin with angular features and a long, dark ponytail. Maybe it was his girlfriend.

Attractive, Chapel decided, *if you're into the whole supermodel thing.*

She realized, then, that she knew basically nothing about the man who knew basically everything about her.

Kacie glanced over Gabe's shoulder at her. She said something to him lowly, her eyes on Chapel. Gabe's chin moved parallel to his shoulder. Chapel stood just inside his periphery. He stepped closer to Kacie and whispered into her ear.

Kacie tugged at her necklace, sliding its pendant from side to side. It caught Chapel's attention because it looked so much like her own, a round eye surrounded by stars. Only Kacie's was done in all silver.

She turned away from Gabe and took two menus from a stack. "Right this way," she said with a stunning smile. Her voice was throaty and rich. "Follow me."

Gabe motioned that Chapel walk ahead of him.

"Thank you, Kacie," Gabe said. "This table is perfect."

Kacie met Chapel's eyes briefly, then walked away.

Gabe shook out a napkin. "I would recommend the homemade cheese sauce," he said causally. "It's quite good."

"Was that your girlfriend?" she asked. The words popped out of her mouth like a verbal Jack-in-the-Box.

Gabe let his napkin hang in the air, suspended above his lap. "No," he said. "Why?"

Their server came to the table and took their drink order. When he left, she leaned forward in her chair so he could pick out her voice among the many others.

"Because I realized that I have no idea who you are," she said. "Because I've taken a huge risk by coming with you tonight. Because I'm wondering if it was a mistake."

"Do you really think I would hurt you?" he asked. "After all the months I spent watching you, protecting you?"

Chapel shrugged. "I don't know what to think about you."

Gabe propped his elbows on the table, balancing his chin on his palm. "What do you want to know?"

Chapel thought she probably shouldn't lead with something too heavy. She needed to warm him up first.

"Well, how was your visit home?"

He shrugged. "It was a much-needed trip."

"When's the last time you were there?"

"A long time ago."

Chapel tapped her fingers along the table. He wasn't really giving her a lot to work with. "So, is your family still there?"

"Yes, they're all still there."

"So, why did you go back? To visit them?"

"Yes. And I needed to think."

"And did you? Think?"

He nodded. "Too much, I'm afraid."

She tapped the side of her head. "Yeah, I'm with you. Thinking can be a real chore. Sometimes I wish I could just throw my thoughts away. Just send them through some type of mental shredder, you know?"

He took a drink and gritted his teeth to swallow. "Yes," he said. "I do."

Chapel closed her eyes and slowly let her head fall on the table. She started to pretend snore, much louder than a dignified girl should.

After a few moments, something hit her in the face—a rolled up napkin, she thought—and she feigned waking up.

"Huh? What?" She smacked with her mouth. "Were you saying something? Because I think I just passed out from boredom over here."

He smiled at her. He was blushing. "Sometimes I forget how young you are."

Chapel crossed her eyes at him. "Oh, yeah? Something tells me I'm going to be this way when I'm forty. What will be my excuse, then?"

"That you're an American, of course."

"Don't be a snob." She flicked the wadded wrapper of her straw at him. "America is rad. We invented hot dogs."

He laughed at that, putting his hand on his chest and letting his head fall back. When he looked back at her, a bit of the old Gabe was there.

"All right, all right. I'll talk—if only to keep you from rattling on so."

Gabe told her about Broken Hill, a mining town in New South Wales. His parents had moved there from a neighboring city in the seventies, looking to cash in on the zinc boom. They were still married, thirty years later, and lived just miles from his older sister in the same house he grew up in.

He talked about his childhood warmly, as if reading about it from his favorite book.

"It was as typical an upbringing as any could be, I guess. Dad worked, Mom stayed home with my sister and I. We played outside a lot." He picked up his drink and finished it. "I'm not sure if you know this," he said with mock-seriousness, "but I grew up in the sticks of Australia."

"Oh, good," she said, "I was really hoping you'd bring *that* up again."

Their waiter brought their meal, and, despite having dinner with Timmy just hours earlier, Chapel dug in, dipping several fries into her cheese sauce at once and shoving them in her mouth.

"What?" she asked once she swallowed. "I burn, like, a million calories a day when I train. Keep talking."

He smiled and continued. "Everything was very run-of-the-mill for me until I was about thirteen," he said. "Then I started having dreams—graphic, vivid dreams. And then they'd come true."

"Mmm. It's all fun and games until that pituitary gland starts firing away."

Gabe's eyebrows flew up. "Yes, it's typical for male Seers to become aware of their exception once puberty begins. You've been studying."

"I'm low on reading materials."

"Oh?"

"Well, I used to read all the time." She licked her fingers before she thought better of it. "Like, all the time. It wasn't always good for me, because I used books to escape my own reality. This, according to Erica, of all people. Anyway, she made me box up my books and put them in the basement."

"So, you've resorted to Genex textbooks?"

"Zay says it's important for me to understand as much as I can about each exception. He never says why, but I think it's so I can exploit their weaknesses if I need to. He worries about me because I'm small."

Gabe turned out his bottom lip. "Isaiah is a cunning adversary. Listen to him."

There was a lull in the conversation for a moment. Their waiter came by with refills, and Chapel wondered what time it was. Would Jackson send someone to Todd's house? How would she explain her absence? She really should have thought this through better.

When she shifted her eyes back to Gabe's, he was looking at her like he had when she got out of Timmy's car—like he was trying to decide something very, very important. It made her squirm.

"What do you like to do for fun?" she blurted, anxious to get out from under his assessing gaze. "You know, besides stalk young girls and see the future?"

He blinked his glazed expression away. "Ha ha. For fun . . . let's see. I like to hike, when the weather's cool. I'm a decent cook. And I like music. Actually, I love music." He fiddled with the seam at the label on his bottle. He smiled at it, not looking at her. "I used to be in a band back home."

Chapel smacked the table. "Shut up. I totally called it. The first time I met you, you had that beard and ponytail and I thought, that guy plays the guitar."

"That's the first thing you thought when you saw me? Seriously?"

She nodded.

Gabe breathed a silent laugh and tucked his chin to his chest. He was quiet for a moment. Then he looked up at her without moving his head, his dark eyelashes skimming the crest of his brow. "Do you want to know what I thought? When you walked into that office?"

Chapel rolled her eyes. She had screamed like an idiot the first day she met Gabe, thinking a cat was a huge rat. "What? What were you thinking?"

"I'd been watching you for a while then, so I knew you were nervous. You were biting the insides of your cheeks— it's your anxious habit."

Chapel glanced at the table and swallowed.

"And then you smiled," he said, "as if you were genuinely happy to see me. I'm sure you were just glad to find the office, or being friendly, but still. I remember thinking," he lowered his voice. "I remember thinking, now that's the kind of smile a guy could lose himself in, and never find his way out again."

Across the table, Gabe went very still. Chapel thought he was freezing up because of what he'd said, but he wasn't looking at her. He was looking over her shoulder at the front door.

"What?" she asked. "What's happening?"

Gabe leaned toward her, so close she could smell his aftershave. "Your use of Tempus will be needed shortly. Are you up for it?"

"My *what?*" She started to turn around, but Gabe grabbed her wrist.

"No, don't look. I don't want them to see your face."

"Who? Who don't—" She stopped talking because he wasn't listening. His eyes scanned the room back and forth, back and forth. A full minute went by, and Chapel watched Gabe's eyes follow someone across the room.

"Three tables to my right is a couple. One is Bellum, the other Thanatos."

"Okay," she said slowly. If there were a point, she was ready for him to make it.

"Just keep that in mind," he whispered. "Get ready."

Chapel's heart hammered behind her ribs. What was going on? Was this part of his plan? Or had something gone wrong?

"My front pocket," he said. "As soon as you Tempus."

She didn't answer. She was concentrating on her breathing technique, filling her body with the energy she'd need to push it back out of her faster than the speed of light—making everything around her seem as if it were frozen.

"Can you do it?" Gabe asked.

She nodded, a fluttering kind of thrill rippling through her.

"Then, whenever you're ready."

She counted down in her head. *Three, two, one. Go.*

Her spine pushed toward her stomach, jerking her body forward. Her elbow popped the table, spilling her water all over her lap and the floor.

Out of instinct, Chapel rose to her feet, trying to step away from the frigid drips. But then her foot got caught on the rung of her chair, and her body tilted at an angle she knew there was no recovering from.

Chapel rolled into the fall, her shoulder and hipbone taking most of the impact.

Everything was still. Everything was silent.

She stayed there for a moment, shaking her head as tiny white lights danced behind her eyelids.

It was the rockiest start to Tempus she'd ever had. She'd rushed it, of course. Maybe trying to impress Gabe. Maybe simply overestimating herself.

"And that," she told the frozen room, "is why my middle name is Grace."

There was a notecard and a small white envelope folded in half inside Gabe's pocket. The card had perfect boxy handwriting on it.

There's an office above the bar. Go there. Open the envelope at nine thirty-seven.

Now that her dress was wet and her body ached, Chapel wasn't in the mood for games. Or fun. Or being out of contact with the people who watched out for her.

A slow ache rose in her throat. *Zay*. She missed him. And when he found out she'd come with Gabe, he would not understand.

For a moment, it crossed her mind to release Tempus and tell Gabe to take her home. She knew she should. In fact, the urge was so strong, she closed her eyes to do so. But when she did, Gabe's face flashed in front of her, wearing the strange expression he'd had several times that evening.

It hit her then that it was the same expression she had felt on her face when she'd studied Timmy earlier that very night.

Gabe was keeping something from her. And either he was trying to decide if she already knew, or he was trying to decide if he should tell her.

At the last second, Chapel's curiosity won out. She skirted around the crowded room to a door just beyond the foyer. She'd seen it when she came in and assessed the room, Zay's soft words in her ears. *Always have two exit strategies.*

The door was metal, and it groaned when she pulled it. Chapel took the narrow stairway to the top where another door sat propped open with a bottle.

She stepped through it cautiously, only to find a small room with a desk at the center. It faced a row of windows that looked out over the restaurant.

She touched the cool glass. It looked like a mirror from the other side, and no one could see her. She was on the inside looking out.

Activity resumed, and if anyone noticed a missing blonde, they didn't react. She did, however, see Gabe assess her chair—askew, her glass—toppled over, and shake his head.

Chapel waited for the nausea to come, but since she'd only used Tempus for a few minutes, it was mild.

She looked at her watch. It read nine-thirty one. She tapped her foot. She wrung out the hem of her dress. She paced along the mirror. She sighed.

At nine thirty-four, she walked back to the door she'd come through and pushed against it. It was locked.

"You better have a good reason for this, Luxe," she mumbled.

Then, at nine thirty-six, she opened the envelope. It was another set of notecards. She read the first one.

I see you, it said. Those three words scattered goose bumps across her skin. *And I knew you would open this early.*

She glanced down at Gabe who was staring right at her as if he could see her. He motioned with his hand to carry on. Chapel flipped to the second card.

Right now a man is approaching the couple I pointed out to you. They call him Night.

Chapel watched as a man with skin the color of an onyx stone approached their table. He was bald and large, and when the boy saw him, his eyes grew wide.

He started to stand, but the man pressed down on his shoulder, settling him back into his chair by force.

Chapel flipped to the next card.

Night recruited Nicholas, the boy you're worried about, to Thanatos.

Back at the table, Nicholas's face was suffused pink. Night gestured to the girl at the table, the Bellum girl, and Nicholas threw his hands in the air. This time when Nicholas went to stand, Night didn't push him back down.

Chapel could hear the steady increase of her own breathing. She flipped the card.

Night disagrees with Nicholas's choice in company. He thinks Bellum are beneath him.

She flipped the card.

And this is how he shows it.

Chapel watched as Night drew back his massive arm and slammed it directly into Nicholas's jaw. Nicholas reeled back, knocking over the waitress behind him, sending a tray of food and drinks scattering everywhere.

Chapel could hear the clatter and gasps sounding from below.

Nicholas' girlfriend rushed toward him, but Night caught her by the back of her dress and flung her out of the way. Her head cracked against a post, and her eyes fell shut.

Chapel's hand flew to her mouth. It muffled her scream.

Nicholas whipped to his feet much faster than Chapel expected. He was smaller than Night, but fast. And his leg jerked out quickly, catching Night at his knees.

Night fell, and Nicholas came behind him, getting him in a headlock and squeezing.

Then, as if materializing out of thin air, two men came up and grabbed Nicholas from behind, dragging him to his feet. He struggled against them, jerking and kicking. But it was no use.

Night slowly lumbered to stand. He took a handkerchief from his back pocket and dabbed at his brow, all the while saying something to Nicholas that Chapel couldn't hear. She squinted, trying to read his lips.

"Know better," she made out. *"Your own kind . . . learn your lesson . . . "*

Then he dropped back slowly, reminding Chapel of a panther stalking his prey. She watched as he smiled at Nicholas, a cold, deadly thing, his white teeth like razors in the dark mask of his head.

His leg jerked back so quickly that Chapel almost missed it until he drove it into Nicholas's stomach for the second time.

"No!" she shouted, slamming her hand into the glass.

Her eyes sought after Gabe, who was standing to his own feet.

Night kicked Nicholas again, and again, and again. Blood dripped from the boy's mouth, and his head lolled to the side. She looked away.

Her hand gripped the cotton of her dress, moving across the raised ridges of the scar on her heart. She saw chocolate brown eyes with tears in them. She smelled burning flesh, the faint sizzle crackling in her ear. She heard a hideous scream, scrambling from her throat. It was hers.

In the moment, all the training, the missions, the glory of being good at something, it all paled in comparison to the bleak reality that the potential for evil lurked beneath the layers of every man, regardless of their affiliation.

Chapel's heart rose higher and higher into her throat. It was difficult for her to grab a full breath.

When she opened her eyes again, Gabe was approaching Night. He pulled on the larger man's shoulder, turning him around.

Night wiped his nose and said something that looked vulgar. Gabe sighed, as if he hoped it wouldn't come to this. Then he lowered his shoulder and barreled into Night, throwing him onto his back, and toppling over the two men holding Nicholas.

The girlfriend, now awake, scrambled to Nicholas's side and pulled him by the arm beneath their table. Her face was streaked with tears and blood.

Chapel watched as Gabe wrestled Night to the ground, the two exchanging blows evenly.

One of Night's lackeys tried to grab for Gabe, but Kacie was there, hitting him over the back of the head with a large black bottle. He fell to the ground in a heavy heap.

The other man helping Night managed to drag Gabe away, but Gabe let his backward motion aid him in slamming the man into the same post Nicholas's girlfriend had hit.

Gabe turned, ready for the punch that Night was aiming at the back of his head, and caught his wrist, twisting it up and around his back. He slammed Night face-first into the back wall with a jarring thud.

Gabe leaned his face to Night's ear and said something Chapel couldn't see. Then he dropped him in a heavy heap on the floor.

The whine of sirens screamed through the restaurant, and Gabe turned to Kacie and said something. She nodded. It looked like she said back to him, *"Any time."*

Gabe disappeared briefly, and Chapel heard footsteps on the stairs. The door swung open.

"We need to go," he said.

Chapel let him grab her hand and lead her down the stairs. They ran into the parking deck and he practically tossed her in his car. His tires screeched beneath them and he flung them onto the black highway.

She wasn't sure exactly why, but she started to cry. She cried and she couldn't stop. She cried hard, leaning over and propping her elbows on her knees.

Gabe's hand rested on her back.

"Don't *touch* me," she snapped, lifting her head to look at him. "What was that all about, huh? Why did I need to see *that?*"

Gabe replaced both hands on the steering wheel and gripped it until his bloody knuckles turned white.

"In D.C., I told you I wanted you to make an informed decision. *That's* what that was about."

Chapel made a frustrated sound deep in her throat. "You think I don't know how hard it will be to date Zay if I'm forced into Bellum? That's what that was about?"

"No, Chapel. That had nothing to do with Isaiah."

"Then, *what*? You want me to hate all of Thanatos because of one thug?"

Gabe's lips formed a hard line. "That's not it, either. I wanted to show you what the Genex society has become. We are obsessed with having the best recruits. We care more about who we get to pledge, and less about the terror we are supposed to prevent."

"So, what? So I refuse to join either sector and become Rogue?"

"That's not what I said," Gabe said quietly. "That's not what I want."

They didn't speak the rest of the way home. Chapel was too horrified, too confused, and too embarrassed.

She was supposed to be a solider in training, and she had cracked. How could she expect herself to stay calm when she was right in the middle of the action, if she couldn't even hold it together on the sidelines?

The moon hung high above her house when they pulled into the driveway.

When she reached for her seatbelt, Gabe put a hand on her arm. "I'm not sorry I took you there," he said. "You have to understand, I *see* a few steps ahead of you."

Chapel didn't respond, but climbed from his car and shut the door.

Timmy had dropped her purse off, and it sat on the top of the porch step. She took out her phone and sent a series of texts.

JACKSON: *I'm home.*

TIMMY: *I'm home.*

MOM: *I'm home.*

ZAY: *Come home.*

CHAPTER TEN

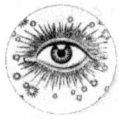

She was in between classes on Tuesday when Zay finally texted.

ZAY: *Come see me.*

A knife of guilt pricked Chapel's chest. She hadn't heard from Gabe since he'd dropped her off Saturday, and the longer she thought about what had happened, the worse she felt about it.

It had been an irrational decision to go with him, and stupid.

She longed to hear the low, velvet voice that would cool the flames of fear that had been growing in her chest.

She was afraid for Timmy. She was afraid for her relationship with Zay. She was afraid for her future.

Chapel tucked herself into the bathroom and called him. He answered on the first ring.

"Hey, babe."

"Hey."

"Skip school and come rub my feet."

She rolled her eyes to herself. "In addition to your phone, did you lose your mind on this mission?"

Zay groaned. "You're mad."

She toyed with her necklace, rolling her bottom lip between her teeth. "I was worried about you."

"Chap, you know better. I don't get caught."

"Everybody says they don't get caught until they get caught."

"How about I make you a deal," he said. "If I get caught, I'll give you one free shot—just not to my face. Obviously."

Chapel slapped her forehead into her hand. "You're a dork."

"Yeah, but I make dork look good."

The bell rang overhead. "I'm late for Office Aid."

Zay gave an exaggerated gasp. "Oh no! Will the secretary run out of tardy slips? Will the copier become inoperably jammed? The *horrors.*"

"Zay. I am not skipping school to come see a boy who can't even text me back."

She heard his body shifting against the phone, and imagined him sitting up in bed. "Wait, you're really upset. Did something happen? Marielle said she checked in with you all the time. If she lied, I'll—"

"No, it's fine, Zay. It's fine." Chapel sagged against the wall. "I handled it."

There was silence on his end for a long stretch. "This conversation isn't over."

She rolled her eyes. "It rarely is."

* * * *

Chapel had ink caked beneath her fingernails. She scrubbed at them again, silently cursing Isaiah Halstead. He'd been right—the copier had gotten jammed, and Chapel had spent the last half hour fishing bits of paper out of crevices too small for human hands to get to.

When she returned to her desk in the front office, Mrs. Wallace was filing her pristine nails.

"Your stepdad called," she said, cracking her gum between her front teeth. "He said he was able to get you the appointment you needed, but you should check out right away to make it on time."

Chapel blinked rapidly. Todd called? About an appointment? *No.* Impossible.

"Did he, um, happen to mention the name of the physician I'm seeing?" Chapel asked cautiously.

Mrs. Wallace waved with her nail file to a yellow square on Chapel's desk. "He spelled it out for me. It's on that Post-it. Must be Russian, or something. I can't pronounce it."

Chapel kept her face smooth as she read the bubbly letters.

Dr. Ivanasay, 11:00am. Ivanasay? Chapel sucked both lips in to keep from laughing. *I want Zay.*

"Hm," Chapel said, nodding her head seriously. "Yes. That's the one. I should go. He's really, really hard to get in with."

When she got into her car, she had a text.

ZAY: *Bennett Park Memorial Gardens.*

To the outside world, a cemetery would be a strange place for a boyfriend and girlfriend to meet. But for Chapel and Zay, *normal* wasn't a word in their vocabulary. And since neither of them fully trusted the privacy of either's house, the small burial grounds just off the square was both peaceful and quiet.

They had ended many training sessions there, sitting on one of the benches and talking until long after the sun went down.

Chapel arrived to a nearly empty parking lot. She was leaning over her trunk to get her jacket out when a rough hand clamped down on her mouth and an arm wrapped around her waist.

She went into self-defense mode, shifting her hips aside to get a shot at the groin. Her attacker anticipated her move, shifting with her, dragging her back between a white van and a truck.

Chapel tried to get a piece of his hand inside her mouth, but couldn't. She did manage to grind her heel into the top of his foot, and she used the brief flinch of pain to shift her hips again and swing the heel of her hand between his legs.

She was within a breath of making contact when a leg wrapped around hers, tangling them. She would have crumbled to the ground if strong arms hadn't scooped her up.

"That was too close for comfort, Sweet Girl," Zay said, grinning down at her.

"Dang it!" she said, laughing and groaning at the same time. "I almost had you."

He squinted at her. "Yes. But our chances of having incredibly gorgeous and intelligent children together would have decreased by at least twenty-five percent."

"Was I kind of awesome, though?" she asked. "Besides missing that first time?"

His gray eyes looked wary. "You had a good teacher." He kissed her between her eyes. "Next time swing your hips and your arm back at the same time."

Always the instructor. Chapel smiled and relaxed, leaning her cheek against the soft leather of his black jacket. "I missed you," she whispered.

Zay propped his back against the van and pulled her close to him again. He took out her ponytail holder and ran his fingers through her tangled hair. "Tell me again."

"I missed you."

His arms tightened around her briefly, and she felt his deep exhale against her chest. Zay seemed to stand in awe of her affection for him. Like he never expected someone to love him, to need him like she did.

"Now," he said, "you made me a promise a few months ago. You promised to never tell me things were fine when they aren't fine."

She kept her face against him so she wouldn't have to look at him. "I was mad," she whispered.

"Promises aren't suspended just because you're *mad.*"

"That's a dumb rule."

"Rules usually are." He ran his hands up and down her back, across her arms, along the sides of her neck "Why don't you start by telling me why you're mad?"

Chapel put her hands over her face. "Do I have to?"

"Generally, that's how conversations work."

Chapel rarely wished she were more like Erica. But in this scenario, she did. By now, Erica would have already cussed out Zay, made up with him, and gotten mad at him about something totally new.

"Can we sit down first?"

Zay led her to a marble bench at the bottom of the hill. She knew he sat facing away from her father's grave on purpose, so she wouldn't have to look at the mockery of her grief.

He took her hand in his and looked at her expectantly.

"Okay," she said, "I'm just going to say it—I went for a run with Marielle, and you called her. I got jealous. Then I texted you Friday night and you didn't respond."

Zay's forehead pinched together. "When did I call Marielle?"

Chapel sighed loudly, and Zay put up both hands.

"Hey, I just spent an entire week tracking a mark in the backwoods of Kentucky. The days kind of run together."

Chapel licked her lips. "It was Thursday."

"Thursday? Thursday, . . . " Zay's knee bounced as he chanted. "Oh, *Thursday* Thursday. Yes, I called Marielle."

"I know, Zay," Chapel snapped. "That's my point. Why do you have time to call her, but not *me*? Did you not want to know how my meeting with Chary and Gabe went?"

"Of course I did," he said. "Jackson sent me an email right after it that was practically a transcript of it. And I had to call Marielle with a work-related question. We talked maybe thirty seconds."

Chapel pulled her hand from his and pretended to adjust the ring on her thumb. "Why does she always want me to think there's something happening between the two of you?"

Zay sighed. "I don't know, Chapel."

"I want to punch her."

"Do you want me to talk to her?"

"Actually, the opposite of that." She flicked her eyes at him from the side. "I want you to never talk to her again."

Zay put both hands on her face and moved it to where he could see her. "I don't want to talk to you about Marielle," he said. "I want to know why you were trying to reach me."

Chapel put a little distance between them, scooting back on the bench to turn toward him. "It doesn't matter anymore," she said. "I told you that I handled it."

She added silently, *If by handling it, you mean pretending like none of my problems exist.*

Zay's cheeks twitched with the grit of his teeth. "You do know," he said, "that you make me angrier than any target, any Rogue ever has?"

She shrugged. "Um, thanks?"

Zay shook his head at her. "What form of torture are you?"

"The good kind?"

He bent his neck and kissed her, the stubble on his jaw brushing along her chin. Chapel wrapped her arms around his neck, pulling the collar of his jacket to reach him.

She wanted to get closer to Zay, to crack the locks of his body and climb inside.

As if he were thinking the same thing, Zay's hand pulled her neck to him, and he slipped a hand beneath her jacket and sweater, gripping her waist.

She kissed him with every fear, every joy, and every unknown pulsing through her heavy heart. No, kissing Zay wouldn't solve any of her problems, but it was the only time her mind was blissfully quiet.

After a while, Zay pulled his face back, just barely. "I know you're hiding something," he said, breathing heavily against her neck. "If you tell me, I promise I won't tell Jackson unless I think he needs to know. Just like the thing with your dad."

Chapel didn't answer immediately—just soaked in every last detail of him. His ink-colored hair, brushed straight back off his high forehead. His face, all planes and hard lines—surprisingly elegant and alarmingly handsome.

"I don't think it's wise," she said, "for me to bargain with you at present."

His mouth tilted up. "And why's that?"

"Let's just say I'm not immune to the nefarious Halstead charm."

"Wait a minute." Zay stood. "Did you just . . . hold on." He cupped his hands around his mouth. "Hear ye, hear ye," he shouted. "All good people of Bennett Park Memorial Gardens. *The* Chapel Ryan just confessed that I may, at least in some part, have some sort of affect on her."

She tugged on his arm, giggling, begging him to be quiet. A woman walking a dog on the sidewalk that hugged the outskirts of the cemetery stared openly.

"I'll be signing autographs later on the public square," Zay continued at full volume, "as well as penning a memoir about my harrowing journey into the uncharted territory of—"

She launched herself onto his back, clamping her hand over his mouth.

Zay leaned over, shucking her off and catching her in one graceful motion. Then, as if she were his child, he gently sat her down on the bench and knelt between her knees, facing her.

His eyes looked almost colorless in the midday sun—orbs of perfect water she wanted to dive into. "One day, you'll trust me with everything," he said seriously. "And I will count it as one of the best days of my entire life."

Chapel's heart ached with the desire to unload. But her head—that always treading, always calculating head of hers—wouldn't allow it.

Where is my father? What if my friends get dragged into this again? What if I fail? Why don't you call me when you're gone? How can I love you this much, and survive it if we don't make it?

"I'm scared," she whispered instead. *"This* is scary."

He took her hands into his, pressing kisses into her palms. "I'm glad," he said. "Because you're right—it's scary. It's unpredictable. I want you to be prepared, and part of that is recognizing the gravity of what you'll commit to if you join us."

"What if I'm not good enough?" she said. "What if, when it's time for the real challenges to begin, I freeze up?"

Zay wrapped a ribbon of her hair around his finger and tucked it behind her ear. "Do you remember the night Hunter broke in to Goodson's? How you tried to run in there without even thinking?"

She nodded. Tamera, a friend from school, had been inside. Along with three Rogues.

"Your instincts are good. It's when you get caught up in your head for too long that you second guess yourself," he said.

She wanted to believe him so badly her chest throbbed.

"It was one of the first things I noticed about you," he said. "That part of you that gets so focused on what you think is *right* that it's all you can think about. That you throw yourself at it even if it's a train coming at you straight on."

Zay took her face in his hands again, and used his thumbs to brush lines down her cheeks.

"I love that about you," he said. The way his eyebrows pulled together made her wonder if he'd meant to use that word. *Love.*

Her entire body tingled. "What else?" she asked. Her breath came out shakily. "Do you love about me?"

He ran his hands down her shoulders and arms. He turned over her fingers and smiled. "I love this part of you." He kissed her wrist. "I love this part of you." He kissed her chin. "I love this part of you. And this part of you." He kissed her eyelids, each one in turn. When his hands reached for the top button of her sweater, she went very, very still.

"I love this part of you." He kissed the hollow of her throat. He unbuttoned the next button. "I love this part of you." He kissed her clavicle.

Chapel could see the jerk of her own heart beneath her chest as Zay exposed the area of skin that was scared. She never let him see it, and her cheeks burned at the hideous sight of it—displayed in the bright sun.

He looked her right in the eye and said, "Chapel, I *love* this part of you."

He said it with such feeling, such conviction, that she felt the effect of each syllable fusing many of the fissures in her wounded heart.

He pressed his mouth against the mangled skin, staying there for a long, long time.

* * * *

She was late by the time she clocked in at Back Porch, but there were only a few tables seated. Chapel checked on them and brought around a few refills before returning to the kitchen.

Erica was leaning over the stainless steel counter that faced the grill and oven area, eating French fries straight from the vat. Chapel followed the line of Erica's laser-steady focus.

Then she dropped the tray of trash she had just brought in from the dining room.

Gabriel Luxe was wearing a red Back Porch apron, standing in front of the grill. He flipped a hamburger patty in the air and caught it on a spatula. The sound of freshly burning meat sizzled around them.

"Chapel, this is our new cook," Erica said without removing her eyes from him. "Gabe. Gabe has an accent. Gabe, this is Chapel. Chapel has a boyfriend."

Gabe glanced over his shoulder, his expression blank. "I know Chapel," he said. "We met when she visited UGA. I used to work there."

Erica groaned. "Don't tell me. You're in love with her. All the pretty boys fall for Chap."

"She's the one who told me about Back Porch," Gabe continued. "I'm in town for a bit working on a special project, and I could use the extra cash."

He met Chapel's eye over Erica's head. *This is the story*, his look said. *Play along.*

Gabe moved the burger into a basket and Erica gave a little clap. Chapel leaned over to be sure—*Yes*. Erica was drooling a little.

Gabe pushed the basket to Erica. "There you go. Perfectly cooked American burger." He stuck a toothpick through its center. "With toasted buns."

Erica giggled. "Did you hear that, Chap? His buns are . . . they're . . . I'm sorry. What do you say about your buns, again?"

The tight look that Gabe handed Chapel told her she was doing a terrible job of acting normal.

She shook her head free of shock, and knocked Erica's hips with her own. "Sober up, Jersey. It's an accent. Not alcohol."

Erica's eyes widened. "Gabe as an adult beverage? There's a thought." She tapped her acrylic nails along the metal counter. "Gabe? What are your thoughts on whipped cream as a garnish?"

Chapel threw a napkin in Erica's face. "I think someone needs a trip to the freezer to cool off."

Gabe laughed, and Chapel noticed a light purple flush at the edge of his jawbones. He shifted his body toward her. "And what for you? Wait—don't tell me. I want to make you something. It's called an Aussie burger. You'll love it."

Then he returned to the grill and started unwrapping ingredients. She had no idea why he was here or how she felt about it.

Meanwhile, however, she *was* kind of hungry.

Chapel snatched one of the French fries and used it to point at Erica's hair. "Looks good."

Finally breaking her stare, Erica stood up straighter and bit into her burger. "My Lord, Gabe," she said, "What's in this thing? Angel tears?" She took another huge bite, then motioned to her hair. "It looks better," she said after she swallowed. "I put a toner on it. I still look like a walking orange sherbet."

"I happen to love orange sherbet," Chapel said. "It's delicious."

Thomas stuck his head in the kitchen. "Erica, table six is asking for you."

Erica rolled her eyes. "Customers. Always wanting something."

As soon as she left, Gabe plopped a basket in front of her. "Your Aussie special," he said, smiling broadly. "I held the pickles."

She took a bite and sighed without meaning to. It really was heavenly. "I am still mad at you," she breathed. "But this helps."

Gage grabbed a rag and tossed it to her. "Soda water," he said. "You've already managed to get ketchup on yourself."

She went to the fountain machine and obeyed, dabbing at the stain.

"I need to talk to you," Gabe said quietly. He'd come around the counter and was standing right behind her. She hadn't even heard him move. "Somewhere safe," he added.

Chapel nodded, darting her eyes to the kitchen door. "When?"

"Soon. After work?"

She shook her head. "I have training. Then I'm watching a movie with Zay."

Gabe was quiet for a moment, then, "Did you tell him?"

She turned around and looked at him, crossing her arms over her chest. "No."

The time they'd spent was too sweet—too needed to sour it with explanations as to why she was out to dinner with Gabe. Explanations that she didn't even *have*.

"Good," Gabe said quickly. "What I have to say won't take long. Why don't we meet here, before you go? Somewhere private?"

Chapel glanced around the narrow room. "The walk-in freezer?" she asked, pointing. "No one ever goes in there because it smells like fish."

Gabe nodded once.

The rest of her shift dragged by. Business was slow, and Chapel was anxious to hear what Gabe had to say.

It was half an hour until quitting time when Thomas came into the empty dining room. "Well, ladies," he said, "I believe everyone is still hibernating. Who wants to go home?"

Chapel looked at Erica, who was picking her teeth in the reflection of a napkin holder.

"Erica? You want to go?"

Erica threw her toothpick into the air. "You don't have to ask me twice. I need to get a mani, anyway." She motioned for Chapel to follow her to the door. "Okay, spill," she said.

Chapel felt her face go from warm, to hot, to cold. "Spill? Spill about what?"

Erica rolled her eyes. "About *Timmy*. What else would I be talking about?"

"Timmy?" Chapel squeaked. Then, she got it. "Ooooh *Timmy.*"

"Yeah, Timmy. I know you guys had dinner the other night. Tell me everything he said."

Chapel bit the insides of her cheeks. "Um . . . "

Erica's face fell. "That bad, huh?"

"No, not at all," Chapel blurted. "He's just afraid, you know?"

Erica's face was very still. "Afraid of what?"

Chapel shrugged. "That you two will end up like Logan and I. And can you blame him? The Logan thing has been kind of a disaster."

Erica pulled at the loose sole to her shoe. "Yeah. Whatever, it's fine."

Chapel grabbed her friend's shoulder and forced Erica to look at her—probably an odd sight—as she was at least six inches shorter than Erica. "Don't say *It's fine,* Jersey. That's my line."

Erica pressed her full lips together in a firm line. She didn't say anything.

"Do you want my advice?" Chapel asked quietly.

"I have a feeling I'll get it either way."

"Yeah," Chapel said. "You will. Here it is—either tell Timmy you love him, or find a way to live with just being friends. I miss us. All three of us."

Erica poofed the back of her hair and threw her shoulders back.

She would be a beautiful woman, Chapel realized. She would grow into her gangly arms and legs; fill out where she was too skinny.

She would meet a boy—probably at the salon she'd get a job at after cosmetology school—and they'd get married. She'd curse a lot. Probably drink too much wine. Wish she got to church more. Maybe have a few kids in her thirties, when she realized the gateway to motherhood was narrowing each year.

And eventually, Erica would lose touch with Chapel, because they'd have very little in common anymore.

Chapel would be a soldier. Her choices would not be her own. Her secrets would not be her own. Her life would not be her own.

The thought unhinged something inside of her. She pressed her toes into the bottom of her boots to keep the pain from reaching her eyes.

"Well, thanks for talking to him," Erica mumbled. "I know it's, like, probably weird for you or whatever."

Chapel nodded. "Sure. But what about what I said? About talking to him?"

Erica flicked her eyes out the window. "I'll take it into consideration." Then she left.

Chapel walked back into the kitchen. Gabe was pushing a greasy oven brick back and forth over the slick metal surface.

"Hey, Thomas," she called over her shoulder. "I'm going to show Gabe how the freezer is organized. Holler if someone comes in."

"Okay," she heard back.

She grabbed her jacket from the hook and opened the freezer's heavy door. Moments later, Gabe joined her.

She pointed to each section. "Bacon. Burgers. Pork. Shrimp. Chicken. Pull from the bottom, because Thomas stacks the new stuff on the top. Now, about what you're doing here?"

He smiled at her. "You hate lying."

"To Thomas, definitely." She wrapped both arms around her chest in a weak effort to conserve body heat.

Gabe put his foot on the stepladder and leaned an arm across his knee. He showed no indication of cold in the freezing air.

"There might be a problem," he said.

"A new problem? Or an old problem?"

Gabe seemed to turn her words over. "An old problem that is becoming a new problem."

"What is it?"

He stepped down and walked closer to her. "We're not sure yet, but a Bellum analyst came across some alarming chatter over the weekend."

"About what?"

Gabe pointed. "You."

"Me?"

"Just your name, but I'm still very concerned. You haven't finished training, you don't have a solid team around you, and your Tempus isn't fully developed. You'd be incredibly vulnerable if your identity got into the wrong hands."

"Does Zay know?"

"He knows I got a job here, but I wasn't specific about why."

"I bet that went over well."

Gabe shook his head. "Better than I thought it would. He wants you taken care of."

Chapel didn't know what to say. Her eyes searched the freezer floor, as if its greasy tiles held the answers to all that plagued her.

"We assume you're safe at school," Gabe said, "because no Genex would expose themselves publically. The Invisibles would descend upon them with the fury of Hades. Thanatos covers your evenings, so work is the only time you're consistently without protection." He indicated his apron. "So, here I am."

She studied his face. It was open and curious and alert.

"I'm still not sure what to think about you," she said. "About why you showed me that Friday night. About what your motives are in helping me."

"I told you why I brought you to The O."

"It still doesn't make sense."

"It will," he said simply. "In time."

Chapel wasn't sure she had much time.

"So, I can still count on you?" she asked. "Are you still trying to help me get out of my oath to Bellum?"

Lines appeared on Gabe's forehead. "I do not believe pledging Bellum is in your best interest. But right now," he sighed, "I'm just trying to keep you alive."

Chapel's hands flew to her mouth. "Did you *see* something? Something happening to me?"

"No. But I saw myself here, at Back Porch, in this apron. I saw it a month ago. Now I know why."

"Oh. Okay." She cleared her throat. "Um, thanks. I guess."

He nodded at her. "Of course."

Chapel knew he was done explaining himself, but Gabe made no move to leave. He stood in her pathway to the door, his arms propped across his chest, the corners of his mouth turned down.

"Is it hard?" she asked. The question had been haunting her since Friday night. "Knowing things that haven't happened yet?"

She lifted her eyes to his. They were assessing her again, warily. She looked right back, holding his gaze a long time. Gabe slid his eyes over her face, as if looking for something.

Just when she thought he wouldn't answer, he dropped his arms.

"It consumes me," he said. "In the worst possible way."

Then he walked out of the freezer, leaving her in the cold.

CHAPTER ELEVEN

Chapel stood in Zay's bathroom, her mouth hanging open.

"Impressive, right?" he said, motioning to the number of pomades and gels stacked in neat rows along a shelf.

"I was thinking *embarrassing,*" she said. "But I guess it's a fine line."

He wrapped her ponytail around his wrist and tugged it playfully, pulling her mouth to his for a quick kiss. "Mmm. You smell good."

"Like sweat?"

He opened his eyes, but didn't move his face. "Like French fries."

She laughed. "Gabe makes these chili cheese fries with jalapeños that I literally can't stop eating. I think he puts crack in them."

"I'll put a crack in Gabe," Zay said seriously. "If that would help matters."

She giggled like an idiot girl and didn't care. "It's not like that and you know it."

He kissed her again, but deeper.

"Hurry up and shower," he said. "Barnabus will have dinner ready for everyone at eight."

Zay left and Chapel stepped out of her sweaty running gear and left it in a pile by the door. While she showered, Zay would run to her house and get something for her to wear to dinner.

There was a quick knock at the door and Chapel froze. "Yes?"

"It's me," Zay said. Then, quieter, "Are you . . . dressed?"

"No." She bent to pick up her shirt. "Is something wrong?"

She heard the soft thud of his head against the door. "No."

She smiled. "You okay?"

There was a shift against the door, and then he cleared his throat. "Thank you for being cool about changing our plans tonight. I know we haven't been on a real date in a while. I'll make it up to you."

It was a Friday, the end of a long week, and Chapel had been looking forward to a trip back to Centennial Park with Zay.

They had been at the gym when Jackson informed them that the fourth member of their team was arriving a week early.

Justin Chon—that was all she knew about him—was moving in that night.

"Yeah, you will," she said. "I'm thinking a foot rub, followed by a back rub, followed by a shoulder rub."

"You got it, babe. I'll be right back, okay? I'll leave your clothes on my bed."

There was something incredibly intimate about using a boyfriend's bathroom to shower. Zay's was tidy, and his scent clung to everything. She stayed inside much longer than she should have.

When she was finished, she snuck a peek inside his bedroom. A stack of clothes sat in the center of his bed, along with a bottle of water.

Chapel dried off and picked through everything Zay had brought her. She was too hot to get dressed—her lungs still burning from her run—so she tucked her towel around herself and walked around, studying the neat clutter of Zay's room.

In the mirror over Zay's dresser, Chapel's cheeks were flushed and the freckles across her nose stood out darker.

She raised her arms above her head and twisted from side to side, hoping to create a breeze that would drain the blood from her face.

"Is this the sort of thing girls do," Zay said, "when men are wondering what's taking them so long to get dressed?"

Chapel flipped around to find him standing in his doorway, one elbow propped against its frame.

She clutched her towel together. "What if I had been naked?" she hissed.

He stepped farther into the room and shut the door behind him. His hair was damp. He must have used Rush's shower.

"I listened in the hallway," Zay said. "I heard you moving around in here. I thought you had your clothes on." He ducked his head. "I'll go downstairs so you can finish your..." He motioned her direction. "Zumba routine."

But she didn't want him to go. "Zay."

His hand stilled on the doorknob.

"I'm just cooling off before I get dressed. Wait with me?"

Instead of turning the knob, Zay pressed in the lock. He paused with his back to her. "Chapel?"

Something in his voice resonated in her gut.

"Yes?"

"I can come over there," he said lowly, "and I can talk to you, and I can keep my hands to myself."

And just like that, Chapel felt her blood thumping everywhere, everywhere, everywhere. "Or?"

Zay turned around and walked to where she stood. "Or I can kiss you."

The buzz of her overactive mind fell silent. She had one, singular, focused thought. "That option sounds good."

"Yeah?" he asked.

"Yeah."

Zay ran a hand over the back of her wet hair, pulling it over one shoulder. "I won't push you. I know your boundaries, okay?"

"Okay."

"You can say stop, you can say anything you need to."

"Zay," she said.

"Hm?"

"Kiss me now."

He smiled down at her, and a sweet ache burned in her core. She didn't recognize it; it was a new kind of hunger.

"Good idea," he said. Then he drew her mouth to his.

Chapel rose on her toes to meet him, one hand gripping the back of his neck, the other on her towel.

Zay's palms came to rest on her waist, then curled around to her back, pressing her into him.

He kissed her lips, her jaw, the hollow of her throat.

His hands traveled down her arms, and his mouth followed, kissing behind her elbows and her wrists. He found her mouth again, and she sighed, making him smile against her cheek.

She stepped back toward the bed and pulled him by the hand after her. He caught himself at the edge, picking up her foot.

"I believe you requested a foot rub?" He pressed his thumb into her arch and made her giggle. "Are you ticklish?" he asked, pressing again and making her squirm.

"Yes! Now, stop."

Zay brought his face down to her foot and pressed his mouth there. "You just have so few weaknesses," he said. "I have to learn every one of them so I can exploit them if you ever try to leave me."

"The tickle-into-submission strategy," she said. "You cruel genius."

His teeth grazed her anklebone, making her jerk. "Don't talk back to me," he said. "If you want me to behave."

Chapel tried not to think about how pale she was, or how the top part of her knees looked fat from a certain angle.

"Relax," Zay said, reading her easily. "It's just me."

He finally came to hover over her, balancing on his forearms. Zay didn't touch her with caution. He didn't touch her like she might break. He touched her like he'd planned out every brush of contact, every whispered word, and committed them to memory.

Just when Chapel thought her body might split down the middle, Zay pulled back, kissed her temple, and flopped on his back beside her.

"Where'd you go?" she asked, connecting their hands between them.

"To safety."

When she looked over at him, he was smiling. She used to think she could tell a guy cared about a girl by how hard he pushed for sex. But watching the rapid rise and fall of his chest, Chapel realized she had it completely backward.

"Should I finish that massage?" he asked. "Back and shoulders?"

"Mmmm," she hummed, turning to lie on her stomach.

The bed shifted as Zay pulled himself up beside her. His fingers pressed into her skin, making her drowsy and content and heavy. She made a little noise that sounded a lot like a purr.

After a while, she felt his lips press into each shoulder blade. "I love this part of you," he whispered.

Chapel's eyes slid open. She turned her body to lay parallel to his, bringing her hand to rest on his cheek.

"You feel warm," she told him.

His cheek moved against her palm, rising in a grin. "That's because I just made out with my hot girlfriend for half an hour."

"Half an hour?" she whispered.

He nodded.

"I've never done anything like that before." The words were out of her mouth before she weighed them. She winced.

"Really?" Zay asked.

"Logan and I . . . " She lifted her shoulder. "It wasn't like *that* for us."

Chapel studied his serious expression as he considered her words. She imagined this was what he looked like when he first woke up, his hair fluffier without anything in it. Younger. Almost boyish.

Zay laid an arm across her waist, resting his palm on her back. "What was it like, then?"

They weren't people who spoke casually about their pasts, and Zay rarely asked questions at all. Chapel paused before answering.

"I mean, we kissed, obviously, but it was never like . . . I don't know. The friendship part was easy with him. But it wasn't . . . "

She let her fingers slip through the back of his hair. It wasn't often she saw him like this—peaceful and unguarded. There was almost always a certain tension to his body—even when she thought he was lounging or resting. Zay was a soldier first, and a boy second.

But right now, he was all boy.

"It wasn't like this with him," she whispered.

"Yeah?" That seemed to please him.

"Yeah."

Through her towel, his fingers traced her vertebrae up her spine and back down again. "So, you guys just kissed?"

She pressed her face into the comforter. This was not a conversation she imagined ever having. Especially with Zay.

"Uh. Yeah."

Zay stared at her quietly for a moment. Then he shook his head, just barely. "Selfishly," he said, "that's exactly what I want to hear. But then there's this other part of me that feels like a tool. Because my story could not be further from that."

"Don't feel that way," she said. Then, after a pause. "Were there . . . a lot of girls?"

He nodded. His eyes looked sad. "But not in a long time."

Chapel didn't say anything, just traced the top curve of his Thanatos tattoo, exposed by the pull of his shirt.

"What are you thinking?" he whispered to her. "Be *honest.*"

Her eyes found his—the color of frozen water. He'd know it if she lied to him.

She filled up her cheeks with air, then pushed it out. "I'm jealous. And I'm sad. For you, though. Because I don't want you to feel like a bad person. Because you're not. You're really not."

"What else?" he pressed.

She dropped her eyes. "I'm thinking I don't know how to be, you know," she licked her lips, "I'm not *sexy.* And maybe *that's* why Logan never . . . I don't know." She hesitated. "I don't know how to like, smolder, or how to walk in a way that gets a guy's attention. I'm not like Brandy and Marielle, I'm not—" She stopped talking.

"Hey." He moved her chin to look at him. "You're right. You're *not* like those girls. They think their looks are all they've got, so they throw them at people." He let his fingers slip down the high curve of her cheekbone. "You're beautiful in so many different ways. In the ways that endure."

"But sometimes I want to be looked at like they're looked at," she said. "Is that stupid?"

Zay brushed her damp hair from her cheek, lacing it behind her ear, fingers resting on her earlobe. Their noses were almost touching.

"I look at you," he whispered. Then, more slowly, "I look at *you.*"

And she knew what he meant by *you. Not just your body. Not just your face. But you.*

This time when he kissed her, Chapel gripped his shoulders, not caring that her hands shook with inexperience, not wishing to be anyone other than herself.

* * * *

"And here the lovebirds are," Rush said grandly when they entered the dining room. He and Marielle sat near the head of the table.

"Hey, Rush," Chapel said. "Marielle."

They sat. Zay leaned back in his chair and propped an ankle on his knee.

Rush leaned forward. "Is my boy treating you right, Peaches?"

"Why?" she asked. "Should I lodge any formal complaints with *you?*"

Marielle snorted and Rush looked offended. "Hey, I know a lot about relationships."

"Relations," Chapel said, "aren't the same as relationships."

Rush laughed, pointing at her. "You just let me know when you've had enough story time with our Reader, here. The Good Doctor Lopez will cure what ails you."

Chapel pushed Zay's shoulder. "Aren't you going to stand up for me?"

He dropped a casual arm across her shoulders. "Your tongue is far sharper than mine."

Jackson walked in with someone at his side. Everyone stood, including Chapel who was the last to scramble to her feet.

"Good evening," he said, bending slightly. "Our guest has arrived."

Justin looked to be about the same age as Rush, early twenties, with short, dark hair and eyes that folded slightly on the corners. His skin was the color of baked cinnamon.

"Justin," Jackson continued, "you know the team."

Justin gave a tight-lipped smile to the others before his eyes came to rest on her. They were dark and assessing.

"And this is Isaiah's girlfriend, Chapel, the one I told you about."

Justin's grip was cool and firm. The same as his expression. She wondered what Jackson had told him.

"Nice to meet you, Justin," she said.

He pressed his lips together in acknowledgement, but didn't say a word.

"Well, then." Jackson pulled his hands together as if in prayer. "Barnabus has something special prepared. Shall we eat?"

Chapel had long-since resigned herself to the fact that she was not a grilled-meat kind of girl. She liked her food battered, fried, and whenever possible, covered in cheese.

But that was not Jackson's way, nor was it the way of someone trying to get in peak physical condition.

While Jackson droned on and on about how happy they were to have Justin on their team, how they hoped he felt like a part of their family, and blah, blah, blah, Chapel forced down bite after bite of salmon, fantasizing that it was really a crispy chicken finger.

Across the table, Marielle was staring at her with her top lip curled as if she knew what Chapel was doing. Chapel glanced at Jackson before looking back at Marielle and opening her mouth, showing her a glob of chewed up fish.

Rush made a noise across from her and started choking on his asparagus, trying to cover up his laugh with a cough.

Zay glanced back at them, as if remembering they were there. He gave Rush a look she couldn't see, then returned his attention to Jackson.

Rush wiped his napkin down his face. *"Troublemaker,"* he mouthed.

Chapel pressed a hand over her lips.

"Do you have any questions?" Jackson asked Justin. She had never seen Zay's uncle so wired. He sat perched on the edge of his chair like a bird leaning over a branch, ready to take flight.

Chapel reached for a knife and another slice of bread. She was fairly certain the butter wasn't real, but it was close enough.

"I do have one question," he said. Chapel felt his eyes on her face again. When she looked up, he was staring at her. "Why do we sharpen the enemy's sword within our own walls?"

Instead of sawing into the load of bread, Chapel sliced the flap of skin between her thumb and forefinger.

She brought the wound to her mouth. She tasted blood. A lot of blood.

"Are you okay?" Zay asked her.

"It's fine," she said, hurriedly. "It's fine."

She reached for a napkin to press against the cut and knocked over a tall sconce. It crashed into Marielle's plate, the candle's wick buried in her untouched sweet potatoes.

"Seriously?" Marielle moaned.

"Oh, like you were going to eat them," Chapel snapped. Her nostrils flared with embarrassment, with anger. "It's just a cut."

"It looked deep," Zay said.

Rush stood. "Let's see it, Peaches."

She didn't answer. She was too busy staring at the jerk at the end of the table.

"I am no one's *sword,*" she said evenly. "Especially Bellum's."

"I meant no disrespect," Justin said, glancing around the table. "But with all the unrest between the factions? You must know you play with fire, letting her stay here."

Zay started to stand.

"Dude," Rush said. Chapel couldn't tell if he was addressing Zay or Justin.

But then Jackson laid his fork very carefully along the side of his plate. It was a small gesture, but it drew everyone's attention.

"We are *quite* aware, actually." His tone was no longer stiff and formal, but calculating and unyielding. He made brief eye contact with every person at the table. "There is little we do without weighing the benefits and risks. And for future reference, Justin, we are not in the habit of questioning one another in this household."

Chapel sat, immobile. She'd never seen Jackson angry before—wasn't even sure if *that was* Jackson being angry. But his presence had quickly shifted from delighted host to cold commander, like a splash of iced water to the face.

Jackson retrieved his fork. He cut into his salmon and everyone was quiet, letting his tone and his words drip, drip, drip like a leaky faucet in a silent room.

Justin slid back from the table and came to stand beside her. He held out a hand. "Let me see it."

She turned down the corners of her mouth. "So you can pour salt in it?"

"Let him," Zay said. "Give him your hand."

Rush sat back down. Chapel met Zay's eyes. He was serious.

"Go ahead," he said.

She moved in her chair, lifting her fingers to Justin. He held her hand up in the dim lighting, studying the injury. A rivulet of blood slipped down her arm, gaining momentum and staining the white fringe along the sleeve of her shirt.

Then he closed his eyes and brought her hand to his face. She thought he was going to press his lips to the injury and she started to draw it back to herself; but instead she felt his breath against her palm. He was whispering something.

Chapel felt a warmth in her hand, not hot like Hunter's touch, but warm like a spot of sunshine on a cool day.

Then Justin's eyes snapped open and he dropped her hand. Chapel brought it back to her face, inspecting it.

The bleeding had stopped. The gash was no longer open, but pressed together like it had been days—not minutes—since she first sliced it.

She looked up at him. "You did this?"

He nodded.

Jackson leaned his elbows on the table and steepled his fingers. He had a gleam in his light eyes. "Isaiah found him last year. "

Chapel blinked several times. "So you're, like, a warlock or something?"

"Chapel," Zay said lowly.

Justin met her steady gaze. "The blood spell is the only one I know. My mother taught it to me. She was a Gypsy. Not Genex."

"Justin's a lot like Rush," Zay explained. "An accelerated learner. But with an aptitude in weaponry."

"Like guns?"

Justin smiled without warmth. "Those, too."

"Justin is going to outfit us for missions. He'll work on some defensive elements, too."

Chapel stared at the dried blood along her arm. A man who could make people bleed in one breath, then stop them from bleeding in another.

How very useful.

CHAPTER TWELVE

She was dreaming about Erica dying again. She'd had the dream so many times now that she memorized each scene as it played before her.

This time, she felt the screams ripping through her throat, making it raw.

"No!" she cried, looking at Erica's slumped and bloody form. *"No!"*

The last cry had been enough to jerk her awake. She stared at the smooth plaster above her, catching her breath, repeating to herself, "Just a dream, just a dream, just a dream."

She never went back to sleep, and the day dragged on.

Seniors had a meeting about graduation that afternoon, so Chapel couldn't go to work. When it was over, Timmy caught her eye.

"I need to ask you something," he said. He glanced over her shoulder. They were still in the crowded auditorium. "Not in here, though."

Chapel followed him outside into the parking lot, her heart rate increasing with every step. *Did he have another dream? Does he remember it all?*

They came to his Beetle and Timmy put his book bag in the back. He picked at some of the peeling blue paint on the doorframe before turning around.

"Timmy, what's up?" she asked, pushing against his arm. "You got a dead body in your trunk, or something? You're acting weird."

When he didn't acknowledge her joke, Chapel's suspicions were confirmed. Something was up.

"Tell me again," he said. "About Thanksgiving."

Chapel squinted against the sun. This was the last conversation she felt like having. "What do you want to know?"

Timmy licked the corner of his mouth. "Tell me about when I called you to come over to your house."

She knew Timmy. He craved answers as if they were oxygen. Problems weren't problems—they were hands that wrapped around his throat, slowly suffocating his mind. There would be no avoiding his question.

Chapel willed her eyes to meet his, forced her hands to hang by her sides. "You called me and said you needed to talk about Erica."

"What time?"

"I don't remember, Timmy. Why? Is she still giving you a hard time?"

"No, she isn't." He looked at the asphalt under their feet as if its black crumbles could fill in the spaces of his missing memories. "I just—" He tugged at the end of his copper curls. "I just keep replaying that day in mind. Everything is so sharp and so clear until I called you. It's just . . . blurry."

"Maybe you were turkey-drunk," she said. "Every time I eat your mother's food, I swear I black out for at least half an hour."

Behind his glasses, his eyes grew round and large. "I'm being serious, Chapel."

Guilt oozed down her face in a heated rush. "I know," she mumbled. "Sorry."

Timmy dug in his back pocket and pulled out a white wad. "I found this," he said, unwrapping it and smoothing it out on the leg of his jeans. "It was in the pocket of my pants. It's been washed once, but I can still read some of it."

Chapel stared at the flimsy rectangle as if it were a rattlesnake. "What is it?"

He handed it to her. Chapel had to cup her hand over the faded words and numbers, but she knew what it was.

"A receipt?" she asked.

He pointed to the date. "On Thanksgiving Day." He moved his hand down to the bottom. "It's from the gas station off Browns Bridge Road."

Chapel knew where he was going with this, but she asked anyway. "What does it mean?"

Timmy removed his glasses and pushed his thumb and forefingers into his eyes. "It *means* I went to the other side of town on my way to your house. Why would I do that?"

Well Timmy, because you were going to check on the hidden camera you had installed for me at my not-so-dead father's grave. Oh, but that was before our former teacher kidnapped you and subsequently stole your memories. Yeah . . . but how about those Braves, huh?

"What do you think is going on?" she asked.

Timmy shook his head. "I don't know. I mean, I remember coming to your house and talking to you about Erica, like, vaguely. But when I try and picture myself there, try and remember a single word I said, it's blank." His eyes found hers. "Like it never really happened."

Chapel throbbed with guilt for not being able to tell him the truth, but she wasn't stupid enough to think that coming clean to Timmy would be to his benefit.

She put a hand on his shoulder, trying to think of what a normal Chapel would say. "Do you think you got abducted by a superior species who used you for your brains then zapped your mind?"

Timmy glanced down at her hand, then back up at her. A slow grin broke through the tension on his face. "Not my brains," he said. "My body."

They laughed—Chapel, probably harder than was necessary. She eased the receipt into her fist, hoping he wouldn't notice.

"You've got company," he said, nodding behind her. Chapel turned to see Zay parked a few rows up, now visible that the lot was emptying. He was waiting for her.

She turned back to Timmy. "You going to be okay?"

He waved her off. "Too many episodes of *X-Files*. Making me crazy."

"Craz*ier*." She surprised both of them by putting her arms around him in a hug. She put her face into his Star Wars sweatshirt, smelling the off-brand detergent his mom used. She had come so close to losing him—*Timmy*—the one constant in her life.

When she pulled away, Timmy batted his hair down. His cheeks were flecked with pink.

"Text me later," she said.

He mumbled something that sounded like *"Sure,"* and opened the door to his Beetle.

When she turned around, Zay was standing outside his car. He had his phone out, and was leaned against the driver's door staring down at it.

The sun's glare winked off the Shelby's black hood, making it hard to look directly at him. But look she did.

Zay was attractive in an obvious way, but it wasn't his smoke-cloud eyes or angular bone structure that she studied.

It was the line of his body, disciplined beyond measure, strong and elegant.

It was the shade of black in his hair, almost blue in richness. The dent of a scar in his lip. The veins on the back of his hands—blue with his life and strength.

"Hey, handsome," she said.

He stood up straight and tucked his phone in his pocket. He gave her a closed-lip smile and slowly shook his head.

"What?" she asked.

He took her wrist and wrapped it behind his neck, pulling her against him. "Here I was," he said, "jealous of you hugging another guy. And then you call me handsome, and I care about nothing else."

She pulled back so she could see him. "Timmy's not another guy. Timmy's Timmy."

"Babe, when it comes to my girl?" He kissed her on the temple, and she felt him smile against her skin. *"Every* guy is another guy."

She lingered next to his face for a moment before looking up at him. "What are you doing here?" she asked. "I thought we were meeting at the gym?"

There was a Dojo facility outside of Bennett Park that was ran by a group of Genex Thanatos. Zay had booked the boxing ring for he and Chapel that afternoon.

But Zay wasn't dressed for training.

"I have a surprise," he said, curling back a piece of her hair. "We're not training today. We're going to do something fun."

Chapel squealed, throwing herself into his arms. "Thank you. Thank you, thank you, thank you."

He rested his hands on her waist. "If that's how you always respond to surprises, I'm going to make this a regular occurrence. Daily. Maybe bi-daily."

"Take a note, Halstead."

"Note taken." He poked her in the ribs, making her squirm. "And don't call me Halstead."

Once inside the Shelby, Chapel wiggled in her seat. "Don't tell me where you're taking me," she said. "Just drive."

He laughed quietly. "You're like a kid at Christmas."

Zay signaled around the courthouse and turned the opposite direction Chapel expected him to.

"I am going to take you home first," he said. "You'll need the thickest jacket you own, gloves, if you have them, and a blanket. I meant to stop on my way here, but . . ." His eyes moved over her face. "I got too excited to see you."

She squeezed his hand. "Zay, have you ever skipped training? Even once?"

He glanced at her sideways. "Not since I started."

Chapel's heart felt mushy and warm and full. He was breaking a rule—his rule—for her. "This may the best moment I've had in a long time. Thank you."

Zay laid an easy hand on her thigh as he drove. "Don't thank me for treating you like a boyfriend should, Chapel. I want to do a better job of making things as normal for us as possible."

When they pulled up to it, Taylor Manor looked like a marble headstone, curving toward the sky on the hilltop.

"When is your mom coming back again?" Zay asked.

It was no secret he thought Todd and Valerie negligent parents to leave Chapel alone so much. In their defense, Chapel had threatened to use the hefty trust fund Michael had given her to get her own apartment if they tried to move her to Capitol Hill.

"I don't know," Chapel said. "Mom's been sketchy about it every time I've asked."

Zay pulled his bottom lip through his teeth. "I don't like it."

Chapel didn't answer.

They went inside and Chapel ran upstairs to grab a jacket. When she swung open the double doors to her closet, every molecule of her body froze in fear.

There was a man just inside dressed in all black, nothing visible except dark irises and bloodshot eyes.

"Surpriiiise," he sang quietly.

Then he launched himself at her, tackling her to the ground. She didn't even have time to scream.

Her head bounced off the floor and stars burst behind her eyelids, along with a blinding pain.

Tempus. She needed to Tempus.

But then he was flipping her over on her back, pinning her down. "You've made someone very unhappy," he whispered in her ear. "And now you're going to pay."

Slanted pictures flashed before her eyes. A slice of ceiling. A slice of bed. A slice of pale yellow wall.

Chapel thrashed wildly, bucking her hips to create a bridge between her and the attacker whose hands were pressing against her throat.

By a miracle, she was able to make contact with a brass lamp just beside her. She caught it with her toe and watched in slow, agonizing silence as it wobbled back and forth on its base. Finally, graciously, the lamp tipped over.

The crash scattered her attacker's attention, and she used the momentum of his flinch to roll out from beneath him. She scooped up the lamp by its neck and spun around.

She heard Zay's feet crashing against the steps. "Chapel!" he yelled.

The masked man jerked toward the door. "You were supposed to be alone."

She pulled the lamp back like a bat. "About that," she breathed. "I'm not."

The lamp was heavy, and she swung it with every ounce of fear, anger, and strength she could muster.

The man must have heard her mid-swing, because he turned just in time for her to catch him in the side of the head, right at his ear. He went down to his knees, screaming.

Zay burst through the door, looking wild-eyed. "What happened? What happened?"

"He attacked me," Chapel gasped. "He was hiding in my closet."

Zay paused and closed his eyes. Chapel knew he was reading the man's energy—trying to see if he were emitting one that might reveal something about his identity, or exceptions, if there were any.

She jerked up a T-shirt from her floor and shrugged into it.

"Nothing," Zay said. "No . . . nothing. He's not Genex." Zay opened his eyes and looked at her. "That makes this a lot easier."

He strode to where the man was, now stumbling to his feet. "Hello," Zay said, almost cordially. "My name is Isaiah Halstead. You may not know this, but that's very, very bad news for you."

The man pulled his mask off, revealing a non-descript face with a nasty looking gash where his ear met his jaw. Zay threw a look back at her.

"You did this?"

"Yeah."

"Babe. Really proud right now. He may never hear out of it again."

The man squinted at both of them. When he spoke, his accent had the broad A of someone from New England. "She was supposed to be alone."

Zay pointed at himself. "She's not."

"Well, I'm not the one you got beef with," he said. "You can take this up with the idiot who hired me."

As the man passed him, Zay gripped his shirt. Chapel was always caught off guard by his precision and strength, but she was left breathless by the effortlessness with which he caught the man's arm and twisted it behind him before flipping him onto his back.

"Let's chat," Zay said. "I feel like a change in scenery. What say you?"

The man groaned.

It made Zay smile. "That's what I like to hear."

Zay dragged the man by his hair into the hallway and slung his back over the wooden banister.

"What the—wait a minute—" The man made a gurgling noise and kicked his feet like a bug turned over on its back.

"Keep struggling," Zay said. "But if I lose my grip, it's on you."

Chapel clamped her hands over her mouth. If Zay dropped him, the man would fall two full stories.

"Zay," she whispered. "Don't."

Zay ignored her. "Tell me everything," he said. "Don't miss a single detail."

The man spat at Zay, but since he was on his back, it landed on his own chest. Zay dipped him back a little farther, making the railing squeak beneath him.

"Okay, okay," the man said. His voice had an edge of fear in it for the first time. He realized, just as Chapel once had, that Zay was capable of unspeakable things. "I got a call from a friend. Said someone was looking for a hit. Not a clean up job—just a hit."

"He's not here to kill you," Zay translated for her. "Just to rough you up." Zay's knuckles tightened on his shirt. "Which *friend?*"

The man laughed. "He'll kill me."

Again, Zay tilted him back. He was almost upside down. "Makes two of us."

"Fine," the man sputtered, flailing helplessly. "Guy's name is Lucky. Lucky Lindtz."

Zay allowed his captive to stand, but still had a hand on his throat. "Lucky Lindtz from . . . ?"

"College Park area."

"And what else did Lucky have to say?"

The man glanced behind him, then jerked his eyes to Zay. "Nothing. Just said there was a rich girl that needed scaring."

"And?"

"Told me not to let her see me first. Said that about ten times. I was supposed to tell her to go away with her mama and never come back. That's it. I swear."

"How did you get in?" Zay said. "How did you know which room was hers?"

"The guy had a map. He had a security code, too."

Zay looked at Chapel for a moment, pursing his lips. She shrugged at him. He shrugged back.

"Okay," Zay said to her, letting the guy slide to the floor. He secured the man's hands behind his back. "I'm thinking chokehold. Because if I start punching this idiot, I will not stop. You want to do it? It'll be good practice"

"Um, no thanks," she said.

"Really?" he asked it as if she were giving him a present.

"He's all yours."

Zay slipped an arm around the man's neck and applied quick and intense pressure to both carotid arteries. In seconds, the attacker's jaw went slack.

Zay shoved him to the ground and looked at Chapel.

She stood in an oversized Braves T-shirt, blood trickled down her neck, and she held the broken lamp by its base.

"So," she asked, pushing sweaty hair off her forehead, "how's that 'normal as possible' thing working out for us so far?"

* * * *

"I tell you what, Peaches," Rush said. "I knew from the moment I saw you that you'd make things around here a lot more exciting." He paused to squirt the air bubbles from the syringe in his hand. "Only, I underestimated you. Seriously. You're better than a new puppy."

"Geez, Rush. You really know how to make a girl feel special." Chapel winced as he inserted the needle into the gash at the back of her head. After a moment, sweet relief rushed through her. It was numb. "I just can't figure out why you're still single. Any insights?"

"You'll feel a little tug," Rush murmured as he started the stitching. "Let me know if there's any pain."

Chapel was still while Rush worked the needle in and out of the back of her head. Zay hovered beside them, hacking away on his laptop. He hadn't spoken much since a black Lincoln Town Car came and picked up her attacker.

According to Zay, he'd be taken to a facility and interviewed by an Invisible representative, slated, if needed, then released to be processed by regular authorities.

"I think chicks are intimidated by me," Rush said. "Too muscular. Too attractive. Gorgeous, shaved head. Latino, so of course I'm a fantastic dancer. Then, when they hear I'm a doctor, too? It's total package overload." She heard the snip of scissors cutting the excess thread, and Rush stood back.

"Yes," Chapel said. "Overload is a very good word for you."

He winked at her. "Good to see the concussion hasn't affected that smart mouth."

Chapel slid off the kitchen counter. "I get few complaints about my mouth, Rush."

"Don't flirt with me, Peaches," Rush said. "Not with your boy standing right here. He's going to catch on to our secret affair."

Zay clapped a hand over Rush's shoulder. "Keep dreaming, Lopez."

"Don't worry," Rush said with a wiggle of his eyebrows. "I do."

"Okay," Zay said. He tapped his computer screen. "Here's what I've been able to dig up on Lucky Lindtz. He's a lifetime criminal. In and out of jail since he was thirteen. Most recently, he did a stint in Georgia State Prison."

Rush smacked a hand on the granite. "Nailed it."

Zay had a grim expression. "I know."

Chapel raised a hand. "Um. What?"

Zay turned the computer screen her way. "When Hunter Carter was processed by the Invisibles, he was held at GSP for two weeks. One of those weeks overlaps Lindtz's stay."

"So, Hunter was the 'friend' who wanted me attacked?"

"He wanted you warned. To go stay with your mom. It makes perfect sense—Hunter has the security code, Hunter could draw a map. He probably still believes he can get out of prison and use you for his plan to unite Genexes, or whatever."

"Did we ever figure out what the Oracle is?" she asked. Hunter had mentioned it to her the night he kidnapped her.

"Nothing," Rush said.

"But we're still looking." Zay shut his computer.

Chapel licked her lips. She had never gotten around to telling Zay about her night out with Gabe. And as the days passed, it got harder and harder to bring it up to him. Because it was no longer something she had forgotten to mention—it was something she was hiding.

"What if it's someone from Bellum?" she asked. "You know, Gabe came to work at Back Porch. He told me it was for my safety. Maybe he knows something."

Rush and Zay exchanged a look. Zay shrugged. "I'll ask him. In the meantime, we need to increase Chap's security detail. She doesn't need to be alone until we secure Lindtz and make sure Hunter ordered the hit."

"I'm in," Rush said. Chapel thought he might add a joke or jab, but he didn't.

The front door to Jackson's house opened and slammed. The clatter of heels on porcelain tile echoed into the kitchen.

"Zay?" Marielle barked. "Isaiah?"

"In here," Zay called.

Marielle flung herself into the kitchen, chest heaving with rapid breaths. "Where were . . . " She leaned over, resting her hands on her knees. "I thought . . . "

"Is something wrong?" Zay asked.

Marielle laughed at that. "Well, if there were, you wouldn't know. I've been trying to call you for the last hour."

Zay's hands went to his back pocket. "My phone is . . . not here. I must have left it at Chapel's."

Marielle's eyes swept across the kitchen. To Chapel, holding a bag of ice against her head, to Rush, packing away medical supplies.

She shook her head. "Does Jackson know you skipped training today?"

Beside her, Chapel felt Zay's posture stiffen. "I don't need his permission to take a day off," he said evenly.

While the sting of the cut was still numb, a throb was forming behind Chapel's eye. She rubbed at it. "You skip training all the time, Marielle," she said. "Why do you care?"

"I wasn't talking to you," Marielle snapped.

"What's your problem?" Chapel said.

"My problem is Isaiah acting like some lovesick idiot. You can't just do whatever you want whenever you want. We're supposed to be a team."

"Rush?" Zay asked. "Do you have any missed calls?"

Rush sighed. "No."

Then Marielle did something Chapel had never seen her do—she burst into tears, turned around, and ran upstairs.

Everyone exchanged looks of utter shock.

"Dude," Rush said. "I've never seen her cry."

Zay scrubbed his hands up and down his face. "I know."

"Should I go?" Chapel asked.

"No." Zay walked over to her and put his arms around her. He tucked her head under his chin. "You've been through enough tonight. I'm sorry she's so . . . "

"Crazy. Mean. Hungry."

"Yes," he said. "To all of the above."

Rush came and wrapped them both in a hug, swaying them from side to side. "Well guys," he said in a mock-whisper. "I guess this mean's Marielle's not going to be up for a security shift. But don't worry, Peaches, I'll do hers and mine. You'll be in good hands. Very good, very capable hands."

Then Zay punched Rush in the stomach and the boys tumbled to the floor in a knot of good-natured wrestling.

Chapel stood to the side, dissolving into a fit of relieved giggles.

CHAPTER THIRTEEN

Chapel checked her rearview mirror and snickered.

Zay was following her and Erica to the mall in a black Jeep, wearing a blonde wig and a burgundy leisure suit.

When Chapel questioned his need for a disguise, Zay said he wanted to remain undetected in order to draw out any potential threats.

When she accused him of only wearing it because he liked the way his butt looked in polyester pants, he didn't deny it.

At the next traffic light, she took out her phone and sent a text.

CHAPEL: The *70s called. It wants its look back.*

His response was quick:

ZAY: *Groovy, baby.*

Erica slapped her on the arm. "The light's been green for, like, half an hour. Wait—are you . . . ? Gross. You're blushing. Put your phone up. I hate love right now."

Chapel did, and then pulled through the intersection. "You hate love? Really?"

"Absolutely. Being single is like being on a diet—everywhere I look, there's a disgustingly huge bowl of ice cream with chocolate and cherries all over it that everyone but me can eat."

Chapel signaled off the interstate. "First of all, I'm not sure that metaphor works. Second of all, did you just call me disgusting?"

Erica smacked the dash. "Wait a minute. Wait. Just. A. Minute. That's Timmy's car, isn't it?"

Chapel looked to where Erica pointed and saw a dusty blue Volkswagen Beetle rounding the corner into the mall parking lot. Timmy was definitely behind the wheel. And in his passenger seat was someone with a long, dark ponytail. A girl.

"Um . . . maybe. There are lots of cars like that around, right?"

Erica gave her a look that communicated just how stupid Chapel's comment sounded. "You know we're about to follow him, so don't even play."

Chapel muttered under her breath, but took the same turn as Timmy.

"Slow down," Erica hissed, slouching in the seat. "He'll see us."

"Okay." Chapel tapped the brakes. "Sorry."

"Haven't you ever followed someone before?"

"Actually, no, Single White Female, I haven't."

Timmy parked in front of a department store. Chapel slung her car into a spot at the end of his row. "What now?"

Erica shrugged. "I usually only do drive-bys."

Chapel laid her head on the steering wheel, then turned to look at Erica. There was a storm of emotion brewing behind her bright hazel eyes. It always shocked her—these moments of rare vulnerability with Erica.

"Okay," she said, placing a hand on Erica's arm. "Let's do this." Looking through the windows of the car beside them, Chapel opened her door. "This way."

She led them through the maze of vehicles and inside the mall. She spotted Timmy and Mystery Girl just as they were getting on the elevator.

Chapel pointed to the escalator just beyond the jewelry counters. "There."

Erica was silent as they rode up, popping her knuckles and looking pale. It hit her then that Erica truly cared about Timmy—maybe even loved him, like she had said. She'd never seen her more anxious.

"Do you want to turn around?" Chapel asked her as they neared the top.

Erica shook her head. "I just want to see how he acts around her. If they're . . . you know."

Chapel understood. Erica wanted to see if Timmy acted with this girl how he'd acted with her. The desire to *know*— it was the worst kind of torture, but the kind that was often insatiable.

They got off the escalator a few seconds before the elevator doors opened. Chapel pulled Erica to hide behind a display of luggage.

"I can't look," Erica said, flinging her arm over her face.

The silver doors slid open with a jerk, and Timmy stepped off. He was smiling over his shoulder.

"Is she pretty?" Erica hissed. "Is she pretty?

"I don't know. I can't see her. Timmy's in the way."

"What's he wearing?"

Chapel squinted. "That stupid shirt with the Table of Elements on it."

"The *I Wear This Periodically* one?"

"Yes."

Her voice lowered. "I actually kind of like that one."

"Me too," Chapel admitted.

"What are they doing?" Erica asked. "Are they holding hands? Does he look happy? Is she prettier than me?"

Chapel would have laughed if Erica's tone weren't so desperate. "No," she said. "They aren't holding hands. They're heading into the food court."

Erica snatched Chapel's arm. "Then we are, too."

"Not that way," Chapel said, pointing to the mirrors above Little Peking's counter. "He'll see us. Here. Let's go this way."

They circled behind a Merry-Go-Round swarming with children and found a tall planter to stand behind. Erica turned her back so she couldn't see.

"Tell me everything," she said. "This is awful."

"They're in line. Timmy is nodding a lot. The girl looks tall, but not as tall as you. Her hair is long. Like, really, really long. And—she looks familiar," Chapel realized.

"Um, Chapel?" Erica said.

Chapel was preoccupied, trying to place the thin frame that was clinging to Timmy's arm and laughing.

"Chap?"

"Hm?"

Erica dipped her head beside Chapel's and whispered, "Don't look now, but there's a creepy old man checking you out. There, over by Chik-fil-A."

Chapel glanced behind her to see Zay holding a bag of food and walking to a table close to them. He had on gold aviators and a fake paunch. He looked ridiculous.

"He's sort of hot," Erica said, turning her head to the side.

But Chapel had turned her attention back to Timmy and Mystery Girl. A face tickled her mind. Someone she'd seen briefly . . .

"Hot in a geriatric, like, Prom-King-of-the-Nursing-Home kind of way," Erica mused.

Timmy finished paying and turned around. With a swing of her ponytail, so did the girl.

And Chapel clamped a hand to her mouth.

"What?" Erica asked, suddenly clamoring to see between two plastic leaves. "What?"

Chapel closed her eyes, focusing her energy on her core. The noises around her grew momentarily sharp, echoing off the edges of her consciousness. A chill wrapped its fingers around her spine and shook her. She breathed in. She breathed out. She felt every nerve ending on her skin.

Then it all stopped.

Chapel opened her eyes. Everyone and everything was suspended in animation. Shopping bags hovered above the ground. Food pouring from spoons hung in the air. Children's legs froze mid-swing.

Chapel shook her head to free it from the momentary shock of having used Tempus. When she looked up, Zay was beside her.

"You okay?"

Chapel pointed across the food court. "That girl with Timmy. Her name is Kacie. I've seen her with Gabe. I think she's Genex."

Zay sighed. "And how would you know this information?"

Chapel tried to take a step away and stumbled, knees still a bit wobbly. She forced them to hold her upright. "Can we fight about this later?"

Zay steadied her. "Most definitely."

Chapel stepped around an elderly lady who appeared to be digging through her purse. A pair of silver frames lay in the floor just beyond her. Chapel scooped them up and placed them gently on the woman's face before joining Zay at Timmy's side.

"What's the plan, babe?" Zay said. "This is your op."

"I want to get a closer look at her to make sure I'm right." Chapel moved the girl's red jacket aside, revealing a silver Eye of Horus necklace. "It's her. It's definitely her. What next?"

"If it were me?" Zay asked. "I'd want to know everything I could about her."

"Everything you need to know about a girl," Chapel said, "you can find in her purse." She pulled the bag hanging from Kacie's arm and took it to a nearby table. She dumped it out. "This feels so wrong," she said. "Going through someone's stuff."

"What are your motives?" Zay came beside her to watch.

"To keep Timmy safe."

"Is that wrong?"

"I guess not. But it still feels dirty." Chapel's hands paused over an envelope. A rush of fear tightened the back of her neck. "Zay." She held it up. "It has my name on it."

His gray eyes held a wary quality. "How much control do you have? Have we got time to read it?"

Chapel felt sick to her stomach already. In her tests, she could hold Tempus for long stretches with no problem. But here, in the mall, with Erica hiding in a plant and Timmy dining with a potential threat, Chapel's insides were tarred with anxiety.

How many times had Kacie hung out with Timmy? And why?

"No," she said. "I can't. I'm sorry."

Zay brushed his thumb down the side of her jaw. "Don't apologize, Chapel. You're not a robot. People, things, it all matters to you. It's why I—." He paused and kissed her on the temple. "It's one of the things that I love about you."

There was that word: love. That sweet syllable on his tongue made her heart feel heavy and light at the same time. She wanted to hear it from him—*I love you.*

"Okay. You take it," she said, shoving it in his hand. "I'll get back to Erica, throw up, and leave. She'll probably be upset and want to hang out, so it may be tonight before I can meet you."

He pushed her hair over her shoulder. "I'll come over as soon as she leaves."

"Read it now, though," Chapel said. "If Timmy's in danger, do whatever you need to do."

"You got it, babe."

Zay swept her up and cradled her in his arms. "Want a ride back to Erica?"

She smiled and he jogged easily back to her position, placing her lightly on the ground. "I haven't forgotten about the thing with Luxe," he said. "We can talk about that tonight, too."

She rolled her eyes. "Oh, goody."

He swatted her bottom and jogged off, sitting just in time for her to grip the slick ceramic of the planter, emptying her insides into its smelly, sludge-filled bowels.

* * * *

"Imagine if Timmy had caught us spying on him?" Erica said, lounging on Chapel's living room floor. "How bad would that have been?"

Chapel held her stomach, which had only settled down in the last half hour. "About as bad as barfing your guts up in front of an entire food court filled with people?"

"Hm," Erica wondered. "Probably not that bad. But close."

Chapel threw a piece of licorice at her and pinged Erica's forehead. "Check yourself, Jersey. Or next time you want to stalk people, you'll fly solo."

Erica leaned up on her elbows. "Whatever. We're like, the Bennett Park version of gangster homies. We're ride or die for life."

A snort pushed through Chapel's nose. "I don't know what that means, but I want to get it tattooed on my body. Should we get matching bandanas?"

"For sure," Erica said seriously. "And maybe some bedazzled holsters."

They both started laughing, and it felt so good that it made Chapel want to cry.

Miraculously, she and Erica had been able to leave the mall unnoticed by Timmy and Kacie. Chapel figured it was probably because the two of them were ogling each other as if they were the main course and not the chicken fried rice.

Erica stood up and stretched. "I better go. It's getting late."

Chapel walked her to the front door. "You good?"

Erica shrugged. "Thanks for today. For following Timmy for me. For listening to me whine all night."

"You would do it for me."

"Steel Magnolia, there's not a lot I wouldn't do for you."

"Yes, but that's mostly because you're from Trenton and you can use a switch blade."

"True." Erica studied her for a beat, as if she wanted to say something more, but didn't. Then she left.

She watched Erica's taillights through the window before walking upstairs. She'd left her phone in her bathroom when she'd changed into pajamas, and she wanted to call Zay and tell him to come out from hiding.

She rounded the corner into her room and came to a dead standstill. Zay was sitting on her bed. He stood up.

"On a guy less hot," she said, "this would be creepy."

His eyes flashed with recognition. She'd said that to him before.

"You think I'm hot?" he asked.

Chapel winked at him. "Maybe."

She was so excited to see him there that she ran across the room, tossing herself into his arms. His flannel shirt felt like velvet beneath her cheek. She rubbed her face against it.

"Mmm," she hummed, burrowing in to his sinewy frame. His arms enveloped her, his right hand coming up and tangling in her hair. "I love it here."

Zay squeezed her. "You fit perfectly."

She lifted her chin to kiss him. When she did, she caught sight of his face for the first time. His expression was drawn and tight—and he didn't immediately bring his mouth to hers.

That was her first indicator that something was wrong.

"What?" she asked. "Is Timmy—?"

Zay pressed his lips to her temple, pausing there before pulling away. His hand came up between them, separating their bodies. In it was the opened envelope from Kacie's purse.

Chapel took it from him, opening the wrinkled page. It had obviously been read several times. She paced back and forth, the words emptying themselves into her like a poison.

My name is Kacie and I'm a Seer.

Chapel paused. Kacie had to be the Seer that Gabriel had been training. The one who never missed. The realization had her hands shaking.

You're pacing in a room that I assume is yours and you're worried about Timothy—don't be. My intentions with him are good. I've seen him. And I know he is beginning to remember what happened to him at Hunter Carter's hands. And while Timothy is not by definition Genex, he is important to our world. I see him playing a vital role in shaping our community. My orders from Bellum are to protect him at all costs.

Isaiah Halstead will read this first, and I've seen many versions of what happens next. Your next question for him will be if he's told Jackson the import of this letter. His answer will lead you down the next turn in your journey. Best of luck, Kacie.

When Chapel raised tired eyes to Zay's, she knew.

"You told him. You told Jackson that Timmy is remembering."

Zay had positioned himself at her door—wisely, because she would have been running out of it to keep Jackson from doing whatever he wanted to do next.

Zay was holding up both hands. "Chapel, think *logically* for a minute. Please."

"Good idea." She picked up an old glass of water and slammed it into the floor with all of her might. The shards careened across her hardwood floor in a cacophony of destruction.

Zay threw his head back and groaned. "I know you'd act like this."

"Like what?" she asked. "Like my boyfriend just put my best friend's life in jeopardy?"

Zay walked to her quickly. "Chapel, don't let this tear us apart. It's what Bellum wants—you have to see that."

She put a hand up to keep him from touching her. "All I see is a guy I'm dying to trust, giving me every reason not to."

"If Bellum can turn you against me," he said, "they know they have you without argument."

"Well they're doing a good job, Halstead. A great job, in fact."

His lips turned up in an angry smile. "Don't. Do not do this."

Chapel dug her fists into her eye sockets. *"Knowing* what the letter said? You did it anyway?"

Zay pulled her wrists down, stooping so his eyes were level with hers. "Look at me," he said. "Please. Look at me." She did. "You know me, Chap." He took her hand and put it on his chest, just over his heart. It was an erratic symphony of emotion. "You know how I feel about you. Don't you?"

She wanted to lash out at him. She wanted to hurt him like he had hurt her by telling Jackson about Timmy. Instead, she met his eyes. She read fear there.

"Yes," she whispered. She knew he loved her, even though he'd never told her.

"And you know I've never told Jackson about your father," Zay said.

"I know."

Zay's jaw tightened. The fear in his eyes melted to hurt. "Then why didn't you trust me?" he whispered. "Why didn't you tell me about Timmy?"

"Because," she said, trying to keep her temper in check. "I know that when it comes to your work, when it comes to doing what Jackson wants, *nothing* else matters."

Her words seemed to light something up inside of him. He took two steps back, shoving his hands into his pockets.

"And *I* know," he said behind gritted teeth, "that when it comes to situations like this, you are un*reasonable.*" He turned to walk away from her, paused, then jerked back around. "Don't you get it? If Timmy remembers what happened to him, it puts *all of us* in danger. He will remember that Marielle, Rush, and *you* are all Genex. He wouldn't hurt you on purpose, Chapel, but revealing who you are by accident? Nothing would be worse for you. *Or him.*"

"So what? I'm supposed to sit quietly and let Jackson do what he thinks is best?"

"Yes," Zay said. "That's exactly what you're supposed to do."

She crossed her arms over her chest. "What's his plan, then? If Timmy remembers. At least tell me that much."

"I could lie to you right now," he said, clenching and unclenching his fists. "I could lie to you and this would all be over. But I won't lie."

Chapel's head felt suddenly warm and buoyant. She heard the solid *THUMP, THUMP, THUMP* of a roaring pulse in her ears. "He'll turn him over to the Invisibles, won't he?"

Zay didn't answer. He just stared at her—unblinking and stoic.

She used both hands to claw the hair back from her face. The noise she made was somewhere between a sob and a scream. "I can't look at you," she said. "I can*not* even look at you."

Zay turned to her door, kicking it so hard that it sounded like a gunshot echoing in the silence around them.

"What has Jackson done to make you so desperately loyal?" she said, her voice growing louder and louder. "You're like a—." She searched for words, anger rolling through her veins like a wave crashing to shore. "You're like his lapdog, or something. Can you even think for yourself, Isaiah?"

He turned toward her, the cold fury on his face telling her she'd gone too far.

"You are constantly asking me to choose," he spat. "Choose between the person I love the most and the person who loves me the most. Jackson took me in, Chapel. Despite the filth that runs through my veins. And then you question *him*? You *keep things from me,*" he said slowly. "And then you question me?"

She hated that he made a good point. "I just want you to think for yourself," she said.

"No you don't." His upper lip curled back. "You want to tell me who to be friends with, who I should listen to, to what *degree* I should rebel." He pointed at her. "You want me to be *your* lapdog. Just like Logan was."

"Get. Out," she hissed, pointing a shaking finger at her bedroom door. "And don't come back."

Zay's expression went strangely placid. He was immobile—a puppet whose strings had been cut.

He shook his head at her. "You're acting like this is some stupid high school relationship." He pointed to the Thanatos tattoo on his chest. "But this isn't a game. This isn't just about you."

Zay walked to the door then turned around. "I've been trying to show you how serious—how dangerous—this is. But I guess I've done a terrible job." His dark eyebrows pushed together and held there. "I won't sit here and watch you destroy everything we've given our lives to build. I won't sit here and watch you self-destruct because you trust the wrong people."

She lashed out at the first thing she came in contact with, her clock, sweeping it and the rest of her nightstand's contents to the floor. She didn't stop there. Her dresser was lined with framed photos. She picked them up one by one, slamming them into the floor.

Next came her desk. Then her walls. She ripped and tore until her room resembled the disaster of her life—of her heart. When she finally looked up, eyes caked with mascara and tears, she found that she was, in every way, alone.

CHAPTER FOURTEEN

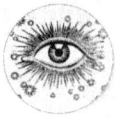

The next morning, Chapel woke feeling like an ax was imbedded behind one eye. On top of nightmares starring Zay and Marielle, she was visited by the Erica death-dream again.

A buzzing noise to her right highlighted the pulse of every ache. She sat up. It took her a few labored breaths to sort out what day it was.

Sunday.

It was Sunday morning, and Chapel's alarm clock wasn't supposed to go off again for a few hours. Someone had set it for earlier.

Chapel's heart leapt in her chest. *Zay.* But then she saw a sticky note pressed to the top. It was her mother's handwriting.

Michael's grave. 7:00 a.m. Tell no one. Come alone.

She didn't even change out of her pajamas before she left. Chapel was shoving her feet into navy rain boots in the foyer when she noticed the sound of a low rumble.

Chapel stuck her head in the guest room off the entryway to find Rush face-first into the mattress. A line of drool hung from his parted lips, puddling on the toile duvet.

If Chapel hadn't felt like her world was disintegrating all around her, she might have taken his picture to text it to everyone later. Instead, she tiptoed backward out of the room and used the door off the kitchen to get outside.

It had started raining by the time Chapel reached Bennett Park Memorial Gardens. She trudged up to the headstone feeling heavy and angry. Once there, Chapel dipped her hands into the potted plant at the base of the headstone, half-hoping the note was actually one from her father.

"He's not going to answer you."

Chapel turned in the direction of her mother's voice.

There, Valerie stood—elegant and poised despite the hideous weather, dressed in a black rain jacket, holding a matching floral umbrella.

She moved like the fog rolling down the hill they stood on top of, the pointed toes of her black boots coming to rest just beside Chapel's knees—now caked in mud.

"Why?" Chapel asked.

Valerie looked off into the distance. "Which why?"

Chapel rose to her feet. Almost as tall as Valerie now, they were eye-level. "Pick one."

"He won't answer you because Todd will have had you followed here. And he's smarter than Todd."

"Why would Todd have me followed?"

Valerie shook her head. "Next question."

Chapel had plenty. "How long have you known he's alive?"

"Two years," Valerie said. "I suspected sooner. There were signs. I used to visit his grave every Sunday afternoon. One of those days he just showed up here. I thought he was a ghost."

"Where is he?" Chapel asked. "Why hasn't he tried to see me?"

"Just because you haven't seen *him* doesn't mean he hasn't seen *you*."

Chapel shivered and pulled her sleeves down over her fists. "What's he doing? Why the fake death?"

"I'd like to know, too." Valerie sighed and switched the umbrella from one hand to the other. "Michael answers few of my questions. He says his absence has served you and I best."

Chapel pressed her lips into a flat, joyless smile.

Valerie shrugged. "I know," she said. "I feel the same as you in that regard. He *has* been worried about you, though. Genuinely worried. I think the main reason he revealed himself to me is you. He said when he turned eighteen his exception began to grow. He said yours would, too. And that I would need his help navigating what came next for you."

"How long have you known I am . . . like this?"

Valerie's hand went to her stomach. She held it there firmly and took a deep breath. "I knew what Michael could do before I married him."

Chapel took a few moments to digest that. "Then why let me grow up feeling like a freak?" she asked. "Why wouldn't you just tell me?"

Valerie's lips thinned into a line. Tears pooled behind her emerald eyes, but none fell. "I was a fool. I thought I could save you from all this. Save you from a life that takes away your choices."

"By sending me to Doctor Forrester?"

"Hunter told me about him," Valerie said. "Hunter said that he had helped other Genex children deal with their exceptions."

"Yeah." Chapel wiped at the spew of rain blurring her vision. "And then Hunter murdered him."

"Hunter did a lot of things wrong," Valerie said. "But he watched out for you your entire life. One bad decision doesn't negate a lifetime of good."

Chapel yanked at the collars of her jacket and shirt, revealing the marred flesh above her heart. Valerie dropped her umbrella to the ground. Removing one glove, she ran light fingers against the scar's raised edges. "He did this?"

Chapel nodded.

Valerie looked at her hard, studying her features. Finally, she put her glove back on. "I imagine Isaiah made him regret it."

"He did."

"Good. As far as your father and I can tell, Isaiah is good. We're both still unsure of Jackson. Time will tell, though."

"Zay and I broke up," Chapel blurted. The word *broke* tasted like bitter fruit on her tongue. "I think."

"I thought your room looked rather ravaged," Valerie said with a tilt of her head. "What happened?"

Chapel found herself describing the previous night's events. Valerie held very still while she spoke, her expression giving away nothing.

When Chapel was quiet, she nodded. "I'm sorry to hear that." She rubbed her lips together for a moment, squinting at her. "But, Chapel, have you ever wondered how it will work in the future? How keeping Timmy close to you might prove a challenge? Not to mention a hazard to him."

Though spoken softly, Valerie's words were like lashes across Chapel's heart. Because she hadn't stopped to think about that.

"It seemed to work out for you and Dad, though," Chapel said. Then, she turned that thought over again in her mind. "Well, until it didn't."

"Just think about it," Valerie added.

The sadness in Valerie's eyes instigated an idea forming in Chapel's mind.

"Two years," Chapel murmured. "You've known Dad was alive for two years. Does that have anything to do with why things are so different between us since then? So . . . distant?"

Valerie retrieved her umbrella from the ground. She inspected its base before responding. "There are many reasons. Complicated reasons, but, in part, yes." She looked behind Chapel, at the marble headstone with a healthy man's name on it.

"You are Michael Ryan's daughter, Chapel. Every bit of you cries out that you belong to him. His return . . . it—" Valerie ground her teeth together. Two fat tears pushed their way down her cheeks. "It nearly killed me, knowing that he's been alive all these years. I loved him like you wouldn't believe. It was a maddening love."

Chapel swallowed her own emotions. She let Valerie cry for herself alone. "You love him still."

Valerie's laugh was as brittle as dead leaves. "It defies reason," she said. Valerie returned her gaze to Chapel. "Learning that he chose to live without me was worse than learning of his death. Being an adult?" She tilted her chin to the side. "It's not like the fairytales, Chapel. There are many bends in the road to happily ever after."

Chapel turned, unable to force her tears back any longer. She spoke with a clenched jaw. "I needed you."

"I know," Valerie said. "And I've done the best I can. It's not enough, but it's my best." She came to stand just in front of Chapel. Using her thumb, her mother rubbed at the dampness beneath Chapel's eyes. Her touch was soft and warm and reminded Chapel of a summer breeze. "Oh, Chapel Grace. You are strong in a way that reminds me so much of Michael Ryan, but there's this . . . *breathtaking* softness just beneath that strength that is totally and wholly *you.*"

Chapel stood in that moment a few beats longer than normal. She indulged herself, lingering under a caring mother's gaze.

Then she cleared her throat. Who knew when Valerie would be forthcoming again? Chapel needed answers. "What does he want me to do? Bellum? Thanatos?"

Valerie took a step back. "He was Bellum at the time of his so-called death, but he was unhappy. He knew something . . . something about Bellum, I think. He never told me what. He just said that when the time came to make the choice, you'd know what to do."

Chapel blew a quick breath out her nose. "That's annoying."

Valerie smiled at her—a true smile. "Quick-tempered. Now, *that* you get from me."

The two women looked at each other as a moment of shared silence passed between them. It wasn't warm, but it wasn't cold, either.

"And Todd?" Chapel said. "You know he speaks Russian, right?"

Valerie raised her eyebrows. "Todd is former military. And, beyond that, a long, long story. I'm afraid it's in your best interest not to know."

Chapel gave a quiet laugh. "When do I get to decide what's in my best interest, huh?"

Valerie reached a gloved hand into her pocket. She pulled out a card. "Now."

"What is this?" On the card was a series of numbers and letters.

"The first set is the number of a safety deposit box at First National bank in Gainesville. The second set is the password to give the on-duty manager to get inside it."

Chapel looked at her mother through squinted eyes. "What will be in there?"

Valerie tilted her chin down. "Not yet. You don't get that answer yet."

Chapel glanced down to the parking lot. Valerie's car was still running. "How will you get word to me? When you find something?"

"Don't worry about that," she said. "Memorize what's on that card, then destroy it." Valerie's eyes looked hard. "Today."

"Okay, okay." Chapel touched her eyebrow. Her mother was speaking in so much code that it was overwhelming. "What about you? What are you going to do?"

"I flew in to get files from my former OB. Or, so I told Todd after I'd boarded the plane. It took extensive planning to get here without his foreknowledge, but it was the only way I could talk to you and know it was in private."

"And . . . the baby?"

Valerie patted the side of her auburn bob. Finally, she looked a little embarrassed. "There is no baby. I need him to keep me close, and there's nothing that man wants more than a son."

Chapel's forehead furrowed. "Wait. So, you're not pregnant."

Valerie actually blushed. "I am *very* not pregnant."

Chapel felt the twinges of a new kind of fear. "Will you be safe?" she asked. "And the twins?"

"Absolutely. Don't worry about us—just focus on your training."

Valerie took a step in Chapel's direction—hesitated— then another and another, until she was wrapping her arms around her and clinging to her—clinging to her like it was the last time she'd ever seen her.

A rush of feelings assailed Chapel: remorse, fear, love, pain, anger, loss. "Mom, I . . . If this is the last time I see you, I want you to know—"

"Shh," Valerie said, tears streaming down her face now. "Don't say that, now. Don't think like that." She pushed Chapel's hair behind her ears—just like she had when she was a little girl. "It's not time for that yet. Just promise me one thing."

"What?"

Valerie released her and stepped back. "Promise me that you'll try to forgive me. Not today, but one day?"

Chapel couldn't tell the difference between her own tears and the rain. A sobbed jerked through her throat as the ache inside of her broke apart.

"I'll try."

Valerie sniffed hard. She picked up her umbrella, shaking the gathered water from its crevices. "The safety deposit box. When it's time, go to it without fail."

"I will."

Valerie nodded once and cinched her coat at the waist. "I need to leave. Todd will no doubt have someone checking on me soon."

They walked without speaking to their respective cars. Chapel swung open her door, pausing at the sound of Valerie's voice.

"Chapel?"

"Yes?" She turned around.

"I love you. One day I hope you understand just how much."

Then Valerie flung her car into reverse and left.

* * * *

Worry about supernatural beings who may want you and/or your friends dead, check.

Get dumped by your boyfriend, check.

Meet your mom by your father's fake grave, check.

It had been an eventful twenty-four hours. But for Chapel, Sunday was just beginning. She still had to teach Sunday school to a classroom full of first graders.

She called Gabe while she drove.

"Hello, Chapel Ryan."

She rolled her eyes at his accent. "Don't *Chapel Ryan* me. What's the deal with Kacie hanging out with Timmy?"

He hesitated for only a moment. "She's observing him. That's all."

"Well tell her to stop," Chapel snapped. "Right now. Call her and tell her to stop."

"She's seen him, Chapel," Gabe said calmly. "She's seen him being involved in our world."

Chapel gripped her steering wheel. "But the visions can change, yes?"

"Sometimes. In some cases. Yes, they can change."

"Well, I'm changing this one," Chapel said. "Right here and right now. If she doesn't back off Timmy, I swear I will use Tempus and I will break her arms."

"Hey, hey," Gabe said, finally sounding alarmed. "Calm down."

"I'm serious, Gabe. I'll do it."

"I'll talk to Kacie. But, Chapel?"

"What?"

"There are some things that can't be changed."

"Then you better pray to God above that this is one of them that *can*."

She hung up and pulled into the church, leaning her head against the headrest. It felt like she'd been awake for forty-eight straight hours.

There was a knock on the window. Chapel jumped when she saw Rush peering at her through the glass. She swung the door open and stepped out.

He ran a hand across his shaved head and looked at her. His eyes had no humor, no amusement in them. "Hey. You snuck out."

"Yeah, I did." Chapel pulled up the lapels of her coat against the wind, leaning against her car. "What?" she asked. "No cracks on my hair?"

She had flung it into a bun in her frenzy to get out of the house after getting drenched at the cemetery. The result teed her up perfectly for a joke about a peach stem.

Rush shook his head slowly. "I figured you weren't in the mood."

Chapel studied the toes of her brown boots. "You've talked to Zay, then?"

"Yeah."

"How is he?"

Rush shoved his hands in his pockets. Despite the forty-degree weather, he had on a thin white shirt and baggy jeans. His shoulders rose in a shrug. "Zay's the suffer-in-silence type."

Chapel bit the insides of her cheeks to keep her emotions in check. "Are you mad at me?"

Rush sighed. "I see it both ways. I didn't grow up in this stuff, either. I know it's heavy. And you're in a bad spot with everybody tugging on you this way, and that. And you're only operating on partial information."

"But . . . "

"But he's my boy. And, I lie to you not, the best person I've ever been around. And, Peaches, I've been around."

Chapel nodded. "I know. But just like Zay is your boy, Timmy is mine."

"Look," Rush said, "no one's going to touch that kid as long as he doesn't remember anything. Zay thinks that Seer's letter was meant to set you off. Personally, I agree."

A gust of wind swirled around them, sending wisps of blonde hair across her face.

"Rush, when we thought my father died, Timmy just knew how to deal with me. I can't explain it any better than that. He just knew me." She gritted her teeth. "And if anything happens to him, it will kill me."

Rush held up his hands. "Look, I get it. He's a good dude. But Zay was looking out for all of us. For you. You're mad at him for doing the exact same thing you would have done for Timmy."

Chapel's throat felt swollen behind her tongue.

Rush tilted his head up at her. "Sucks, huh?"

Chapel squinted up at him. "It's like that moment when you cut yourself badly, just before the pain starts, and you know it's going to hurt. Like really, really hurt. That's where I am right now. Holding my breath, waiting to bleed."

"Uh, Chapel?"

Rush and Chapel both turned in the direction of Timmy's voice.

"What's up, Timmy," Rush said easily, leaning to shake his hand. "We met once before at Roosters? I'm Zay's friend."

Timmy met Rush's hand in the middle, studying him just a beat too long. Chapel's chest tightened. Was he remembering something more about Rush?

"Yeah, I remember," Timmy said finally. "Rush, right? Did you ever upgrade your phone?"

Rush pulled a thin device from his back pocket and held it out, showing it to Timmy. "Absolutely, dude. It's killer."

Timmy slid his finger across the screen. "I've read the reviews on it. It looks pretty sick. I just can't make up my mind, you know?"

"Oh, we know," Erica said, coming to stand beside Chapel. Her pleather pants squeaked when she put her hands on her hips. "That mind of yours never knows what it wants, does it?"

"What are you doing here?" Timmy asked, crossing his arms. "You never get here this early."

Erica rolled her eyes. "I would say it's because God is good, because," she motioned to Rush's biceps, "well, obviously. But it's actually because Chapel asked me to help her teach the lesson. She said it has two parts."

Timmy pulled his glasses off his face and rubbed his eyes. "That's funny. She asked me to be here for the same reason."

Chapel smacked her forehead into her hand. "I think I accidentally asked both of you to help me teach Sunday school. I'm sorry. I've had a lot on my mind." She threw out something she knew they couldn't get mad about. "Zay and I may have broken up last night. That's why Rush is here. He's checking on me."

Erica and Timmy exchanged a long look. *No, we can't get mad at her*, it said.

Erica was the first to speak. "I'll personally take care of castrating him," she said calmly.

"Sorry," Timmy mumbled.

"Erica, you don't have to stay," Chapel said. "I know how much you like your sleep."

Erica's spine straightened. "Why? You think Timmy knows more about kids than me?"

"Not at—"

"Wait a minute," Timmy said, turning to face Erica. "What are *you* trying to say? I know a ton about kids."

"Oh, right," Erica said, stepping toward him. "Like the time you did that experiment on Mikey that made his pee blue for a week."

Timmy closed the distance between them. Chapel had always thought he and Erica were the same height, but looking at them standing toe to toe she noticed Timmy was now much taller.

"I don't think," Timmy said, "that you should talk about turning things the incorrect color." His eyes flicked meaningfully to Erica's pale orange hair.

Erica gasped. "Don't you talk about my hair," she hissed. "Don't you ever talk about my hair."

Chapel closed her eyes and prayed God would suck her through a massive vortex into the ground. But when she opened them, she had three people staring at her—obviously waiting on her to fix things.

"Okay, okay." She pulled apart her two best friends. "Are you guys eight years old?" She sighed. "If you had any idea what kind of morning I've had . . . How about this? You're both going to help me teach Sunday school. Now, march." She pointed to the basement entrance.

"She started it," Timmy mumbled as he passed.

"My bad, Steel," Erica added in a whisper. "But seriously, he brought up the hair."

Chapel and Rush followed them inside. Before she opened the door to her classroom, she sagged against the wall. "There's an empty room beside mine," she told Rush. "You can nap in there. I'll wake you when it's over."

Rush laughed. "And miss all the fun, Peaches? No way."

In the silence of the hallway, Chapel whispered a word she rarely said aloud.

Helen Horrowitz picked that exact moment to hobble around the corner. She pointed at Chapel with her cane. "I heard that, little lady." Then she limped off.

When Chapel swung through the door, Timmy was handing out the beginning activity while Erica stood in the corner taking attendance. They were shooting intermittent looks of rage at each other.

Chapel wondered briefly if she should pull the fire alarm and avoid the inevitable, but decided against it. If the volcano of their friendship was about to erupt, maybe being in God's house would keep them all from going up in flames.

Mikey Valentine stood from his seat and came over to Chapel. "Psst," he said in a loud whisper. "There's a giant in the corner."

Chapel looked over at Rush, sitting in two chairs at once, his legs stretched out halfway across the room.

"Does he bite?" Mikey asked.

Chapel shrugged. "I don't think so. Go sit back down. We're about to tell the Bible story."

Chapel went to the front of the room, scraping the bottom of her emotional barrel to find some warmth. "Hey, everybody! Today we have some special guests who are going to help me tell our Bible story. Ms. Erica is going to be Friend One, and Mr. Timmy is going to be Friend Two." She handed them cardboard cutouts of their respective numbers, decorated in glitter and her tears—she'd made them at two in the morning when she couldn't sleep.

Chapel continued. "One night, very, very late, Friend One was fast asleep in her bed."

Erica, reading from her script, started fake snoring.

"All of a sudden, there was a knock at her door."

Timmy banged the wall by Erica's head, making her jerk. She narrowed her hazel eyes at him like a cat about to pounce.

"Hello, friend," Timmy read robotically. "I had another friend show up at my house. I have no food for them. May I borrow some bread to feed them?"

Erica cocked an eyebrow. "Is your 'friend' that trick from the mall the other day? If so, she can go hungry. As for you, you can go—"

"Um, Ms. Erica?" Chapel interrupted. "Do you want to try that line again? What did *Friend One* say when *Friend Two* needed some bread?"

Erica cleared her throat and looked down at the script. "Don't bother me," she read. "My family is asleep and my door is locked. It's late."

"Please let me in?" Timmy said, glancing at his sheet of paper. "I need your help."

"I said no," Erica read. "If you don't stop banging on my doors, you're going to wake the neighbors."

"But Friend Two was determined," Chapel interjected. "The Bible says Friend Two had shameless persistence. That means he never gave up—no matter what."

Timmy stared at his script so long that Chapel began to wonder if he had fallen asleep. But when he spoke again, his words came out a little softer.

"Friend One," he said, "I can't help my hungry friend without you. Please, let me in."

Erica's hand slid from her hip. Her jaw unclenched. "Okay," she said. "I will help you. Tell me what you need and I will give it to you."

Chapel turned to the class. "Jesus told this story to teach us that we should never give up on something—or someone—that's important to us. Let's clap for Mr. Timmy and Ms. Erica."

Erica curtsied and Timmy gave a quick salute. They spent the rest of the class on opposite sides of the room, but Chapel noted a significant decrease in hateful looks and eye rolls.

After church, Rush walked her out to her car. Chapel got in immediately and cranked it. Rush surprised her by climbing in beside her.

"Do you think they caught on to you, Peaches?" he asked. "That little 'Oh, I accidentally invited you both,' thing?"

"Absolutely," Chapel said. "Maybe not at first, but they've realized it by now. Well, Timmy at least."

Rush raised his hand for a high-five. "I have to admire the orchestration. Getting them in the same room and making them read a Bible story that you more or less manipulated for your purposes."

Chapel smiled. "Look at you, Rush Lopez. Knowing your New Testament parables."

"You're looking at the best-looking altar boy Holy Trinity Catholic Church has ever had the pleasure of hosting." He flexed his biceps, kissing them one by one.

"You're going to make Helen pass out," Chapel told him, jerking her head to the old lady gazing blatantly from behind the wheel of her Buick.

Rush winked at her, giving a little wave. He turned back to Chapel. "You know something, Peaches? You talk a big game about being tough. But you ain't tough."

She made a face at him. "You going to follow me the rest of the day?"

"Actually, I'll be around a lot this week. Right now, it's just Gabe and me on rotation."

"Gabe?"

Rush shifted in his seat. He didn't meet her eye. "Marielle and Justin are with Jackson on an op and Zay . . ."

Chapel's heart sank like a stone dropped into still waters. "He doesn't want to see me?"

He thought a moment before he spoke. "Here's the thing about Zay, Peaches. He's too good for his own good. If he had to decide between cutting off his own arm and disappointing our team, we both know he'd lunge for the knife. It's not you he's denying—it's himself."

Chapel pulled at a thread on her steering wheel and didn't answer. She felt like two people were on either side of her, pulling her apart at the spine.

Rush stilled her hand. "You've never had someone to look up to, have you?"

She shook her head. Her eyes stung, so she blinked several times.

"Jackson gave Zay something to believe in," Rush said. "Something to *hope* in. You know, people say that love is the greatest emotion of all. But I think they're wrong. I think it's hope, because hope makes you strong."

Chapel didn't complete the thought, but she felt it: *And love makes you weak.*

CHAPTER FIFTEEN

Chapel woke in the middle of the night with a strangled cry choking through her throat. She sat up in a rush, gripping her heaving chest.

Erica. Blood. Casket.

"Just a dream," she whispered, looking down to see her hands were clean and not slathered in Erica's blood. "Just a dream."

A light knock came at her door.

"Peaches?" Rush leaned his head in. "You okay?"

"Just a dream." She said it for the third time, but it still felt so *real*.

Rush gave her one quick nod, then went back to the guest room next to hers. He and Gabe had taken turns sleeping at Taylor Manor for the last week since her attack five days ago.

Five days and no word on the whereabouts of Lucky Lindtz.

Five days of Timmy casting suspicious glances her direction.

Five days and no word from Zay.

Chapel's footsteps fell silently as she made her way to the set of windows that faced Jackson's house. Zay's light was on. She watched for a few minutes until she saw a shadow move; then the light went out.

Should she text him? Would he answer? What would she say?

She was no good at this—at weighing the cost of a sentence tapped out on a screen and knowing its worth. It seemed her dignity was the price to be paid, and Chapel clung to her pride with a terrible determination.

But her phone was in her hand and her heart was in her throat and something had to *give*.

She typed out a message and hit send before she could think better of it. It was a rare moment of emotional indulgence. And it terrified her.

CHAPEL: *You awake?*

Chapel learned something new then. She learned that the seconds between sending a text and receiving its response could scrape by at an exponentially slower rate than normal seconds.

Normal seconds, those blessed units. She decided, while waiting, that she'd never take normal seconds for granted again.

One minute passed.

Two minutes passed.

Three minutes passed.

Chapel got up from the window seat and got into bed.

Four minutes passed.

She hated him.

She pulled her soft yellow blanket over her head.

Five minutes passed.

She loved him. Why had she never told him?

Chapel checked to make sure her cellphone had service. She flipped to the text application to make sure she hadn't missed his answer. Nothing.

Six minutes passed.

She got out of bed and started pacing. She hated him again.

He wouldn't *not* answer her. And there was no way he was asleep. The light had gone out in his room six minutes ago.

Seven minutes passed and Chapel got back in bed again. She squeezed her jaws together and stared at the ceiling, trying to make her mind as blank as its cold, white landscape.

She would not cry.

The soft vibrate of his response had her jumping from the bed and staring at her phone as if it were a tiny UFO that had just landed on her nightstand. She picked it up.

ZAY: *Yes.*

"One word?" she hissed back at the phone's screen. "Seven minutes for *one word?*"

Chapel typed out and deleted several responses before choosing one. He answered more quickly then.

CHAPEL: *I had a bad dream.*
ZAY: *I hate that.*
CHAPEL: *I hate THIS.*
ZAY: *Me too . . .*
CHAPEL: *Are we broken up?*
ZAY: *I don't know.*
ZAY: *If what you said about me is how you really feel, then yes.*

What had she said again? *Oh, right.* That Zay was a lapdog that couldn't think for himself. *Quick-tempered,* Valerie had said. *You get that from me.*

ZAY: *Maybe we need space.*

Space? Chapel stared at the word *space* and hated it. Loathed every letter.

In her mind, it was simple:

He'd put Timmy in danger.

She'd reacted emotionally.

He had done what he thought was best.

She had done what she thought was best.

He'd gotten frustrated and called her a child.

She'd pitched a tantrum and acted like a child.

Why did he want *space?* Couldn't they just say they were sorry and act like it never happened?

Chapel turned her phone off and threw it across the room. *This* is why she didn't date. *Feeling. Ugh.* It was draining and confusing and awful.

She made herself as small as possible in the bed and hugged her knees to her chest.

The urge to crumble was strong, like two strong hands on her shoulders pushing her down, down, down. But Chapel resisted.

She slaked the burning in her sinuses with calm, steady breathing.

"Space," she repeated the word to her empty room. *I will give him space.*

* * * *

Chapel scanned Back Porch's parking lot, but didn't see Rush's Jeep anywhere.

She took off her apron and sat on one of the pastel rocking chairs and closed her eyes. It was Friday, and Chapel had never been more ready for a week to be over.

The flexing of the wood beneath her feet had her turning around. It was Gabe.

"Rush isn't coming," he said. "He got held up. I'm taking you to training today."

Chapel followed Gabe to his car. She got in and leaned her forehead against the window. He pulled out of the parking lot and started to drive.

She felt his eyes on the side of her face. She looked over at him.

"What?" she asked.

He put his eyes back on the road. "Are you going to tell me why you've been moping around all week like someone shot your puppy?"

Chapel sighed and leaned her head against the headrest. "Don't act like you don't know."

He was quiet for a moment. "You and Halstead still on the rocks, then?"

"On the rocks." She made a noise that was somewhere between a laugh and a sigh. "That's a good way to put it. But they're *sharp* rocks this time." She tilted her head from side to side. "No, I think . . . speared by the sword of life is more accurate. *Gutted* by the sword of life." She nodded. "That's better."

Gabe whistled. "I forget how *quite* dramatic everything is at eighteen."

She turned to look at him. "Don't do that."

"What?"

She tried to imitate his accent, "Don't, *you're-eighteen-and-young-and-sometimes-I-forget-until-you-act-like-a-dork* me. I know I'm a teenager, but hurt still hurts."

Gabe's eyebrows pressed down quickly. He rubbed the back of his hair. She would never get used to seeing it so short, and yet . . . she liked it. A lot.

"Sorry," he said.

Chapel rubbed at her temples. "I don't want to talk about it anyway."

They rode in silence and Chapel closed her eyes. Suddenly, a bang to her right had her jumping in her seat.

"You're fine," Gabe's voice said calmly. "We just got here. You fell asleep."

Gabe pointed to the window on the other side of her. Justin Chon had his fist raised against the glass. His dark eyes were level with hers, making her jump again. She rolled down the window.

"Why did you park in the back?" he asked.

Chapel looked up and saw a tall sign looming on the other side of the building. *Bulls Eye*, it said. They were at a shooting range.

Chapel turned to make a joke to Gabe, but he was digging behind them in the backseat. His shirt had come untucked, revealing a slice of skin almost as brown as Justin's.

Chapel fumbled with the door handle and got out.

"Hey, Justin," she said, hoping her smile didn't look like a grimace. "My hand looks really good." She showed him the cut, almost completely healed.

His eyes darted from her face, to her hand, back to her face again. He nodded once. "Let's go."

Justin picked up a duffel bag at his feet and started walking around the store to the front door.

Gabe stood beside her. "I don't think he likes you very much."

"And he's about to have a gun in his hand," she murmured.

"Any last words?"

"Yeah." She looked up at him. "I liked your hair better long."

The inside of Bulls Eye smelled like fireworks and rubber. They followed Justin until they came into an empty room with a series of partitions and hanging targets.

"Where is everybody?" she asked, her echo repeating her words back to her.

"Jackson rented it out," Justin said. He started unloading guns, knives, and other metallic objects she didn't recognize onto a table in the back.

"For training?"

He looked at her like it should be obvious. "No. For fun."

"Chapel, come here." Gabe opened the box in his hand. Inside was a small revolver. She picked it up, inspecting its silver barrel. "Smith and Wesson," she said, running her finger over the inscription.

"You've heard of it?"

Chapel rolled her eyes. "Have you *met* Timmy Valentine? He's obsessed with weapons. His dad used to let us shoot guns off the back porch."

"Used to?"

Chapel scratched her eyebrow. "Right up until Timmy almost shot up the propane tank when he sneezed and pulled the trigger at the same time."

Gabe look mildly horrified. "That'll do it, hm?"

"Quite so," she said, doing a terrible job at an Australian accent. "You carry this in your car with you?"

"Yes. And a smaller one, too, in my glove box. It's illegal to knowingly *kill* a Genex, but there's no law against *shooting* an errant Rogue."

She wrapped her hand around the cool handle, surprised at how heavy it was, at how easily it fit in her small hands.

"I want you to shoot with it tonight," he said, lowering his voice. "I think you'll like it."

He was probably afraid she'd ruin one of Justin's guns and then he'd scalp her for it. She smiled at him. "Thank you."

A screech from the front of the store drew everyone's attention. Chapel stuck her head around the corner to see Zay, Marielle, Rush, and Jackson walking in together from the parking lot.

Well, walking up wasn't the correct word.

Zay was charging in with Marielle on his back. Rush was chasing after them with a water gun in his hand. Jackson stood off to the side, chuckling softly as if watching his children at play.

She stepped back while they ran inside, giggling and squealing. When Zay zoomed by her, Marielle had her hands wrapped around his neck, hugging him tightly.

"Direct shot," Rush said, squirting her back with a splattered X. "And further proof that I, Rush Lopez, am the Super Soaker Sultan. And *you* two are . . . Peaches?" He started when he saw her. "How did you get here?"

She couldn't see him anymore, but Chapel knew Zay must have frozen at the sound of her nickname.

"I brought her," Gabe said. He was right behind her. "Like you asked me to."

"They parked out back," Justin said as he stared down the barrel of a gun that looked bigger than her. "I told them not to."

Chapel's eyes were like magnets when she turned around, drawn to Zay's hands cupped firmly around Marielle's thighs.

"I'm ready," she said, to whom, she wasn't sure. "I'd like to shoot something now."

Jackson raised both hands. "Now, now, eager little huntress. We will all get our turn. But first, I thought it might be fun for Justin to do a little exposé for us."

Chapel thought maybe she and Jackson had different definitions of *fun*, but she kept her mouth shut. Instead, she joined the others in the back of the room while Justin finished setting up.

From the corner of her eye, she watched as Zay leaned Marielle off his back and onto a stool. Her ankle was wrapped in a bandage.

"Relax," Gabe murmured, standing on the other side of her. He glanced down at her hand. She still held the revolver, her knuckles white around the handle. He reached down and extricated it from her clutch.

Embarrassment made her duck her head.

"It's okay," he said. Then whispered, motioning to the gun, "I feel the same way about her."

The boys who attacked Marielle had been recruited by Gabe. And though he had nothing to do with their actions, Marielle placed a lot of the blame on him.

He smirked at Chapel and it made her laugh.

"Luxe," Zay said, coming to stand beside them. He glanced down at her briefly, and Chapel couldn't read his expression. "Thank you for helping out with Chapel."

Chapel had seen Gabe and Zay interact only a handful of times, and Gabe always seemed to treat him with a sense of deference, though Zay was five years his junior.

But today, Gabe's eyes met Zay's squarely, confidently. "Chapel is my friend," he said. Then, to Chapel, "I'll see you tomorrow at work."

"Wait." Suddenly she didn't want him to go. The thought of being left alone with no one else to commiserate with over Marielle filled her with a great sense of dread. She turned around to Jackson. "Can Gabe stay? We're just having fun, right? No work stuff?"

Jackson showed no surprise or hesitation before he spread his arms open. "Certainly, he can stay. Gabriel is a welcomed ally."

"Ready," Justin called. Everyone moved his direction, but Zay tugged Chapel's elbow, drawing her back.

"She has a hurt ankle," he said. "Rush couldn't carry her in because he pulled his back out this morning. That's why he brought a water gun. He can't even shoot with us tonight."

In the shadows of the back room, his gray eyes looked metallic. Chapel was tempted to fist her hand in the front of his navy shirt and dismiss any questions Marielle may have about where Zay's heart was.

But she wasn't a dog, and Zay wasn't her territory. Besides, she felt Gabe glancing back at them periodically and it made her feel on display.

"Zay," Marielle's voice sang. "I need you to help me move my stool so I can see better."

"Are you going to say something?" he whispered, ignoring Marielle.

Chapel wasn't used to the tension in her chest—to the heat in her lungs that struggled to expand far enough to give her adequate oxygen.

Jealousy, her mind identified the emotion. She realized, with a sinking feeling, that she had never been jealous before. Not truly. Not like this.

Chapel disliked jealousy almost as much as she disliked Marielle.

"Why don't I take a number?" She brushed by him. "You just let me know when you're freed up."

There were a series of tables set up in intervals down the length of the room. On each of them was a different weapon: guns, knives, a handful of silver stars, things Chapel didn't have names for.

Justin had also adjusted the targets that hung across from each table. He had turned them around, revealing the outline of a body. He had added a few dummies between the tables and the targets, and had marked on all of them in different locations with a blood red X.

"Is the timer set?" Justin asked.

Jackson held up his cellphone. "Yes, I've got it at one minute."

"What?" Chapel couldn't keep the exclamation in. "You're going to hit all those marks in less than a minute?" She didn't count them all, but there had to be at least fifty.

Justin pulled something from his back pocket. A black bandana. He walked up to Chapel and held it out. "Yes," he said. "But I'm going to do it blind."

She took the material from his hands, wondering why he chose her to tie it on his head. A message, maybe? But what? She knotted it as tightly as it would go.

Once he was in position, Jackson counted down from three. "Three, two, one."

The first table held a handgun. Justin picked it up and fired off several shots, then hopped over the table and rolled to the first dummy.

Chapel hadn't seen him pick it up, but a knife appeared in his hand. He shoved it into every red X, under the ribs, and across the neck, with flawless precision.

Then his leg drew an upward arc and he kicked the dummy over. At the same time his arm flicked, the knife slicing into the red X over the hanging target's heart.

Bull's-eye.

He did a forward handspring over the next table, putting him on their side of the room again. He picked up a bow, pulled it back and shot one, two, three perfectly aimed arrows at the target.

The next table had five silver stars. He immediately threw three. Before they even hit the target, Justin had launched himself over the table and tossed the other two at the dummy. They found their mark in each of its eyes.

Justin threw himself their direction again, doing a back tuck over the table and stepping out of it.

The next table had something on it Chapel didn't recognize. It looked like a large sickle with a chain attached to the bottom. A silver rectangle hung from the chain's other end. A weight.

Justin picked up the object and swung the chain over his head. He took two steps back before he leapt over the table. As soon as his feet hit the ground, he let the chain fly, wrapping itself around the legs of the dummy.

With a jerk, it was on the ground and the sickle was buried directly in the center of its forehead.

He left it there, then ran and slid under the last table. On it was a whip.

Justin cracked it across the table, snapping the plastic down the middle. He jumped on top of it, forcing the two pieces apart.

His body was flung forward into an aerial—a cartwheel with no hands—that Chapel had learned how to do when she was a gymnast. Except he stepped out of his with the whip already in motion.

The snap made her flinch each and every time. He whipped the dummy, sending stitches and cotton flying in every direction.

Jackson held up his cellphone and started counting. "And ten, nine, eight . . . "

Justin kept whipping.

"Seven, six, five . . . "

Justin *kept* whipping.

"Three, two—"

Justin yanked the whip back one last time and caught its tail in the air. He pulled it to his side just as Jackson said, "Time's up."

When he stepped away from the dummy, Chapel saw what he had done. In the center of its mutilated cotton chest were the initials *JC.*

Justin's body rocked with the deep gulps of breaths he now took. No one made a sound as he slipped off his bandana.

For the first time since she'd met him, he wore a new expression—*excitement.*

He had enjoyed that. Maybe a little too much for Chapel's taste. And yet, she couldn't tear her eyes away from the destruction he had created. It was ugly and impressive and *precise.*

Her hands were the first to come together in a clap, then everyone followed.

Genius had to be appreciated. Even the darker variety.

They all cleaned up and reset the tables, targets, and dummies.

Chapel caught Gabe's eye. "Let's shoot."

She pulled him to the far end of the room where targets had been rehung.

"It's been a while since I've done this," she said. "Show me again?"

Gabe came and stood beside her. Over his shoulder, Chapel saw Zay watching.

"How jealous do you want to make him?" Gabe asked quietly. "Mild irritation? Or blind with rage?"

Chapel's smile was wide. "Somewhere in the middle, I think."

"Very well."

Gabe showed her how to stand with two hands squaring her hips. Then he showed her how to hold the gun, and where to rest her hands. Then he taught her when to shoot.

"Inhale and put your finger on the trigger," he said. "On the exhale, pull. Let me see you."

Chapel assumed the position. Gabe came and shifted her half an inch toward the center. He let his hands linger.

"Now you're ready," he whispered.

At first, she was very aware of Zay—wherever he was in the room, how long he looked at her, and when.

But when she started hitting the target in its center, she forgot to care.

Chapel shot Gabe's gun until her hands felt numb. "I think I need a break," she told Gabe. Chapel walked to where Justin sat organizing his knives.

"Teach me," she said.

Justin looked around the room as if someone might tell him she was joking. "Are you being serious?"

"I can shoot a gun," she said. "I have no interest in whips and chains, and I'll probably put someone's eye out with one of those stars. So, yes. Knives."

Justin taught her a few basic techniques, including the best place to stab someone for maximum impact.

"In the throat," he said, moving her arm over the dummy's neck. "But don't slice. Stab."

It took her several attempts to get the knife through the cotton, but when she did, it gave her a sickening feeling of accomplishment.

"Teach me again, but add the aerial," she said. "I know how to do one."

He didn't question her. "Hand me the knife."

She gave it to him and he showed her how to position her fingers over the handle while flipping.

"Try the aerial with nothing in your hand," he said.

She started off a little rusty, putting one hand down the first few attempts.

When he was satisfied she had the technical aspects of the flip down, he showed her how to measure the distance between herself and the dummy.

"When your shadow grazes their feet, start your lunge. Watch." He showed her. "Now try it with this." He handed her the knife's empty sheath.

Chapel gripped it just like he showed her and backed up. Her first try was a near-disaster, and she almost landed on top of the dummy's feet.

She gritted her teeth and paused to unbutton her flannel shirt to the black tank top she wore beneath. She flicked it to the ground and scraped her hair into a ponytail.

The sides of her vision warped gently, like they were curtains billowing in the wind.

Tempus. She recognized it and pushed it back. Chapel's encounter with Hunter had taught her many things, perhaps the most important of which was that Tempus could not be her crutch.

And she tried again. And again. And again. Her calves ached. Her ankles felt jarred. She'd come up short, or lose her balance, or miss the step out. But Chapel had made up her mind that she wasn't leaving until she'd mastered this *one* move.

She had to be able to do *something* besides Tempus.

"Do you want a break?" Justin asked.

"No."

She tried again. And then, finally, Chapel was able to land the flip, step out, and bring the sheath to the side of the dummy's neck in one fluid movement.

When she did, she became suddenly aware of how quiet the room had grown. Everyone had put down their weapons, and stood in the back of the room talking quietly.

"Give me the knife," she told Justin.

He shook his head. "You landed it one time. One time out of about thirty."

She put out her hand. "The knife."

"Look, you did okay, but—"

"Don't act like you care if I get hurt," she said lowly. "And hand me the knife."

Justin pursed his lips and tilted his head to the side. She literally felt his assessment of her, piece by piece. Then he tossed the knife into the air and caught it by the tip of its blade, offering her the black handle.

"Chapel, wait." Gabe crossed to them. "Do you really think this is a good idea?"

His light eyes were a sea of concern, and they seemed to search her face for something—maybe a reason why she would be so determined to do this.

"It's probably not a good idea," she admitted. "But I'm going to do it anyway."

He crossed his arms over his chest. "Why? What are you trying to prove?"

She glanced behind him at everyone watching her.

"He's right, Peaches," Rush said. "Let's drive through Dairy Queen and eat our feelings instead."

"It isn't prudent, I'm afraid," Jackson added.

Marielle lifted a dainty finger. "I'd like to see her try."

Then she met Zay's eyes. *I look at you*, he had said. And she had felt it then, just like she felt it now. He saw something in her that no one else saw. Maybe it was something he saw in himself, too. A self-belief, a mad determination.

"She can do it," he said. Then louder, "She can do it."

He walked over, plucking the knife from Justin's hand. He moved her back to the spot on the floor she had landed her jump from and stood behind her, pressing the length of her side against him.

"It's a Rogue," he said, lips by her ear. He ran his hand down her arm, letting the knife slip into her fingers. "And he has Timmy, and this is your one shot to save him."

He nudged her back leg with his knee. "Don't whip this leg down so fast," he said. "That's what made the difference when you landed it."

So, he *had* been watching her.

"Two more things . . ." He leaned so close she tasted his breath, "You look good holding that knife, and I'm driving you home."

She met his eye.

"Go at it hard," he said.

It didn't take Chapel's imagination long to conjure up panic on Timmy's behalf. She pictured him just beyond the dummy, unconscious and bound.

Her head was filled with a ringing silence when she began the lunge; her eyes saw nothing but stuffing spilling from a seam.

Chapel's muscles contracted and her body was spurned forward. Her legs swung around, then down, slightly slower, as Zay had suggested. At the same time, she spiraled her arm around, blade out, and sunk it solidly into the thick material.

She hit the dummy in the shoulder. It wasn't perfect, but it was close enough.

Chapel told herself to be cool, but when she turned around, she rose up on her toes and squealed. She found Justin, and she launched herself at him, hugging him and laughing like she'd actually just saved Timmy's life.

Justin didn't exactly hug her back, but when she pulled away, there was a hint of amusement on his stoic features. "You did well," he said.

"Thank you," she said. "For teaching me."

It was late and time to pack up. They helped Justin load his Jeep. When they were finished, she walked with Gabe to his SUV to get her purse and book bag.

It was late-March, and the nights were getting slightly warmer. Chapel sat on the back bumper while he unlocked his doors.

"Feel good?" he asked, dropping her bags at her feet.

She nodded. "Yeah."

He sat beside her. "I'm sorry I questioned you earlier. It's just . . ." He leaned forward on his knees and glanced up at the night sky. A new moon hung right over their heads, as if pinned there. Gabe looked back at her. "I like watching you rise to the occasion."

For a breath, all she saw was Gabe. Tan skin. Long lashes brushing the top of his brow. The full shape of his bottom lip. Eyes that looked softer than she'd seen in quite some time.

A familiar growl crept around the corner, and they were washed in headlights. Zay's Shelby came to a rolling stop and the lingering moment was snuffed out like a candle.

"See you tomorrow, Gabe," she called over her shoulder.

"See you." His next words came to her back. "Don't let him off the hook too easily."

The inside of the Shelby was warm and it smelled like Zay. She slipped into the seat and he threw her bags in the back. Neither spoke as he gunned the gas, propelling them into the clear-skied night.

He had brought the knife with him. It sat between them in the console, and when a streetlight hit it just right, she could see both their faces in its reflection, separated by its raised center.

He glanced over at her. "I want to take you somewhere before we go home and talk. Is that okay?"

She watched the way his blue veins shifted beneath the taut skin of his arm and he shifted into another gear.

"I guess," she said. What she really meant was, *I'd follow you anywhere.*

Zay pulled around the square and into the Goodson's Pharmacy parking lot. It was closed, but she didn't question him when he got out and opened her door.

Zay never did anything without intention. He was deliberate to the point of neurosis.

Taking her by the hand, he pulled her around back.

The way his thumb rubbed over her knuckles told her he was worked up. She sensed that there was something building up inside of him. Like a soda that had been shaken up. He was fizzling, ready to spew.

"Do you see that wall?" he asked, pointing.

"Yes."

"Do you want to know why I think about that wall? All the time?"

She shook her head, her heart gaining momentum behind her ribs. "Tell me."

He walked up to the brick and splayed his hand across it, looking back at her.

"This is the wall I pushed you up against the night that Hunter broke into this store. And this," he pointed to a specific rectangle, "is the exact brick I looked at when you bit into my hand to get away from me."

She swallowed. "In my defense, I was trying to get to Tamera. To help her."

"I know." Zay walked to where she stood. He was so close that her head tilted back to look up at him. "That was when

I knew you were more than just a girl with a gift. That was the night I knew you had *courage.*"

He pressed his hand to her chest, just over her scar. The blood inside pumped erratically behind his touch. "I could feel how scared you were," he said. "Terrified. As you should have been. But when you set this mind on something." He moved his hand to her temple. "Like you did tonight? Chapel, you are *magic.*"

His lips were wet with quick speech and excitement, and she couldn't resist them one syllable longer.

Like she had wanted to earlier, Chapel twisted her fingers into his shirt and jerked his mouth to hers, crushing their bodies together as if any space between them was intolerable.

His hand came behind her head and spun her back against the wall. This time she welcomed its cold and gritty embrace.

It wasn't a gentle kiss they shared. It was passionate; it was desperate.

She had to break away to breathe, but Zay continued kissing her. Her neck, the bottom of her chin, her collarbone. He kept a hand pressed to her bare back, pulling her to him and holding her upright as she angled her body against him.

As their breathing slowed down, Zay started speaking between kisses.

"I know . . . we need to talk . . . should be talking right now. But you had that knife." He ran his nose along the edge of hers. "It was so hot. And I'm just a boy. You with a weapon turns me into nothing but a stupid, silly boy."

Chapel's mind picked that moment to replay Gabe's words. *"Don't let him off the hook too easily."*

Gently, she made some space between them. "About that talk?"

He leaned his forehead against hers and held it there for several long moments. Then he kissed her one last time on the temple and pulled away.

"You're right. Let's go."

They had been on the road fewer than five minutes when her phone started ringing in her purse. She reached to get it and saw that it was Gabe.

Zay must have read the screen over her shoulder. "Ah. Luxe. He touched you enough during that shooting lesson, don't you think?"

Chapel sent the call to voicemail. "When I start carrying him around on my back like he's my personal koala bear, you can have an opinion about Gabe."

Then her phone started vibrating again. This time with a text.

Zay stopped at a red light and held out a hand. "Give it to me," he said. "I'll answer it."

"I'm sure he just wants to make sure I'm okay," Chapel said. "I'll tell him that I'll text when I get home."

"You should tell him we had to pull over on the side of the road to make out," Zay said. "That we got sidetracked having a hardcore, sloppy, wet make-out session."

"Sloppy?" she said. "Speak for your . . ." She trailed off. Gabe's message was typed in all capital letters. "Don't stop at the light." She looked over at Zay who was bathed in the bright red glow of the light they sat under. "Gabe says don't stop at the light."

Zay's arms tensed, straightening at the wheel. His foot came down on the gas with a squeal.

To her right she saw a blinding light. A car was coming at them quickly. She threw her arm up at the last second, as if that might be enough to save her.

She heard her name on Zay's lips, heard the crunch of tearing metal, and her own scream, ripping through her throat.

There was glass, and pain, and darkness.

Then nothing.

CHAPTER SIXTEEN

She was having a dream.

Her body was floating down a stream. She was weightless, a feather in the wind.

Then it changed, and she was heavy. Sinking, sinking, sinking like an anchor into warm waters.

Then she wasn't dreaming anymore. She was lying on something soft. She willed her eyes open, but they wouldn't move.

She heard voices.

"Is she waking up?" *Gabe.*

There was a pause, a hand on her cheek. The callused fingertips she knew so well. *Zay.* "No. They gave her some pretty strong pain meds. She's out."

A chair slid back. "I should go," Gabe said. Chapel heard him stand.

"Wait." Zay said. "Look. Without your text, she might be dead. I moved just in time. So . . . thank you."

"Yes, well." Gabe cleared his throat. "I didn't do it for you."

The door opened and a wedge of light pressed itself against her closed eyelids.

"I know why you did it," Zay said. "And it's not because she's your friend."

The door stayed open.

"Is this the bit," Gabe said, "where you tell me that she's yours?"

There was a pause. "We both know better than that. Chapel belongs to no one." Two fingers curled hair behind her ear. "Chapel belongs to herself."

The door closed.

* * * *

Her eyelids slid open once, twice, three times before she could keep them there. It hurt, but the sting told her she was really alive and not dead, like she was sure she would be when those headlights had careened into the side of Zay's car.

"Chapel?" It was her mother's voice. "She's awake. Go tell the others."

It took a moment, but Chapel was able to move her head and look at Valerie's face—tears-stained and drawn, without a brush of makeup on it. She looked beautiful.

"Mom?"

Valerie moved to her side, pushing hair off her forehead.

"Hey sweetie," she murmured, a sob bubbling from her lips. She pressed a hand over her mouth, and Chapel saw she was holding a fist of crumbled tissues.

Chapel's throat felt raw and dry. She tried to push a swallow down it, but couldn't. "Zay?" she croaked.

"He's fine. He moved the car just in time. It was . . . a miracle."

Gabe's text. It had saved her life.

A nurse came in and checked Chapel's machines. "Everything looks great," she said. "The doctor will want to look at you when he makes his rounds, but I think we can have you discharged by tonight."

"Where is Zay?" she whispered when they were alone.

"You'll see him soon," Valerie said. "How do you feel?"

Chapel studied her body. There were cuts along her arm, and the side of her head throbbed lightly. But she was *whole.*

"My arm hurts. But that's it."

Valerie shook her head. "There was a piece of glass in your shoulder. They removed it. You had to have some stitches. Other than that, you're fine."

Chapel closed her eyes, those last heartbeats before the crash playing there. It had seemed so familiar. Darkness and crunching glass. "Who was it?" she asked.

"We don't know." Valerie said. "They were driving a—" Her breath caught. "A highly specialized car. Isaiah got out to chase them, but he didn't want to leave you, so he returned before he saw the driver."

"Highly specialized?"

Valerie nodded somberly. "Outfitted with a brush guard and a lift kit." There was a tic in her mother's jaw. "The attack was premeditated, Chapel."

Chapel's only response was recorded by the increased beeping of her blood pressure machine beside the bed.

"You're going to be fine, though," Valerie said, and Chapel thought she might have been reassuring herself, too. "You got knocked unconscious, and they gave you a sedative to sleep. But you're fine. You're fine."

Out in the hallway, Chapel heard a familiar voice. "I *am* family," Erica was saying. "What? You don't see the resemblance?"

"Mom?" Chapel nodded to the door.

Valerie stuck her head outside. When she came back in, Timmy and Erica were with her.

"I'm going to call Todd," Valerie said, and exited.

Erica rushed right to her and pointed a finger in her chest. "If you ever scare us like this again, Steel, I will be forced take drastic action."

Chapel smiled. Erica's face was stern, but her hazel eyes were red-rimmed and swollen.

"Deal," she said, squeezing her friend's arm.

Timmy stood at the foot of her bed, staring at her like he'd seen a ghost. "They're saying it was an accident," he said slowly. "But how does a car on a deserted street run over a curb and hit another car squarely in the side?"

Chapel was saved from that answer when a knock came at the door. "Chapel? I'm Dr. Sullivan."

"We'll come back," Timmy said.

Chapel nodded. "I'll catch up with you two later."

"I was terrified," Erica said quietly.

Chapel squeezed Erica's hand, her own eyes clouding with tears. "I'm fine."

Timmy came and put his arm along Erica's shoulders. "Come on. I'll buy you a Snickers from the vending machine."

When they were gone, the doctor came to stand beside her bed. "Dr. Lopez is coming right behind me," he said. "We did our residency together."

Dr. Lopez? It took Chapel a beat to realize he meant Rush.

"Ah," she said. "Was *Doctor* Lopez as charming then as he is now?"

A smile turned up Dr. Sullivan's face. "His nickname was Doctor Suave. Because he thought he was so smooth."

She laughed. It hurt her stomach muscles, but it felt good, too. "Dr. Suave," she repeated. "I can't thank you enough for that tidbit."

As if on cue, Rush pushed open the door with a tap of his knuckles.

"Peaches? You alive in there?"

Chapel sat up as much as she could. If Rush were here, that meant Zay was nearby. "Hey, Dr. Suave. Feeling rough today? Or *smooth?*"

Rush met Dr. Sullivan's eyes over her bed. "Cool, Sully."

Dr. Sullivan laughed as he rolled a laptop to her bedside. He asked Chapel a few questions about her pain level and explained her at-home care. He checked her stitches before excusing himself.

When they were alone, Rush flopped like a fish in the chair beside her bed. "You okay?" he asked her.

She rolled her head along the bed to face him. "I'm sore. But alive. Where is Zay?"

Rush sat up and pushed his feet onto the floor. When he clasped his hands between his knees, she knew something was wrong.

"What? What is it?"

Rush stood and walked to the end of her bed. He gripped the rail and leaned against it. "I have to tell you something."

No jokes. No cracks. No humor.

Chapel's heart began to sink inside her chest. "What? Tell me what?"

Rush pushed off from the bed and crossed thick arms over his chest. "Hunter broke out of jail," he said simply.

She could tell by the look on his face that he wasn't finished. "And . . . what else?"

"And Zay's gone to find him."

CHAPTER SEVENTEEN

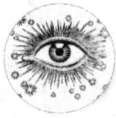

Chapel was discharged later that evening. Besides a bruise down her right arm and a little stiffness from her stitches, she was fine.

Valerie and the twins stayed the night at Taylor Manor. Despite the ache in her arm, Chapel played with the girls all evening. When the car came around the next morning to pick them up for the airport, Chapel cried.

"You can come with us?" Valerie said. But Chapel heard the doubt in her tone. Valerie knew Chapel wouldn't leave Zay, and couldn't leave Timmy and Erica.

Instead of answering, she chased the twins down until she could press kisses into their hair. She tried to memorize their scent, the way their baby fat curved up on their cheeks when they grinned at her.

Someone was trying to kill her. And she would not draw danger to the twins by going to D.C.

Chapel walked over to Jackson's and knocked on the door. Barnabus answered.

"Is anyone home?" she asked.

His gloved fingers came together in front of him. "What am I?" he asked. "Chopped liver?"

Chapel laughed. "Barnabus, was that a joke?"

"Perhaps." He wore a tiny smile. "No one is here, at present. Shall I write down a message?"

Chapel scuffed the bottom of her shoe against the door jam in frustration. "Nah. Thanks, though, Barnabus."

Chapel went back home and tried Zay's cell again. He answered breathlessly on the third ring. "Hey. You okay?"

Chapel's hand gripped the phone. "I'm fine. How are you? Where are you?"

"I can't talk long," he said. "I'm tracking a lead on Carter."

"What happened? How did Hunter break out of a Genex prison?" Chapel had never seen one, but she'd read about them. They were as impenetrable as anything she'd ever heard of.

"He didn't break out," Zay said. "He walked out."

"What? How?"

"It appears a guard helped him escape." Zay coughed. "Evidence indicates they had been . . . together."

Chapel wasn't surprised by that fact. Hunter had a certain charm that made him the most perilous type of villain. The one who you found yourself commiserating with, even though you know they're wrong.

"When can I see you?" she asked. "I want to see you."

"Babe." His breath pushed into the phone. "Don't use that tone right now."

"What tone?"

"The come-make-out-with-me tone."

"I wasn't—"

"Hey, I've got to go," he said in a rush. Chapel heard muffled voices in the background. "Gabe's coming to take you to church."

"Well. Okay." She felt so out of control. "Be careful."

"I will." She thought he had hung up until he added, "And, Chapel?"

"Yeah?"

"Don't use that tone with Gabe, either."

* * * *

174

Chapel managed to teach her class without anyone attempting to murder her.

During church, she sat between Erica and Timmy. Gabe lingered in the back, but she wasn't sure where.

About halfway through the service, something caught Chapel's eye. Helen Horrowitz sat in her usual position, the first seat on the second row. But her posture was off. It was slouched, and she wasn't craning her neck to make sure everybody was awake and paying attention.

She's going to have a seizure. The thought burst into Chapel's mind. *Those navy pumps she's wearing are going to slip on the hardwood, taking her to the floor with a heavy-sounding fall.* She could see it, too. As if it were happening.

Chapel wanted to find Gabe. She wondered if she were about to use Tempus. She felt hot and fuzzy and strange. But she couldn't take her eyes off Helen. She couldn't get the image out of her mind of Helen's body slumping to the floor with a solid *THUD.*

The service ended and everyone started standing, including Helen, who appeared to be just fine. Chapel promised herself no more pain meds. None. She was cut off.

"Where should we eat?" Erica asked. "I'm thinking somewhere greasy and disgusting. Thoughts?"

Chapel opened her mouth to agree, when there was a flurry of activity at the front of the church. People were rushing toward the altar, and the pianist stopped playing with a sharp-sounding chord.

Timmy used her shoulder to push up and stand on the pew.

"What is it?" she asked. But she already knew.

"It's Helen," he said, straining to see on his toes. "It looks like she's had a seizure or something."

CHAPTER EIGHTEEN

The next night Chapel was sleeping in Zay's room, pressing her cheek into his pillow and smelling him there. In the constantly shifting chaos of her life, she wanted something to hold onto—someone, actually. *Him.*

She had nightmares all night. Of glass shattering and Erica's blood and Helen falling and a burning sensation at the center of her chest.

When she woke up, she heard voices downstairs.

Zay's. She threw a sweatshirt on over her pajamas and ran downstairs.

The entire team had just come through the front door. They looked tired and walked with burdened feet.

Chapel went straight to Zay, wrapping her arms around his waist. His response was foreign. He patted her back two times stiffly, then stepped out of her grasp.

"I'm going to shower," he said. Then he walked upstairs without another word.

"What's wrong with him?" Chapel asked, turning to find Rush unlacing his boots.

Rush shook his head. "No idea. We all just got here at the same time. But Chon and I weren't with him. He was with Marielle."

Marielle's body didn't hold the same exhaustion as everyone else's. She stood in the foyer with her thin arms crossed over her chest. Her gaze devoured Chapel.

It was almost laughable, how different the two of them were. Where Marielle was tall and lean, Chapel was petite and curvy. Where Marielle was dark and porcelain, Chapel was fair and pink-cheeked.

"What happened?" Chapel asked.

Marielle smiled. A true smile. It warmed her perpetually chilly eyes. "We'll debrief when Jackson gets home. He's on his way."

* * * *

When they assembled in the basement conference room, Jackson motioned toward Zay. "I've allowed Isaiah to treat this specific situation as an unofficial Field Team op. As its leader, he will provide you with a debrief."

Zay stood with the tablet in his hand. "Here's Carter as of Friday at oh three hundred hours."

The image was the grainy black and green of a night vision shot. Hunter wore ill-fitting clothes, and his sandy hair had been shaved. Other than that, he appeared exactly the same. Handsome. Controlled.

"The guard who aided in his escape took her own life an hour later, leaving no one to question about Carter's plan." Zay turned around. "After Chapel was abducted last fall, I looked into all of Carter's known associates in order to evaluate potential threats."

"You did?" Chapel asked, interrupting him. Everyone looked at her. Including Zay, for the first time since he'd walked inside the house.

When had Zay had time to do that? He was working constantly and spent the rest of his time training or with her. When did he sleep?

I made time, his expression said. *To keep you safe.* Then he looked away.

"That's when I learned about Emily Banks." The image on the screen changed to a young girl. "Emily was a love interest of Carter's when he was in college. She lives a few hours from the facility he escaped from, so she was a logical place to start."

The image changed again to a broken blue phone.

"Rush and Chon found this prepaid cell in her garbage can Saturday morning. She had crushed it and removed its SIM card, but we were able to get it into a lab for analysis."

Jackson lifted a finger. "A lab?"

Zay nodded. "The Invisibles also have a team searching for Carter. I agreed to trade intelligence with them in exchange for two things. One of them was for someone to extract information from the phone for us."

"And the second?" Jackson asked.

Zay paused. "For information on my mother's whereabouts."

Chapel felt the shock register on her face. It mirrored Jackson's across the table. She'd never heard Zay mention his mother.

The silence in the room hummed for several moments. Then Zay continued. "There was data on the cellphone that led us to this man." An image of someone she didn't recognize came on the screen. "This is Frank Agnello," Zay said. "Agnello is non-Genex, but has ties to thug activity in the city, including ties to Lucky Lindtz. They did time together twice."

The image changed again. This time, the man it showed looked familiar.

"Agnello has recently been spotted around the city with someone new. He has just recently defected from Thanatos to the Rogues. His name is Night."

Chapel felt a sharp sickness. She knew what was about to happen. She looked across the table to Marielle, whose expression was as placid as a pond on a windless day.

"Like many Genexes," Zay continued, "Night is a frequenter of the downtown restaurant called The O. Marielle and I went last night to pay him a visit."

Chapel bit the insides of her cheeks. *That's why Marielle looks like she just won a gold medal.*

"Though we did not find Night on the premises, we were given access to the security footage from the last evening he was there."

Another image came up on the screen. It was a full color shot of Night sitting at a table with the man named Agnello.

But she wasn't looking at Night and the man. She was looking beyond them, at another couple on the edge of the image.

The photo showed Gabe leaning across the table toward her, staring at her intently. She remembered the moment— remembered when Gabe had told her to be ready to use Tempus. She hadn't realized how close his face had been to hers.

Zay motioned to the man Night was meeting with. "This is just two weeks ago. Night is meeting with Agnello."

Zay's words registered, but all Chapel could think about was the fact that he knew she had gone to The O with Gabe. And that she hadn't told him about it.

The image changed again. It showed a decrepit-looking building surrounded by a chain-link fence. Graffiti littered every surface.

"Agnello owns a chop shop in College Park. They're known for outfitting vehicles for jobs." Zay turned off the screen and faced the room. "In some cases, for hits."

"Well, there you go," Rush said, uncrossing his arms to motion to the screen. "Carter uses his sissy-boy appeal to get his ex to make the calls for him. Lucky can't get the job done, so he suggests Agnello. Agnello teams up with his new friend Night, who has sources inside Thanatos. Somebody knows Zay's patterns. They know the make and model of his Shelby." He smacked his hands together, making Chapel flinch. "And Peaches is done for."

Jackson tapped his fingers across his chin. "I am inclined to agree with Rush. It all lines up."

Everyone murmured their assent. But something about the situation didn't sit well with Chapel.

She tapped her knuckles on the table. "I actually disagree." Everyone looked at her. "The two attacks are different in their intent. One was meant as a warning, and one was meant to hurt me. I think there's two sources of threat."

Marielle rolled her eyes. "The first guy Lucky sent just *said* it was supposed to be a warning. Do you think he was going to admit to trying to kill you? With Zay there about to snap his spine?"

Chapel shook her head. "I believed him."

Marielle snorted. "You *would*."

Zay cleared his throat. "Ryan is right." His use of her last name felt like a chastisement. "I don't think Carter wants her dead. I think he's our guy for the Lucky job, but not for the accident."

"So, what's our move?" Justin asked, joining the conversation for the first time.

"The Invisibles have Emily Banks in custody. They're in pursuit of Night and Agnello as we speak. We believe they're together and still in the area. I'm going to join them after I sleep a few hours. I suggest the rest of you get some sleep, too."

"What about Lucky?" Chapel asked. "Who will look for him?"

Zay met Marielle's eyes briefly. "He's dead. They found his body in downtown Atlanta last night."

"What happened?"

"Burned to death." He turned off the screen. "With handprints all over his body."

* * * *

180

Everyone went upstairs except for she and Zay. He stood in front of the screen with his arms crossed. The flicker of the light overhead pulsed over his olive skin, making his body look like veined marble.

Tension radiated from his every pore. He stared at her, his cold gaze dissecting her right down the middle.

Panic. Chapel felt it like a knife against her throat.

The creak of her chair rolling back from the table sounded like a screaming whine in the reverberating silence.

"Well," he said, "at least now I know how you recognized Kacie."

"Zay," she said. "It's not—"

"Are you cheating on me?" he snapped. His fingers gripped his elbows. "And don't think about lying to me. You're a terrible liar."

"No." Chapel took two steps toward him. He mirrored her, taking two steps back. "It was just dinner. He took me to see some fight that he foresaw happening. He wanted me to see how unstable things are with Genexes . . . " She trailed off.

It sounded like a stupid excuse, even to her own ears.

"How many dates with him?"

"It wasn't a date."

Zay dropped his arms and walked right up in front of her. He ticked off the stabbing sentences on his fingers. "Did he pick you up at your house? Did he buy you dinner? Did you talk about each other's lives? Tell me it was strictly work, Chapel. Tell me."

She couldn't.

Zay leaned so his nose was almost touching hers. "Now that Luxe has some status, did you like being the girl on his arm?"

Chapel felt her own anger simmering, like a pot of water ready to boil. "I was angry at you for not answering your phone," she said. "I was upset about Timmy. He had just recognized Gabe, and I freaked out. It was . . . impulsive."

"And stupid, and dangerous, and it—" He pushed his jaw forward. "There is no way to know who saw you there, who connected the dots between Gabe and Bellum's secret new recruit."

"Zay." She reached for his arm, but he pulled it away.

"It's not that you *went*, Chapel. Though I can't *stand* the thought of him—" He blew out a breath. "You didn't tell me. It just shows how messed up things are between us. Much more so than I thought."

Chapel didn't know what to say. She could point out that he'd dined countless times with Marielle. Or that *he* was the one who asked Gabe to take extra shifts watching over her. She could say that he worked *all the time,* and what did he expect her to do—stay at home every weekend?

But his somber expression—disappointed, sad—it quieted the roar of bitter reasoning inside of her.

"I should have told you," she said. "There's no excuse."

He flinched as if surprised. He probably was. Chapel had an argument for everything. Her mother had taught her that—how to be defensive or to be aloof in the face of accusations.

But her mother didn't teach her her how to look a man in the eye and see so much love there that it made her forget all the rules, and all the looks that had come before.

"I am sorry, Zay." He let her put her hand on his cheek. "I don't want Gabe. I want you."

She was terrible at expressing her emotions. She knew the words missed the mark of how she felt, of what he needed to hear right then, but it was the best she could do.

He closed his eyes briefly, then opened them again. He pulled her hand away and used it to spin her around. "Let's see your stitches."

She shrugged out of her sweatshirt and pulled aside her tank top. He ran a light finger over her skin. "I will find them," he said quietly. "And I will crush them."

She turned to face him. She wanted to ask him to spare Hunter, but she also knew there was no chance he would do that.

"Will we make it through this?" she asked. "Us?"

His fierce expression faded, and his eyes found the floor.

"There's a reason there are few married Genexes, Chapel. It's not an easy way of life."

"So, what does that mean?"

He tilted his eyes up at her. "It means we have to stop doing this." Anger seeped back into his tone. "Not trusting each other. Not communicating."

"Isaiah?" Barnabus's voice traveled down to them. "Erin Stephens is here to see you."

"Who is that?" Chapel asked.

"My liaison to the Invisibles. I haven't spoken with her since Lucky's body was found. I need to talk to her. Alone," he added.

Chapel nodded. "Then go."

"Do you still have Luxe's gun?"

"Yes."

"Good." He nodded, not making eye contact. "Don't hesitate if you need to use it."

Then he left her there in Jackson's cold basement without so much as a hug goodbye.

CHAPTER NINETEEN

At work on Friday, Chapel was in the kitchen checking her phone. The week had crept by, and Chapel had held her breath every day for word on the search for Carter, Agnello, and Night. For word from Zay.

But there was none.

Something wet popped her from behind. Chapel squealed and turned around to find Erica holding a dripping rag.

"Ouch." Chapel rubbed her backside. "That hurt."

Erica raised both eyebrows at her. "Duh."

"What did I do to deserve that?"

Erica slid up on the counter, squinting at her. "You've just seemed off lately." She snatched a French fry from the vat beneath the warmer. "Doesn't she, Gabe?"

Though Erica had stopped throwing herself at him, she managed to work Gabe in to just about every conversation they had at Back Porch.

"I think you need to eat more," Erica continued. "All this running and weird boy-fighting stuff Zay has you doing is making you too skinny."

"It's not boy-fighting, it's—okay, well. Maybe it's a little bit boy-fighting. But I am not too skinny." To highlight her point, Chapel shoved a handful of fries in her mouth. She chewed half of them, then opened up to show Erica. "See?"

Gabe looked up from the grill. "I think she's just nervous," he said. "She got a letter from UGA that she has yet to open."

Chapel shot a look at him across the kitchen.

Erica placed both hands on her hips. "Excuse *me?*" she said. "How would *you* know something like that and I don't?"

"Yeah, Gabe," Chapel called to him. "How *do* you know that?"

Gabe finished pushing residual grease over the lip of the cook top and walked over. "Because the letter's been in the front seat of your car since Tuesday. I've seen it every day on my way in."

Chapel fidgeted. "Oh." He was right.

Gabe's cellphone rang in his pocket. He made eye contact with Chapel over Erica's head. "I need to take this. I'll be right back." He pushed through the back door and stepped outside.

Erica swung back around to face Chapel. "He's got it so bad for you."

Chapel wrinkled her nose. "Stop it."

Erica shrugged. "Zay works so much, I doubt he'd notice if you got a little TLC on the side."

Chapel sighed. "I don't even know if Zay and I are together, Jersey."

Erica tapped the side of Chapel's head. "Duuuuuh, Steel. That's what I'm saying. Get while the getting's good."

Chapel pushed Erica's arm playfully. "Yeah. I'm going to take advice from someone who won't even tell the guy she loves that she loves him."

Erica picked up a crispy fry and threw it at her. "Hey. Timmy and I are just now talking like people who *don't* want to murder each other. Give it time."

"Then what's your plan?" Chapel asked. "You going to pretend to choke on something so he'll do CPR on you and you can shove your tongue in his mouth?"

"Hey." Erica dipped a fry in salad dressing before launching it at her. "I only did that once."

Chapel ducked and the fry slid down the wall behind her. "You did it twice," Chapel reminded her. "Once to that poor lifeguard when we were eleven. And once to—"

"Marshall Preston's dad," they said together.

"The summer I turned sixteen," Erica said, all dreamily. "He was so hot. Not even dad-hot. But like, hot-hot."

Chapel had to agree. "If you hadn't pulled that move first, I might have stolen it from you."

"Whatever, Steel. You'd feel so guilty that you'd, like, have to go pray eleven times and confess your sins to a priest even though you're not Catholic. I can just see you now, soaking your tongue in bleach as punishment."

Chapel's mouth fell open. "You don't think I can be bad?"

Erica gave her a look that said, *Absolutely not, you idiot.*

Chapel didn't know whether to feel guilty or glad that her best friend had no idea she'd been lying to her. Not just for the last six months, but for their *entire lives.*

"Tell you what." Chapel looked at the Ranch dressing. "How about I start off by proving you wrong?"

She snatched the ladle out of the dressing and flung it at Erica. Creamy white sauce sprayed across her face, chest, and hair.

Erica squealed. "You did *not* just get that in my hair."

Chapel nodded. "I kind of did. You look like an orange soda now with whipped cream on top."

Erica responded by snatching the tea pitcher and jerking its contents toward Chapel's face. Chapel gasped at its coldness, already reaching for the ketchup bottle on the counter. At the same time, Erica reached for the mustard.

They were running around the kitchen in an all-out food war when Gabe came inside. Chapel accidently ran smack into his chest.

She pulled away and grimaced. "Sorry." She pointed to his now-stained shirt and apron. "I got some mustard on you." She squinted. "And maybe some tea and ketchup, too."

She expected Gabe to make a crack about her age or silliness, but he didn't. He just stared at her somberly.

"Who was on the phone?" she asked.

But then Erica jumped out from around the corner and shot a line of mustard right inside her mouth.

Gabe did crack a small smile that time.

"It can wait," he said quietly. "Until after work."

* * * *

"Okay," she said. "Spill."

Gabe hadn't even shut the door to his car yet when Chapel made the demand.

"It was Chary," he said. "There's been news."

"What?"

"Night and Agnello were apprehended this morning trying to cross into Mexico."

"By who?"

"By the team the Invisibles put together." Gabe looked over at her. "Halstead is not formally on a Field Team. Or, he isn't yet. He was nearby, but not in on the actual arrest."

Chapel sucked in a breath through her teeth. "I bet he *loved* that."

Gabe nodded. "Yes, but it was his contacts and footwork that put together the clues that helped the Invisibles. Chary spoke with Jackson this morning. He's seriously considering applying for the entire team to be raised to Field status."

"Wow," Chapel said "Good for them."

She wondered if Zay knew. And when he would call her to tell the news about the arrest. Or *if* he would.

Gabe's news unraveled one of the tightly rolled coils in her chest. "We can make them talk and find out who wants me dead," she said. "That's good, right?"

"Very good."

Chapel turned in her seat to look at him. "What's up? Why don't you seem as happy about this as me?"

Gabe shifted. "Chary didn't call Jackson about Halstead."

"Okay . . ."

"She called him about you."

Chapel didn't like the sound of that. "What's going on?"

"We're eight weeks away from your Bellum examination. Bellum thinks it's time to bring you in to one of our camps for a practice test."

"A Bellum camp?"

"Yes. It's where most Bellum train. We need to ease you into our community. And you need to familiarize yourself with the facility before your actual exam."

Chapel swallowed as anxiety ran icy fingertips across her sternum.

"Don't worry," Gabe said. "I've arranged to escort you."

"I really may have to go through with it," she whispered. She'd had so much else to worry about that she'd forgotten to worry about *this*. "Not the exam. The . . . Bellum. All of it."

Gabe moved his arm from behind her headrest and squeezed her shoulder. "I'm not sure. I was counting on my new position giving me a bit more clout."

"What exactly *is* your new position?" She'd meant to ask that sooner.

A light red flush washed up the back of Gabe's neck. He tugged at the collar of his shirt. "The official title is Master of Recruits."

A laugh pushed through her mouth before she could suck it back in. "*Master* of recruits? Wow."

Gabe didn't answer. He checked the rearview mirror several times. Chapel thought it was so he wouldn't have to look at her.

She put a hand on his arm. "I'm sorry, Gabe. It's a big deal."

She'd read about the different levels of Genex leadership in one of the books Jackson had given her. And she was being honest—it *was* a big promotion. It put Gabe over a number of recruiting groups and gave him a chair in meetings that were presided over by a liaison to the Invisibles.

He was on the same level as Jackson now.

"I didn't mean to laugh. It's just . . . the word *master*, you know?"

He glanced over at her finally, a small smile on his face. "I know." He sighed. "But it's done me little good. It seems the more I hint that you aren't Bellum material, the more they cling to the idea that you can somehow save us from the mess we're in."

"Mess?" Chapel asked.

Gabe pulled around the square. He paused at a stop sign and looked at her.

"Things have been very contentious in the Genex arena the last few months. Chapel, I'm afraid you're entering our fold during a season of instability."

Gabe's words settled in her stomach like she'd eaten something rotten. She shook her head. "Justin. Um, Justin Chon—the new guy on Zay's team. He mentioned unrest?"

Gabe nodded. "You saw the fight at The O. And this thing with Agnello and Night? I'm sure it's related to the tensions between Bellum and Thanatos, too. And then there's the riots at the Capital."

"The Capital?"

"The Invisibles have a post in D.C.," Gabe said. "Though no one knows where. I suppose it's so they can easily congregate with the nation's leadership over assignments and strategy."

Chapel was genuinely shocked. Gabe was talking to her. Like an equal. She was so used to having information withheld from her. It was like a sip of water to a thirsty man.

"What's happening there?" she asked.

Gabe stared at her a moment before answering. "There's a group of people—people with exceptions—they're calling them Unifists. It's Rogues, mostly. But many former Bellum and Thanatos as well. They've been looking for the Invisibles there."

"Looking for them how?"

"They've posted billboards, taken out entire pages of newspapers and magazines. Last week they drew all over the Washington Monument with sidewalk chalk."

There was a hint of a smile on Gabe's lips, so Chapel let hers come forward. "That sounds kind of funny and crazy. What do they want?"

"They want the Invisibles to come forward. To listen to their ideas."

"What are their ideas?"

Gabe's green eyes held hers. "They want to unite Genexes under one order."

His words flicked a shiver down her back. "Just like Hunter Carter."

"No." Gabe shook his head. "Hunter wanted to *control* all Genexes. The Unifists want to control themselves. They want more options. Take yourself, for example," he said, motioning to her. "Let's say you don't want to pledge Bellum. You want to pledge Thanatos, but you can't. Or let's say you wanted to be a teacher, but moonlight for Genexes during the summer—"

That made her laugh.

"No, but seriously," Gabe said. "Think of it. Your options—our options—they're very limited. It worked when there were only a hundred or so of us, but now there are many more. Our leadership has no face," he said simply. "It has no accountability."

190

Chapel's chin tilted to the side. There was a question on the edge of her lips, but it fell away when Gabe signaled onto the interstate. "Where are we going?" she asked.

He didn't look at her when he answered. "An airport."

"A *huh?*"

"Your practice test for Bellum." Gabe glanced at her. "It's tomorrow."

She uncrossed her legs, slamming her feet onto the floorboard. *"What?"*

"The decision was made last night by the President of Bellum, himself."

"Gabe, my mom will flip out if Sheriff Carter tells her my car isn't home."

"Your mother knows. Chary contacted her this morning. You're eighteen, however. And we don't need her consent."

Chapel pulled her bottom lip through her teeth. "What about Zay?"

There was a pause. "Yes, I assume he knows. Chary talked to Jackson first thing this morning."

And Zay hadn't thought to warn her? Anger jockeyed with hurt for control of her emotions.

"What kind of test are we talking about?" she asked.

"Nothing that Jackson hasn't already had you do. You'll do well. There's no need to worry."

Chapel was quiet the rest of the ride. She *was* worried about it. Worried about leaving Timmy and Erica. Worried about Zay.

If Zay had known about this, why hadn't he called and warned her? And why did his silence bother her more than the idea that she was about to walk into the enemy's camp? The enemy who had manipulated her into joining them by dangling Timmy's life in front of her?

Instead of driving them to the Atlanta airport, Gabe got off the highway much sooner. He turned down a dirt road that looked like it had seen better days. They followed it around a bend and down a hill that led into a densely wooded area.

After several miles, the asphalt returned. The longer they drove, the nicer the landscape became. The two-lane road became a four-lane road. The ditches became bush-lined sidewalks.

Finally, they came to a massive iron gate. A turret-like building sat in the middle. Chapel studied it more closely. It wasn't shaped like a turret. It was shaped like a *bell*— Bellum's symbol.

"I'm guessing I have no say in whether or not this happens, right?" she asked.

Gabe used his thumbs to crack each of his knuckles, one by one. "No."

A man with a gun the size of a baby elephant walked up to Gabe's window. Despite the fact that he had a barrel leveled at their faces, he was smiling.

"Mr. Luxe," the guard said, shifting his weapon so he could shake Gabe's hand through the window. "Good to see you again."

"You as well, Harold. I have the newest transport, here."

"Hi," Chapel said.

Harold gave her a bland smile that said Gabe did this kind of thing every day, and she was just another one in a long line of females he transported via aircraft to unknown locations.

Harold had Gabe press a thumb to a small device before allowing them through the gate.

There was a bright white, long and low building to the left. It had branches jutting out at intervals. *Terminals.* A huge glass bell sat on its roof, catching the sun's rays and throwing them back at her. It hurt her eyes to look at it.

Across from the low building was a tall tower, and between the two stretched a pristine runway.

Gabe pulled them up to a set of double doors. They opened as he parked, revealing an empty interior whose ivory walls and floor literally sparkled.

"Okay." She unbuckled her seatbelt and looked at him. "You guys have your own *airport?*"

Gabe got out of the car and opened her door for her. "Yes."

She gave him a look that said, *You're not getting off that easily.*

"Come on," he said, motioning to the door. "Our plane is waiting. We'll talk there."

"What about our luggage?" she asked as they walked inside. She was wearing jeans and a purple blouse with sweet tea and mustard on it.

Gabe's eyes darted around her. "I already have things where we're going. We can pick up something for you when we get there. Here, this way."

Chapel moaned. There was no getting out of this. They walked down the achromatic corridor in silence. After a few turns, Gabe pushed open a door that led them into a small foyer-like area. The outer wall was glass, and Chapel saw steps leading down from it to a small plane.

Gabe pressed against the wall and it slid open. "I'm going to talk to Ricky, our pilot, and see what the ETD is." Then he left.

Chapel became sharply aware of the fact that she was about to get on a plane with Gabe and fly to a Genex facility to be tested by strangers who would likely determine the fate of the rest of her life.

She pushed against the door they'd just come through, but it was locked. Chapel checked to make sure Gabe was still busy talking to Ricky before she used her phone to call her mom.

"Hello?" Valerie answered on the first ring as if she knew Chapel would call.

"Mom, did Chary talk to you about me going somewhere this weekend?"

"Yes, Rebecca, I got your email," she said, slightly louder than normal. "Sorry I haven't gotten back to you yet on those samples. Todd and I are in Virginia meeting with contractors. How is the project coming along?"

Rebecca? Rebecca . . . Chapel thought that sounded familiar. She thought it might be the name of the designer Todd had hired to decorate their new apartment.

Chapel lowered her voice. "Mom, Gabe is taking me to a Bellum camp. Did you know that?"

"Yes, that's fine. Personally, I preferred to wait on another shipment, but I understand if they have to be ordered today."

She knew.

"You haven't heard from Dad, right?"

"Unfortunately, that pattern just won't work for us. It's too busy."

Chapel wanted to say a really, really vulgar curse word.

"Mom, is there any way Luke can look in on Timmy while I'm gone? I'm worried . . . " Chapel didn't finish. What if the room were bugged? Or her phone?

"Certainly. Oh, and Rebecca?"

"Yes?"

There was a pause. "Take care of yourself."

Chapel's free hand curled into a fist. Nothing she wanted to say would fit through the tightness in her throat, so she mumbled a goodbye and hung up.

She texted Erica and Timmy quickly, telling them she was going to D.C. to see the twins. She realized, with a squeeze of her heart, how much she wished that were true.

Then, she didn't give her fingers time to think before she dialed Zay's number. If he had known about this and didn't tell her because of their fight, she was going to explain in graphic detail just how low that made him.

But the voice that answered wasn't his. "Yes?" Marielle's greeting was soaked in a knowing tone.

"Marielle, I need to speak with Zay. It's an emergency."

"Aren't the two of you broken up?" Marielle asked.

Gabe appeared on the bottom step. He looked right at the phone in her hand and picked up his pace.

"I don't have time to describe all the ways I loathe you," she said quickly. "But when I see you again, I will make you sorry."

Gabe opened the door and waved her down. Outside, the plane's engine was already working its way into a frenzy.

He spoke right into her ear. "Don't say anything about Thanatos on this flight. It's not safe."

She nodded.

"Also, I have to take your phone and shut it down. You're not allowed to communicate with anyone while on Bellum property."

Irritated, Chapel reached for the edges of her blouse and pulled it over her head. She had on a dark tank top underneath. It wasn't very cute, but at least it didn't smell like lunch.

Two perfectly round pink patches had shown up on Gabe's cheeks. She rolled up the shirt and threw it at him.

Her hair whipped across her face and she shoved it back. "Don't look at me that way."

He batted the shirt to the side. "What way?"

"You know what way. I'm mad at you right now."

He looked like he wanted to say something, but he didn't. They got on the plane and she stared out the window.

Chapel had always been the kind of girl who could compartmentalize almost as well as a boy. But right now, everything in her mind felt scattered. Felt mixed up, disorganized, chaotic.

She tried not to think about Zay and Marielle. Marielle could easily have let that call go to voicemail. She had only answered to piss her off.

It had worked.

After about an hour of flying, the pilot turned the seatbelt light back on. After trying unsuccessfully to make small talk with her on the plane, Gabe had spent most of the journey on his laptop. He put it away then and turned to her.

"We're in Florida," he said. "Sorry I couldn't tell you more sooner. I wanted your location to be as secure as possible."

"Got it."

"Do you have any questions?"

She gave him a hard look. "I'd say I have a few."

He gave her a look that said *Not here*, and she rolled her eyes.

"*Duh*," she mouthed.

His lips twitched. He had wanted to smile.

"How do all of you have so much money?" she asked. "Airports, bases all over the world, nice cars?"

Gabe settled back in his seat and crossed his hands over his stomach. "You might be surprised to learn all the things Genexes have done for our country, and others. Many good things." He glanced out the window. "Some not as good." He looked back at her. "We are paid well. Very, very well."

That explained the money her father had left her. He must have saved every dime he'd made and given it to her.

What is he living off of now? she wondered.

The thought made her shiver.

"You okay?" Gabe asked.

She shot him a look. She had no idea where they were going, what she was going to do, or whom she was going to do it with.

And Marielle had answered Zay's phone.

"Yeah," she said. "Just peachy."

* * * *

A car was waiting for them at the airport. It drove them down the coast to a small town with white beaches and old architecture.

"Rosemary Beach." Chapel read the name off a welcome sign on their way in. "Sounds pleasant."

Gabe actually looked a little excited. Like the old Gabe. "It is."

The driver dropped them off in front of a two-story carriage house on a secluded road that faced the beach. When Chapel inhaled, she tasted ocean and sand and sun.

When she opened her eyes again, Gabe had already scaled the porch steps.

"Come inside." He pushed open the two wooden doors and Chapel walked into paradise. The furniture was sparse, but sumptuous. The colors were earthy, but rich. It smelled like vanilla and salt.

There were knickknacks on shelves, magnets on the fridge, and framed photos on side tables. One, just off the entryway, caught Chapel's eye. In it was Gabe and a woman. A beautiful woman. With kinky dark hair and a breathtaking smile.

"What do you think?" Gabe asked. And she realized he was staring at her with his hands clasped in front of him. He shifted his weight from one foot to the other.

Was he *nervous*?

Then it hit her. This was his *home*. "You . . . live here?"

He nodded. "Chary and I used to split our time between New York and Rosemary. There's a Bellum training facility close by."

Chapel dropped onto a stool at the island. Gabe stood across from her, his arms propped wide on the white quartz counter.

"Is it safe?" Chapel mouthed.

"Yes. I have bug detectors that would scramble anything someone might plant here. Besides, Bellum thinks you're coming tomorrow. They won't be looking for you any earlier."

"Then why did you bring me today? Could you get in trouble?"

His shoulders lifted. "By whom? I'm the boss."

That only halfway answered her question, but she didn't press. "So, you never worked at UGA?"

He shook his head. "We commandeered that office about thirty minutes before you got there."

She had thought it seemed strange—no photos on the walls.

"And . . . Midnight?"

He cleared his throat over a laugh that made her cheeks tingle. "The cat actually caught me off guard, too. Only my reaction was a little less extreme than yours."

"I'm such an idiot," she said, shaking her head slowly. "About the cat, the office, the study." She sighed. "Everything."

Gabe looked down at his hands. His fingers pressed into the counter, white tipped with tension. "You're not an idiot," he said finally. "It's ridiculous, all the lies we have to tell these days." He looked at her, unblinking. "It makes the nights long."

Chapel knew a thing or two about long nights. They shared a knowing look before Gabe clasped his hands together.

"We should go."

Chapel glanced around. "But we just got here."

"Yes, and you have nothing to wear and I'm quite famished."

She held up two hands. "Wait. Are you saying we're about to eat and shop?"

He smiled. "That's what I'm saying."

Chapel bounced off the stool and grabbed him by the shoulders. "Gabriel Luxe," she breathed, "I could kiss you right now."

It was one of those comments she said that sped by her filter without pausing for approval. And immediately, a pop of pink bloomed on each of Gabe's tan cheeks. He didn't move, though, and he didn't say a word. His eyes fell to her mouth.

Whoa.

Chapel felt something move between them then. Like a shadow shifting, or a light going from dim to bright. She dropped her arms and stepped back.

He was teasing her, right? He was kidding. He brought up her youth and immaturity in basically every conversation they had. She wasn't naive enough to think Gabe never looked at her—she looked at him, too.

But not like *that*. Like he was looking at her right now.

She covered up her confusion and embarrassment by laughing. "I know what you're thinking." She put on his Australian accent. "How *quite* eighteen you are, Chapel. It's just gear and sustenance."

He brushed his thumb down the center of his lips. "That's not what I'm thinking."

Now, she was the one blushing. It was ridiculous. Chapel pretended to adjust her boots. "Well, I'm thinking food first."

"That's perfect," he said. "The garage is this way."

He had a small black SUV in there, something much more Gabe than the Porsche back in Georgia. They chatted about their favorite beaches while they drove.

They ate dinner in Pier Park. There were restaurants, stores, and a small amusement park in the back corner.

Chapel was grateful that their time together wasn't ruined by her stupid comment. They finished eating and walked along the sidewalk, looking for a place for her to shop.

They talked a lot about music, something she was only beginning to understand Gabe's passion for. When he told her he actually wrote most of the songs his band used to perform, she was intrigued.

"So, what do you like better?" she asked. "Writing music or playing it?"

He tucked his hands into his pockets. "I don't like writing at all, actually."

"But you do it anyway?"

His chest rose with a deep breath. "It's quite tragic," he said on the exhale, "to be a writer. You find yourself in your head too often, and spend most of your time wishing you could extricate a feeling or a memory onto paper, and mostly failing at it miserably."

"I want to hear you play," she said.

His eyes studied his shoes. "It's been a long time since I've picked up the guitar."

"How long?"

His lips pushed together. "Two years."

Chapel stopped walking *"Two years?"*

He didn't answer and pointed into a store that sold athletic apparel. "We need to pick you up something you can move in tomorrow."

Chapel chose dry fit leggings, a sports tank, a pullover, and a pair of shoes. All in black. It made her think of Zay, and a lightning strike of hurt flashed inside her chest.

She allowed herself to be sad and angry until she counted to ten, then she opened her eyes and kept shopping.

They made a few more stops for necessities and something to fly home in, then they went back to Gabe's.

He showed her to the bedroom on the third floor. It took up the entire upstairs, and had nothing but a huge bed in the middle. It didn't take her long to realize that it was Gabe's personal bedroom.

He lingered by the door. "Are you nervous about tomorrow?"

"I haven't allowed myself to believe it's really happening," she said. "I have no context for any of this. "

He nodded. "Follow our plan closely, and all will be well."

At dinner they had come up with the idea that she would perform at a very basic level to downplay her skills. The last thing she wanted was to make Bellum want her *more*.

"The entrance exam is a simple endurance test," Gabe reminded her. "Then you'll demonstrate your Tempus for a small group of people, and I'll be among them."

"Good." She was glad he would be there. "Thanks for making this as painless as possible."

"It's not over yet." He gave her a close-lipped smile, patted the doorframe twice. "Sleep well."

She took a long shower and dried off. She'd gotten mousse to run through her hair so it would be curly the next day. It was how she always wore it at the beach, and much easier than fighting the humidity.

Standing in her towel, she sorted through the shopping bags.

"Where is it?" she mumbled, looking for the one with the pajamas she'd picked up. But she couldn't find it anywhere. *Probably still in the car*, she thought to herself.

Instead of traipsing around Gabe's house in a towel, she swung open the closet door on the other side of the room. She skipped all the clothes on hangers and went for the dresser. In the bottom drawer she found a T-shirt with orange sleeves and a gray body that had Ted Nugent on the front.

She put it on. It smelled like vanilla and salt, too. She realized, then, that it was also how Gabe smelled.

Sleep didn't come fast for her, but when it did, it barreled over her, taking her into a numbing darkness that her exhausted mind craved.

CHAPTER TWENTY

Chapel had spent a lot of her life wanting to look beautiful. But as she stretched her limbs through the clothes she would test in, she wanted to shed any semblance of fragility, of softness.

In her mind, Bellum was an enemy. And though she couldn't unleash the fury of Tempus on them in full, she wanted them to make no mistake about the strength of her spirit.

Chapel wore no makeup, save for darkly lined eyes and lashes. She left her hair down and curly, wild and restless, like the look she saw in her eyes just before she walked down to meet Gabe.

"How do I look?" she asked.

His eyes moved from her gym shoes to her eyes. They lingered there. "Fearless."

Gabe talked idly while they drove the half hour to the Bellum facility. He was telling her about his entrance exam, and some funny bit about misunderstanding a cue and leaving before he was finished.

Chapel felt an automatic smile lift the corners of her mouth. But her knees shifted, her thumbs gently cracked knuckle after knuckle, and her eyes roved over the obscure landscape whipping by.

Chapel couldn't concentrate—not on his voice, not on the highway beneath them, not on what unknown task was ahead of her.

It was one of the main differences between Gabe and Zay. Zay spoke as if he had a limited number of words to use each day and he couldn't stand the inefficiency of wasting one single syllable. He could also sense when she wanted to turn inward, like now, and he let her. Sometimes she thought Zay knew her better than she knew herself.

Then she remembered that Zay was an idiot who had girls like Marielle answering his phone and tried not to be annoyed with Gabe's stream-of-consciousness monologue.

After what felt like hours, not minutes, Gabe pulled into a complex and stopped at a gate. He offered his thumb to a guard who scanned it and allowed them inside. They were then taken by ferry to a small island about half an hour off the coast.

The exterior of the facility was similar to the airport— bright white and chrome with a huge bell in a center courtyard. This bell, too, was made of glass, and the effect of the new day's sun piercing its surface was prismatic and bright.

Chapel's feet slowed as she approached it. The colors of the rainbow danced in pale beams across the pavement as she came to a stop in front of a plaque at the bell's base.

Gabe read the words over her shoulder, "Si vis pacem, para bellum."

She recognized it as Latin. "What does it mean?" she asked.

He put a hand on her shoulder and squeezed. "If you want peace," he whispered by her ear, "prepare for war."

* * * *

"Welcome, darlings," Chary said, sweeping her arms open as she greeted Chapel and Gabe in the foyer. Tiny bells dangled from her sleeves, making her jingle lightly with each fluid motion. "How was your flight?"

"Fine, thank you," Chapel answered, letting Chary brush a kiss on either of her cheeks.

A group who looked to be around Chapel's age passed by them laughing and pushing one another. A few glanced curiously in her direction. A tall brunette's eyes lingered on Gabe.

"Look at you, Gabriel," Chary said, oblivious. She ran a hand down his chocolate brown tie and matching suit jacket. "You've certainly polished up for the brass today." She winked at Chapel like they were sharing a big joke together. "He's a vision in brown, yes, Chapel?"

The no-teeth smile Gabe was giving her told Chapel that Chary was making him uncomfortable.

Chapel stepped forward and lightly pulled on Chary's shoulder. "Let's get this thing done," she said.

Chary's lips pulled together in a perfect, dark bow. "Someone's anxious, I see." She laid an arm along the back of Chapel's shoulders and ushered her to a bank of elevators. "No worries, dear. They're going to *love* you."

Chapel met Gabe's eyes over Chary's shoulder. *That's what I'm afraid of,* his said.

Me too, she thought back.

Chary used a key card to take them all the way to the top floor. As they rose, the back wall of the elevator became glass, and Chapel could see straight through to the other side of the building.

"The first five floors are dormitories and classrooms," Chary said.

Chapel saw blips of faces, backpacks, lockers, doorways, hallways. And she imagined, for a moment, that this had been her life. She would have grown up so differently, feeling like she fit in. Maybe even feeling special.

But she would have missed out, too. On Timmy. On Erica. On the times when her family felt like a family. Maybe on Zay.

Zay. What was he doing right now? Did he worry about her? Did he miss her?

"There is a large training facility in the basement," Chary said. Her jovial tone jarred Chapel back to the present. "That's where the practice exams are typically held, but *you* are the exception."

Gabe's hands jumped from his pockets. "Where are they testing her?"

Chary waved her fingers in the air. "Oh, no need to get dramatic, Gabriel. Daniel and I met this morning, and we decided to use the Chamber."

The Chamber? That sounded ominous to Chapel. Gabe's face showed surprise, but not concern.

The elevator doors spit them out into a hallway with floors so white they gleamed lavender in places. They came to a doorway with a polished C hanging in its center.

"Here we are," Chary said, spinning around. She pressed her clasped hands to her chest, the tiny bells on her sleeves scattering a tinkling sound into the air. "Now remember, your scores will determine your ranking coming in to Bellum. The better your score, the better assignment you get. Though, this is just a practice run, you'll still want to try your very best."

Chary reached as if to smooth some of Chapel's curls, but Chapel jerked back.

Over Chary's shoulder, Gabe seemed to be trying to communicate something with his eyes.

As if she sensed it, Chary turned around. "Gabriel, we'll see you in the Anteroom later."

Gabe rubbed the back of his head and nodded. "Yes." He took two steps back as if to leave, then paused. He walked over to Chapel and touched her shoulder. "Fearless," he said. "Remember that." Then he left.

* * * *

The Chamber was just as creepy as Chapel predicted. The walls and floors were made of galvanized steel, save for one, which had a one-way mirror in its center.

A voice came over a speaker. "Hello, Miss Ryan," it said. "My name is Proctor Q, and I'll be running your practice examination today."

Chapel lifted her fingers in a small wave. "Oh, um, hi. Am I supposed to answer out loud?" She licked her dry lips. Proctor Q was silent. "Sorry, I'm not sure what the protocol is for clandestine pre-examination etiquette."

She laughed at her own joke, and the sound was garish against the cool steel of her surroundings. A bead of sweat tickled down her back. She tugged off the pullover, revealing the black sports tank underneath.

"A red timer will appear on the mirror," Proctor Q finally said. "When it reaches zero, please begin doing as many pushups as you can until you hear three short beeps."

The timer appeared and Chapel steadied herself on the floor. She watched the red number count off three, two, one.

Chapel was taken through a battery of similar challenges. And, just as she and Gabe had planned, she only performed at about seventy-five percent of her actual capacity.

Everything was going accordingly until the door flew open behind her. The sound of the handle ricocheting off the wall sounded like a small explosion inside Chapel's head. She was in the middle of running a series of sprints, and she snapped around in response.

Chary rushed in, grabbing her by the shoulders.

"I'm sorry," she said to the glass mirrors. "But there's an emergency." She dragged Chapel into the hallway, her round eyes looking panicked and desperate. "It's *Isaiah*," she hissed.

Chapel's heart squeezed behind her ribs. "What about him?"

"A security camera just caught him breaking into the basement training room. Him being here will be treated as an act of *war*, Chapel. You have to get to him before he is apprehended."

The oxygen seemed to evaporate from her lungs. "Are you serious?"

Chary nodded. "Chapel, he will go to prison for this. Or worse."

"He's such an idiot."

But even as she said the words, Chapel was already rolling her shoulders back to prepare for Tempus. He'd come for her. *For her.*

The impulsivity of it, the romance of it, the stupidity of it—it all fueled her, and before Chary could respond, Chapel shuddered and thrust her energy forward, sending the molecules around her into an almost paralytic state.

Most electrical systems did not respond during Tempus, so Chapel didn't waste time trying to get the elevators to work. Instead, she immediately shot the other direction. She had noticed a door on the way in that looked fireproof, which meant it likely led to the stairwell.

Chapel was rewarded when she swung through it. Five flights of stairs later, and Chapel bounded into the lobby. It took her a moment to orient herself to the new vantage, but once she had her bearings, she started trying doors.

She found bathrooms, break rooms, offices, and an indoor swimming pool. But no access to the basement.

She ran outside and made a circuit around the building. It must have been a mile she ran, looking for windows, for doors, for anything that might indicate a lower passage.

Nothing.

Chapel kicked at the white, smooth landscaping stones that hugged the complex and tried to think. The hot sun pressed against her, squeezing out her sweat and energy. The inside of her mouth tasted sour.

Chapel returned inside with her exertion dripping down her forehead and back. She stood motionless in the center of the atrium, and pressed against the sides of her head.

Think, think, think.

When there isn't a way, Zay's voice whispered in her memory, *make a way.*

Chapel's sneakers squeaked against the tiles as she ran back to the bank of elevators. A fire extinguisher encased in glass hung on the wall to the right. Chapel kicked at the face of the unit until it shattered.

She walked around to the elevator doors and hoisted the extinguisher over her head. It was heavier than she thought it would be, and she had to pause a moment to maintain her balance.

The mirrored doors of the elevator threw her reflection back at her. Her eyes were bright, her hair was wind-blown from running, and her eyeliner was smeared. Her cheeks were flushed, she was sweating, and her ankle was bleeding from kicking through the glass.

It struck Chapel then that she liked the way she looked. She liked the way she felt. *Doing* something. For someone. And not just anyone. But *Zay.* He'd saved her life, but more than that, he'd saved *her.*

With that thought, Chapel brought the extinguisher down with so much force that the first strike reverberated through her arms and into her chest painfully. But she braced herself again and slammed into the doors two, three, four times before there was a dent between the two sliding doors.

Chapel pushed her body into the doorframe for leverage and wedged her foot into the crevice created by the dent. Gritting her teeth, she used every ounce of leg-strength she had to force the doors apart.

She almost cried with relief when they opened just enough to allow her hips to squeeze through. The metal dug into her bones when she shimmied to peer down the shaft.

The light from the widows above filtered down. Chapel's eyes searched the dimness until she saw an iron service ladder hung against the wall opposite her.

She felt confident that she could jump and land on it—it wasn't much different from tossing her body from the high bar to the low bar in gymnastics. But she didn't know how slippery it was, or how stable.

But what other choice did she have? Zay's life could be on the line.

Chapel pictured it before she jumped—envisioned her legs lunging, her arms reaching. She even picked out the rungs she'd aim for.

Without much more thought, she rocked back on one heel, then used her other foot to push off the narrow ledge. Her stomach fell to the floor, but her body slammed into the ladder headfirst.

The impact of the pain across her face made her lose her composure briefly, and her foot slipped. Her hands clawed at the cool steel slipping through her fingers as she slid down.

I'm going to die, she thought. *Or be so injured I wish I were dead.*

By a miracle, about halfway down, Chapel was able to gain a grip along a rung with her right arm. She cried out as she caught it, a burning sensation tearing up her bicep.

That was close, she thought, pressing herself against the ladder. *Too close.*

Over-confidence. That was what Zay had called it. She had been overconfident and had nearly paid for it with her life.

She moved down one rung and whimpered.

"Zay," she yelled. Her voice was thrown back at her as a shrill echo. "I'm coming."

The climb down was agonizing. Chapel double-checked her grip on each rung, lowering herself to the basement, inch by precious inch. When she reached solid ground, she leaned over and kissed it.

There was an emergency bar at the top of the bottom set of doors, and Chapel smacked against it with both hands. They popped apart and she fell into the basement.

"Zay?" she called. "*Isaiah?*"

The first door she came to was locked. So were the second, and the third.

"Zay?" she yelled again, panic creeping into her voice. "It's just me, here. I need you to make some noise."

She worked like a woman possessed, trying another door, and another, and another, until finally, one clicked open.

"Zay, are you—" Chapel's words died on her lips.

The room was full of people, Gabe included. And they were all facing a screen with a ticking red clock.

32:11:31, it read. And it kept ticking. Thirty-two minutes. She'd been using Tempus for thirty-two minutes.

Nausea slammed into her. She cupped a hand over her mouth.

They had tricked her.

She fell to her knees.

Zay wasn't there.

Relief flooded her veins. Fury followed closely after.

She heard the hitch in her breathing, felt the stutter of her heart.

And they knew her secret. The secret even *she* didn't know.

She could hold Tempus much longer than she thought.

She saw red just before things went black.

CHAPTER TWENTY-ONE

Inside her head there played a broken record. There were stretches of sound, disjointed and sharp, then abrupt lulls where there was nothing but a pulsing bass, a thud behind her eyes.

Then noise would return in screeching syncopations, clattering in her head like stones through glass.

The mast of a helicopter rotated nearby.

Thump thump thump thump thump thump thump thump thump thump.

She saw the tips of shoes, white with no scuffs. Struggled to sit up.

Gabe was standing over her, telling her to lie still.

It wasn't a helicopter.

The people in the room . . . they were *clapping* for her. Clapping as if she had actually saved someone, and not nearly killed herself for the sake of study.

There was something cool and damp on her cheek.

Chapel forced her eyes open. There she was. Her. Or a picture of her on the wall. On a poster. There were a series of them.

Bellum's Belle, one caption said. She looked pretty.

A woman was wiping at Chapel's mouth and telling her to breathe through her nose.

My nose? Chapel felt it now—the ache in her face that stung as if a thousand bees were shoved into her sinuses.

She tried to sit up again, but a man with a red face glowered at her. No, it was a balloon. A bunch of balloons. Everywhere. They were having a party. A party for her.

Chapel swung out with her fist, connecting with something warm and smooth. She hoped it was Chary.

That was her last conscious thought.

* * * *

Chapel woke up to the sound of beeping. It was slow at first, then faster as she remembered what had happened.

"You're okay," Gabe's voice said. He was sitting beside her in a chair. "You're in the infirmary."

"What the—"

He widened his eyes at her and wiped a hand across his lips. *Not here*, the gesture said. She returned her eyes back to the ceiling, her speeding pulse clipping on the monitor above her head.

She shifted the direction of her thoughts. "My face hurts."

Gabe winced. "You broke your nose. The doctor reset it, though. It should heal nicely."

Chapel pushed her eyes closed then opened them again. She blinked several times at Gabe. "What happened to you?" she asked, pointing with a shaky hand to a bright red welt below his eye.

"You happened, I'm afraid." Gabe looked like he didn't want to smile, but he did anyway. "That's quite a right hook you have there,"

"Oops." Chapel licked her dry lips. "Would it make you feel better if I said you looked really tough with that huge gash on your face?"

"I wouldn't call it *huge.*" Gabe stood and walked until his hands rested on the cool steel of her bedrail. "Are you okay?" he asked quietly.

In the fluorescent lights of the small room, Gabe's tan skin appeared pallid. The fine lines at the corner of his light eyes betrayed the warm smile he sent her way.

Chapel lifted her fingers and brushed them lightly beside the cut. Gabe flinched slightly.

"I should be asking you that, apparently," she said.

Gabe caught her wrist and slowly lowered it to the bed. Chapel was having difficulty swallowing.

"I'll go tell them you're awake," Gabe said. Then he left.

Chapel was examined and allowed to change. Her clothes were still damp from her perspiration, and covered in a thin layer of dust from inside the elevator shaft.

Chapel winced as she lifted her arms to shrug into her shirt. The stitches from the car accident had only been removed days ago, and already she had a new injury. Or injuries. Her body felt as if every bone inside it had been tweaked during the exercise.

When Chapel came out of the bathroom, she found Chary, Gabe, and a man she'd never seen before standing in a semicircle looking at an open file.

The man looked up. He was of average height and build, with hair and eyes the color of black coffee. He lifted his chin to acknowledge her.

"Chapel," he said as if they'd been friends for years. "How are you feeling?"

Gabe shot her a look. She was pretty sure it was a warning. She ignored it.

"Like an idiot, actually." She ripped the remaining IV tape from her arm. "Can I go, now?"

The man took off his frameless glasses and stuck out a hand. "My apologies, Chapel. My name is Daniel. I should have introduced myself sooner."

She looked at his hand for a few beats before she reached over and took it in hers. His handshake was stern and cool, just like his expression. As she stepped closer to him, she realized he was probably younger than she first thought.

Daniel leaned his head on his palm for a moment and studied her. Something about the way he held himself, about the cut of his jaw, it was familiar.

"Have we met before?" she asked.

His dark eyebrows twitched. "No. Believe me. I would have remembered." He opened the file containing her charts. "You, Chapel Ryan, are a modern day mystery."

He pointed to a graph with numbers. The corresponding line started off as a plateau, then shot up sharply, tapering off before plateauing again, but not a low as the previous line.

"This is a representation of your brain's activity before, during, and after Tempus. See how your new rate of activity is still higher than its former positioning? And that's when you were *passed out."*

He flipped to another page. It was an image of a brain. It was colored in hues of the rainbow that Chapel didn't understand.

"Here is your brain when you used Tempus back in November. The colors represent—"

"Wait," she cut in. "Back in November?"

Daniel's eyes flicked over to Gabe. Gabe's eyes were on anything but her.

"Gabe?" she asked.

He rubbed the back of his head. "I planted a monitor on you while you slept on the airplane en route to D.C."

"You *what?"* she spat as if the words tasted bad.

"He did his job," Daniel said simply. "And today, Chary planted another monitor on you."

The kiss on both cheeks, Chapel remembered. She thought it had been a bit over the top. Her jaws ached with the effort it took not to open them and use the worst words she could think of to tell them what she thought of their subversive methods.

"The digital clock in the room," she said. "It was working. How?"

"Solar powered," Daniel said. "My idea, actually." He flipped to another page. *"Here* is your brain activity during today's trial. See how the red portion has doubled in size from one experience to the next?"

She nodded.

"Your neuron transmissions are increasing, and with it, the amount of energy you release. In tandem, your resting energy rate is increasing." Daniel's eyes were dark orbs of fascination. "You're getting exponentially stronger, far faster than we predicted."

His words made her throat burn with anxiety. She had done the opposite of underwhelm Bellum. She had wooed them.

"And the posters?" she asked. "Were you guys having a . . . party?"

Daniel clasped his wrists behind his back. "We were, in fact. A party in your honor. I am happy to say, Chapel, that after today's exhibition, there will be no need for further testing. Congratulations." Daniel smiled at her as if he were presenting her with a million-dollar check. "Come May, you will be the Belle of Bellum."

Chapel stood frozen, feet rooted into place, with her fists opening and closing at her sides. The room was too small.

"Can I leave now?" she asked.

Daniel adjusted his glasses. He appeared mildly surprised. "Of course. You'll need to rest for this evening."

Gabe's eyes shifted over her face. There was confusion in them.

"This evening?" he asked.

Chary lifted a dainty finger. "Yes, well. I didn't tell you sooner because I didn't want to get Chapel's hopes up." She turned to Chapel. "But since you've astounded us all and won over our Daniel, here, tonight is our annual Bellum Gala and *you* will be in attendance."

"I will be in attendance?" Chapel repeated flatly.

"Yes," Daniel said, stepping between she and Chary and taking off his glasses. His eyes, they were so intense when he looked at her. And she wondered again if she'd ever met him.

"It's time your introductions are made," he said. "We need to fast-track you into integration. Your skills are . . . " He glanced at the charts on the wall. "Exemplary. And needed."

Chary laughed, but it sounded forced. *"Dear,* don't look so downtrodden. It's a *Gala,* not a beheading."

Chapel swallowed. *Actually,* she thought, *it's both.*

"Many people want to meet you," Daniel said. "And it will be good for you to mingle with some of the others you'll be working with very soon."

Chapel didn't have words. But she knew this news was bad. Bad because it exposed her identity to a group of people she didn't trust. And bad because it pushed her further into Bellum's community.

Chary walked them out to where Gabe's car had been pulled to a back entrance. The sun was dripping into the ocean, and a warm breeze lifted her tangled curls off her shoulders.

Once they were outside, Gabe spun on Chary. They spoke over each other in jabs of sentences.

"Did you know—"

"I had no idea—"

"She could have been *killed—*"

"Daniel insisted it stay a secret—"

"Now, she'll have *no* choice."

The last sentence was the only one Chapel followed every word of, and Chary went still upon hearing it. She glanced back at the doors they had exited through, then back at Gabe.

"You and I both know," Chary hissed, "that she *never* had a choice."

Gabe tilted his head at Chary. Chapel counted thirty-six full seconds of staring before he looked away, shoving his hands in his pockets.

"Get in the car, Chapel," he said lowly.

She had never heard him speak so angrily. She obeyed without question. Chapel watched through the window as Gabe said something quietly to Chary. Chary lifted her shoulders in response and spun around, leaving Gabe to stare at her back.

Chapel waited until they were a safe distance from the training facility before turning in her seat. "You good?"

Gabe's jaw tightened, then released. "I'm good. You?"

"Fine."

Gabe slid a sideways look at her. They were both lying, but neither acknowledged it.

"Who is Daniel, *exactly?*" Chapel asked.

Gabe sighed. "You don't want to know."

"Your boss?"

He rubbed the back of his head. "Everyone's boss. He's the President of Bellum."

Chapel didn't have the energy to react. "I'm so screwed," she mumbled.

"Yes." Gabe gripped the steering wheel until his knuckles were white. *"Quite* so."

* * * *

The silver lining to the black and ominous thunderclouds of the day were that Bellum sent a team to get her dressed for the Gala. Gerome and his assistant, Jean.

"Should I be offended right now?" she asked Gabe as she was ushered upstairs.

Gabe didn't answer. Gabe looked worried.

Two hours later, Chapel had been thoroughly plucked, curled, and mascaraed. Her broken nose looked puffy near the bridge, but the two men had made makeup magic and covered the cut masterfully.

"That stuff is amazing," Chapel said, pointing at a dish of cream foundation. "You can barely tell I broke my nose."

"It'll look worse tomorrow," Jean said. "Be glad you broke it today."

Glad? Chapel rolled her eyes. "Yeah, that's the word I'd use."

Gerome surprised her by giggling. "Girl, you feisty," he growled. "I like you."

They were a lot nicer to her after that.

"Are you nervous?" Jean asked at one point, rolling a piece of hair around the barrel of a curling iron.

Chapel lifted her shoulders. "I have no idea what to expect."

Gerome moaned. "Oh, it will be *lovely*. There'll be wine, and dancing, and all the Bellum elite will be there, flouncing in their finery."

"Will you be there?"

Jean picked up another section of hair. "Heavens, no. This event is invite-only. Gerome and I are still training."

Chapel gulped. She'd be the only non-Bellum in attendance.

Finally, they led her to a full-length mirror inside Gabe's closet. Gerome clicked on the light.

Over her shoulder, Chapel saw them rise on their toes, clenching their hands over open mouths.

The girl across from her was actually not a girl. She was woman. With hips. And legs. And lips. And eyelashes. The dress she wore was gold and fitted. It had a sweetheart neckline and hit just above her knees.

Her hair was twisted and braided back into a low bun with pieces curled softly around her face. When she moved her head, they tickled the sides of her cheeks.

Her fingers traced the top edge of her scar. Hunter's thumb and pointer finger.

Gerome sucked in a breath through his teeth. "Honey, you sure you don't want us to cover that up? It'll just take a sec."

Chapel answered the same way she had the first time he asked. "No. I want them to see it."

There was a little flutter in her chest when she slipped the champagne-colored heels on.

Gerome squealed. "It's time," he said, offering her his arm.

She let him usher her down the stairs. She was laughing at something he said about the best kind of lipstick for kissing when they got to the landing. A noise in the kitchen drew her attention.

Gabe was staring at her with a bottle pulled halfway to his lips. His eyes were hooded in the dim light, and when they connected with hers, she waited for his reaction. Slowly, greedily, he drank her in.

She waited for his words. *You look beautiful.* Or, *Good job, boys.* Or even, *Quite lovely.* But instead of reacting, Gabe turned and poured the beer in the sink without saying a word.

Disappointment deflated the buoyant moment. Embarrassment warmed her cheeks. He couldn't even muster up a *You look nice.*

She knew she looked nice. He should have said she looked nice.

She turned to Jean and Gerome. "Thank you so much."

Gerome was staring over her shoulder at Gabe. It took him a moment to return his attention to her. "Ignore him," he said loud enough for Gabe to hear. "You're a doll, babe."

They waved goodbye and Chapel was alone with Gabe.

She turned to find him behind her in the foyer. He was holding the photograph of him and the beautiful woman in his hands. His fingers touched the image. Where, she couldn't see.

He was handsome in a black tuxedo, his short hair styled straight back, opening his broad face. Why wouldn't he look at her? She knew he felt her staring.

She didn't fully understand why, but it made her angry.

"I'll be in the car," she said flatly. She didn't wait for him to respond.

It was a few minutes before he joined her. When he did, he didn't crank the car right away.

"Stay by my side the entire night. Don't leave my sight."

Lifting her head from the window it rested on, Chapel curled her lip back at him. "You're not my keeper," she said.

"Is that so?" Gabe rubbed his hands down his suit pants. "Well then, who is?"

Her voice was the temperature of ice. "I keep me."

The drive was silent and strained. It was the longest Gabe had ever been quiet in her presence. Instead of relishing in it, it grated against her ears, making her even *angrier*.

On the ferry ride, Chapel stood at the helm of the boat, as far away from Gabe as possible. The emotions swarming inside of her sloshed around like the waters they pushed through. Hurt. Sadness. Anxiety. Fear.

She let the cooling night's air fill her lungs, easing their burn, and something became suddenly clear: she loved Zay. But she liked Gabe. How much? And in what way, specifically? She couldn't be sure.

They were taken by car to another building near the back of the island. Gabe slowed as the valet stepped through glass doors that automatically opened. Chapel reached for her seatbelt, but Gabe touched her arm.

"Chapel."

She waited for him to say something else. To look at her. He did neither. So when the valet swung open her door, she got out and walked inside without waiting for him.

Music thumped through the hall she entered. It was surprising—in its volume and its intensity. It sounded like a nightclub inside. Which is exactly what the scene she walked into looked like.

The lights were brighter, and the clothes were fancier, but the dance floor was crowded with young people dancing, talking, and laughing. She was stunned.

"Not what you expected?" Gabe said into her ear.

She shook her head.

Someone touched her arm and pulled her to the side. It was Daniel. He motioned she follow him to the edge of the room. She noticed now that there were tables set up along the perimeter that looked like they'd just been eaten on.

"Am I late?" she asked.

He shook his head. "I asked Gabriel to bring you after the speeches. I didn't want you to be bored." He took a silver serving lid off a plate. "I did have them bring you two some steaks out."

Chapel turned to see Gabe over her shoulder.

"Thank you," Gabe said. "I'm famished." He pulled out a chair and began opening his napkin.

Chapel turned back to Daniel. "I'm not hungry. Thank you, though."

Daniel gestured toward her dress. "Well, you look gorgeous. Like an angel. Literally."

She smiled at him. "That is *so* good to hear, Daniel. Thank you."

Gabe's shoulders stiffened.

Daniel offered her his arm. "Let us see about some introductions, hm?"

Chapel was taken around the room and introduced to more people than she could keep up with. Everyone seemed to know her name, her exception, and about her test.

The men and women she met smiled at her adoringly. They were all so positive and enthusiastic—it made it hard not to have a nice time. People she could openly be herself around who were glad to see her? She couldn't recall the last time that happened.

A large crowd had gathered on the edge of the room, and Daniel pressed through the throng to the head of it. Chapel was surprised to see Chary at the center, looking stunning in a pale pink sari. She was in the middle of telling a story about some trip to the dessert, and everyone stood around her, rapt.

Chary paused mid-sentence when she saw Chapel and Daniel approaching.

"Oh, there she is," Chary said. She reached out an arm to Chapel. "Our little Belle of Bellum."

Chapel was drawn to Chary's side in a fierce hug that pressed their cheeks together. It made Chapel wince.

"Isn't she a beauty?" Chary asked, stroking Chapel's arm.

The crowd around her murmured and Chapel stepped away a little too quickly, stumbling slightly into a couple standing to the side.

"Don't worry," Chary said behind her, "she uses Tempus *much* better than she walks."

It felt like the whole room roared in laughter and Chapel's insides felt like they were on fire. Daniel arrived at her side and took her elbow.

"Excuse her," he said. "She is the life of the party when she's drunk," he said. "And that life just happens to be centered around *her.*"

He led her back around to Gabe who sat in the same place. Before they reached the table, however, Daniel tugged her elbow and they stopped at a small recess in the wall. She realized he did so purposefully. He wanted to speak with her in private.

"You did well," Daniel said.

"Oh." She hadn't realized it had been a test. "Thanks."

"I know how you feel about Bellum," he continued. "But I want you to put yourself in my position for a moment." He motioned his arm across the room. "These people are my family. My children, really." He turned his dark eyes to her. "What would you be willing to do to protect your family, Chapel?"

She studied his jaw, his eyelashes, the curve of his lips. He looked so familiar.

"Anything," she said at last. "I would do anything to keep them safe."

Daniel nodded, lifted a finger and a boy and a girl peeled off from a group on the edge of the dance floor. They both smiled at her as they shook Daniel's hand.

"This is Jack and Mia," he introduced them. "They are the top recruits for Bellum's next training class. Them," he said, "and you."

Jack and Mia looked like siblings. They were tall with copper hair and pale skin. Baby blue eyes shone from both of their lean faces. They were striking.

"I heard about your times today," Jack said. "Wow." He scratched behind his ear. "Just, wow."

Mia pushed Jack's shoulder. "Jack is a little star struck. Don't mind him. Do you like to dance?"

Chapel's eye wandered to Daniel's. He smiled at her. "I wanted you to come here tonight to have *fun*. To meet the people you will soon do life with." He leaned toward her. "I know we're not your first choice. But we will treat you well. I give you my word."

Taking the hand Mia had stretched out to her, Chapel was led to the center of the room where the bodies were pressed together like sheets of paper.

She looked back one time to where Gabe sat. Through the shifting masses, she saw Chary hunched beside him, speaking animatedly. She looked angry. For some reason, that made Chapel laugh.

Join the freaking club, she thought. Then she looked around and took her own advice.

* * * *

By the time that Chapel took a break from dancing, her feet hurt, her hair was falling, and her nose ached again. She had some pain pills in her purse.

She disentangled herself from the arms and legs that did not belong to her, and she made her way to the table. Gabe was gone, but her plate remained. So she took a few cold bites of a baked potato and washed her pills down with someone's tepid water.

She'd had better dinners.

The tempo of the music changed. Couples started pairing off and people exited the dance floor. Chapel sat at the table and lifted her ankle to her knee to take off her heels.

A hand touched hers, right on her leg. She looked up—it belonged to Gabe. He had dropped into the seat beside her. And finally, he was looking at her.

"Would you like to dance?" he asked.

She lifted an eyebrow. "Are you speaking to me again?"

He tilted his chin. "Please?"

She wanted to say no. If it had been Zay, she would have said no and walked outside and made him chase her. But Gabe was different. He couldn't fight like they could.

Gabe set her foot back on the ground and helped her stand.

When his hands settled on her hips, Chapel lifted her arms around his neck. He wasn't as tall Zay, but almost.

Zay. She closed her eyes against that thought, too emotionally tapped out to consider where he was, what he was doing. And who he was doing it with.

Gabe must have misinterpreted her actions for exhaustion, because he sighed before pressing her face against his chest. He left his other hand against her back.

"Your nose hurt?" he said into her ear.

She nodded.

"I'm sorry," he said.

"About my nose?"

"Yes," he said, his breath warming her neck. "And for earlier."

Chapel didn't speak. She just left her eyes closed and clung to him. He smelled like vanilla and salt and alcohol.

"I had a fiancé," he said.

Chapel couldn't mask the jerk that touched her body. She steadied herself before asking. "Who?"

"Her name was Cecily," he said. "I called her Cess."

"Cess," Chapel repeated. "Pretty."

A laugh hummed in Gabe's chest. "She was. Inside and out."

Chapel realized then, that Gabe didn't have an *ex* fiancé. He had a *late fiancé*. She lifted her face to his. "What happened?"

She didn't miss the wince that pinched the corners of his eyes. "I'd rather not talk about her," he said. "If you don't mind."

Chapel lifted one side of her mouth. "I can talk for hours about not talking about things."

Gabe smiled at her.

"There it is," she said quietly. "I haven't seen *that* in a long time."

He laughed quietly. "Ah, Chapel."

Then he leaned his forehead against hers, and suddenly the smiles were gone.

His lips started moving, and it took Chapel a moment to hear his words. He was singing to the song that played overhead.

"Something about the way you look tonight. Takes my breath away."

His voice was low at first, but then got clearer. He moved his face beside her ear, and that was when she knew he was singing to *her*.

"It's that feeling I get about you, deep inside. And I can't describe. But it's something about the way you look tonight."

When the song was over, Chapel leaned back. "Beautiful," she said.

Gabe stared at her, long and steady. "You are," he said. "And I should have already told you."

As he led her away from the dance floor, Chapel got a prickling sensation along the back of her neck. Her eyes moved over her shoulder. But no—that's not where she needed to be looking. Up, higher, there was a movement in the balcony area.

She couldn't be sure, but through the folds of golden curtains, it looked like someone was *staring* at her. Chapel paused.

In the shadows, Chapel's eyes met angry, dark ones above. She gasped. There was a swirl of pale fabric and dark hair, and the moment was gone.

Chary?

Gabe was tugging on her wrist. "You okay?" he asked.

She looked down at their hands, still joined. And it was either the pain medicine or something she wanted desperately to ignore, but her entire body filled with a sense of cool relief—the first of its kind in days.

CHAPTER TWENTY-TWO

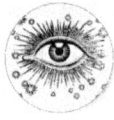

Chapel was too wired to sleep when they got back to Gabe's. She took a shower and went out to the beach in a pair of cotton shorts and a tank top. The air coming off the ocean was cool and misty, and it felt good against the sting inside her nose.

The momentary breath of air she had at the Gala was now replaced by the weight of the daunting unknown before her, laid out in thick blackness, just like the edges of the ocean she stared across.

She sat down at the edge of the shore, letting the water lap over her bare toes. She closed her eyes, her fingers sifting through clumps of damp sand.

Words emerged from some hidden place inside of her.

How precious are your thoughts, O God! How vast is the sum of them. Were I to count them, they would outnumber the grains of sand.

God, she prayed, *I don't know what I'm doing. I don't know what you're doing. It feels like you've forgotten about me.*

She pushed down the knot rising like vomit in her throat. She couldn't imagine how badly it would hurt her nose to start sobbing, but the truth was that Chapel didn't even feel like *Chapel* anymore. She felt like *Tempus*.

She missed her friends. She missed Zay and Rush. She missed her mother and the twins. And, yes, maybe even Todd, a little.

What would happen with her and Zay? What would happen with Timmy? What would happen with Gabe?

If everything continued its current trajectory, would she join Bellum and still be able to have normal friends? Would she end up like Zay's group, working constantly, never making a choice again that was wholly *hers?*

Guilt and anger clashed inside of her, chipping at the foundation of all she knew to be true. It felt heavy and scary and real.

She heard Gabe's approach, but didn't look at him until he stood beside her. His hair was damp and he had on shorts and T-shirt. He looked like he'd just showered.

He sat without a word, and the only sound between them was the breathy lapping of waves, exhaling and inhaling at their feet.

Finally, she felt Gabe's shoulders relax beside her. He pushed his legs to the ground and leaned back on his palms. A sigh unraveled on his lips.

"When was the last time you came to the beach?" he asked.

Chapel closed one eye and thought. "We never had enough money for vacations," she said. "But this one summer, my mom let me come with the Valentines. I think I was, like, twelve."

"Which beach did you go to?"

"Daytona Beach, Florida," Chapel said, a faint smile appearing. "I begged her all summer. Timmy begged her. Even Mrs. Valentine begged her. It was weird, because I knew my mom trusted them, but it was like she was afraid for me to spend the night somewhere that wasn't *home.*"

"She may have been frightened that you'd use Tempus while you were gone. Or that someone from Bellum or Thanatos would find you and take you."

Chapel hadn't thought of that. In fact, in light of the fact that her mother *knew* what she was, Chapel would have to reexamine many of her childhood memories to see how this new truth might have affected her relationship with Valerie.

"Did you have fun?" Gabe asked.

Chapel closed her eyes and grinned at the pictures she saw there. She laughed quietly, remembering Timmy's face the first time she'd come out of the bathroom in her bikini. His ears had turned a color so red they looked violet at the tips.

He had taught her how to dig for crabs and skim board. She had tried shrimp for the first time. They'd stayed up late and watched shows on MTV that neither of them were supposed to watch. It had felt incredibly scandalous and normal. She had craved that then, *normalcy*.

Now she would never have it.

"Yes," she whispered.

Chapel needed to shove the emotions back down her throat before they poured out of her mouth and down her face. She coughed into her fist.

"What about you?" She turned over her shoulder to look back at him. "What's the best vacation you've ever taken?"

Gabe's eyes looked down the beach. His eyes went slightly unfocused, and she could tell he was remembering something.

"Two years ago," he murmured.

When he didn't say anything more, she nudged his leg. "Who did you go with?"

He turned to look at her then, as if remembering she were there. "Cess."

Chapel bit her tongue. She could be so stupid sometimes. Of course that was who he went with.

"I'm sorry," she said.

Her mind went to the photo of the beautiful girl with dark, kinky hair and warm eyes. *Cess*. Like her name, Cecily had been lovely and exotic.

Gabe was quiet for a stretch. Then he shifted beside her. He leaned up and dusted off his hands. She looked over at him. His expression was soft.

"We went to a beach in Vietnam called Doc Let," he said. His eyes strayed from her face and landed on the water. He smiled to himself, remembering something. "We didn't make it to the ocean a single time."

"Oh." Chapel couldn't suck the word in fast enough. She didn't know what else to say. "That sounds relaxing. Or, well, maybe not *relaxing*. Because, I mean . . . just . . . um." She slammed her forehead into her hands. "I'm an idiot."

Gabe laughed quietly beside her. "I'm sorry. I shouldn't have said that. I don't know why I did." He pulled her hands away from her face. "I forget that about you. That you're..."

"Young and dumb and innocent." She filled in his words. "Yes. You remind me of that every chance you get."

"I've never said that you are dumb." His chin tilted, and he pushed the hair off her shoulder, revealing more of her face. "But you are in some ways—ways that I wish I were—innocent."

"And young," she added.

His eyes fell to her lips, to her arms where her nervous energy pressed against her skin in flushed goose bumps.

"And young," he repeated, so quietly that she almost didn't hear him. "It's good for me to remind myself of that."

There were five or six heartbeats when she thought he was going to kiss her. And then there were two more when she was terrified that she was going to let him. She even lowered her eyelids, leaning slightly toward him.

Then something clattered behind them, making them both jerk around.

"It's just the gate," he breathed. It sounded shaky. "The wind must have blown it shut. The gate," he said again. "Just the wind."

"Yeah," she said. "You said that."

They were both quiet then.

Did that just happen?

When she dared another glance at Gabe, his eyebrows were pressed down and his head was leaned to the side. It looked like he was asking himself that exact same question.

He must have felt her gaze, because he lifted his eyes to hers. He pressed his lips together in a shy smile and it felt like her heart grew a little inside her chest.

"What were we saying?" he asked.

Chapel told her tongue to form words. It took a moment for it to obey. "I think we were talking about my youth," she said at last. "Though I feel pretty old tonight."

Gabe's shoulders lifted into a shrug. "Experience ages us more than years. And you've had *quite* the number of experiences lately."

She looked at him and made her voice like his. "Yes," she said, *"quite."*

He elbowed her gently. "You're getting better at that, I'm afraid."

She smiled, looking up at the night sky. "The Gala wasn't so bad."

"No," Gabe said. "They never are. Since we are not government-regulated, we get to spend our profits how we like. We're a wilder bunch than Thanatos, though Daniel is working to correct that."

"But wasn't it dangerous to have me there?" she asked.

"Daniel's idea," Gabe said. "You're our best advertisement."

Chapel read between the lines: revealing her identity was worth the risk, as long as it got more recruits.

"A commercial with legs," she mumbled.

"Yes," he said. "And not bad legs at that." He made a hissing sound between his teeth. "That was cheesy. Wasn't it?"

Chapel nudged his knee with her foot. "A little." She bit down on the insides of her cheeks. "Gabe?"

"Hm?"

"I'm going to pledge Bellum, aren't I?"

"Unless you defect," he said with a sigh. "At which point you'd become a Rogue and a fugitive, and the Invisibles would hunt you down until they found you."

"Why?" she asked, banging the sand with her fist. "Why is it such a big deal?"

Gabe shook his head. "The Invisibles would say it's their way of decreasing interfaction violence. They would say that you struck a deal, and that its terms are irreversible."

His tone was edged and sharp, and she wondered just when he became so bitter at the Invisibles, and why.

"That's what the Invisibles would say," she said, "But what would *you* say?"

Before he could answer, a frigid wave lapped higher than the others, licking at the back of her calves. She squealed and stood up.

"That's cold," she breathed.

"It is." Gabe stood and dusted off the back of his pants. "Pity we weren't able to come out here during the daytime." He glanced down the beach. "It's beautiful."

Chapel followed his gaze. When she got back, she'd have Timmy, Erica, Zay, and midterms to contend with. Not to mention coming to terms with the fact that she would be Bellum.

"I almost wish I could just stay here," she said. "And pretend none of this is actually happening."

Gabe looked at her. "Really?"

She nodded.

His eyes returned to the water. "Then I have an idea."

CHAPTER TWENTY-THREE

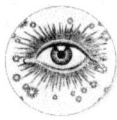

They spent the first half of the day on the beach.

When she woke up, Gabe had already walked around the corner to buy her a bikini. It fit perfectly.

On side-by-side towels, she read a book she found on Gabe's shelf while he worked on his phone beside her. There wasn't another moment like last night, when she wondered if he were going to kiss her. But she was more aware of him now. Of how he looked at her and when he touched her.

Maybe he had feelings for her, she decided. But they weren't strong. It was likely just an attraction. An attraction she returned, in part. She wasn't *blind*.

But when she closed her eyes, it was Zay's face she saw, his voice she heard. It had been his words, after all, that had spoken in her head, urging her onward in the fake mission to rescue him.

He made her stronger. There was so much about *that* that mattered.

The flight home was quick and uneventful—except for the part when Gabe took out his guitar and tuned it. She begged him to play for her, but he waved her off.

"It's been too long. I'm only bringing it because I'm not sure when I'll be back."

Two years. He'd stopped playing when Cecily died. And again she wondered what had happened.

He handed her her cellphone when they exited the Bellum airport. When she turned it on, it lit up in her hand with missed calls and messages.

Almost all of them were from Zay. She opened the texts firsts. They started on Saturday morning.

ZAY: *I just got back from an op to hear you're gone.*
ZAY: *Tell me where you are, and I'll come get you.*
ZAY: *I can't believe Jackson let him take you.*
ZAY: *Why didn't you tell me you were going?*
ZAY: *I finally got it out of Marielle that you called. Please answer me.*
ZAY: *I drove to the Bellum camp in Alabama. You're not here, are you?*
ZAY: *I am assuming they took your phone from you? Please call me as soon as you can.*
ZAY: *I taught your class for you this morning. Katie prayed you would come back next week. I prayed, too.*

Her Sunday school class. She had totally forgotten. But not Zay. And he had *prayed* for her? That did something different to her stomach. She felt it dip, and turn, and warm all in one breath.

Gabe pressed his lips together. "You can call him, if you'd like."

Zay answered on the first ring. "Chapel? Where are you?"

His voice sounded so panicked, so stricken, so *rattled*. It wasn't a voice she'd ever heard him use before. And it took her a moment to answer.

"I'm with Gabe," she finally said. "We just landed. I'll be home in half an hour."

"Can I meet you there?"

She glanced over at Gabe, suddenly wishing she were somewhere more private. "Actually, no. I think we need to meet with Jackson. In the basement conference room."

It was late afternoon by the time Gabe pulled into the driveway. They shared a heavy look before she got out.

Zay was leaning against the porch. She felt his steady gaze like a touch on her face. His expression was guarded.

"Hey," she said, unsure of what to do with her hands.

He studied her face for a beat, then Gabe's. "Is it broken?"

She lifted a finger to her nose. It had a slit on the bridge and was blue in the corners of her eyes. "Yes."

He nodded. "They're already downstairs."

The entire team was in the basement. Justin and Marielle sat at the end of the table, looking bored. Rush and Jackson had their backs turned, looking at the large screen at the front of the room. When they turned and saw Chapel, the conversation halted.

Rush smiled. "Peaches with a tan." He whistled. "Should I call you Prunes, now?"

He gave her a hug that nearly constricted her airways.

"Is that your way of saying you missed me?" she asked.

Jackson made a noise at the front of the room. For a normal person, it would have sounded like a throat clearing. For Jackson, it sounded like he was humming.

Chapel looked up to see the scans of her brain on the wall. That was what they had been studying when she walked in.

"How did you get these?" she asked.

"Gabriel emailed them to us early this morning," Jackson said. "For which we are thankful."

Zay shifted against the wall behind them, drawing her eye. She tried to get him to look at her, but he wouldn't. He just stared at the projection as if it were a piece of thought-provoking artwork.

Jackson slid into the chair across from her. "Isaiah, will you join us at the table?"

His response was quick: "No."

Chapel almost laughed at how absurd it sounded—his direct refusal of an order from Jackson. What had happened while she was gone?

Ignoring him, Jackson motioned to the screen. "We have these images, which are beyond impressive, but no further explanation. Please, tell us what happened."

Chapel started talking. As she did, Zay walked over to the table. He stood beside it, but didn't sit down.

"I was just finishing the physical portion when the door opened. It was Chary."

Chapel paused, briefly reliving the terror of that moment. "She said there was an emergency. That Zay had broken into the basement. She insinuated that he would be arrested, or hurt, if I didn't use Tempus and save him."

For some reason, that made Marielle sit up in her seat. Justin also looked mildly interested.

"I didn't even stop to *consider* the fact that she was playing me. I did *exactly* what they wanted me to do."

She told them about her search for entry into the basement, about her circuit around the building and back inside again. When she got to the part about breaking into the elevator, Marielle held up a hand.

"Let me stop you right there," she said. "Are you telling me you forced open metal doors?"

"Does she have to be in here?" Chapel asked. "Marielle, don't you have some innocent animals to maim? A voodoo doll to fashion? Maybe an elderly person to trip or scam?"

"Hold on," Rush said. He stood and walked over to the screen. "Okay. Does everybody see this purple section right here?" He pointed to something that looked to be about the size of a grape. "That's Chapel's hypothalamus. That's the part of the brain in charge of communicating with her adrenals." He turned to them, and for a second, Chapel almost didn't recognize him. His serious face was . . . serious.

"I'm just hypothesizing here," he said, "but judging by the levels displayed in her blood work, combined with the representations here, Chapel's body was producing a serious amount of adrenaline." His eyes found hers, pausing there. "An insane amount, actually."

"Continue, please," Jackson said to her.

"Once inside the elevator shaft, I took a service ladder to the basement. They were waiting for me there."

"Hold up." Zay stabbed the table with a finger. "I've seen that elevator before. It's encased in glass from the first floor up. How did you get to the ladder in the first place?" He looked at her nose, as if he already knew the answer.

She met his eyes. "I jumped."

Zay pursed his lips and nodded. "You jumped," he repeated. He looked around the room. "She *jumped,*" he yelled, slamming both fists on the table. Everybody flinched. "Good. No, that's great. *Perfect.*"

"I knew I could land it," she said with clenched teeth. "I knew I could do it."

Zay shook his head. "Chapel, you're smart. You took a calculated risk. That's not what I'm worried about." He pushed up the sleeves on his black thermal shirt as if the room had just gotten ten degrees warmer. "What I'm *worried* about is the fact that now *they* know that about you."

"Isaiah," Jackson started.

"No." Zay pointed at him. "Don't try and gloss this over. They're going to make her pledge Bellum. They'll never let her go now."

He pressed his thumb and forefinger into his eyes and yelled a curse word, stilling the entire room with his shouted expletive. Zay rarely lost control like this. Actually—never.

"This could have been *avoided!*" he yelled. He turned on Gabe. "You could have rescheduled this until we had a chance to strategize. Unless the rules have changed, she gets two opportunities to reschedule her pre-test. Why didn't you wait?"

Chapel's eyes zeroed in on Gabe. "Is that true?"

The blood seemed to seep from Gabe's tan cheeks. "I thought it prudent for her to take it before her skills were any sharper."

Zay laughed, but there was no humor in it. "No, you saw a way *in* with her, and you took it. Look at her." Zay motioned to her, the veins on his arms standing out angrily. "She's tan and her hair smells like salt water, for godsake. You took her on a vacation, Luxe. A vacation that may cost her *her life.*"

"Zay," Chapel said. She'd never seen him like this before—his handsome face twisted in disgust.

"And *you.*" Zay shoved the table toward Marielle, who jerked back in surprise. "If you had just given me the *phone*, we wouldn't even be having this conversation. I could have told Chapel to reschedule. Or at least assured her of us. She would have known I wasn't in that basement. She would have known it was a trap."

Marielle's upper lip curled in a snarl and she opened her mouth to say something.

"Don't." Zay cut her off. "I am sick of you acting like you have some sort of claim on me." Spit flew from his lips as he his voice raised with each word. "It was *hooking up*, Marielle. Get. Over. It!"

Jackson rose to his feet. By that time, Zay had made it to the other side of the table. He stood right in front of Jackson, toe to toe. Tension expanded like a balloon inside her chest, and Chapel was certain that it was about to burst.

"But out of everybody?" Zay said, barely loud enough for Chapel to hear. This voice, this scraping and dark voice, was much more frightening than the yelling. Chapel watched Zay's pulse thump wildly in the hollow of his throat. "I blame *you* the most," Zay said. "Not only did you let him take her, but you didn't even have the decency to *tell me* about it. I had to hear it from some contact while I'm on a job!"

"Isaiah." Jackson's voice was calm.

Zay turned quickly, shoving Jackson's chair onto its side and kicking the back of it, popping open the leather seam. "You want her to end up with Bellum, don't you?" Zay's eyes swiveled back to his uncle. "All that talk about my 'attention being divided.' That's what this is about. I wasn't your *slave* anymore?"

Chapel watched as Jackson's mouth went tight at the corners.

Thoughts and questions ricocheted off the inside of Chapel's mind: What talk of divided attention had gone on? Was Zay right? Had Jackson sent her to Bellum to get rid of her?

Rush stood and Zay shook his head at him. "Did you know, Lopez?" he asked. "Before Saturday? Did you know about Chapel?"

Rush didn't answer. He only swallowed.

Zay's head ticked back and he rocked on his heels. "Seriously?" he asked. "You were supposed to be my boy. All of you. You were supposed to be my *family.*"

The room held its breath.

"Ah. Now I remember," Zay said. "I have no family. You know what?" He shook his head. "Screw it. Screw all of you."

Then he left out the back door, leaving it open behind him.

Gabe looked pale. Marielle was crying into both of her upturned hands. Jackson stared at his feet. Rush cracked his knuckles. Justin flipped a pocketknife between his fingers back and forth, back and forth.

"What was that?" Chapel whispered, more to herself than anyone else.

Jackson was the first to answer. He looked at her without any expression on his face. "That was the old Isaiah."

* * * *

The room cleared out pretty quickly after Zay's exit. It seemed he took all the energy with him, and everyone's feet fell heavily as they moved.

Chapel followed Gabe out to his car to get her stuff.

"Is what he said true?" she asked. "About rescheduling my test?"

Gabe crossed his arms over his chest. "Yes. But why I took you there has nothing to do with how I feel about you."

"Great. Then tell me why you took me."

He shook his head. "I have my reasons."

Chapel slammed her open palm against the hood of his car. Pain radiated up her arm—it was the one she'd pulled when falling down the ladder. "Oh, goody," she said. "More talking in code. I was hoping we'd get back to that."

"Lashing out at me will not help you now."

"Oh, please," she moaned. "Spare me the tired lecture, Gabe. I *trusted* you."

He stepped toward her quickly, surprising her by taking her face between his two hands. His eyes roved over her greedily. She watched the internal struggle in his conflicted expression, the clash of his will, a decision he needed to make.

It built, it built, it built and then . . . he stepped away from her, leaving her legs feeling boneless and her throat feeling raw. She put a hand at her heart. It was racing.

"I wanted to kiss you, too," he said. "On the beach last night." He licked his lips. "And now. I want to kiss you now. But I can't *see* where that path takes us." He pressed two hands against his head. "I don't know if it takes me off the journey that I'm on now. And I must stay this course, Chapel. For both of us."

She was immobile. He was talking about the future. He was talking about destiny.

"What do you see?" she asked. "Is it the same vision from last fall? Do you see me as Bellum and Zay as Rogue?"

Gabe stared at her for several long moments, his chest rising and falling faster than normal.

"It changes," he said. "With every passing day. Some days yes, some days no. But the days I resist you . . ." He pinched his lips. "This is the path I have to stay on. She deserves it."

"Cecily?" Chapel whispered.

His eyes closed at the sound of her name. He said nothing else, and left.

CHAPTER TWENTY-FOUR

It wasn't a bad dream that woke Chapel up in the middle of the night, but the sound of someone banging on her front door.

The worst thoughts possible rushed to the front of her brain as she ran down the steps in a flurry. Images of Timmy's mind melting down, or Erica with a gun to her own head.

What she found instead was Marielle, Rush, and Justin. She swung open the door.

"It's Zay," Rush said. "He didn't come back tonight, and we can't find him. He won't answer his phone."

Chapel blinked the bleariness from her eyes. Three faces stared at her expectantly. She knew her expression must have been surly, because even Marielle looked sheepish.

"Peaches," Rush said. "You're the only one he'll listen to."

Chapel rolled her eyes with a heavy sigh. She took two steps backward. "Come in."

She showed them to the kitchen then ran up and got her robe and phone. She shut herself in her bathroom to call him. When he answered, the music in the background swelled above the sound of his voice.

"Hey," she thought he said. He sounded strange.

"Zay? Are you okay?"

The noise grew slightly less deafening, and Chapel thought he had probably walked to the back of whatever room he was in.

"You . . . there?" he asked, his words spaced further out than they should be.

"Yeah, I'm here. Where are you?"

"They . . . make . . . you call? Or you call me . . . for me?"

"Zay," she said slowly, "have you been drinking?"

"Me . . . who?"

"Oh my." She looked at the phone to check the time. It was just after midnight. "Tell me where you are."

"No."

"I'm getting in my car in five minutes. Tell me where you are, or I'll visit every bar between here and Atlanta looking for you."

He groaned, probably knowing that she was just stubborn enough to try.

"I just . . . I want to be . . . left."

There was an ache in his tone. He was hurting. Chapel shoved the robe off her shoulders and headed for her closet. Something protective rose up in her, in her chest and neck and limbs.

There were voices in the background. "Oh, there you are," said a girl.

Then a guy Chapel didn't recognize said, "Bro, we thought you'd passed out."

An announcer's voice split through the ambient noise. "*Welcoooooome to the Club Palace stage, DJ Murdeeeeerrrrrrr!*"

Zay mumbled something she couldn't hear. Then his voice came back again. "I'm . . . not . . . I'm fine." Then he hung up.

It took her approximately eight minutes to whip her hair into a bun, throw on some mascara and jeans, and slip into her gray leather jacket.

Zay had bought it for her for Christmas. She rubbed her cheek against the soft lapel. How could things get so complicated so quickly?

All eyes were on her when she pushed into the kitchen. She tilted her chin up. "I hope one of you has a fake ID for me."

Rush glanced at Marielle who shrugged, then nodded. "What do I look like, an amateur?"

"Good then." Chapel rubbed her hands together. "Because we're all going clubbing."

* * * *

The car ride was about as comfortable as a straightjacket.

"Look, Peaches," Rush said as they pulled out of the driveway. "Jackson didn't want Zay to know where you were until he was back from Mexico. A lot was riding on getting Agnello and Night locked up, including your safety. You and I both know he would have dropped everything to come get you if we'd told him sooner."

Chapel met his eyes in the rearview mirror. "I don't care why you did it. It was the wrong call." She looked away. "Not because of what happened to me. But because it broke his trust in *you.*"

Marielle sat silently in the front seat, her eyes unseeing as she faced the passenger window.

Justin sat in the back beside her, digging beneath his thumbnail with a knife.

"Why did you even come?" Chapel asked him.

He didn't look up when he said, "I was bored."

Chapel leaned her head back against the headrest. "This is the most dysfunctional rescue crew ever."

* * * *

The inside of Club Palace smelled like smoke and sweat and sin.

Chapel's boots stuck to the floor as she shuffled through the narrow hallway that spilled into an unexpectedly large and crowded dance floor.

A long bar curved around the back wall. It looked like the line was two or three people deep behind every stool.

Chapel craned her neck to the second floor where a balcony ran the entire circuit of the room. Bodies dangled against its gold bannister, dancing, leaning, lounging.

"We'll never find him," Rush bellowed in her ear.

Chapel pointed to herself. "Why do you think I'm here? Eye candy?" She joked to let him know she didn't hate his guts permanently.

He grinned. "That, too."

Marielle shook her head. "No need for Tempus," she shouted. "I know where he'll be."

They followed Marielle to the back of the room where she led them into a dark corridor. She turned around. "I asked the bouncer where the VIP lounge is. I've partied with Zay more times than I can count. Or remember. That's where he'll be."

"Let's do it, then," Rush said.

Marielle gave him a look. "This is a woman's job. You and Justin stay and make sure no one comes back here. It may get ugly." She looked over at Chapel. "Take your hair down and give Rush your jacket."

Chapel didn't ask any questions. She was too amazed at Marielle's taking control of the situation. She'd never seen her do much besides sulk and complain.

Marielle came and sifted through Chapel's hair, pushing it behind her shoulders. She tilted Chapel's chin to the side, looking at her nose.

"You jumped down an elevator shaft for him," Marielle said.

"I'd do it again."

Marielle blinked at her. "In another life," she said, "we could have gotten along."

Chapel pulled her face from Marielle's hands. "I doubt it."

Marielle gave her a wicked smile. "Follow me."

They turned down a corridor before coming to a velvet rope. Two men the size of small rhinos stood in front of it.

Marielle toyed with the stringy strap of her tank top. "Is there room for two more?"

Chapel stood off to the side, hoping she looked moderately cool and not like a twelve-year-old watching The Miracle of Life birthing video in Health class.

Rhino One looked at Rhino Two. They said something with their eyes and one unfastened the rope from a stanchion and motioned for the girls to enter the room.

Marielle's hand rested on the knob. She looked back at Chapel. "Be warned," she said, "he can be a nasty drunk."

The room was larger than Chapel anticipated. It had music blaring, a few booths along the back wall, and a small dance floor in its center. Chapel averted her eyes from the girls who were dancing there. She felt embarrassed for them.

Marielle walked straight back to the bartender and dropped a wad of cash on the counter. "I'm looking for a guy. Black hair, good-looking. Just over six feet tall?"

The bartender paused the set of shakers in her hands and thought for a moment. "Delicious scar on his upper lip?"

Marielle looked at Chapel. "That's the one."

"He's in that back booth."

"Does he have a tab I can close?" Marielle asked, reaching for more money.

The bartender turned and yanked a receipt from a clip. When Chapel saw the total, her eyes bulged. "That can't be right."

Marielle shook her head. "Oh, ye of little faith."

Chapel heard Zay before she saw him. A rumble of his laughter came from the back. Then a girl squealed.

She touched Marielle's eyes with hers. "Did you hear that?"

Marielle turned around. When she looked back to Chapel, she ran her tongue over her front teeth. "You don't have any firearms on you, do you?"

Chapel whipped around and charged in the direction of Zay's laugh.

"Chapel?" Marielle called behind her back. "We need to keep a low profile. We need to . . . oh, screw it. I'm in the mood for a good fight."

Chapel watched the U-shaped booth as she approached it. Zay sat in its center, a cigar in his mouth, and a drink in his hand. It looked like a poker game was underway, and judging by the stacks of chips in front of him, Zay was winning.

A woman in a white dress was draped along Zay's right side. He was pointing to the curve of cards in his hand as if explaining something to her.

Like he could sense her presence, Zay's eyes flicked up to Chapel when she was still about ten steps away. His cigar wavered between his teeth before he snapped it from his lips and exhaled slowly.

Chapel stopped just short of the table and stared at him, stared at the woman's blood red fingernails digging into his arm.

"Let's go," she said.

No one paid much attention to her. Except for Zay. His bloodshot eyes were locked onto hers as if they were connected by steel cables. His face was impassive—blank.

Tired, sore, hurt, jealous, and just plain *pissed off,* Chapel did the most logical thing she could think of. She picked up a full glass and launched it his direction, drenching Zay and the leach in a white dress in the process.

White Dress squealed and brushed at her thighs. The other men at the table looked up at her with hazy expressions of surprise and confusion. Zay's only reaction was to rearrange the cards in his hand, shuffling one on the end behind another.

A man with a beard ran a hand down her arm. "Honey, if you wanted in, all you had to do was ask."

Chapel jerked back. "If you value your hand, you'll never touch me with it again."

"I could touch you with something else," he said, darting his tongue to the edge of his mouth.

Chapel made a gagging sound in the back of her throat. "Please don't procreate. Like, I'm seriously begging you."

Marielle appeared at her side. "Zay, we're leaving. I need a bubble bath."

White Dress pulled her soaked dress from her body. "Do you know these skanks?" She laid narrowed eyes on Chapel. "Are you even old enough to drive yet?"

Zay took a long drink and threw a few black chips into the center of the table. "I'll raise the pot by fifty," he said lazily.

"He's already got a friend," The Beard said to Chapel. "Share the love." His hand snaked around her hips and Chapel smacked him away.

"*Halstead*," she hissed. "Get. Up."

He lounged back against the gaudy red vinyl. "Or what?"

She lifted the end of the table. "Or this," She said, shoving up, sending drinks, ashtrays, and poker chips careening to the floor in an ear-splitting fit of shatters and slams.

Chapel heard a few gasps and somebody laughed. She looked up. It was Marielle.

"You trashy, redneck—"White Dress began.

Then several things happened at once.

In her periphery, Chapel saw Rhinos One and Two heading their direction.

The man with the beard stood and jerked her against his chest by her arm. He breathed in her face and it smelled stale and sharp. He pressed crusted lips to hers.

White Dress's hand tangled in the back of Chapel's hair.

Marielle lunged for White Dress.

And Zay's expression *finally* changed.

One second her face was pressed against a stranger's, then it wasn't. Chapel blinked and Zay was shoving The Beard against a wall and sliding him up by his collar.

Someone whistled behind her and Chapel turned around. Marielle and White Dress were rolling in the floor, punching and pulling hair. A crowd had gathered around them, mostly men, but no one looked like they were going to intervene.

Chapel turned back to make sure Zay wasn't slaughtering The Beard, and saw that Rhinos One and Two had Zay by the shoulders. She watched as he allowed them to draw him back. When they thought the fight was gone from him, he jumped straight up and down, using his weight to break their hold.

That was Chapel's move.

He caught her eye as he kicked out with his legs to stand upright again.

"It was a good move," he said with a shrug.

Then Rhino One shoved him, making him stumble. Rhino Two charged from the side and barreled over him, sending Zay careening into the wall behind them. Chapel heard Zay's head slam against it.

Then Rhino Two was on top of Zay with his rhino arm jerked back. Chapel watched Zay's hips, waited for them to shift and arch, but they didn't. He wasn't conscious.

From somewhere behind her, she heard Rush yell. She didn't wait for him though, before she threw herself onto Rhino Two's back. She clawed at his arms and sank her teeth into his shoulder.

"When you're bested in size or strength," Zay had taught her, *"fight dirty."*

It didn't take him long to break free from her, but it gave Zay time to come to. Their eyes met again just before Rhino Two shook her off.

With a growl, Zay's hand shot up. Chapel couldn't see what he connected with, but blood sprayed down on his neck and shirt. He got one more shot in before Rush and Justin got there, dragging the Rhino off Zay.

Behind her she saw Rhino One out cold on the ground. Rush or Justin must have taken care of him already.

Beside his body, White Dress sat on the ground, holding both hands over her nose. It was gushing blood. The Beard sat slumped against the wall, cupping between his legs and moaning.

Someone grabbed her shoulder. "Let's go," Rush said, breathless. "I heard the bartender call security."

Just then the door burst open and two uniformed officers entered with guns drawn.

Rush cursed. "They must have been here on duty. We need another exit."

"This way," Zay said, wiping blood from his chin. Chapel couldn't tell if it belonged to him.

The five of them ran with Zay behind the bar and into a small kitchen. He led them through an emergency exit that poured them out into an alley.

He took Chapel by the hand. "Can you run?" he asked.

"Yeah."

"Marielle?"

She nodded.

Then they broke out into a full on sprint.

Chapel heard shouts at their backs as they dashed into the night. "Stop! Atlanta PD! Stop right now!"

For some reason, it made her giggle. She could imagine the headlines: STATE SENATOR'S DAUGHTER CHAPEL

RYAN ARRESTED AFTER HEATED ALTERCATION WITH RHINOS AT CLUB PALACE

Zay glanced down at her and a smile ghosted his lips. He gripped her hand harder.

They cut across a side street, then ran a block, cut across another side street, then ran two blocks. They ran silently, swiftly.

Chapel's thighs screamed against the burn, and her lungs ached. But she kept pushing one leg down, then the other, keeping pace as best she could.

Finally, Marielle held up a hand, slowing her steps until she stopped behind them.

Chapel pulled Zay's arm. "Stop. Marielle stopped."

"Go ahead," Marielle said, holding her side. "I'll slate them if they find me."

But Chapel had already stopped. Rush and Justin, too.

"This way," Zay said.

They walked behind a strip mall whose parking lot had a small patch of grass behind it.

Rush threw himself to the ground face first. Justin plunked down beside him, caramel skin flushed pink under the fluorescent streetlight. Marielle sat too, massaging her calves.

Chapel's quivering legs told her she should join them. She sank to the curb, breathing hard, her heart still thundering in her chest.

Zay stood, shifting his weight from foot to foot. He was not winded.

They were quiet for a long stretch, all probably thinking about how they could be sitting in jail right now, or a hospital bed.

Rush was the first one to start laughing. Chapel followed, then Marielle, and Justin. Even Zay lifted his eyes from the pavement, a grin curling his lips.

"That was freaking awesome," Rush said.

"It wasn't terrible," Justin added.

Marielle gave a rare smile. "It actually wasn't."

"Once we're an official Field Team," Rush said, "this is what we'll get to do all day, every day."

"Guys—" Zay started.

But Rush cut him off. "No, dude. No apologies. We let you down, man. We owed you."

Zay ran a hand down the side of his face. "You guys are all I have," he said at last.

Chapel understood the sentiment behind his words. Families hurt each other, but families forgive.

Marielle stood up and walked over to Chapel. "We square, now?" she asked.

Chapel took in the welt below her eye and the split in her lip. She let Marielle help her to her feet. "No," she said after a pause. "But closer."

They sent Rush to the parking deck to bring the Jeep around. He picked them up and drove to Zay's Jeep. The Shelby was still in the shop.

"Will you drive me home?" Zay asked her.

They were quiet as he helped her navigate them to the interstate. His speech was still slower than it should have been, and as the adrenaline seeped out of him, his lethargy resumed.

She thought he was asleep until he spoke. "That was crazy."

She glanced over at him. He was looking out the window. "Yeah," she said. "It sure was."

"Not the fight," he said, shifting toward her. "But the fact that I couldn't turn it off. I tried. I've always been so good at turning it off. Now I can't."

He wasn't making sense. "Turn *what* off?"

He pointed to his chest, right over his heart. "This."

Chapel didn't answer. Then next time she looked over at him, he was asleep.

CHAPTER TWENTY-FIVE

Chapel slept at Jackson's house in the guest room. Everyone was tired, and Chapel didn't want someone having to come stay at her house.

The next morning, she woke up to find a pile of her clothes inside the door. *Zay.* They needed to talk. But first, Chapel had school.

She didn't want to go, but she needed to put her eyes on Timmy. She needed to talk to him. Things had been awkward since their conversation in the parking lot, and that worried her.

Also. That whole graduating thing. She needed to do that.

She showered quickly and tried not to look at herself too closely in the mirror. Her nose was a little less swollen, but was still light blue along the bridge with a small gash.

When she came out of her room, Zay was coming out of his, too.

He reopened his door. "Can we talk for a minute?"

"I have, like, ten minutes before I need to leave for school."

He nodded. "I'll make it fast."

Zay's room was neat and smelled like soap. Warmth radiated from his bathroom, and she could tell from his damp hair that he'd just showered.

She sat on his bed. "You feeling okay?"

He came to kneel in front of her. "I wanted you to know that nothing happened with that girl last night. The one in the white dress."

Chapel looked at her hands. "Okay."

He shifted. "Did you and Luxe . . . did he . . . "

Heat crept up her neck. She was so glad she could answer honestly. "No." She raised her eyes to his. "But almost."

Zay's jaws clenched for a full ten seconds before he spoke again. "I don't think I'd like to know the details. Right now, at least."

"Okay," she said. It came out like a squeak. Then, "What's going on with us, Zay?"

He looked at her hands a full five seconds before picking one up in his. "I don't want to be broken up with you," he said. A crease formed between his eyebrows. "But I also don't want us to keep hurting each other, either."

With a finger, Chapel smoothed down the wrinkles in the center of his forehead "What are we going to do?"

"Well, I can't tell you what to do, but I can tell you what I want."

She nodded for him to continue. He stood up and sat beside her.

"I know I can do better. Here's where I'm going to start." Zay took out a phone that Chapel had never seen before. "I got this just for you and me. I give you my word, as long as I'm not in the middle of a fight to the death, I will answer your call or text as soon as humanly possible."

That made her smile a little. "What's the number?"

He nudged her. "Already stored it in your phone."

"On a guy less hot," she said, "that would be creepy."

He grinned at her widely. "You think I'm hot?"

She leaned against his shoulder. "Maybe."

Zay's arm came around her waist. "There's more," he said. "I told you once that I wasn't the hero in one of your books. I meant that. I'm not the perfect boyfriend, and I'm never going to be."

"I don't want you to be perfect," she mumbled.

"Yes, Chapel," he said softly. "You do."

The urge to be defensive blossomed in her chest, but she hesitated. He wasn't trying to be mean. He was just trying to talk to her. When she was quiet for a moment, he continued.

"I want to talk to you about the Jackson thing, but not right now. I'm too . . . " He shook his head. "I need to think about it a little more." His top lip spread thin in disgust. "I sound like such a girl. I need to go hit something or spit."

When he stood to get up, Chapel caught his wrist. He looked down at her.

"I've been thinking about it, too. And I wanted you to know something." She stood up. "You're not the same guy that you used to be." She pointed to his chest, where he had last night. "Something has changed inside of you. You are a *good* person. I wish you believed that about yourself."

He stared at her for a long time, the early morning sunlight pouring in sideways across his face. "Do you really think that?" he asked roughly.

She nodded. "Yes."

He pulled her up and leaned his forehead against hers. "No one has ever told me that before. No one has ever thought that I was good . . . " He placed his hand over hers, flattening them both across his chest. *"Here."*

Under her hand, his heart was racing.

"You looked so good last night," he said. "Tough. You flipped that table over and I thought, 'I am a complete mess over this girl.' And I was glad. Because I wasn't numb."

Chapel closed her eyes for a moment, savoring the feel of him against her. She wanted to kiss him so much and so hard, but she didn't. Physical attraction wasn't their issue, and they still had a lot to figure out.

"We can talk more after I get off work," she said. "Yes, the threat to my life is gone. For now. But the whole me-joining-Bellum thing is real. The situation with Timmy is real. The

255

amount of work you do is real. And as much as we'd like to ignore all of that, we just can't anymore."

They stayed that way for a long time, forehead to forehead, with her hand over his heart, sharing the same measured breaths for as long as she could stand it.

* * * *

Timmy was waiting for her in the parking lot when she got to school. His shirt had a pair of glasses on the front that looked a lot like his. The caption beneath said, *Talk Nerdy To Me.*

Chapel told her feet to walk at a normal pace, but she couldn't help it—when she saw him, she jogged to where he was slouched against his car, reading on his phone.

"How was—" He stopped talking when he saw her nose. "Who did you piss off?"

Chapel laughed awkwardly and touched the raised cut. She decided on a mild version of the truth. "I got up close and personal with a ladder."

Timmy touched his in the same place, as if he were trying to determine the corresponding location on his own nose. "It looks like it hurts."

"I think you just told me my face looks terrible."

That earned her a small smile that made her heart contract.

"Let's skip school," she said.

Timmy pressed his chin to his neck. "What? Are you serious?"

"As a heart attack."

"I don't know . . . I've got AP Chem and. . . . " He stopped, realizing she was giving him her best puppy-dog eyes and sad face. "You look so weird when you do that. Like a combination of you have to pee and maybe there's something in your eye."

She smacked his shoulder. "Is that a yes?"

He shook his head, but allowed her to pull him back down to the parking lot. They drove to Waffle House where they ate delicious grease and fat and talked about nothing that mattered.

It was medicine to her. It made her heart feel lighter. *How will I survive in this world without Timmy?* she wondered. Then she crammed that thought back down quickly. It was a question she had no answer for.

After breakfast, they decided on a walk around the square.

"What about you?" she asked him. "Did you have a good weekend?"

He made a face. "It was fine."

Chapel grabbed his arm. "Cool. Well, how about we try this again. Did you have a good weekend? And this time, no crap responses."

He leaned into her side. "God, I hate how much you know about me."

She leaned right back. "You don't have to tell me."

Timmy tugged at a tuft of his hair. "There was this girl. We had a lot of fun together, but she stopped answering my calls." He stopped walking and Chapel did, too. Her stomach was starting to feel sour. He was talking about Kacie, the girl she'd basically blackmailed into leaving Timmy alone.

"I don't know," he said with a shrug. "She was probably too pretty for me, anyway."

Chapel's eyebrows pulled down in the center. She took two hands and shoved Timmy hard. "Don't be an idiot."

He stumbled sideways, an embarrassed-sounding laugh bubbling up his throat. "Was that necessary?"

She yanked him by his sleeve back to her. "Yes," she said. "It was. You are awesome, Timothy Valentine. You're freaking hilarious. You're smart. No one can touch you on the Xbox."

She pointed a finger into his sternum. "And I've seen you without your shirt on recently, and I felt like I needed to look away because you looked man-ish—which is weird. And weirder for me to say, but I've already said it."

He was full on laughing at her, and she cracked up a little, too. Then they quieted, and she touched his arm.

"Don't say a girl is too pretty for you. That's impossible."

Timmy studied his scuffed sneakers before looking back at her. He cleared his throat twice. "Thanks for saying that, Chap."

And, like an idiot, her nose started burning and moisture filled the bottoms of her eyelids. She hooked an arm around him and pressed her face into his neck.

"I'm going to miss you," Timmy whispered, his breath burning in her ear. "After we graduate, it's never going to be like this again."

His words broke a dam inside her, and the tears started falling. She let them—let them slip down her face and into the crook of Timmy's shoulder. He hadn't held her like that since they were six or seven, and she was surprised by how strong he felt—how solid.

She kept her face hidden when she whispered, "I love you, Valentine. You know that, right?"

He nodded beside her face. "I know."

They stood in front of the courthouse, clinging to each other for a long time. When she finally pulled away, her mascara was a wreck and Timmy's eyes looked red.

She opened her mouth to make a joke about him looking high, when something in her periphery drew her attention: A shaved head, but a familiar build. She froze.

Hunter Carter? *No.* He wouldn't be stupid enough to be seen in the center of the town he had tormented.

But was he the stupid one? *No.* She reminded herself that she was the idiot who'd just left the protection of her secure school campus without telling anyone. And more than that, she'd brought Timmy with her.

Timmy who had no idea how much danger he was in.

"You okay?" he asked, sensing her tension. His big brown eyes widened. "Chap?"

Several things occurred to her at once.

One, not thinking about the future didn't mean the future would never come. She wasn't always going to be around to protect Timmy.

And, two, she was going to tell him everything. Because out of everyone in the entire world, she trusted him the most.

"Hold on," she murmured. She walked to the edge of the building where she thought she'd seen Hunter. No one was there.

"Timmy?" She turned back to him. "Can we go somewhere to talk?"

* * * *

They drove to The Ruins—the charred field on the edge of town where people went to make out—because she didn't know where else was safe.

She made him get out of his car while she told him, because she didn't want to mar its interior with this memory—the memory where everything he knew about her changed.

With his back against an old pine tree, Chapel told Timmy the truth. She talked for close to an hour, telling him every last detail.

He stopped her often at first—to ask her if she were serious, to demand that she wasn't being serious—but after a while, he quieted.

When she was finished, he stood immobile. "Show me," he said. And she knew why. Timmy was a man of science. Of proof.

Part of her was hurt that he didn't take her word for it, but she dismissed that as petty. She'd just told him she was basically the equivalent of a mutant.

"Okay." She sighed. "Get out your phone and look at the time."

Timmy did. Chapel took a deep breath, feeling the threads of Tempus outlining her body. Once she had used it, she ran to the other side of the field. Then she let it go.

It took her energy a moment to dissipate, but when she drew it back to herself, time resumed at normal speed with a snap.

"Timmy," she yelled. "Over here."

His eyes found hers and he jerked. He glanced down at his phone. No time had passed, and yet, Chapel was fifty yards away.

When she walked back to him, she could see that he was noticeably paler. His expression was wary. He hadn't believed her, she realized. But now he was afraid that he did.

"My nightmares," he said. "Those things really happened?"

She nodded. "I'm so sorry."

Timmy looked at her feet. He looked at the sky. He looked at the grass. He did not look at her.

"What makes *these people* think they have the right to play with somebody's mind?" he asked, voice fierce.

She did not fail to notice he had lumped her in to *these people.*

"I don't know."

He scowled. "Why didn't you tell me sooner? You let me think I was *losing* it, Chapel."

"I just wanted to keep you safe."

His jaw contracted. "What makes you think you know what's best for *me?* For anyone?"

"Timmy, I'm just doing the best I can." She moved toward him, but he moved back. "Why won't you look at me?"

"Because I don't even know *you!*" he shouted, his voice bouncing off the trees and sky. He took off his glasses and rubbed his shoulder across his face. "I don't even know you," he whispered.

Chapel's throat squeezed. He'd taken it so well when he had found out about her for the first time in Hunter's warehouse. She never expected him to react like *this*.

"Timmy, I'm still me." Panic made her feel sweaty. "And I'm telling you now. That has to count for something."

He gnawed on his bottom lip. He shook his head. "Do you have your phone?" he asked.

She pulled it from her pocket. "Yeah, why?"

He held up two hands. "Because I can't . . . I can't . . ." He starting walking toward his car. "You need to find someone to come get you, Chapel. I just . . . I can't."

She watched him get in his car and drive away.

Out of everything that had happened in her life, that moment was one of her worst.

＊ ＊ ＊ ＊

When Zay answered his phone, she was already choking on a sob.

"What happened?" he asked. "Chapel? What happened?"

"I'm okay. I just—" She wheezed. "I need you to come get me. I'm at The Ruins." She couldn't admit what she'd done over the phone, so she hung up.

Not long after, Zay drove up and got out of the Jeep before he'd barely had time to put it in park. She had only cried like this one other time in recent memory—the day after she'd found out she was Genex.

She'd needed him then, too.

He hugged her, letting her cry for a while before he leaned her away from him. "You're scaring me," he said quietly.

She sniffed and nodded. "I know. It's just—" Another sob jerked from her gut. "You're going to be so mad at me. And I'm scared what you might do about it."

He led her by the hand to the back of the Jeep where he opened the gate and pulled her beside him to sit on its edge.

He didn't ask her again, but she knew he was waiting. She looked up at him and swallowed. "I told Timmy."

He sucked in a heavy breath before he let it out. "Wow." He ran a hand down the side of his jaw. "I thought you and Luxe . . ."

Chapel grimaced. "He's really bothering you, isn't he?"

His dark eyebrows pushed to the center of his forehead. "That night—the night at Palace. I saw the possibility of Luxe's vision become real for the first time."

"What do you mean?"

"I mean, I could picture it—me, hating Jackson for letting Bellum get you. Our separation pushing you toward Luxe. And the combination of those two things . . . it would be enough," he said. "To make me want to be Rogue. To make want to do something crazy enough to get on the kill list."

"It would?"

"Yes. And I'm an idiot because you even have to ask that." Zay pulled both lips in his mouth. "All this time I've been telling myself my attitude toward work and toward Jackson was about *honor*. About doing what was *right*. But now . . ." He shook his head. "Now I think it may have been about me. And not trusting myself to make the right decisions on my own."

"Yeah?"

"Yeah." Zay sighed. "I've been thinking about the Bible today."

That made her mouth pop open. "Uh. What?"

"About the lesson I taught on Sunday. It was about David. And Bathsheba."

"Yikes. That one was probably a little tricky to tell to a room full of first graders."

"Yeah. You may get a few strongly-worded emails from parents." Zay pushed his thumb and forefinger into his eyes. "Katie Monroe had a lot of questions about how David and Bathsheba met."

She leaned her head onto his shoulder. He laid his arm across her back, resting his hand on her hip. "That's funny."

His mouth pressed into her hair, and she closed her eyes, waiting on him to continue.

"David slept with a married woman, got her pregnant, and then basically had her husband killed. And yet . . . " Zay's head shook. "God said that David was a man after his own heart. God still saw goodness inside of him. Even after all he'd done."

Chapel moved so she could look at his face. There was boyish wonder there. He was so handsome.

"And?" she prompted.

"And then today, you told me that *I* was good. And I wanted to reject it right away." He put his hand on his chest. "Because I have this past that I can't forget. I won't let myself forget, because I'm afraid if I do, I'll repeat it. But last night I saw you and I knew that I could never be that guy again. Because how I feel about you has changed me."

He paused and she kissed his cheek gently.

"So, I started thinking," he said. "I started thinking, what if I *am* like David? What if my goodness isn't based on the worst thing I ever did?"

Chapel touched the scar on his lip with the tips of her fingers. "People, we—we're all capable of good and bad things. That's what makes us human." She studied his eyes, trying to slow down her speech, wanting him to understand. "But choosing the good thing, especially after you've chosen a bad thing? *That's* what makes a person exceptional. Not a chromosome. Not an ability."

He leaned his forehead against hers. His eyes were shut so tightly she couldn't see his eyelids. "You make me believe

I can trust myself," he said roughly. "You make me *feel* good."

She put two hands on his cheeks, rough from days on the field chasing her attackers. "I didn't change you," she whispered. "I just helped you see what was there all along."

His mouth opened over hers slowly and held, hovering, connecting at all points. She sighed and he brought his hand to the back of her head, crushing the space between them.

When he pulled away, she tugged at his shirt for more. She felt his smile on her lips, and after a few more moments, finally let him pull away.

"What did I do to earn *that?*" he asked.

She kissed him again, not gently. "When you talk Old Testament, the good girl in me gets . . . bad."

He laughed softly. "I need to call Mikey for some tips, then. He knows this books of the Bible song that I think you'd enjoy."

At the sound of Timmy's brother's name, Chapel's chest deflated. "Timmy." She smacked her forehead into her hand. "I shouldn't have told him."

Zay tilted his eyes back to hers. They looked bluer than normal. "Talk to me about Timmy. Why did you tell him?"

"Because he deserves to know that his life is in danger," she said simply. "I may not be around forever to protect him, and he needs to know to be careful. And, most of all, I trust him."

Zay filled his cheeks with air. "How did he take it?"

"Terribly. He said he doesn't know me anymore." She fisted her hands, remembering his words. "I don't get it. He took it so well at Hunter's warehouse. He was *laughing.*"

Zay leaned forward on the palms of his hands. "They probably gave him something. A narcotic to calm him down."

That, she thought, *would have been helpful to know.*

"What happens now?" She was afraid to ask.

"Can I think about this?" he asked. "About what the best thing to do is?"

She nodded. "I'll think about it, too. And before either of us does anything, let's talk about it first."

Zay put his hand over hers, tangling their fingers into knots. "We'll make the decision together," he said.

Warmth splashed over her face and chest, the first relief she'd known for days. "Yes," she repeated. "Together."

CHAPTER TWENTY-SIX

Chapel went to school the next day and immediately looked for Timmy's car in the parking lot. It wasn't there.

She had texted him several times last night, but he wouldn't answer. Finally, she'd called the house phone. Mrs. Valentine had gone to get him, but then returned sounding flustered.

"He's not, um . . ." Chapel could imagine Mrs. Valentine tugging the ends of her copper curls just like Timmy. "He's not available right now, Chapel. I'm so sorry."

Timmy was screening her calls.

She went through the school day feeling agitated. Then, agitation digressed into mild rage when Chapel got stuck in traffic—traffic when she only had to drive half a mile—on her way to Back Porch.

She stopped her car beside a police officer waving traffic flow around the square instead of straight through it.

"What's going on?" she asked.

The kid looked no older than she did. He adjusted his sunglasses, smacking his gum between his jaws as if it were steak. "Rotary Club. Fundraiser set up. Main Street closed."

Chapel's fingers squeezed her steering wheel until she thought she might dislodge it from its base. "I need to get to Back Porch," said. "For work."

And maybe the guy felt sorry for her, or maybe he imagined that steering wheel could be his neck shortly, because he moved two cones to the side and allowed her through.

The place was a madhouse. After the long winter, spring had finally warmed Bennett Park, and the natives were in full celebration mode. Rotary Club members in all their navy and white filled up almost every table.

And just to top off the horrendousness of the day, Gabe kept giving her pointed looks every time she entered the kitchen.

Ugh. She had forgotten, in the emotional haze of her reunion with Zay, that she had come down with a case of severe attraction to Gabriel Luxe. And that frustrated her.

When Chapel had gotten a particularly perky woman's order wrong, she slammed her tray onto the counter, making the incorrectly cooked hamburger flap open.

"Dang, Steel," Erica said, slinging her hand on her hip. "What did that tray ever do to you?"

Gabe's eyes met hers across the room. She hadn't spoken to him since he'd told her he had wanted to kiss her. Kiss her *too*, he had said.

She wanted to stick out her tongue. She wanted to give him the middle finger. She wanted to tell him that *of course* she hadn't wanted to kiss him.

But that was a lie.

She loved Zay. But Gabe had entered her heart on some level. A level she wanted to extract him from immediately.

"I am a little angry," she allowed, not breaking eye contact with Gabe. "But not at the tray. With men. All of them."

Erica squealed. "I love it when you get all angry and riled up. You can be a real B, you know. When you want to be."

Chapel looked at her. "You said that like it was a compliment."

Erica's squinted. "Um. That's because it was."

Chapel glanced back to Gabe. "I need another one of these," she said, holding up the burger. "Only, no cheese."

Erica slid up on the counter beside her. "What's up?"

She had finally fixed her hair. It was blonde now—just a few shades lighter than Chapel's. It looked good.

Chapel waved a hand in the air. "You know. Stuff. Life."

Erica nodded. "I know what you need."

"What?"

"You need a plan." Erica slid down. "I've seen this look in your eye before. You're all scattered and frustrated. Like that time I accidently lost our schedule at cheerleading camp. Girls like you need a plan."

Huh. Chapel considered that. She *had* been sitting back and allowing everything to just *happen* to her. She had been reactive, not proactive.

What she hadn't done was mapped out what she could do. What she could control.

"Oh my gosh." Chapel looked at her best friend's wide, hazel eyes. "I think you're right."

"Duh." Erica headed to the back door.

"Where are you going?"

"To get that letter from UGA," she said over her shoulder. "We all know you haven't opened it yet."

Chapel felt her lips pull into a smile. Oh, Jersey. *I'm going to miss her.*

"You're going to miss her," Gabe said. She looked up. He was staring at her. And, apparently, reading her mind.

"Yes."

"You wouldn't have to," he said quietly. "If things were different. If you had more choices."

Something clicked into place at his words. Something she had known, or suspected, but had never said out loud. But she knew it. She knew it like she knew her own name.

"Gabe," she said, "you're a Unifist."

His response was drowned out by the most horrific noise Chapel had ever heard in her entire life.

A scream.

Three loud pops.

Then a deafening silence.

Erica.

Chapel sprinted for the back door, pushing through it and rounding into the parking lot.

"Oh God, no. Oh, God."

The door to her car was open. Erica's legs hung out the bottom. They weren't moving. She wasn't moving.

I've seen this, she thought. Then her vision tunneled. Black dots crowded out all other colors, replacing the scene before her with fuzzy snapshots from her memory.

The dream. This was the dream she'd been having. Erica being shot. Erica dying.

"No," she whispered. Then she yelled, *"No!"*

She moved to run, but two arms pulled her back. "Wait a minute, just wait." It was Gabe. "They could still be out here."

Chapel's body had memorized the moves and she reacted without thinking.

"Bring the heel of your shoe on their instep."

She did.

"Swing your hips to the side," Zay said. *"Those lovely hips."*

She did.

"At the same time, draw your hand back, find that money spot, and run."

She did.

"Erica!" Her voice cracked into the eerie silence. *"Erica!"*

She stumbled to the open car door. A strangled sound choked through her when she saw her best friend's lifeless form.

Erica's body was splayed across the center console, blood already soaking through the back of her hot pink shirt.

"Chapel?" Thomas's voice came from the back door. "Is everything okay?"

"No," she sobbed. "Call nine-one-one-one. Erica's been—"

Gabe came to stand beside her. She was vaguely aware of a shrill scream and of high-pitched voices over her shoulder.

"Should we move her?" Chapel asked. "Should we—"

But Gabe was on the phone. "We need an ambulance. And fast. She's . . . she may not have much longer."

Erica made a gurgling sound and anguish bit Chapel in two.

They meant to shoot me. The blonde hair. *They meant to shoot me.* Leaning over in her car. *They meant to shoot me.*

Chapel reached in her apron.

"Hey, Sweet Girl." Zay's voice was warm. But Chapel was cold. She was cold all over.

"Zay, Erica's been shot behind Back Porch. There's a lot of blood. Where are you, and where is Justin?"

Zay paused, probably interpreting the flood of words and information.

"I'm home. I was about to leave to come pick you up for training."

"And Justin?"

"He's here, too. I just passed him in the hall. What's your plan?"

"Can you get him here? If I can Tempus, can you get him here so he can make Erica stop bleeding?"

"Stand back," Gabe was shouting behind her. "Everyone stand back."

There was another long pause. They hadn't practiced a great deal of Tempus-related missions together. It hit her then that Jackson had never encouraged it, and that there must be a reason for that.

Jackson had been always more concerned with how long she could maintain the episode, and not how far it reached, or what it affected.

"I'll drive as far as I can," he said. "Then I'll have to carry him the rest of the way. *Chon!*" he yelled. "Chon, where are you?" There was a muffled response in the background. Zay's voice came back clearer. "Do you remember the night I helped you move that car so Timmy wouldn't wreck? Do you remember that night?"

"Yes."

"Tempus doesn't affect me like it does everyone else, but it *does* affect me. The longer you hold it, the harder it is for me to move. That's why I didn't help you push that car. I could barely stand up."

"Make your point, Zay."

"My point is that it could take me a while to get there. And even if you managed to hold Tempus that long, Justin may not be able to save her."

She saw the casket. The black lid closing. Smelled the freshly dug Georgia clay.

Gabe was leaning over Erica now, and he glanced back at Chapel. His tan had vanished. In its place was a stricken-looking ash. He shook his head slightly.

"Then I will die trying," Chapel said.

She closed her eyes and pushed her energy out. It rushed through her body and burst out her pores with such a violent force that it threw her backward onto the cement.

She caught herself on her palms and struggled to stand. She needed to get to the other side of the car. She needed to do *something* while she waited.

Running inside Back Porch, Chapel felt no burn in her thighs or ache in her lungs. She moved without realizing she was moving.

She had to shimmy by Thomas, who was just hanging up the phone in the office. She grabbed the first aid kit and a few other supplies, then ran back to the car and opened the other car door.

Gabe had taken his shirt off and was pressing it against Erica's back. When Chapel pushed the fabric aside, she whimpered. There was already so much blood.

She used the scissors to carefully cut away Erica's soiled shirt. She gritted her teeth and pulled it back. There were two holes there, just beneath Erica's left shoulder blade. They looked purpled around the edges, and oozed with blood.

Chapel stared at the two wounds for several horrific presses of her own heart. The blood that was on Erica's back was old blood. She was no longer actively bleeding.

"Your energy," Rush had told her, *"it has a paralytic effect on everything around you that has energy or potential energy. Time hasn't stopped, it's just slowed down to an almost indiscernible pace."*

Chapel took the alcohol pads out of the first aid kit and pressed two squares directly to Erica's wounds.

The linens truck had just brought a sealed bundle of freshly sanitized napkins and towels that morning. Chapel used her teeth to break open the plastic and dropped the first one directly on Erica's back. She held it there with both trembling hands, pressing down.

Though she couldn't hear her, Chapel leaned her lips to Erica's ear. "I love you," she said. "You are my best friend. You are beautiful. You are funny. I love you. I love you."

Her throat constricted with each uttered syllable. She stopped talking. She was afraid that she would stop being able to control Tempus if she started to sob. So instead of talking, instead of sobbing, Chapel decided to count.

She reached one thousand and started over again.

One, two, three.

Erica's smile.

Four, five, six.

The sound of her laugh.

Seven, eight, nine.

How she never smoked with Chapel in the car.

Ten, eleven, twelve.

How mean she was to Logan after he started dating Brandy.

Thirteen, fourteen, fifteen.

She remembered hundreds of small things about her best friend and reached one thousand for the third time before she heard any noises but the sound of her own unsteady breathing.

Seven hundred fifty-six.

"Chap?"

Seven hundred fifty-seven.

"*Chapel!*"

She sat up and looked over her shoulder. Zay was walking up Main Street with Justin resting on the top of his shoulders. Well. Walking wasn't exactly the right word. Zay was trudging, slowly, clumsily. His damp T-shirt clung to his body as he dug his chin into his chest and barely lifted his legs to take the next step.

"Zay," she yelled at him, not willing to leave Erica. "I'm going to let it go."

As she said the word *go*, Chapel imagined her body like a sponge, soaking, sucking, sopping up every scrap of energy around her.

Noise exploded inside her head. Shouts, wind, an ambulance, Gabe's voice.

"Chapel?" he was saying. "Chapel?"

Her head swiveled from one side to the other. "No," she heard her voice say. "Stay awake."

She imagined her consciousness as if it were a rope. And she gripped it with both arms, tugging it back her direction. She gagged and let herself throw up in the floorboard, but she did not pass out.

"Move." Justin's voice came from behind her. He was pulling on a pair of Latex gloves when Chapel shuffled out of the way. Gabe came around and picked her up.

"Take me," she managed, and he understood. He half-supported, half-carried her to the other side of the car so Chapel could see. "Keep the people away."

Zay appeared behind Justin and his eyes met hers. They were strained and tired, and sweat slipped down his upper lip and neck.

"Thank you," she mouthed, and he shook his head. She knew what he was thinking. *You don't have to thank me.*

Chapel's focus moved to Justin, and the way his hands applied pressure directly over the wounds, pushing and creating an airtight seal.

His lips moved, but no words came out. At the same time, Chapel prayed out loud. "Please, God. God, please. Please, please, please."

An ambulance screamed closer in the background.

Chapel stared at Justin's lips. They moved faster. And faster. And faster and faster and faster until they weren't moving anymore.

He sucked in a breath, his Adam's apple rising up, then down. His eyelids fluttered like a hummingbird's wings. He gasped again and then his eyes were open.

They were bloodshot.

Chapel took three excruciating breaths before he spoke.

"I did what I can," he said. "But I'm not sure it will be enough."

Then two hands were drawing her back and a woman in a uniform was bending over Erica's lifeless body and Zay's face hovered over hers and she was choking on the fact that she knew to be true.

Erica was going to die.

CHAPTER TWENTY-SEVEN

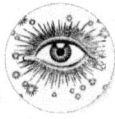

The ride to the hospital was long and tense. They'd taken Erica to a nearby hospital where they had assessed her injuries before having her life-flighted to Emory University in Atlanta.

Since Chapel had had to stay behind and answer questions from the police, she and Zay didn't leave until Erica was already in the air.

"It's a good thing they moved her," Zay told her as he drove. "It means they think she's stable enough to make the trip."

Chapel didn't say anything. She sat in the passenger seat and gripped her purse to her chest as if it might be enough to keep Erica's rising and falling.

Once they got to Emory, it was hard to get any information. Erica's parents and older sister were back with the doctors, and no one would let Chapel pass.

That was when she had broken down. When the nurse had put a sympathetic hand on her shoulder and said, "I'm sorry. We can't disclose her status to anyone who isn't family."

Something animalistic chased through her at those words, and Chapel slung the lady's arm off her shoulder as if it were a snake.

"You don't know me!" she yelled, drawing startled gazes in the crowded waiting room. Then she choked and whispered, "She is my family."

Zay had wrapped his arms around her from behind and held her tightly. She turned and let her emotions loose, burying her face in his neck and sobbing.

Zay held her still. And the feel of his steady heartbeat was the only thing keeping her tethered to the present.

She felt him nudge her and she turned around. The elevator doors had just opened and Timmy stepped out. He looked lost.

Chapel walked toward him and didn't question anything as she threw herself at him. His hands came around her shoulders and he squeezed her tightly. He squeezed her like she might disappear. Just like Erica might.

"I'm so sorry," she cried into his neck. "This is all my fault. This is all my fault."

He didn't respond at first, but then his hand came to the back of her head. His chest jerked and he put his face by her ear. "I'm still mad at you," he said, "I am so *freaking* pissed off at you. And I don't know what to think about it. I don't know what to think. But that doesn't matter right now."

She couldn't speak, so she just nodded. The elevator opened again and Logan Breeze appeared behind Timmy. His eyes were wide and red-rimmed.

"Is she—?"

Chapel shook her head. "She's in surgery. She's still—. She's still here."

Logan's face twisted and he walked over and Chapel shifted to the side. He put a hand on Timmy's shoulder and wrapped his other arm around Chapel's waist.

They stood there, in the threshold of the dingy waiting room that smelled like urine and bleach, leaning into each other in ways they always had.

Chapel didn't know how much time had passed when a hand touched her back. She spun around. It was Erica's sister. Her face was puffy and red and Chapel wanted to cut herself wide open because it was all her fault.

"How is she?" Chapel managed.

Zay materialized and he reached down to grip her hand.

Annalisa Monroe pressed a tissue to her lips and closed her eyes. Two tears escaped their tight crevices.

"She is . . . " She cleared her throat and shook her head. "She is out of surgery." Annalissa opened her eyes. "She is stable. They—. They said that she is going to make it."

Chapel fell to her knees. She fell to her knees and she didn't care that she looked like a fool because God had answered her prayers.

Thank you, thank you, she prayed. *I will make this up to You. I will fix all of this. Thank you.*

Zay helped her to her feet and Annalissa hugged her hard.

"You saved her life," she said, and it came out muffled with emotion. "I don't know how you did it. The paramedics said the wounds had been cleaned out and that first aid had been administered perfectly. They said the risk for infection was very small because of that. And that the blood loss should have been so much worse." She pulled away, and her smile pushed crinkles beside her eyes—so much like Erica's. "It's a miracle."

"Can I see her?" Chapel asked.

Annalissa shook her head. "Not now. She's being moved to ICU for recovery, and they only allow two people at a time. Mom and Dad are with her."

Chapel's disappointment must have shown, because Annalissa squeezed her shoulders. "Come back tomorrow morning," she said. "First thing. If she's still good, I'll make Mom and Dad go home and rest. I don't think any of us can stand to leave her until then."

It felt so wrong to leave the hospital, but Chapel knew there was nothing she could do while she was there. She walked Logan and Timmy outside where she explained to them what had happened.

"This is crazy," Logan muttered. "A shooting? In *Bennett Park?* I don't get it."

Chapel met Timmy's eyes awkwardly. Neither of them responded.

"Anyway," Logan scratched behind his ear. "I'm going to head out. What time are y'all coming back tomorrow?"

They made plans to meet up the next day and said goodbye.

Zay pulled the Jeep around and Chapel turned to Timmy. "I'm not going home," she said. "I'm going to get a hotel room so I can be close. I think you should come. I think we should talk."

He took off his glasses and rubbed his eyes. "Yeah," he said. "Yeah, okay. Text me the info. I need to call my mom and I'll be right there."

* * * *

They checked into a room just a block from the hospital. When she'd told Zay that she wanted to tell Timmy everything about Erica's attack, he had only hesitated a moment.

"It exposes Chon," he said. "That's the part I don't like about it. But if you trust Timmy, I trust Timmy. I'd just like to be there. So I can troubleshoot any potential problems."

She nodded. It was so much better than fighting with him. "Okay."

Timmy found their room just minutes after they did. He tugged the tips of his hair as he sat on one of the beds. Chapel slid on top of the dresser, and Zay propped himself against the door.

Chapel launched into the unedited version of the afternoon's events, sparing no detail. Timmy listened quietly, without interruption. His eyes kept sliding over to Zay.

"You can ask me," Zay said.

Timmy swallowed. A crinkle appeared between his eyes. "How does it work? Your . . . thing?"

"My exception, right?" Zay touched the side of his head. "Well, everyone emits a certain energy. And everyone's energies are different. My mind picks up on these differences and translates their frequencies into a code."

"Is that how you found Chapel? Is that why y'all live next door to her?"

Zay shifted against the wall. "That's not why I wanted to live beside her, no. But I think it'd be ignorant of me to think that Jackson did not know about her beforehand."

Chapel hadn't thought of that. She wondered what else Zay had been thinking about Jackson, now that his confidence in him was cracked at its foundation.

Timmy groaned. "This is so messed up." He stood up and started pacing at the end of the bed. "It's so hard to believe. If you hadn't proved it, I wouldn't. But you did, and the dreams, and now Erica. This is so messed up," he repeated.

"I'm sorry Timmy," she said again. Her throat was raw. "I am so sorry."

Zay's fingers tapped along the tops of his thighs. He cleared his throat. "I think you've apologized enough, Chapel. Don't you, Valentine?"

Timmy's mouth came open a little, and it looked like he swallowed back his first response.

"If you had seen the way she has tortured herself," Zay said to him. "You wouldn't be acting so selfishly right now."

She didn't say anything. She *was* sorry, but Zay was right. She had done the best she could. She had done what she thought was best for Timmy.

A bright red hue blossomed on Timmy's cheeks. He sat back down on the bed. He lifted conflicted eyes to Chapel. "You tortured yourself."

"I broke up with Zay," she whispered. "Because of it."

The red crept from Timmy's cheeks to his ears. He stared at the floor. "I'm sorry," he mumbled. "I wasn't thinking about . . ."

Chapel slid from the dresser and stopped just shy of his feet. "None of this is easy. And I don't expect you to just shrug and accept it without question. But—"

He looked up at her, waiting.

"But I need you." The words were out of her throat right before it squeezed together. "I need you, Timmy."

His jaw moved forward and his eyes grew clouded behind his glasses. "I'm here, aren't I?" He still didn't meet her eye. No, he hadn't forgiven her yet. But maybe he was closer.

She moved back to the dresser and looked at Zay. "Has the team found anything yet?"

Rush and Marielle had come to pick up Justin at the hospital to chase down any leads on the gunman. Neither she nor Gabe had seen anyone, and there hadn't been any eyewitnesses the last Chapel had heard.

Zay untucked his phone from a pocket and checked the screen. He grimaced. "Nothing yet."

Timmy stood. "I can't just sit here and wait," he said. "I'm going to go home and hack into some traffic cameras."

Chapel wanted to tell him not to do something dangerous or anything that could get him into trouble, but she bit it back. He was a part of this world now. Just like Kacie had said he would be. He had a role to play, too.

"Be smart," she said.

When he was gone, Zay came and stood between her knees. He kissed her on the forehead.

"You hungry?" he asked.

"Not really. You?"

"No. Not really." He pulled back. "But we should both eat. Tomorrow could be a long day."

"Can we get room service, then? I don't want you to go."

Zay ran a hand down the length of her ponytail, pulling out her hair tie and massaging her achy skull. "I'm not going anywhere, babe. I promise."

She hummed and he kissed her temple.

"Why don't you take a shower while I call?" he said.

Chapel looked at her hands. They were dirtied with streaks of Erica's blood.

"Okay." She pulled at her stained shirt. "I just wish I had something clean to change into."

Zay's forehead puckered as he stepped back. He unbuttoned his flannel shirt, then handed it to her. He wore a thin gray T-shirt underneath. The curve of his Thanatos tattoo reached out from its center V.

"I tied it around my waist when I was carrying Justin, so I've barely worn it today."

Chapel took it and stood.

"One more thing." Zay handed her a gun. Gabe's gun. "Keep this with you at all times. Just in case."

She showered quickly, scrubbing at her hands and face until the skin felt angry beneath her nails. She dried off and raked her hair to the side and put it in a thick braid.

With Zay's shirt skimming her mid-thigh, she opened the bathroom door. Zay was laying on one of the beds with his head propped back against the wall.

She thought he might be sleeping until she got closer. His eyes fell open and she felt his gaze brush her body before it moved to her face.

"Feel better?" he asked.

"Much."

The food service arrived and they set up a picnic at the small table on the edge of the room.

"It looks like you ordered one of everything," she told him.

Zay shrugged. "I wanted you to have options."

That reminded her of something. "Zay, I forgot to tell you this earlier. I think that Gabe might be . . . I *know* that Gabe is a Unifist."

Zay's expression did not register surprise. "I was afraid of that," he said.

"What happened to Cecily?"

Now *that* did surprise Zay. "He told you about her?"

"No. Sort of. He didn't really want to talk about her."

Zay toyed with his fork, studying her for a few seconds longer than normal. "She was killed," he said finally. "Accidently. Two years ago. There was an altercation between a Bellum recruit and a Thanatos recruiter. Things got out of hand, and she . . . she didn't make it."

"So that's why," Chapel said. "He wants neither faction to have me. He wants me to be a Unifist, too."

She can change things. That was what he had said to Chary.

Zay pushed his tongue into the side of his mouth. "If you've figured this out," he said, "what if Bellum has, too? What if they think *you're* a Unifist? What if *they're* the ones trying to kill you, and not Hunter Carter?"

It made sense. Jackson had referred to her once as a loaded gun, and Justin had called her a sword. In the wrong hands, she could be dangerous.

They finished eating and Zay pushed the room service trays into the hallway. When he came back inside, he motioned to her.

"Come on. Let's get you in bed."

She stood and walked to one of the double beds and peeled back the comforter and sheets.

Zay picked up the remote and found a show about home renovation that she loved.

"Mind if I grab a quick shower?" he asked, not looking at her.

She studied his body language. His fingers punched the volume up then down, up then down, up then down. Was he nervous to be in a hotel room alone with her?

"Of course not," she said.

He placed the gun on the side table. "I won't be long."

Chapel tried to keep her eyes open, but the day's events combined with her extended use of Tempus had her eyelids feeling heavy and thick.

Sleep came with a blistering darkness, and she dreamed of nothing but blood, and screams, and hospital beds.

CHAPTER TWENTY-EIGHT

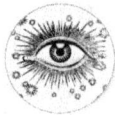

Some time just before daybreak, her eyelids fluttered open. There was a movement at the edge of the bed, and Chapel looked down to find Zay on his knees, whispering.

She watched his lips move silently, the silver scar at the edge of his mouth dancing like a feather floating in air.

He stayed that way for several minutes, and she indulged to observe him. Then, without warning, his eyes blinked open. He looked right at her.

"Hey," she said.

"Hi."

"What were you doing?"

Zay came and sat beside her. He touched her cheek. "I was praying."

Chapel pushed herself into a sitting position, bringing them forehead to forehead. The light filtering through the window cast lavender shadows on the thick white comforter. He traced their square patterns with his finger.

"What were you praying about?" she asked.

"You."

"Me?" She placed a hand on top of his, stilling his anxious motions.

"Do you believe in destiny, Chapel?" he whispered.

Her head felt a little too foggy for a conversation this serious, but she squinted and tried to concentrate. "I believe God has a plan for our lives, yes."

"I didn't," Zay said. "Not really. I've seen too much. Or, maybe I haven't seen enough."

He looked at her, his expression a mirror of the night he'd first kissed her: somber and soft and heartbreakingly handsome.

"But then there's you. And everything that's led up to me finding you. And I know it makes me a terrible human being, but I am *so glad* it wasn't you that was shot. Because we wouldn't have been able to save you like we saved Erica. And you would be *dead.*"

She leaned toward him and pressed her lips to his scar. His skin felt cold to her feverish mouth.

"What are you saying?" she murmured.

Zay took her face in his hands. "Ever since I joined Jackson's team, I've been waiting to be Field Team—waiting on the heroic part of my life to start. I've been restless to do something *great*. Something that made me feel *worthy.*"

His breath caught and Chapel shakily sucked in some air of her own.

"But I think I've realized that . . . " He touched his nose to hers. "That *that* part of my life has already started. And it started when I met *you.*"

"Zay, I—"

"No, no, no. Let me finish. I should have told you this sooner."

"Tell me what?"

He looked up at her, silver eyes warm and wide with wonder. "Chapel, I think I was put on this Earth to protect

284

you. That maybe that's the greatest thing I'll do with my life. Protect you. Protect you and *love you*. Because I love you." He kissed her gently. "I love you, Chapel Ryan. And this whole time I've been thinking that you're the girl I want to rescue at the end of my story. But that's not it at all. You *are* my story."

Chapel never thought she'd see Zay cry. And he wasn't crying now, but his eyes were shining and his lips trembled against hers.

A heady glee yawned its way through her, making her smile against his mouth. She leaned away from him because she wanted to be sure he heard her clearly.

"I love you, too, Zay."

His breath slipped quietly from his lungs, tickling her face. "You love me?"

She nodded. "So much. Too much. Your voice?" She closed her eyes. "Your face. It's all I hear. It's all I see."

Warm lips pressed over hers. Slow at first, a physical manifestation of the words just spoken. Usually, she let her mind shut off when Zay kissed her, but this time the noise wouldn't go away.

She should be *dead.* Erica should be dead. But neither of them was. And Zay's talk of destiny had woken up a part of her that had been sleeping.

Thanatos had a plan for her. Bellum had a plan for her. The Unifists likely had a plan for her. But all those dimmed to irrelevancy in the shadows of what *God* had planned for her.

She didn't know what it was, but she would fight to the death for it. Because Zay was right—the fact that she had Tempus, the fact that they had found each other—their abilities the perfect compliment, the fact that she was alive?

This was her destiny.

She must have deepened the kiss with Zay at that thought, because he made a happy noise with his throat and dug his fingers into the back of her head.

Her hands reached to his shoulders and pulled him back with her against the pillows. He pressed his knees into the mattress and it dipped as he lay beside her, still dressed in jeans and his shirt.

He flattened his hand against her stomach. "I like this. You in my clothes."

Her head had no idea what to do, but her body seemed to understand its own needs anyway. Her fingers brushed against the skin of his stomach. He was warm again. She fumbled with the hem of his shirt, pushing it up. She needed to *see* it. The tattoo. The way his body was marked with death.

Zay moved his hand from her leg to the back of his collar, pulling the thin material from between them.

"Thank you," she whispered, and his stomach contracted with a quiet laugh.

She dipped her mouth to the black edges of the theta and kissed him.

The dark nature of Zay would always be there—just like it would always be in her nature to resist love. But together, they could find reasons to choose good.

"I love this part of you," she whispered.

Then they lay facing each other, watching the sun spill its brand new light across their strong bodies.

* * * *

A loud bang on the hotel door jerked her awake. They must have fallen asleep again.

Chapel looked at the clock beside the bed—it wasn't even eight o'clock. She still had an hour before she needed to meet Timmy and Logan.

"Peaches? Zay?" Rush's voice echoed inside their room. "Rise and freaking shine!"

"Quit yelling," Marielle hissed. "Have some decency."

Rush snorted. *"Decency?* Marielle. Do you know what that word even means?"

Justin's cough sounded uncomfortable.

Zay groaned. "If we ignore them," he murmured, "do you think it'll stop?"

Chapel moved to get up, but Zay's arm tightened around her waist. She turned and looked down at him.

His light eyes were alert and wide. She wondered if he'd fallen back asleep at all. "You're beautiful. You know that?"

She slipped back down beside him, running a hand down the edge of his jaw, just like he did when he got frustrated or nervous.

He leaned his forehead to hers. "This is the part where you tell me I'm beautiful, too," he said. "Then you get embarrassed, because you don't mean *beautiful* like a girl. You mean devastatingly handsome. Like, *beyond compare* handsome."

Chapel smiled. "Well, obviously I'm not kicking you out of bed."

Another round of pounds assailed the door. "I'm about to kick this thing in," Rush said in a singsong voice. "And I would say *get your clothes on*, but we all know the two of you are—"

Chapel swung open the door. Rush turned around and his eyes immediately dropped to the edge of Zay's shirt along her bare thighs.

Marielle's mouth fell open. Justin's eyebrows twitched. Rush just stared.

Zay came behind her, wrapping the comforter around her.

"You were saying, Dr. Suave?" she asked.

Rush's mouth formed a hesitant smile, and Chapel laughed out loud.

"I never thought I'd see the day," Zay said. "I think Rush is speechless."

"There *is* a God," Marielle moaned.

Chapel gripped the blanket around her shoulders and took a step toward Justin. "I'm going to hug you now," she said. She figured he was probably the kind of guy who needed a warning. "Thank you," she said. "You saved her. Erica would be . . . *dead* if it weren't for you."

When she stepped back, the tips of Justin's ears were pink. "It was a team effort," he mumbled.

"Yeah," Rush said from behind her. "Ain't no 'I' in team, Peaches, so spread the love."

She punched him in the kidney on her way back into the room. "Love ya, Rush. Mean it."

Chapel went into the bathroom to change into clean clothes—a pair of jeans and gray T-shirt. Apparently, Zay had texted Marielle at some point and asked her to bring them something clean to wear.

Before she went back into the room, she called Annalissa and checked on Erica. The night brought no changes, but the doctors had announced they'd take Erica off her ventilator at noon, then begin ebbing off her medication.

Erica should be awake by that night.

When Chapel came out, she found that Timmy had joined the group. He had unfolded a laptop on the table. He looked up when she opened the door.

"Hey," she said to him. Her fingers worked her hair into a thick braid. "What are you doing here?"

He motioned to his computer. "I think I found something."

She looked at him more closely. His hair was flat against his head and he had the same shirt on as yesterday. She caught Marielle eyeing it suspiciously. It said *Adorakable* across the front in large blue letters.

"Did you sleep last night?" Chapel asked him.

"Yes, Mother," he said, focusing on the computer. "For an hour or so."

"What did you find?" Zay asked.

They all gathered around as Timmy opened several files. "I hacked into the traffic cameras in the area to see if there was something the police missed."

"Was there?"

Timmy shook his head. He snapped his fingers while the blue download bar moved across the screen. "Not that I saw. But then I remembered that yesterday they were setting up for something on the square. The Rotary Club."

"That's right," Zay said. "I saw some of them standing around after the ambulance left."

Several windows finally opened at once and Timmy blew out a gust of air. "Freaking *finally*." He pointed to them. "I went on Twitter and Instagram last night and I searched the fundraiser's hashtag. There were thirty-six hits, so I took screenshots of them all. "

He dragged the images into the photo application and clicked on the View As Slideshow option.

"We know the gunman had to be on foot," he said. "That means he had to walk right through their set up to get behind Back Porch."

"Valentine," Zay said. "You're a genius."

"Yes." Timmy nodded. "Literally."

"They're all wearing navy," Marielle said, leaning closer. "Creepy."

"Yes," Chapel said. "But good for us. Anyone not wearing navy will stand out."

Most of the shots were from the same woman—@BPRotaryQueen—a very busty blonde who took an insane amount of selfies.

"Come to Papa," Rush murmured, and Zay flicked the back of his ear.

"Stop right there." Chapel pointed to Rotary Queen's shot of a centerpiece. In the background was a partial view of a man's back and hand.

Zay hunkered down beside her. "He's got on a jacket. It was seventy degrees yesterday."

Rush pointed to his back. "Dude's packing, for sure. Look at that bulge."

They clicked through the rest of the photos, but there was no other shot of a man in a dark jacket.

"Go back to it," Zay said quietly. Chapel knew by his tone that he was thinking about something—turning a thought over in his mind. "There." He touched the image at the man's wrist. "It looks like a tattoo. Can you enhance it?"

Timmy made a scoffing sound and opened a photo-editing suite. He pulled the image inside it and clicked around for a bit.

"It looks like an oval," Timmy said. "With something in the middle."

Chapel's gut clenched as she made eye contact with Zay. That sounded very similar to the description of the tattoo that he had over his heart.

"Let me just insta-alpha this," Timmy muttered. He clicked his mouse, dragged it across the image, then stood back.

What Chapel saw stole the strength from her knees. She would have fallen, but Timmy's hand came up and caught her by the elbow. Their gazes connected, then dropped at the same time to her necklace.

"Your father, he—."

"Gave it to me," she finished.

The tattoo was simple. It was the Eye of Horus—just like the one she wore around her neck—but instead of an iris inside the eyelid, it had three sets of initials ringed inside its center. *MBR, VGR,* and *CGR.*

Michael Benjamin Ryan, Victoria Grace Ryan, Chapel Grace Ryan.

"That's my—." She stopped and restarted, the truth of it no longer crippling her. The truth of it making her insides bubble like molten lava. "That's Michael Ryan," she said. "My father tried to kill me."

* * * *

Zay came up with a plan.

Marielle would locate Rotary Queen and ask if there were any photos from yesterday that she didn't post. She would also ask to see all the uncropped versions of the posted images.

Rush and Justin would canvas the area looking for Michael Ryan.

Timmy and Chapel would visit Erica—because she insisted without exception—before getting Chapel to a safe location.

"We know Michael Ryan can use Tempus," Zay said, pacing at the head of the conference room like a teacher, "What we don't know is how strong it is, how it will affect Chapel, or how it will affect me."

He paused and looked at Chapel. "The threat he poses is immeasurable," he said. "And those are the worst kinds of threats. If you're anywhere in the vicinity when he uses Tempus, he could grab you and leave and none of us would know."

"I'm sure I sound like Captain Obvious," Timmy said, "but shouldn't we take this picture to the police?"

"They may already have this same photograph," Zay said. He shared a quick look with Rush where they communicated something with their eyes. "But at any rate, we think Bennett Park PD has been compromised."

"Because Luke is the Sheriff," Chapel said for Timmy's benefit. She remembered the last time she'd seen Hunter's mom in the grocery store. Her eyes had cut through Chapel like a blade. "If it comes down to my—. To Michael or myself," she amended, unable to call him her dad any longer, "Sheriff Carter won't choose me."

"But this is about Erica," Timmy argued. "And catching whoever shot her."

Zay put a hand on Timmy's shoulder. "I'm not going to stop you from going to the police with this," he said. "But if you tell them we expect it's Michael Ryan, one of their own that they buried fifteen years ago, do you think they'll believe you?"

Timmy was quiet for a beat. "Okay." He nodded. "You're right."

Chapel looked at her phone. "Timmy, we need to go. Annalissa said the Monroes are going home to shower and there's a window for us."

They all went their separate ways, and Timmy said he'd drive over to the hospital alone. She didn't miss how his eyes kept moving to the one bed that had been slept in.

Awkward.

Rush had brought them Barnabus' car to drive so they wouldn't be easily identifiable.

"An *Escalade?*" Chapel said a little incredulously. "With rims?"

Rush shrugged. "Maybe Barnabus has a little gangster in him. I think he wears a gold chain under his sweater vests."

On the ride over, Zay held her hand tightly. He only glanced heavily at her once. She met his eye and he knew exactly what she was thinking: *I don't want to talk about it.*

Zay pulled into the parking deck and got out of the car. He met her at the tailgate.

"Luxe's gun is still in your purse," he said. "Don't let it out of your sight the entire time we're in here."

She appreciated that he didn't try and talk her out of coming. She wasn't stupid—she knew whoever had attacked her would be watching the hospital. But she had to see Erica once. She had to leave her the note she'd written her last night at the hotel. She had to say goodbye.

Because until the source of the threat was found, Chapel was getting far, far away from the people she loved.

"What about you?" Chapel asked.

Zay lifted the edge of dark green flannel shirt. There was a black pistol shoved in the waistband of his jeans.

"Dang." She looked at him. "Is it sick that I think that's kind of hot?"

He smiled and grabbed her chin to kiss her swiftly. "Babe. It's hot that you think it's hot."

Chapel stepped away from Zay and drew Tempus to her quickly. In a few measured breaths, the rhythm of time slowed and they made their way inside the hospital.

They used a side door to enter the building, and then took the stairs to Erica's unit.

"Here," Zay said, pulling her hand and leading her into the family bathroom right outside the ICU waiting room. "You can let go of Tempus in here."

When they emerged, time had resumed at a normal pace. They waited for Logan and Timmy to get off the elevator before walking inside the waiting room together.

There was only one slightly awkward moment when Zay hesitated before shaking Logan's outstretched hand, but Chapel was grateful the four of them got through the first thirty seconds without anyone getting punched. Or shot.

"I'll be right here." Zay pointed to a chair. He brushed a kiss against her cheek, but it was just an excuse to whisper lowly, "If anything happens, if you even get nervous . . ."

She mentally finished his sentence, *Use Tempus.*

She, Logan, and Timmy went inside the ICU area and found Erica's glass cubicle. Annalissa stood when Chapel stuck her head in.

"Oh, good," she said, stepping outside. "I'm starving. Mom and Dad should be back in about an hour."

"Go," Chapel said, pulling her into a hug. "We'll stay here until one of you gets back."

When Annalissa was gone, an extremely young-looking nurse approached them. "Only two people at a time," she said.

Then Logan batted his eyelashes and did this thing to his lips that looked like he was cleaning food off of them with his teeth and they were all allowed inside.

"If Timmy's the brains, and you're the beauty," Chapel said, pointing at Logan, "what role do *I* play in this operation?"

Timmy and Logan exchanged a look. "The muscle?" Timmy said.

Then they both cracked up. Chapel felt the weight of the gun in her purse and grinned. *If they only knew.*

The teasing ceased once inside Erica's room. It was dark and warm, but a cool jerk shook down Chapel's shoulders and back. She was fine until that moment. Fine in the sense that she had blocked out what she'd find on the narrow hospital bed.

She made no noise when her eyes fell on Erica's lifeless body, but Timmy sucked in a gasp so loud, they all three flinched.

She was pale, and her newly-golden hair was matted on the sides. There was a clear plastic tube down Erica's throat. Chapel hated that. Mostly because Erica's mouth was rarely shut, and now there was tape closing her full lips.

Timmy sniffed several times and Chapel grabbed his hand. Logan pressed his fingers into his eyes. No one moved.

"Let's go sit down," Chapel said quietly. "And no crying. If she can hear us, the crying may scare her."

Logan sat beside Chapel on a narrow bench to Erica's right and Timmy sat in the chair on the other side of the bed. It was the closest position to Erica, and Chapel knew he needed that right now.

They were all three quiet for a while, the only sound in the room the suck and blow of the ventilator and the steady beeps of her heart monitor.

Chapel closed her eyes and listened to the steady pulse of Erica's life all around her—it sounded like poetry.

The nurse came in and checked the readouts before winking at Logan and sashaying out the door. Her exit stirred the somber tone in the room.

"Remember that time you and Erica entered the talent show?" Logan asked. He was looking at the stark white linoleum beneath his feet, rubbing his red knuckles.

Chapel had her knees hugged to her chest. She hid her face behind them. "No. I don't remember."

Timmy snorted. "What was that song you guys danced to? Something by Madonna?"

"No," Chapel groaned. "Worse. Paula Abdul."

"*Straight up now tell me,*" Logan sang in a high falsetto.

"*Do you really want to love me forever,*" Chapel sang back.

"*Oh, oh, oh,*" they sang together.

Then they both looked at Timmy for the next line. He pointed to himself. "Wait, seriously? No."

Chapel threw a notepad at him. "Lame."

"Why did you do that, anyway?" Logan asked. "You got so nervous before you went out that you almost puked on me."

Chapel closed her eyes and remembered the day with ease. Erica's mom had made them the most hideous costumes to grace the Bennett Park Middle School Assembly Hall stage—mostly nylon and sequins—and Erica had begged her to wear her hair in a side ponytail like hers.

They had performed the dance routine Erica had choreographed down to the order of when they'd enter, exit, and bow. It was the first and last time Erica had executed a plan of her very own.

Chapel opened her eyes before they filled with tears.

"I did it for the costume," she said.

"No, you didn't." Timmy shook his head. "You did it for Erica. She would have never gone through with it without you."

Chapel rubbed her lips together so hard it hurt. It matched the sting in her chest and eyes.

"That's what you are, Chapel," Timmy said quietly. "I'm the brains, Logan is the beauty, Erica is the fun, but you're the heart. You keep all of us beating."

They were quiet for a long time again, but Chapel breathed easier in the silence. Because she knew that Timmy had finally forgiven her.

They recalled a few more Erica-stories, and Chapel tried really hard not to laugh so loudly that she got them all kicked out.

Timmy had grown quiet across from her, and she saw him working furiously on his phone. She figured he was probably researching every piece of technology in the room, so she left him alone about it.

Before long, the Monroes were back. Annalissa was with them, and she promised to keep Chapel posted on Erica's progress.

When Chapel got back to the waiting room, Zay stood from his seat. "You okay?" he asked.

She shrugged. There was no use in lying to Zay. He saw through her as if she were glass.

Zay glanced at Timmy and Logan over her shoulder. "I need to go to the restroom before we leave. We'll see you guys around."

Which of course was code for, *Let's go somewhere you can use Tempus to get out of here safely.*

Chapel hugged her two friends and watched their elevator doors slide close before she joined Zay in the bathroom.

"I'm worried about leaving Timmy," she told him once inside. "And Erica, too. And even Logan, for that matter. What if someone tries to get to them to hurt me?"

Zay's eyebrows drew together. "If someone wanted to take that route, they would have already done it, don't you think?"

Chapel bit the insides of her cheeks. Zay leaned down.

"Babe, whoever this is, they straight up want you *dead*. This isn't like when Hunter just wanted to take you. This isn't like Hunter hiring that thug to scare you into moving. This is a planned execution."

Chapel pressed a hand to each of her cheeks. They felt warm. "Dang, Zay. You don't have to be so casual about it."

He kissed her on the forehead, but his expression did not soften. "Downplaying the gravity of this would be a mistake. I'm not Gabriel Luxe. I won't soften this to spare your feelings. Not with your life at risk."

Chapel took a moment to digest his words, then nodded. It made sense.

"You're right. I'm—"

The words were snatched out of her mouth by Zay's arms clamping around her body and pinning her against the wall opposite the door. She couldn't move her neck to see his face, but she heard his whispers beside her ear.

"*Six, two, three, B, K, six, four, four, R ...*" Then he cursed and moved back. "They're here."

Fear stabbed through her chest. "Who?"

"Kacie, the Seer," he said, pulling out his gun and removing the safety. "Her necklace. It's like your dad's tattoo. I think he's using her to try and find you."

Chapel's lungs wouldn't fully expand. She was short of breath. "What's our plan?"

"There are a few options," Zay said. "But once we decide, we have to take action right away. Kacie may be seeing several different paths, and I don't want her to have a definite intuition with enough margin to act accordingly."

"Okay." She swallowed. "What are the options?"

"Put your hand in your purse with your finger on the trigger." Zay opened his phone and hammered out a text. His head jerked up. "She's getting closer. No more time to wait."

Chapel knew the only decision to make. She closed her eyes and fisted her hands. At the same moment, Zay's body jerked, and he went down on one knee, both hands over his ears.

"What? What?" she asked.

He bared his teeth, clearly in pain. He reached a hand out to her before falling to the floor, squeezing his head between his palms. Chapel had never even see Zay *wince* from an injury. Her stomach turned, and the sour taste of fear coated her dry mouth.

"Zay, what's happening?"

He was being very still now, but there was a tremble at his jaw that told her he was still very much in pain.

"Zay?" Her voice sounded shrill, so she made it softer. "Zay, tell me what to do."

His eyelids raised suddenly, but he stared at the wall in such a way that she was sure he wasn't actually seeing anything. He made a noise like a grunt and slid his jaw forward.

"Tempus," he mumbled. "His . . . Tempus."

She grabbed his shoulders and helped him to his feet. With his elbow, he gestured toward the toilet paper roll. "Ears," he said. "Hurt."

Chapel took two small wads and quickly folded them both into plugs. Zay fitted them into his ears and shook his head from side to side.

"Better," he breathed. "But not great." He took her by the shoulders. "Your dad's here, and he's . . . " Zay grimaced, "using Tempus. When the edge of his energy touches yours . . ."

She knew the end of *that* sentence. No one knew what would happen. They had hypothesized last night that the person with the weakest Tempus would be affected.

Zay shook his head again. "It's getting . . . easier," he mumbled. "At first, it was like . . . sharp . . . like . . . feedback in an amp." He looked at her, but his eyes were barely open. "And I think he's getting closer."

Chapel turned to the wall so she wouldn't see him hurting. She ground her jaws together and pictured her body like a shaken up soda can. Her spine arched and she threw her neck back at the moment of release.

Zay's sigh was audible. "Much better," he said. "Only if he's with a Reader, they know we're still here."

Zay picked up his gun and pointed to her purse. Chapel got the Smith and Wesson out and gripped it. It didn't feel cold or heavy in her hands. It felt solid and stabilizing. Like an anchor.

Zay tucked her behind him as he opened the door a sliver and peered out. Anger and fear collided inside of her. The questions pressed against the walls of her heart—why? When did her father start hating her? What kind of man could *hunt* his own child?

Chapel felt her arms starting to shake and her teeth rattled in her head. She wanted to tell Zay to stay behind, to stay safe, because someone had to protect her friends and family, but she knew that was pointless.

She knew she needed him beside her.

She knew there was a good chance they could die.

Her arms came around Zay's waist from the back, and she pressed her face against him. One hand slid beneath his shirt and rested on his heart. She tapped it three times.

"I love you," she whispered.

Zay turned around and ran a hand down the back of her hair. "Say it again," he whispered.

"I. Love. You."

He watched her mouth before he kissed it.

"I'm scared, Zay."

Instead of answering, he kissed her again and turned back around.

Like his shadow, Chapel edged out of the bathroom behind him. As they crept up the corridor, she felt a charge in the air. It was like static electricity, like a hand pressed lightly to the back of her head. She could feel *it*—her father's energy resting against the bubble she had created with her own.

Zay led them into the ICU waiting room. In the back corner, there was a sofa. Zay removed the cushions from its back and stacked them in its center. He hopped on top of the teetering pile and reached toward the ceiling.

There was an air vent there, and he pulled a red knife from his pocket and shimmied it between the metal grate until it fell open on one side.

"You first," he said. He helped steady her on the pile of cushions before hoisting her up and into the ceiling. They must have been moving in the opposite direction as Michael, because she was feeling an ease in the pressure around her.

Chapel wiped the cobwebs from her face and moved so Zay could climb in. He swung himself in the airshaft soundlessly and slid by her.

"Try and spread your weight out between your hands and knees," he whispered. "And follow me."

After several long, tense moments, Chapel touched his ankle.

"How do you know where we're going?" she whispered.

Zay paused to remove the toilet paper from his ears. He rubbed them gently, then glanced over his shoulder. "Timmy sent me a map. I memorized it."

"What? Timmy sent you a map?"

The duct split two ways. Zay went left. "I texted him while you guys were with Erica. I asked for a map of the airways, the maintenance stairs, and the general schematics of the building. He emailed them to me before you left her room."

"Dang." Chapel paused to wipe a bead of sweat from her temple. "I knew Timmy was kind of a genius, but he *hacked* into the hospital's records from his cellphone?"

"Yup." Zay paused. "Here's our exit."

Chapel looked at where he pointed. "But there's no vent there."

He took his knife out again and flicked open a long blade. He shoved it into the flimsy metal and started sawing.

"Well, thanks for including him," Chapel said, watching his forearm strain as he ripped through the metal. "I know it makes him feel useful."

Zay paused and flexed his wrist. "Timmy's really good." He squinted at her. "One of the best hackers I've ever seen."

Chapel started shaking her head. "No."

"What?"

"I said *no.*"

Zay went back to cutting. "There's a great training cell out by MIT. He wouldn't see any combat. He'd be behind a computer."

She punched him in the arm as hard as she could. He flicked an annoyed look at her. "I could have sawed my arm off by accident."

"Zay, Timmy cannot be involved in this."

Zay stopped sawing and yanked at his shirt, scattering buttons. "Would you mind terribly," he said, "if we fought about this after I save our lives?"

With that, he wrapped his shirt around his knuckles and punched through the floor until a rough square-shaped hole was opened. He dangled and dropped, then caught her at the waist and placed her feet on the floor.

"Where are we?" she asked.

"Get your gun ready," he said. "You're handling that thing like it's a hair brush."

She rolled her eyes and held the gun up. "You're awfully bossy, hero."

He laughed quietly and shoved his arms back into his shirt. "I've told you this before, babe. I'm not the hero in this story."

He motioned that she get behind him again. "And to answer your question, I don't know where we are. I didn't want to decide beforehand. It makes it easier for the Seer. But it looks like someone's office."

There was a desk in the center of the room scattered with files and paper and medical utensils. The framed photographs showed a happy family—two kids, mom and dad—smiling and peaceful. Shame flashed through Chapel and it made her eyes sting.

"I just moved in the opposite direction of the noise that hurt my ears," Zay said. "It's not as loud now. But it's also not moving."

Chapel blinked back her emotions. She watched him check his gun's clip for the second time. It was his only nervous tell. "What does that mean?"

He looked at her. "It means wherever he is, he's probably waiting for us."

"Oh, goody," Chapel murmured. "This just keeps getting better and better."

Zay raised on his toes to look out the slim strip of window at the top of the door. "How much longer do you have in you?"

"I'm good," she said.

Zay nodded once and moved out of the office with his gun leading the way, swinging around every corner before he'd let her follow him. He took them to a set of service stairs and they walked down.

Their shoes squeaked on the slick floors. Besides that, everything was silent.

Everything was clear.

Everything was fine.

On the landing of the first floor, Zay froze. "Something's not right," he said. He closed his eyes.

As soon as he said it, she felt it. Like falling face first into water, a light weight poured over her. Michael Ryan's Tempus was pushing against hers, harder and faster than the first time she'd felt it.

How had they not felt it moving? Why had they no warning?

Zay bent at the waist and grabbed his head again, an animalistic sound dragging through his throat.

"Run," he managed. "Out . . . door . . . then . . . right."

She went and knelt in front of him. "No," she said simply.

He blinked at her rapidly, but she wasn't sure he saw her. "Run. Just . . . *run!*"

A protective notion crashed over Chapel's consciousness and without understanding what she was doing, she bared her chin to her chest and breathed heavily, concentrating on pushing out any energy, any breath, any *thing* inside of her.

Her temple ached with the effort, but she didn't relent. It was almost like a game of mental tug-of-war. But Chapel was just as mad as she was scared, and those emotions fueled her ability. Slowly, she sensed the pressure of her father's energy easing.

Zay staggered to his feet. Chapel put an arm under his shoulder and together they exited the stairwell.

Using his body as a shield, Zay moved to the right. There was an emergency exit at the end of the long corridor, its red letters looking like the gates to heaven. A sliding door would take too long to force open—they needed something they could push.

"It's getting harder to move," Zay murmured. Chapel felt it, too. Her thighs burned, and the effort to put one foot in front of the other had her ducking her head as if she were sprinting. They were both working every muscle in their body to move at a fast walk's pace—like running underwater.

When Zay's hands pushed against the cool metal of the door, Chapel whimpered. Maybe they were going to make it after all.

He grabbed her hand and moved her along the edge of the hospital. They came to a corner at the edge of the courtyard. They were fewer than fifty yards from the parking deck.

Like a breeze against her skin, Chapel felt another press of energy all around her. She pushed back with all her strength—which wasn't much.

With a moan, Zay leaned his head against the brick. "Chapel," he whispered. "This isn't going to work."

"Don't say that." She squeezed his hand. "We're almost there."

They tried to take a few more steps, but it was almost impossible to move.

Zay shook his head, releasing her hand and pressing against his ears. "No."

The pressure increased on all edges of Chapel's awareness, and she knew what Michael was doing. He was looking for her.

"He's close," he said. "My guess is he's gaining ground."

"Stop, Zay. Don't. Please."

"It's not me . . . they want to kill," he said. He gasped, and she knew it was taking everything he had to remain coherent. The muscles in his neck stood out like strained wires. "There's a   car . . . at the drop off. Keys under . . . mat."

Chapel's breathing had increased, and with it, her lack of focus. Her hands started trembling again, rattling the gun against her leg. "Please don't do this." She swallowed, but her throat was dry and she choked on it. "Please don't."

Zay closed his eyes and moved to lean his forehead on hers. "I love you," he whispered, and crushed his mouth to hers, cracking their teeth together and kissing her deeply.

Then he pushed her back against the wall and took off running far faster than they had just been moving.

"Where are you, Ryan?" he shouted, spinning in the center of the courtyard. His shirt swung open, and Chapel could see every line in his strained stomach—every vein bulging to push blood all the places it needed to.

"I said," Zay yelled again, "where—" A sound of agony raked from his throat, and he fell to one knee before careening to the ground.

Chapel pushed off the wall and ran as quickly as she could. The effort made her dizzy, but she saw nothing but his strong body curling in on itself.

She made it to him and gripped his arm. "No," he moaned. "No, no, no. I . . . told . . . you. Never . . . listen."

She kissed his forehead. His cheek. His nose. His eyes. She realized, in that moment, that she would take a hundred bullets to the back before she'd let someone take him.

Then her breath was pushed from her lungs as the weight of the world plunged on top of her, paralyzing her on her knees. She could barely draw in a breath.

"You know," a voice said from behind her, "the two of you are going to get killed trying to keep one another alive."

A hand gripped her shoulder, rolling her over. She scraped together just enough strength to force her eyelids apart.

She saw her coloring. Her freckles. Her smile. All on the face of a stranger.

"Hello, Chapel," he said. "It's me, Dad."

CHAPTER TWENTY-NINE

She wasn't sure if she threw up or not, but when Chapel woke up, there was a steady thud of pain pulsing behind both her eyes, and her mouth felt like it'd been stuffed with cotton balls.

Chapel tried to swallow, but couldn't. She coughed instead and reached for Zay. Wasn't he just beside her?

Zay.

Chapel sat up so quickly that it felt like she left her stomach behind her. She waited as it roiled, gurgled, then quieted. No, Zay wasn't there. She looked around, unsure of where *there* even was.

She was in a bed. In a house. There was an alarm clock. An empty glass. A box of tissues. Everything looked so *normal.* It could be anyone's house.

Chapel lifted her hands to rub at the ache in her skull. It wasn't until that moment that she realized she was unrestrained.

Her purse lay on the table beside the bed. She looked inside. Of course—the gun was missing.

A window in the corner of the room drew her attention. It was dark outside.

How long was I out?

Chapel hadn't passed out this long after Erica's shooting. And she hadn't felt this bad, either. What had *happened?*

Voices rumbled from somewhere in the house and Chapel rose shakily to her feet. She paused, one hand out to balance herself, while the sharp dizziness passed. When she thought she could move without vomiting or blacking out, she crept toward the echoes of the conversation.

"—Of my team was dispatched immediately after the shooting." It was Michael Ryan's voice, and she felt it in her gut. "I don't know who is trying to kill my daughter, but I will find out. I promise you that."

There was a familiar sound—a throat being cleared. "And you expect her to stay here until you do so?"

Zay. The sigh of relief that flushed through her was like a salve on a fresh wound. He was there. And obviously not in grave danger.

"I expect you to help me keep her here," Michael said.

The sound of his voice—so alien yet so familiar—it scattered Chapel's emotions in different directions, making her grip the bannister she leaned against.

The sound of Zay's quiet laugh rose to her ears. "You do not know your daughter very well, if you think she will take orders from you. Furthermore, neither will I."

Her heart was not ready to see her father, the man who had abandoned her and chased her around the hospital, forcing his Tempus on her. But her feet disagreed. They pushed her farther down the stairs, faster than she should have been moving.

There was a pause, and Zay laughed again. "I can't wait to see what she does when she sees *you.*"

Who is you? she wondered. But then her eyes answered the question for her as she turned the corner and saw a familiar photograph in the foyer.

Gabe and Cess.

She knew it then—recognized the minimalist approach to décor and the smell of disuse. They were in Gabe's house. The one he had been staying in while in Bennett Park.

That meant Gabe had known about her father.

That meant Gabe had been lying to her.

About *everything.*

She rushed into the kitchen with anger blinding her to anything but that single truth.

Zay was leaned against the doorframe she passed through. Michael Ryan sat at the kitchen table with his foot propped on his thigh.

And Gabriel Luxe—traitor that he was—sat on the kitchen counter. He had the audacity to have his ankles crossed. Like this were a leisurely conversation and not the ultimate betrayal.

She charged at him just as he slid to his feet. "I'm going to kill you," she seethed. "I'm going to literally *murder* you."

She shoved as hard as she could with two palms at his chest. He jerked back and his eyes shot wide.

"How long have you known he's alive?" she shouted, pointing back at Michael. "How long have you been *lying to me?*" She shoved him again and he let her. "How long have you been a snake in the grass, Luxe? Tell me."

His jaw twitched, and his eyes looked deep and somber.

Zay's sneakers squeaked on the floor behind her. She knew he wouldn't stop her. He just wanted her to know he was there.

"Answer me!" she shouted, spit flipping out of her mouth. "I deserve an answer."

He said nothing. But his eyes got misty and he met her punishing gaze as if he craved her chastisement. It made her angrier.

Her arm swung back and smacked his face so hard that the effect of it radiated through her knuckles and elbow.

"Chapel," Michael started.

"No," she yelled over her back. Then, to Gabe, "He doesn't answer for you. He is *nothing* to me. But you were . . . " She faltered for a moment. "You were . . . more."

Zay's hand came down on her shoulder then, and he pressed her back against his chest. Her insides felt erratic and out of control. Zay must have sensed that—the throbbing of Tempus begging to be set free.

She tugged in three calming breaths.

"You don't get to be a martyr," she whispered. "You be a *man* and talk to me."

Gabe's face and neck were flushed red—especially where her handprint now rose against his cheek. He truly looked tortured.

"I found out just after Christmas," he said quietly. He looked her in the eye, and she knew that that must have cost him something. "Michael came to me and presented me with an offer. That's why I went home, Chapel. It wasn't easy to agree to lie to you." He stepped toward her. "It took me six weeks to convince myself that I should do it. That I *could* do it."

Chapel allowed her gaze to finally land on Michael's. He was standing now—taller than she expected, and older. His hair was lighter than hers, closer to Hunter's color. But his eyes—green and piercing and observant—studied her openly. As if she were a cadaver to be dissected on his examination table.

She made a face at him, and his lips tipped up in a grin. She rolled her eyes.

"What was the offer?" she asked, finally returning her attention to Gabe. "Try and get me to fall in love with you so that I'll join Bellum after all?"

Zay coughed into his fist. "*What?*"

Gabe shot him a look, then tilted his head at her. "No," he said firmly. "Your father's reach is far higher than Bellum."

"He's not my father," Chapel said.

Michael sighed. "Actually," he said, "I am."

Chapel rounded on Zay, turning to face Michael. "I'm sure you mean that in a very biological sense of the word," she spat, "so I won't waste our time by detailing all the ways you aren't. You're as much my father as Todd Taylor is."

Michael's eyes narrowed, and Chapel sensed she hit a nerve. Unbridled anger trounced through her. She had no control.

"Actually." She tilted her head slowly. "I've known Todd a lot longer than I've known you. Mom loves him. And at least he's stuck around."

Michael twisted his lips for a moment. Then he looked at her with a raised eyebrow. "Are you finished with your little tantrum?"

Zay stepped beside her and took her hand. "Don't patronize her," he said quietly. He looked at Gabe. "Besides me, you're the person she trusted the most in this world." Then he looked to Michael. "And you're the person she should be able to trust the most in this world."

He said nothing else. He didn't need to. The other two men in the room sagged back into sitting positions. Chapel squeezed his hand.

"About the deal," Zay said to Michael. "Please explain."

Michael brushed a finger across the bridge of his nose—just like Chapel did when she was irritated or anxious. It made her skin crawl.

"I was Bellum for many years," Michael began. He looked at Chapel when he spoke, his eyes unwavering. "This was before the days of Daniel's leadership, and the group was even more out of control than it is now. I saw a better way—a new way for our people to live. For you to live, Chapel. You'll never believe me, but I left our family to create that world for you."

He looked to Zay now.

"Isaiah, you know as well as I do that conditions are intolerable for all Genexes. Your workload, the tension between factions, career limitations, everyone's suspicious nature."

Beside her she felt Zay stiffen. He hated to agree with her father, and she loved him for that. She leaned into his body, letting him wrap an arm around her waist.

She felt Gabe's eyes on her and she shook her head just slightly. *No.* Whatever he was thinking, wanting, or needing, the answer was: *Heck. No.*

Michael continued. "So, with Luke Carter's help, I faked my death and left the country. I traveled the world in search of Genexes who hadn't been contacted or documented by Thanatos or Bellum. I began to recruit them, train them, and indoctrinate them with a new dream—a new people—a *free* people. Who operate as one."

"You're a Unifist," Chapel said.

Michael nodded. He flitted his hand in the air. "They call me the Oracle." He rolled his eyes. "A little dramatic, but our people insisted."

Chapel touched her necklace. His eyes followed her actions.

"The Eye of Horas," he said. "That's our symbol. It's on our flag, actually."

Chapel snickered without meaning to. "You have a flag? What are you, a country?"

Gabe and Michael exchanged a look. "Not a country, no. But we have purchased several thousand acres that we plan to settle with any Genex who wishes to join us. A community—a town, more than a country. But we can live openly. We can be teachers, lawyers, doctors. And Genex, too. If Bellum, Thanatos, or even a government or institution wants to contract us for work, wonderful. We will be owned of no one but ourselves. We will be free."

Chapel's mouth fell open. In all her wildest dreams, she never imagined *this*. Her father was a mutant George Washington.

The puzzle pieces began to slide together slowly. "So, Gabe's job was to expose me to the horrors of the factions so I'd be conditioned like a dog to do whatever you wanted?" she asked.

Michael's eyebrows jumped. He even laughed a little. "So much like Valerie." He sighed. "No. I wanted him to educate you. We actually had a very good plan. But someone is trying to murder you and I can't possibly keep an eye on you and finish the projects before we go public with our agenda."

"We," Zay repeated. "The Unifists."

Michael nodded.

"Why did you go to Gabe?" Chapel asked. "And not Zay?"

Michael shifted in his chair. "Hunter Carter was my first charge." His eyes fell to Chapel's T-shirt. An inch of raised skin sat hot and angry above it's collar. "He failed. And when I find him, he will suffer."

Chapel swallowed.

"And," Michael added, "Isaiah would never lie to you."

"But Gabe would," she said needlessly.

"Only for Cess," Gabe said, breaking his silence. "Michael knows who killed her. He's going to hand them over to me." He met her eyes fiercely. "She deserves to be avenged. They—did things to her. Before they killed her. And—"

He didn't finish. Of the miles of her anger toward him, she allowed him one foot of grace. Not forgiveness. Just a margin of understanding.

Chapel's head was beginning to pound again. Or maybe it had been pounding all along and she was unaware of it. She rubbed her temple.

"That would be the sedative," Michael said. "I had to drug you to get you away from the hospital. Gabriel?"

Gabe opened a cabinet above the oven and took out two pills from a bottle. "Advil," he said. When she pushed them away, he opened her hands and dropped them inside. "It's for your headache."

It pained her, but not enough to turn them away.

"What now?" she asked, swallowing the pills.

Michael looked at Zay. "I was hoping you and Isaiah might stay here for the evening while Gabriel and I join a team who is pursuing leads on the attempts on your life."

"It's not Hunter, is it?" she asked.

Michael shook his head. "I'm afraid not. We have eyes on him."

"Where are Erica and Timmy?" she asked.

Michael nodded. "Erica's awake and well, though she isn't taking visitors. As for Timothy, I am aware that you have told him of our world, yes?"

She squared her shoulders. "Yes." Her eyes touched Gabe's. "I find it very difficult to lie to people I love."

Michael rapped the wall beside his head. "I'll have him brought here, if you want," he said. "If it will make you stay inside for one single evening."

Chapel thought about his offer. She looked to Zay. "What does Jackson think?"

Zay lifted his shoulders. "I don't care. Where you go, I go. Where you sleep, I sleep."

"It's secure here," Gabe said. "My name isn't on the deed. I have cameras installed all over the exterior. The windows are wired, so are the doors. It's very secure, and no one will suspect you're here."

She looked at Zay again. She just wanted him to tell her what to do. He must have read her expression, because he cupped her cheek. "You need rest," he said.

She nodded. "One night." She turned to her father. "And I want Timmy here as soon as possible."

Michael sighed and walked over to her. She took a step back, and he flinched. For the first time, pain tightened his expression—but briefly.

"Just wait," he said quietly. "When we have our world— *our* world—the way it should be . . . you'll see." He looked at her again for a long moment. "It will have all been worth it then. All of it."

But it sounded like he was trying to convince himself.

CHAPTER THIRTY

The first thing she wanted was a shower. Hot and scalding and long. When she got out, her towel smelled like Gabe, and *that* made her want to vomit.

On the bed was a folded stack of clothes. She recognized them as things Gabe had bought for her in Florida. She'd left that bag in his car. He had washed them, obviously, and laid them out carefully.

After choosing cotton shorts and a T-shirt, Chapel pulled her wet hair into a bun and sat on the bed.

She felt restless and fidgety and exhausted and worn. She'd had some water and a banana before the shower, and her headache was getting a little better.

There was a knock on the door before Zay poked his head in. "Dressed?" he asked, eyes closed.

"Yeah."

He smiled at her and came inside. Instead of sitting beside her, he knelt in front of her and put his hands on her knees. "How we doing, babe?"

She took a deep breath. "Fi—" She cut off after a look from him. "Not fine," she amended. "I actually feel . . ." She tried to think of a word. "Confused? Angry? Sleepy? Worried? Hungry?"

His thumbs brushed the tops of her thighs. "I'm here," he said. Not, *It's going to be okay,* not, *I'm sorry.* He always knew what to say.

"That's enough," she said.

He leaned up and kissed her temple. "Come here."

He moved to put his back against the headboard and pulled her across his lap. She burrowed her face against his shirt.

"Say it," he whispered.

She smiled. "I love you."

She felt his chest rise and fall with a breath. "I know you won't want to talk about it," he said. "But at some point, you need to."

The tears bubbled at the corner of her eyes, making her throat tight and her sinuses burn. But she was afraid if she started crying, she wouldn't stop.

Zay's lips touched the top of her ear. "I love you so much."

That was the last thing she remembered before she fell asleep.

* * * *

She knew she was dreaming, but it didn't feel like a dream. She could *smell* things. Gasoline and rubber and something tangy. She was in a parking lot. One she'd never been in.

To the left was a jewelry store and to the right was a fast food restaurant—Thai food. And it was like she knew what to do without knowing why.

Her feet pushed her forward. Glass doors swooshed open, blowing her hair behind her and making her cold. She was in a small vestibule. Someone brushed by her with a fistful of envelopes.

A bank. She was at a bank.

As she took another step, she winced. Her ankle was sore. *From jumping from the window*, she reminded herself.

She took a right and walked down a narrow hallway. Small gold doors lined both sides of the walls.

She stopped in front of three-one-one-B and reached in her pocket. There was a smooth key there, the one the manager had given her after she had recited the code.

"You'll know when it's time," Valerie had said.

It's time, Chapel thought

The key turned over inside the slot, and the door swung open. Chapel reached inside and pulled out a thin envelope.

"What's in it?" someone said behind her. *Timmy.*

"Give her a minute," another voice said. *Zay.*

But Chapel knew what it was before she opened it—a picture of the person trying to kill her.

As her fingers pulled back the envelope, her vision started to blur.

No, she thought. *Not yet. I have to see.*

But it was no use. Black holes started to burn through the picture, through the walls, through the slick marble-tiled floor. The envelope dropped, and just before it hit the floor, her spine jerked.

She was awake again.

"You okay?" Zay's voice was thick with sleep. Something shifted beneath her, making her tense.

"It's just me," he said, putting a hand on her back. "We both fell asleep."

"Timmy?" she asked.

"He's here. He's watching TV in the other room."

Chapel heard it then—the laugh track followed by a high-pitched squeal. *Seinfeld.* One of his favorite episodes.

Chapel sat up, stretching across the bed and clicking on the lamp.

Zay's eyes were swollen and red-rimmed, and he gave her a half-smile that made her want to crawl back into his lap and sleep for a week.

But she couldn't.

"Zay," she said, "I know how to find the person who is trying to kill me. And . . . "

He moved to the edge of the bed and took her hand. "And?" he asked.

She licked her lips. "And I think my mother is a Seer."

* * * *

Her knuckles came up lightly against the door. Timmy swung it open before her hand was back by her side.

"Hey," she said. "Any word from Erica?"

He rubbed a hand over his frizzy hair. "Stable, but still no visitors. They don't want her over-stimulated now that she's awake." His eyes moved over her hastily. "What's up?"

"Weird stuff."

He rolled his eyes. "What else is new?"

Zay stepped out of the bedroom across the hall and raised his eyebrows at her. She turned her attention back to Timmy.

"Timmy, do you want to sneak out of this house? Without asking any questions about why?"

He smiled. "I was hoping it was something like that."

Zay found the live feed of Gabe's security system in the master bedroom closet.

"Why do we have to sneak out again?" Timmy asked when he saw how thoroughly the house was monitored.

"I don't know," Chapel answered honestly. "I just know we have to go out through a window."

"This is a sophisticated system," Zay said. "Solar powered. Isn't that what Daniel used during your Tempus evaluation?"

She nodded. "Yes. So, it looks like we're getting out of here the old fashioned way. Is it possible?"

Zay lifted one corner of his mouth. "Who are you talking to?" He pointed to a screen at the edge of the display. "There's a small lapse between the swings of cameras D and E."

"How long is the lapse?" Timmy asked.

Zay looked over his shoulder. "Eight seconds."

Timmy coughed. Chapel sighed. Zay laughed.

The window they needed to exit from was in the guest bathroom at the front of the house. It led to the roof of the porch. Zay had the timer on his phone set to beep every time the lapse in coverage started.

They stood in the bathroom, shifting feet and eyes, finding the rhythm of their escape.

"Okay, can we just review what's about to happen?" Timmy asked.

Zay motioned to the window. He had opened it during one of the first lapses. The curtains billowed slightly in the breeze. It was just after seven in the morning, and the air that filtered in was cool.

"I'm going down first," Zay said. "You're second, and Chapel's third. She'll bring the phone down with her." He handed it to her then. "Wait for the first beep, move through the opening quickly, and make it to the edge of the roof and drop down before the next beep."

"In eight seconds," Timmy said flatly.

Zay grinned. "Or less." He gripped the edge of the window frame. "The hard part is getting through without messing up the curtains. They need to look the same."

Then the phone beeped and Chapel blinked and Zay was gone. Two breaths later, she heard the light thud of feet on the ground.

Timmy swiveled his eyes to hers. "That was a little crazy, right?"

She nodded, mouth hanging open. "Uh. Yeah. A lot crazy."

The phone beeped again and they both flinched.

"Just wait for the next one," she said. "But get ready."

Timmy's hands rose to the sides of the window. Chapel saw from behind him that they trembled slightly.

"Timmy, you don't have to—."

Then the phone beeped again and Timmy shot through the window. It wasn't nearly as graceful as Zay's exit, but it wasn't bad looking, either.

"Huh," she said to an empty bathroom. A moment later, the phone beeped. She wasn't ready, but her legs flung her through the narrow opening anyway. Her off-kilter exit had her sliding down the roof clumsily.

She reached the edge on her bottom, and thought for sure that she was going to flip off entirely.

Then, at the last moment, she caught the gutter with her ankle. She flipped over on her stomach, but a burn rising up her leg made her hesitate.

"Three, two," she heard below, and she dropped just as Zay said, "one."

"You okay?" he asked. He steadied her at the elbow as she rolled her ankle around and around. It stung.

"Yeah," she said, remembering her dream. "This is how it's supposed to be."

* * * *

They had an hour before the bank opened and they needed to get a car.

"Where are we?" Chapel asked. She got out her phone to look at the map application.

"We're in Nichols Landing," Zay said. "It's just over two miles back to Todd's."

"Oh." Of course. Zay would have made it his business to know where Gabe lived. But Chapel was beginning to think she'd never known anything about him at all.

Chapel's heart throbbed for several beats and she tried to ignore the ache. The deal Gabe made with her father wasn't an act that she could make a judgment on right away. She'd need to mentally peel through the layers of hurt before she decided to what degree she hated him.

"Let's go through the woods," Zay said, pointing. "I'm sure they'll realize we're gone soon, and we need to already be in

319

the car when that happens." He looked at Chapel. "I'll carry you."

Chapel didn't protest. Her ankle pulsed beneath her. She climbed on his back and he gripped her beneath the thighs.

Then they were off.

Zay jogged, oblivious to her added weight. She could tell he was pacing himself for Timmy's sake, but he still pushed pretty hard.

Before long, Chapel could see the back of a house inside her neighborhood. That was when her phone started ringing.

She pulled it from her pocket. Her battery warning flashed at the same time as Gabe's number.

"It's Gabe," she said. "He knows we're gone."

Zay stopped running and so did Timmy. "What do you guys think about staying here while I go get the Jeep?"

Timmy leaned over on his knees. He tilted his head back and squinted at them. "I think that idea would have been a lot better a mile and a half ago."

Zay's lips twitched. "I wanted to get you guys away from his cameras." He put a hand on Timmy's shoulder. "You did good." He turned to Chapel. "I know you're going to answer it if he calls again," he said. "Just keep it under twenty seconds."

He kissed her lips hard and took off running.

Her phone immediately started ringing again.

"Is he psychic?" Timmy asked. It sounded like he was half-serious.

Chapel shrugged. "If he weren't so attractive, it'd be unsettling."

Timmy gagged and she laughed. Then she answered the phone.

"What's up, traitor?" she said to Gabe.

Across from her, Timmy's eyes went wide before he chuckled.

"Chapel?" Gabe sounded confused for a moment. "Where are you?"

She breathed a quick breath of relief. He hadn't seen where they were headed. Yet.

"Gone, Gabe. I'm gone."

There was a pause on the other end where she heard steady breaths. He was thinking about something.

"They've started, then? The visions?"

Chapel put a hand to her other ear to block out all the ambient noises.

"Visions?" He knew. *He knew.*

"Your visions, Chapel. I can't always see when it happens, but most of the time, you haven't found out yet . . . But it seems that perhaps you have?"

"Yeah," she said. "No thanks to *you.*"

He was quiet again, and she knew he was trying to get a read on what she was doing. "I can't see you," he said roughly. "I can't *see you* anymore. Chapel, you have to understand I—"

Then her phone went dead.

"You okay?" Timmy asked. His hand was gripping his side and his pale skin was flushed pink. But his eyes were bright and he had a goofy smile on his face.

"I'm fine. What about you?"

He shrugged. "I suck at running. But don't lie—I looked pretty good jumping out of that window, right?"

She rolled her eyes. "You looked *decent.*"

"I looked like a ninja. Like a ginger ninja."

Zay rolled up then, the Jeep's engine swallowing her laugh. They climbed inside and Chapel gave Zay directions to the bank. When her mother had given her the code, she had memorized it, the mailbox number, and the bank's address.

They were quiet as they drove. The sun was pushing its way farther over the horizon, warming the sky to a hazy purplish blue.

About halfway to the bank, Zay's phone started ringing in his pocket. He pulled it out and looked at the screen. It was Jackson. Zay sent it to voicemail and took Chapel's hand.

"He's going to track this Jeep," Zay said. "We can ditch it and walk the rest of the way or risk it."

Chapel looked in the rearview mirror. Timmy's head leaned against the seat, his eyes were closed, and his breathing was steady and deep.

Her feet and body already ached, and it felt like there were shards of glass behind her own eyelids.

"What do you think?" she asked him.

He squeezed her hand. "I think we drive."

She wanted to kiss him. So she leaned over and did, right where his jaw met his neck. It felt so good to be close to him that she left her head on his shoulder.

The next thing she knew, she was gently being lifted. "Babe," Zay was whispering. "We're here."

She jerked up and looked from left to right. Behind her, she heard Timmy smacking.

Chapel looked at the door handle to get out of the Jeep. She already knew how her fingers would look curled around its silver edges. She knew how the ground would feel beneath her feet. How her ankle would sting. How her right toe would be sore.

She would ask for Samantha, the manager on-duty, and she would take the twenty-seven steps from her office door to the box with a cool key in the palm of her hand.

Zay touched her arm. "Ready?"

She was. It was like it had already happened. And just like she saw in her mind's eye, Chapel walked to the glass door with *Samantha Carnes* written on it and knocked.

A tall woman with dark hair answered. She already had the key in her hand. "Your mother just called," she said. "Please let me know if you have any issues."

Almost robotically, Chapel turned and took her first step toward the truth.

The key turned over inside the slot, and the door swung open. Chapel pulled out a thin envelope.

"What's in it?" Timmy asked.

"Give her a minute," Zay answered.

As her fingers pulled back the envelope, her vision sharpened. She tugged back the sticky edges and pulled out a sheath of paper. She fanned them out and flicked through them one by one.

With each movement, her heart dropped lower and lower in her gut.

Her killer. The person who had been trying to take her life for the last month wore a warm smile and an ice blue tunic. Dr. Battacharya—Chary.

No.

Chapel tried to make the evidence fit another scenario, but it was all there. In emails, photos, and credit card transactions. Chary was behind the hits to Zay's car and at Back Porch.

Chapel turned without speaking and handed everything to Zay. His chest rose and fell more quickly with every page he ingested, too. And Timmy, over his shoulder, grew pink-cheeked and sweat broke out over his forehead.

Zay finished looking at the documents and shoved them back in the envelope.

"She wasn't behind the attack at my house," Chapel said.

"I still think that was Hunter," Zay said.

Chapel shook her head. "I disagree."

Zay folded the envelope and shoved it in the back band of his jeans. "While I'd love to sit here and argue," he said, "anyone wanting to find us is probably going to be here in the next five minutes. What do you want to do?"

Chapel touched her eyebrow with a finger. "I *want* to gag and tie up Chary and throw her into a pit of venomous snakes and watch as they give her a thousand tiny bite marks all over her worthless body."

Timmy lifted a hand. "That could be arranged. I know a guy."

Chapel and Zay made eye contact briefly. Timmy was going to be better at this world than she ever would be.

"I need to get this in front of Daniel," Chapel said. "Chary is very well-known in the Bellum community. He would rather die than let any more bad press get out about his people."

Zay's eyes widened. "You're right," he said. He touched the envelope at his back. "This isn't just the answer to who's trying to kill you. This is your way out of your oath to Bellum."

"It is," she confirmed. "Now take me to Florida before my father ruins everything."

CHAPTER THIRTY-ONE

They walked several blocks down the road and found a Waffle House. Chapel whimpered when she smelled the batter, and Zay pressed a kiss to her temple.

"I need to feed you, don't I?" he asked.

She ordered two meals, an orange juice, a coffee, and chocolate milk. Even Timmy looked sort of impressed.

When they were alone, Zay propped his elbows on the table. "Okay," he said, "so we're going to need help getting a meeting with Daniel. There's no way I can get you to Florida without someone intervening, and even if I do, there's no guarantee that he's there."

Chapel chewed on her waffle and thought. There were only two people who could get her in touch with Daniel. One was trying to kill her and the other she sort of wanted dead.

Timmy stole a piece of Chapel's bacon and bit into it. She snatched the rest before he could devour it, too.

"We need Luxe," she said.

Zay nodded. "Unfortunately."

Timmy lifted a finger. "If I may? I have a few thoughts."

Zay crossed his hands over his chest and smiled. "The floor is all yours, Valentine."

Timmy pushed his glasses up his nose. "Every time Chapel has been attacked, it's been when she's with one other person, or alone. I actually think it might be safest to keep her out in the open. As long as that Chary bi—sorry—

lady doesn't know that we know, she should keep her M.O. the same."

Zay pushed out his bottom lip. "I agree."

Chapel sighed. "What about school?" she asked. "It's Thursday and I haven't been a single day this week."

Timmy shrugged. "Fixing our attendance record will take me all of thirty seconds. Don't worry about that."

"And I can't keep an eye on you at school," Zay said.

They were all quiet while they ate. The waitress came and cleared their dishes and Zay ran a hand down the side of his jaw.

"What?" Chapel asked. "What are you about to say that I'm not going to like?"

He smiled at her. "I think we need to call a meeting," he said. "With everyone. Including Jackson. Including Michael Ryan. Including Luxe."

"Why?" she asked.

He put his hand on her back. "Because I can't protect you enough on my own. Because we can't keep running. Because you need sleep. You couldn't Tempus right now, could you?"

Chapel closed her eyes. She didn't even feel a flutter. Without opening her eyes, she shook her head.

"It's settled, then," Zay said. "No hiding. Keep you out in the open." He stood. "I'll go make the call."

* * * *

Gabriel was the first to arrive. He must have been in the area, because it only took him about five minutes. Zay stood from their table.

"Can I speak with him first?" he asked, looking down at Chapel. "I'm not going to tell him about Chary yet, but I have a few questions for him."

Chapel nodded. "Sure."

When he was gone, Timmy rolled his eyes. "Dude, those guys are in freaking love with you. It's so messed up."

Chapel threw a sugar packet at his head. "Shut up. You love Erica."

His mouth swung open, but he didn't say anything. Chapel had been sort of kidding, but the look on Timmy's face told her she had hit a nerve.

"Wait," she whispered. "You love Erica?"

He brushed a hand over his copper hair and sniffed. "A little."

Chapel sucked in both of her lips, her eyes going wide. "A little," she said, "as in a *lot?*"

Timmy finally looked at her. "Yes. A lot. Happy?"

Chapel shot up from the booth to her feet. "You love Erica? You love Erica!"

Her voice was probably a little louder than normal, but she didn't care. Her two best friends were in love. She clapped. "Can I be the Maid of Honor *and* the Best Man?" she asked. "I mean, has that ever been done?"

Timmy covered his face with his hands and groaned. "I knew I should've kept it a secret."

"I could probably just stand between the two of you at the altar. Maybe I should be your officiate, actually. I mean, I have taught Sunday school for the last few years, and—"

"Chapel?" Zay's voice came from the door. "Everybody's here, now."

"Thank *God*," Timmy muttered, grabbing her arm and dragging her to the door. "Please forget I said anything."

Once outside, Chapel's good mood came to an abrupt end. At the corner of the parking lot, in an awkward-looking semi-circle, stood Michael, Gabe, Rush, Marielle, Justin, and Jackson.

Most notable was the fact that Jackson was staring at Michael like he was seeing a ghost, and Michael was staring at Chapel as if he'd seen one, too. Gabe's back was turned, Marielle looked bored, Rush was spitting the lyrics to a rap song, and Justin was inspecting the sharp tip of a long knife.

"Your new friends are weird," Timmy said in a low voice.

"Our new friends," Chapel corrected him. "You've already been more helpful than me. They're not cutting you free after this. You get that, right?"

Timmy's thick eyebrows pushed up his forehead as he considered that. A slow, silly grin tilted up his mouth. "You know what that means, right?" He looked at her. "You *have* to start calling me Ginger Ninja, now."

Chapel punched Timmy in the arm and he winced.

"That *hurt,*" he whined.

"I didn't mean for it to tickle." She pulled him by the elbow. "Let's go. I'm not facing this firing squad alone."

"We need somewhere to meet," Zay said, addressing the group. "Somewhere secure and neutral. Any ideas?"

Michael lifted his chin. "I have a place. Follow me."

Chapel moved to get in Zay's Jeep, but Zay held up a hand. "As much as I hate this, they'll be looking for you to be with me." His eyes moved over her shoulder. "Chary worships Luxe. She'd never hurt him. I think you should ride with him."

Chapel's spine automatically straightened. "Well, then Valentine can come with me."

Zay shook his head. "He needs to ride in the front with me. He's more of a giveaway at your side than I am."

Chapel felt Gabe's eyes on her face as Zay came and cradled her cheeks between his hands. "I've already spoken with him," he said. "I'm not going to let anyone hurt you, okay? Especially him."

He kissed her again, this time letting it linger long enough to make Rush whistle. He smiled against her mouth and stepped away.

"Chapel rides with Luxe," he said, loud enough for everyone to hear. "Valentine with me. Rush and Marielle, you guys drive Jackson. We'll all take alternate routes, leaving in ten-minute waves. We'll meet in forty minutes."

Michael studied Zay for a moment, and Chapel figured he was probably trying to find something to pick apart about the plan. But eventually he just nodded.

"What's the address, Michael?" Zay asked.

"It's on Lighthouse Way," Michael said slowly. "Our old house together."

Chapel's eyes met Zay's, then Timmy's. His words felt like heavy stones in her stomach. "Fine," she said stiffly. "Let's go."

The inside of Gabe's Porsche looked like it had been ransacked. Clothes were rolled up and scattered over seats and in the floor, papers were shoved in corners, and half-drank cups and bottles of water teetered in nearly every available crevice.

Chapel threw a brown banana peel in the woods to make room to sit in the front seat. When they left the parking lot, a file folder slid across the dash and spilled into her lap.

Gabe cursed. "Sorry," he mumbled.

Chapel shoved the papers back inside and stuck it in a compartment at the door. She turned in her seat.

"Okay," she said. "You're taking this sad, like, tortured lover thing a step too far." She pointed to the mold on a muffin in his cup holder. "Seriously? I don't know the girl, but something tells me this would gross Cess the heck out."

Chapel leaned behind his chair and found a plastic grocery bag. It was empty. Chapel rolled down her window and started collecting garbage.

Gabe stuck his thumb and forefinger in his eyes and pressed. He groaned. "Don't be nice to me," he said. "I can't stand it."

"I'm not being nice," she said. "I seriously might get a disease in here. This is for my own safety."

Her body jerked against the door when Gabe slammed on the brakes. He turned off the main road and accelerated quickly down a gravel drive. Dust rose behind them as he brought the SUV to a jittery stop.

At least ten horrific scenarios played themselves inside her mind and Chapel was completely frozen.

He unbuckled his seat belt and spun to her. "You have to know something." His light eyes were wide with wonder. "Chapel," he said slowly, "I love you."

Chapel blinked. "You *what* me?"

Gabe nodded. "I love you. I do. Quite so, I'm afraid."

Chapel's chest rose and fell beneath her chin in rapid succession. She knew that this moment would change the trajectory of their paths. She felt it in her bones—a tingling sensation, a gentle roar in her mind like quiet static.

"And you care for me," Gabe said, watching her carefully. "You being mine is not so far from reality. Just one lapse in my restraint. Just one missed phone call. Just one minute early. Just one half-decision. And you would have been mine. See it, Chapel. *See it.*"

It was like she had no control over her own mind. She saw it. *Saw* it. Like she had seen what would happen at the bank.

The day Gabe had met her at UGA. Instead of leaving her at her car, he walked her to a coffee shop on campus. They talked for hours and he called her later that night. Her relationship with Zay was so new. She pulled away from Zay and closer to Gabe.

In this version of her life, she was Gabe's.

Then the day she learned she was Genex. Gabe had answered the phone when she called to cancel the meeting they had. He had been expecting her call—he had *seen* it. But in this version, he hadn't answered. Instead, he'd driven to her house and met her there. He had been waiting on her porch and not Zay.

In this version of her life, she was Gabe's.

Another set of images unfolded in her mind.

Gabe beating Zay to Hunter's warehouse and saving her.

Gabe coming to her house the night Zay went missing. He had picked her up in this version and confessed his love for her, kissing her against her front door until she couldn't breathe.

Gabe in her room.

Gabe in her car.

Gabe in her heart.

Everywhere, everywhere.

Destiny had brought them together and forced them apart in a hundred different versions of their story.

"Since I was sixteen years old," Gabe said. "You've been the one I dreamed about. When he calls you *his*, Chapel . . . " Gabe shook his head. "It sets my heart on fire. Because you were *mine* first."

Then in a move so fast she couldn't have prepared for it, Gabe leaned over and put his mouth on hers. Her reaction was mixed. It was a kiss she had kissed a thousand times and yet never at all.

Like a slow yawn, her body opened up to him. Betraying her heart, she leaned forward, drinking in his kiss cautiously as if it might sting. But it didn't. It warmed her—that was certain. But it was a gentle kind of warmth—like tilting your face to the sun.

Gabe moaned lightly and the sound snapped against her senses. Her hands drew up between them and pushed him away hard.

He didn't look surprised. "That's what I thought," he said quietly. She had no idea what he meant.

"Why?" she whispered.

He understood her.

"Cess." He said her name almost reverently. "I never saw Cess coming. She was my tangent, Chapel. Everyone has them in life. Moments or relationships whose impact divert our orbit irrevocably."

He put his hand on his chest, right over his heart and gripped it there.

"And I loved her in a way that wrecked me. Because I could never *see* her. Not once did I see anything that might happen between Cess and I. She was unpredictable and wild and full of surprises." He gritted his teeth together and two thick tears appeared on his cheeks. "And then she was tortured and murdered and I swore to myself I'd find no happiness until I avenged her death."

Chapel's face and neck were hot and sticky. She felt sick. "Gabe," she whispered.

He licked his lips. "I've always been able to see you until today." She watched his Adam's apple rise and fall. "It scared me. It terrified me. I've always known we had a future—a thread—a possibility. Until today. And then it was gone."

Chapel felt the loss behind her ribcage, too. Despite her love for Zay, it made her sad.

"I've killed it, haven't I?" Gabe asked. This time the tear that moved down his face was for her. "Us?"

She bit the insides of her cheeks as hard as she could. The bitter taste of blood and regret lingered on her tongue. She turned back in her seat, facing the window.

"We need to get to the house, Gabe," she said. "Zay will be there soon and I don't feel like dragging him off of you if you get me there late."

He stared at her a few moments longer before he straightened in his seat and re-buckled his belt.

"I will make this up to you," he said. "To us."

CHAPTER THIRTY-TWO

Chapel wasn't sure what to do with her thoughts about Gabe. The new, almost-memories of the two of them floated around the hallways of her mind like dust particles in the sunlight.

She couldn't shake them.

Not when Zay got there, tucking her to his side. Not when Rush got out of the car and hugged her until her chest hurt. Not when Marielle actually greeted her civilly. Not even when Justin lifted a hand of "hello" to her and asked if she wanted to borrow one of his knives.

They waited for Michael to arrive before they went inside the house. The sight of her foyer, the one with peeling wallpaper with apples and houses on it, was the only thing that could pierce the fog created by her encounter with Gabe.

A melody started playing from the recesses of a distant memory. A song that Valerie used to sing to her. Chapel closed her eyes, reaching for it.

Valerie's voice—softer than she had heard it in a long time—filled her senses.

"Oh my little, precious Chapel, you're the apple of my eye."

A preschool-aged Chapel stuck a chubby finger at her own chest.

"I'm Chapel," she said.

"Yes," Valerie said, a wide smile pulling at her lips. "You're Chapel."

Chapel scrunched her forehead into tiny lines. "And I a apple, too?"

The sound of her mother's laugh was like sunshine on her face. "You're not an apple, silly girl. But you are pretty sweet." Valerie lifted Chapel's arm. "Maybe I should take a bite out of you just to be sure."

Chapel giggled as Valerie pretended to sink her teeth into the folds of her skin, thinking her mother was the best mother in the whole world, and feeling loved, and safe, and warm.

Chapel opened her eyes, reluctantly untangling herself from the emotions of the resurfaced memory. She touched a faded apple on the yellowed wallpaper and her heart suddenly started beating again.

Zay put a hand on her shoulder. "You still with me?"

"Sort of," she whispered.

He pressed his mouth to the top of her head and steered her behind Michael. "Let's get this meeting over with," he said. "And I'll take you home."

But where was home? She wanted to ask. It wasn't Taylor Manor. It wasn't Jackson's. This place that she was in right now? It was the closest thing she'd ever had to a home.

Michael led them into the kitchen with its beige laminate countertops. They congregated around the island and every eye moved to Zay.

He held out the envelope they'd just retrieved. "We know who wants Chapel dead." He started laying out each sheet one by one.

Gabe was the first to react, stringing together several curse words and shaking his head.

Jackson paled.

Initially, Michael had no physical reaction whatsoever. After a few heavy moments, he sighed and crossed his arms casually. "I'll have her dead within the hour."

Zay seemed to take a steadying breath before answering. "If I wanted her dead, I'd kill her myself."

Everyone in the room flinched at his tone. No one said it, but Michael Ryan emitted a soft hum of prowess that was intimidating. But Zay didn't seem to notice. Or maybe he didn't care. Chapel shuffled closer to him.

"We know who it is," Zay continued. "But we don't know why."

"Are we *sure?*" Gabe asked. He sounded pained.

Chapel waved an arm over the paperwork on the counter. "Um. Yeah, Gabe. A picture of her with a freaking gun in her hand pretty much rules out any question."

He looked dazed. "I don't believe it."

Rush laughed without humor and pointed. "Dude. Believe that. It's real."

Justin surprised Chapel by talking next. "I'm up for some target practice if we need information." He twirled his knife in the air and caught it with the other hand. "I can be persuasive."

Chapel watched Timmy's face across the room. He didn't look afraid. He looked fascinated.

"Isaiah is right," Jackson said, apparently finding his voice. "If Chary wants Chapel dead, we need to know why. She could be working for someone else. Or she could know something about Chapel that we don't."

Chapel met Michael's gaze. The dark pupils of his eyes stretched momentarily. He knew something. And she could guess what—Valerie was a Seer. And so was Chapel.

"I need to see Chary," Chapel said. "I need to meet with her *alone.*"

"No," Zay said. At the same time Michael said, *"What?"* and Gabe said, "Are you *quite* insane?"

"She's right," Marielle spoke up. "Women don't work like men. There's a complex reason driving this affidavit. Chapel is likely the only person Chary will admit it to."

Rush brushed a hand down his mouth. "I don't like it, Peaches. But Marielle might be right."

"She is," Timmy chimed in. "It's been my experience that girls tell men about sixty percent of the truth, while they'll be over-expressive to members of the same sex."

If the moment hadn't felt so heavy, Chapel would have laughed out loud. Timmy Valentine, the walking factoid generator.

Zay looked at Chapel. "Are you sure about this?"

She wanted to cower. She wanted to shrug. She wanted to close her eyes until it all went away. But she was beyond the point of avoiding conflict.

Someone had put two holes in her best friend's back. That type of anger cancelled out the gravest of fears.

"I'm sure," she said.

"Okay," his mouth said at last. But his face said, *No, no, no.*

Chapel looked away from his somber gray eyes. "Gabe, set it up," she said. "Tomorrow night. I have to get some sleep in case I need Tempus. Let her pick the place, though," she added, tapping her fingers across the counter. "That will put her at ease. I need her to feel like she has me right where she wants me."

Gabe leaned against the cabinet and crossed his ankles. "I think Daniel needs to be there, too," he said. "I think we need solid, indisputable proof that she's trying to kill you."

Michael and Zay communicated something to each other with their eyes. Chapel thought it looked like acquiescence.

Zay looked at Gabe. "Can you make Chary believe you?"

Gabe was staring off, unfocused, his forehead pinched. He was trying to see where that phone call might go. Chapel could tell by the cloudy look in his eyes that he was unsure.

"I'll do it," he said. His tone rang skeptical. His eyes found Chapel's and he held them steadily. "This is what you think is best?"

Beside her, Zay's body went taut. He stepped forward just barely, blocking Gabe's view of her.

"She's already said it's what she wants," Zay snapped. "Make the call."

Everyone in the room became suddenly very curious about the floor beneath their feet. Chapel leaned back to see Gabe's jaw clenched.

"Isaiah, a word outside, please?" he said.

Zay's hands fisted by his side. "Good idea."

They both walked out the front door.

Michael took his phone from his pocket and walked to the back of the house. Marielle and Jackson had their heads huddled close and were whispering. Timmy was pointing at something on Justin's knife, looking at it longingly.

Only Rush made eye contact with her. He walked over. "Peaches," he said. "Another day, another drama, huh?"

Chapel didn't even have the energy to verbally spar with him. She just leaned her head against his shoulder and sighed. "Should you go make sure Zay doesn't kill him?"

Justin whistled at Rush. "Did you bid on that Spanish dagger we saw on eBay?"

Rush darted his eyes to Chapel. "You got this," he said. "Holler if you need me." Then he crossed to Justin and Timmy.

Chapel trained her eyes on her shoes. It stung to look at the walls and ceiling that housed her formative years. And there was enough emotion pressing in on all sides of her.

She left out of the same door as Zay and Gabe and followed their voices to the backyard. She tried very hard not to think about the countless games of hide-and-seek that had occurred there, or the hours of stargazing, or the nights she and Logan had spent curled together on the swing at the edge of the woods.

She couldn't see him, but Gabe was speaking. She paused at the corner of the house to listen.

"Was there for her every time you've left," he was saying. "*Me*, that's who. You never called her. You let Marielle treat her terribly. What did you think was going to happen?"

"So you're openly admitting this to me," Zay said. His tone was flat. "You're openly admitting that you're in love with my girlfriend."

"You know that I am," Gabe said, raising his voice. "Don't act surprised."

There was a pause, then the sound of knuckles against bone. "That's for not telling her about her dad," Zay said. Then there was another punch—and a groan—Gabe's. "That's not for loving her," Zay said, "It's for not loving her *enough.*"

The sound of boots coming her direction had Chapel skittering back. Something scraped against the sidewalk and then there was a thud that jarred the window by her head.

Chapel moved back toward the noises and leaned her head around the corner. Gabe had Zay pressed against the side of the house. Zay's elbow came up and caught Gabe in the chin, breaking his hold.

They stood staring at each other for several tense moments, breathing heavily. Zay rubbed the back of his head and Gabe touched his jaw.

"Neither do you," Gabe said. "You don't love her nearly enough."

"I haven't," Zay said quietly. "Not until I saw Erica bleeding to death in Chapel's car. Losing her. It would . . . " He was quiet before he spoke again. "I would never love again. Chapel is not my Cecily, Luxe. Chapel is my Chapel."

* * * *

Gabe set up the meeting and the group of them stayed up late devising a plan. Several more calls were made, supplies were gathered, and tasks were delegated.

It was beyond late when it was decided that everyone should return to his or her homes to keep Chary from suspecting anything was amiss.

Chapel was bone tired when Zay took her hand to lead her out to the car, so when her father stopped her at the door, she couldn't suppress a groan.

"Not tonight," she begged. "Or actually, not this *morning* is more accurate."

Michael shook his head once. "It won't take long," he said. "It's about Valerie."

That got Chapel's attention. "Zay comes," she said.

"Fine."

They followed him back into the old guest bedroom. Chapel was glad he hadn't chosen one of theirs. He flicked on the light and turned to study her.

"You look so much like her right now," he said with a shake of his head. "Determined and angry."

Chapel switched her weight from one foot to the other. "Mom is a Seer?"

Michael crossed his arms over his chest. He was in good shape for a man his age. Great shape, actually. The veins on his forearms strained against his pale skin.

"She is," he said. "It didn't show itself until she turned eighteen. The year I met her."

"Who else knows?"

He shook his head. "The three of us and Gabriel." His eyes tightened and he took a step her direction. "Valerie has always distanced herself from you for this reason. Her being in Virginia right now, as much as it has hurt you, has served you well. She is out of sight, out of mind."

A wave of emotion spread itself over her like a warm blanket and the corners of her eyes moistened. Could it be true? Could Valerie's separation have really been *for* her and not *because* of her?

Zay put a hand on her shoulder and squeezed. "How do her visions work?" he asked.

"They're not as strong as Gabriel's. It's more of a sense of déjà vu, or recurring dreams," Michael explained. "But we have no idea how it will manifest itself with Chapel."

"Are we sure Luxe hasn't told Bellum?" Zay asked.

Michael shrugged. "He promises he hasn't. I'm inclined to believe him." His green eyes surveyed Zay's. "What do you think?"

Zay sighed. "He wouldn't lie to us about Chapel."

Chapel bit the insides of her cheeks. "Has Mom seen anything about tomorrow?" She squeezed her eyes shut then opened them again. "I'm not sure how this whole thing works, but I'm getting nothing."

Michael's jaw clenched. "I can't get in touch with her," he said. "With your mother. Todd hasn't, either. She's been gone for two days now."

Chapel's mouth flew open. *"What?* The twins?"

"They're fine," Michael said. He scratched the strawberry blond stubble along his jaw. "They're staying with Todd's mother. She hasn't contacted you, right?"

It took her a moment to answer. "No. I mean, my cell phone has been dead for hours. I can charge it in Zay's car."

Across from her, Michael was chewing the insides of his cheeks. They made eye contact at the same moment that she realized she was doing the exact same thing.

"Let me know if you hear from her," Michael said after a moment. "Regardless of what time it is. Do you promise?"

Chapel nodded. "Of course."

Michael flicked his eyes to Zay's. "Take care of her."

Then he walked from the room and left them alone.

* * * *

Chapel knew she needed to rest, but her mind wouldn't shut off. Just after sunrise, she pushed from her bed in Jackson's house and tiptoed down the hallway to Zay's room.

He must have been sleeping lightly, because his head raised as soon as she stepped in his room.

"Did she call?" he asked, voice thick and heavy.

She shook her head. "Couldn't sleep."

Zay pressed a fist into his eye with one hand and lifted the edge of his blanket with the other. "Come here."

It was warm beside him. He wrapped a hand around her waist and pulled her against him. She fit there like a key inside a lock.

"I could get used to this," he said into her ear. "Three nights in a row."

She knew what he meant. It was getting harder not to need him. It was getting harder not to depend on him.

"Love you," he murmured. And she knew he was on the edge of sleep.

"Love you, too," she whispered. And jumped into the abyss right alongside of him.

CHAPTER THIRTY-THREE

Jackson led them into the basement. No one spoke as their feet traveled across freshly vacuumed carpet. He moved through the conference room to a door Chapel had never entered.

Against the wall, there was a keypad. Jackson flipped the cover of it and pressed two fingers in its center. The door clicked open and he shifted so she, Zay, Rush, Marielle, and Justin could move inside.

The room was like an oversized walk-in closet. Lockers lined either side and a low bench split the center. Jackson stood at the head of the room and rubbed his hands together.

"I am not a perfect leader," he said. "I have made mistakes, and I am sure to make more. But I will promise you this." He paused and briefly touched everyone's eyes with his own. "I want what's best for you. And starting tonight, I want what's best for you more than I want what's best for Thanatos."

Zay's pinky reached over and wrapped around hers. Chapel's heart moved outside her chest for a few tight breaths.

"And as of right now," Jackson continued, "it is my honor to elevate this Training Cell to a Field Team. We will have the formal ceremony later, but it's already been approved by the Invisibles."

Zay squeezed her hand before going over and clasping Rush on the back and nodding to Marielle and Justin. It was a big moment for them. And though she wasn't a part of their team, Chapel didn't feel excluded from it.

"Justin will take it from here," Jackson said, and he stepped away and into the shadows.

Justin lifted his honey-colored eyes. A current of electricity ran just behind them. "Everyone's equipment is inside their locker," he said. "If you have any questions, let me know."

Then he placed his phone on a speaker dock and pressed a button. A heavy beat dropped, and the thud of bass swelled around them.

Zay nodded and even Marielle swayed her lithe frame as she flicked through the contents of her locker.

Chapel felt her own body shift in sync to the pulsating rhythm. She turned and touched her name printed on a strip of tape across one of the doors. Then she swung it open. A feeling rose inside her chest like a balloon being inflated.

It was all about to be over. She was about to be free of Bellum once and for all. Free from the threat of an assassin at her back. Free.

Justin came to stand beside her. He spoke close to her ear so she could hear.

"You can't wear anything that might indicate you expect an attack," he said, pulling out a flannel shirt. "But I sewed a pocket here in the hem for you. It's just big enough for a knife."

Chapel scrunched up her face. "You *sewed?*"

A small smile touched Justin's lips. The silver ring there caught the overhead fluorescent light and winked at her. "I like needles," he said.

Chapel buttoned the shirt over her tank top and slipped the knife into its pocket.

Around her Justin pointed out gear and wardrobe enhancements to the others. The track changed and Chapel was surprised to hear a familiar song in her ears. She finished dressing and turned in to the bench at the same time Rush did.

He dropped a hand to his leg and the other he danced in the air while singing the chorus, *"Life's a game but it's not fair. I break the rules so I don't care."*

"So I keep doing my own thing," Chapel answered, making Rush laugh out loud. *"Walking tall against the rain."*

Justin shook his head at her and Marielle smirked.

Rush cupped a hand over his mouth and hollered. "Peaches knows her some Jay Z! Zay, if you don't bag this girl up, I'ma do it for you!"

Zay's hand came around her waist and his breath was hot in her ear, finishing the song, *"Only thing that's on my mind, is who's gonna run this town tonight."*

* * * *

Chapel checked her lip-gloss in the mirror. Chary was obviously shrewder than anyone had thought her to be. It was important that Chapel appear normal. Poised. Probably a little annoyed—that's how Chary typically made her feel.

"I'm going in," she said under her breath. Justin had also sewn a cordless microphone into the collar of her shirt. It transmitted her voice wirelessly to a white van a few blocks away where Jackson, Daniel, Marielle, and Timmy listened to the recording.

Chapel opened the door to her Jetta and pushed her hands down her jeans.

Her palms were dry.

Her boots scuffed against the cement floor of the parking deck as she crossed toward the entrance to O's. Chapel was surprised when Chary suggested such a public meeting location. But the worried look that Gabe and Zay had shared stopped that relief in its tracks.

"It's well-known among Genexes," Gabe had said. "There will be plenty of rooms she can take you to."

Zay had stood and popped his knuckles. "And plenty of pockets to line if she needed someone to look the other way."

Cool air washed over her body when she swung open the heavy steel door. Music vibrated the wooden floors beneath her feet and she immediately made eye contact with Kacie.

Kacie's Eye of Horas necklace caught the lights from the bar. She worked for Michael Ryan, too. She would be Chapel's only contact inside the building. Zay, Justin, Rush, and Gabe all waited closeby for a word from Jackson's van to come inside. Kacie would communicate Chapel's exact location after she delivered her.

"Right this way," Kacie said, her expression betraying nothing as she escorted Chapel through the dining room. "Dr. Battacharya arrived a few minutes ago."

With those words, Chapel's heart plummeted to the floor beneath her hesitant feet. She stopped moving. "Chary's *here?*" Chapel asked. "Already?"

Kacie's wide eyes confirmed Chapel's incredulity. *Chary? On time?*

Chapel hadn't taken the time to consider the fact that she was walking into the lion's den. That she could open the door and get a gun in her face and a bullet to her brain before she said the first word.

"She's waiting," Kacie reminded her quietly.

"Right."

Chapel started walking again, but her boots felt as if they were filled with water. *Whose idea was this? Oh, yeah,* she thought. *Mine.*

Kacie took her down a narrow hallway, past the kitchen doors to a bank of elevators. They didn't speak as she pressed the button with the letter B on it. Chapel could only assume it stood for basement.

Not good.

Chapel opened her mouth to say something, but Kacie's eyes darted to the camera in the corner. The red light on it was blinking.

Chapel's teeth clicked together. Chary could have people watching and listening, just like she did.

The elevator doors opened and Chapel stepped onto dingy black and white linoleum tiles. The sheet-rocked walls were water-stained and pot-marked, and the one light in the hallway buzzed with the weakness of neglect.

It was a far cry from the high gloss sheen of upstairs.

And it looked exactly like a place where someone would get murdered.

There was one door at the end of the corridor that Kacie stuck her head around. "Here she is, Dr. Battacharya."

Chapel's pulse thundered in her ears as she stepped by Kacie and over the threshold into the small room. It appeared to be an office, and Chary sat on top of a wide desk in a black and silver sari. Her ankles were crossed as if this were a leisurely picnic and not the standoff they both knew it was.

Kacie would alert everyone to her position as soon as possible. As long as Chapel could keep herself alive, she would expose Chary, get out of her oath to Bellum, and discover why Chary wanted her dead.

No big deal. Chapel almost cracked a sarcastic smile at the thought.

"Hello, Chapel," Chary said, sliding from the desk like an oil-slicked eel. The two air kisses she gave Chapel had the name *Judas* resting on the tip of Chapel's disobedient tongue.

But instead of blurting out profanities and shoving the knife pressed into her hip right between Chary's shoulder blades, Chapel lifted her lips into a nervous smile.

"Chary," she said. "Thank you for meeting me on such short notice." The script they'd written yesterday poured from her lips. "I didn't want anyone else in our meeting because I don't know who to trust anymore."

Chary's thin eyebrows lifted over honey-colored eyes. She clicked her tongue. "Tsk, tsk, tsk. Trust is a terrible thing, isn't it?" She shook her head, the tinkle of her silver earrings sounding morbidly out of place in the squalor of their surroundings. "Trust is so hard to give," Chary said. "And so easy to lose."

Chapel detected a knowing tone in Chary's response. Or a suspicion at the very least. Chary was smart. She knew something was amiss.

When Chary had come to kiss her, she'd turned Chapel's shoulders toward the back of the room. Now she stood between Chapel and the exit. That had to change.

"I wanted to show you this in person," Chapel said. She pulled her cellphone from her back pocket and walked Chary's direction. She made sure to position her body where Chary had to turn. Now the exit was to Chapel's left and Chary's right.

They were on equal footing. Chary's eyes met hers over the cell phone and Chapel could tell her movement didn't go unnoticed.

"What is it?" she asked, taking the phone and rocking to the side closest to the exit.

"It's a text from Jackson. I wanted to forward it to you, but I think he's tracking my phone."

Chary accepted the phone and studied the screen. Chapel knew what she would see there: *I know who is trying to harm you. Tell no one, not even Isaiah, and meet me at Bennett Park Memorial Gardens tomorrow night at eleven.*

Jackson had sent the fake message last night just fifteen minutes before they had Gabe make the call to Chary.

"It seemed strange," Chapel said. "That he would want me to meet with him alone and not tell anyone about it," Chapel said.

Chary tapped the screen with a long, naked fingernail. "Hm. Yes. This is interesting." She lifted her chin and stared at Chapel for a moment. "And you haven't spoken to Jackson? You . . . haven't any idea who he suspects?"

Chapel commanded her breath to stay steady. "No," she said. "I haven't."

Chary surprised her then by leaning over and jerking open the door. "Very good. If you'll come with me, we'll get to the bottom of this."

Chapel stared out into the dim hallway. She couldn't leave. Everyone was positioning themselves based on where Kacie had told them Chapel would be. But Chary was already floating out in the hallway, an expectant look on her face.

"Let's go," Chary said, and her tone indicated it wasn't the first time she said it.

"We're leaving?" Chapel said for the benefit of her microphone. "Where are we going?"

Chary wafted her fingers in the air and laughed. "Darling, you sound nervous. We're going out to my car, of course. I only chose this as our meet-up location so we wouldn't be followed to our next destination."

"Our next destination?"

Chary sighed grandly. "Love, it's time we brought you in for good. All this back and forth isn't good for anyone. Your life is in constant peril, you don't even trust the people you live with." She pursed her dark lips. They were chapped and had bits of white at their center. "You are Bellum and that is the end of your story. Come, now."

Chapel had a choice. She could run and hope that Chary didn't catch her or have a gun. Or she could stay just one interaction longer. If she left, there was a good chance she'd be caught. And she'd be right where she started—pledged to Bellum without knowing why Chary had tried to kill her.

Chapel followed after the smack of Chary's sandals against the floor. She was leading her in the opposite direction of the elevators. They were heading toward the back of the restaurant two stories overhead.

And if the schematics she had studied last night were accurate, they were about to be at the back loading docks. Chapel had seen movies. Nothing good happened at loading docks.

She acted as if she was straightening her shirt, but Chapel's fingers unclipped the belt from inside the hem and released the small knife. Chary spun around just as Chapel slipped the blade inside her shirtsleeve.

She paused for a terrible moment and Chapel was sure Chary had seen her. But instead, Chary tickled the air with her fingers. "Watch your step," she sang.

She led them down a corridor that spilled into an area that looked like it used to be a factory of some sort. Scattered across the floor were rusted pieces of machinery that lay at odd angles. The air tasted of disuse and cobwebs clung to every surface.

Chapel knew in that moment that she didn't want to get wherever they were going. Being Bellum was not nearly as bad as being dead.

Her feet stopped moving. One step later, so did Chary's. The woman turned around slowly. "Darling?"

Chapel felt her lip curl in disgust. "Don't *darling* me."

Chary clasped her hands to her chest. "So, we're done playing nice, now?"

"Said the psycho trying to kill me."

Chary tilted her head. "If you had listened to my first warning and left town, none of this would have happened."

"Oh yeah," Chapel said, rolling her eyes. "It's *my* fault you're trying to kill me. Did you read that line in Villains For Dummies?"

Chary's jawbone flexed. "Tsk, tsk, tsk." She shook her head. "It's a shame you must be disposed of. Such *spirit*." Chary's eyes looked over Chapel's shoulder. "Do it."

Chapel turned to see who Chary was talking to. When she did, her blood pressure rocketed, taking her stomach with it.

Her hair was a different color, but the look of disdain in her eyes was the same.

Chapel groaned. "Seriously? *You?*"

There was movement in the periphery of her vision, then a slice of pain against her temple. The last thing she saw before her knees cracked against the floor was a look of pure hatred tightened against Brandy Miller's shadowed features.

CHAPTER THIRTY-FOUR

Chapel wasn't out long. Her shirt was being pulled from her arms.

"She had a knife. And there's something here in the collar," Brandy was saying. "They'll be close."

"I've got someone at every entry point," Chary said. "It will slow them enough to get her in the truck."

Chapel barely opened her eyes. She had been dragged in front of a galvanized door that looked like a gate. Chary smacked a red button against the wall and it rolled open to reveal the trailer of a truck pulled flush against its opening.

"Get the sedative in her now. If she wakes up and uses Tempus, we're done."

There was a sting at Chapel's neck. A warmth ignited inside her veins, begging her to come under. She bit the insides of her cheeks to remain conscious.

"And get her naked," Chary added. "In case she has a tracking device in her clothes. Then put her in the truck. I have to check in with Daniel to cover us."

Chapel heard a sound in the distance. Someone yelling. Gun shots. Grunts. Metal against metal.

The jerking against her body stopped. "They're here already?" Brandy asked.

"Kacie." Chary made a growl in the back of her throat. "I thought her feelings for Gabriel would keep her loyal to me. Apparently, I was wrong."

"What should we do?" Brandy asked. "Should we just do it here?"

"No," Chary snapped. "She knew about me. I need to question her. To find out who else knows. There's still a chance we can keep this contained."

Chapel felt a tug at the button of her jeans. Instinctively, her stomach sucked in. Brandy's cool fingers paused.

She knew Chapel was awake.

Chapel used what little strength she had and rolled away from Brandy, coming to her feet. Her shirt had been thrown just a few yards away. She needed the knife that lay on top of it.

"How are you still alive?" Brandy asked, shaking her now dark hair. "It's annoying."

Chapel pressed a finger against the tender injection spot on her neck. The medicine was rushing through her system, but it hadn't reached every limb yet. She needed to act quickly.

"Good to see you too, Brandy. Tell me something. Does it get old? Having your hate for me run your entire life?"

Brandy's arrogant expression faltered. "Shut up."

Chapel laughed. It sounded ugly in the empty room. "You don't care whose team you're on, do you? As long as they're against me. I didn't realize I had that much power over you." Chapel touched her tongue to her dry lips. "I'm just going to take your obsession with me as compliment. Really."

And just as she'd hoped, Brandy lashed out, bending at the waist and charging at Chapel like a bull.

Emotional weaknesses can be used as leverage in the same way as physical weaknesses, Zay had taught her. *Exploit them.*

Chapel was slower than she would have been, but was still quick enough to drop and roll out of the way, sending Brandy skittering behind her.

She shook her head, feeling heavier by the heartbeat, and lunged for the knife just as Brandy threw herself on Chapel's back.

"I hate you, I hate you, I hate *you,*" Brandy hissed in Chapel's ear, ripping at Chapel's tank top and hair.

Chapel pushed her knees to the ground and bucked Brandy back. It took two tries, but she was stronger than the other girl, especially from that position.

When Chapel stood, she held the knife out in front of her, pointed right at Brandy's heaving chest.

"The feeling is mutual," Chapel breathed. "Now, get on your knees."

Chapel felt around in her core for the thread she so desperately needed, but came up with nothing. The sedative was making her sluggish, and her tongue felt swollen in her mouth.

"You don't have the guts to kill me," Brandy said, stepping toward Chapel and letting the blade pierce the fabric of her black shirt.

Chapel felt a cruel smile slither across her lips. "You sure about that?" She pressed the knife until Brandy jumped back.

"You *cut* me," Brandy yelled. She reached down her shirt and removed a red-slicked finger. "You *cut* me!"

Chapel waved the knife in the air. It glinted in the yellowed light. "I didn't bring this to check my lip gloss in."

There was a commotion behind Brandy, and both girls moved to see what it was. Two figures wrestled in the dark against a far wall. Grunts and the echoes of punches rang out.

The silk of Chary's sari rustled against the ground as she pinned a figure to the floor. But then a leg twisted up and pushed Chary off, rolling on top of her.

Chary was wrestling with someone . . . but who?

A flash of auburn had Chapel's feet moving in the direction of the scuffle. The two figures separated and there was no denying who Chary's attacker was.

"Mom?"

Valerie's hair was pulled into a low bun with pieces floating around her face. She had a red welt along her right eye and she was massaging her lower back with one hand.

Valerie's eyes slid over her briefly before turning back to Chary. "Chapel, stay back. The drug they gave you will take full effect any second now. If you aren't careful, you'll trip over your own feet and they'll kill you."

Chapel paused just as her ankle came in contact with a decayed pipe. One more inch that direction and Chapel would have tripped and landed headfirst into an upturned office chair.

"How did you . . . " Chapel stopped.

Of course. Valerie had *seen* this. That meant Chapel needed to listen. That meant she needed to follow Valerie's lead.

"Get behind me, Chapel," Valerie said. Chapel moved much slower than she wanted to. She looked around Valerie to see Chary's eyes tighten.

"You're a Seer, then," Chary said. "Perfect. Just perfect."

"I tried to tell you," Brandy said, coming to Chary's side. "Hunter always acted weird about the mom. Wouldn't talk about her."

Chapel's blood was a wild fire inside her body. "You sold out *Hunter* for Bellum?"

Brandy threw back her lean shoulders. "Hunter and Michael sold *me* out. I was displaced. A Rogue. Chary agreed to get me in with Bellum in exchange for information. Which I would have given her for nothing, by the way, if it meant you were *dead*."

"You're sick," Chapel said. "You're insane."

Valerie moved fractionally closer to Chapel. Chary's head fell to the side.

"You're not sure how this will end?" Chary murmured. "You are nervous. There are many variations, yes? That's how the visions work?"

Valerie remained on the balls of her feet, and Chapel detected the practiced nervous energy of a fighter ready to pounce. Valerie was biding her time. But for what?

"There are no definites in life," Valerie said. Her voice sounded strong. It sounded brave. "Every road we travel down has a thousand side roads. Each one we take brings us a set of new and unique decisions." Valerie paused. "Didn't losing Cecily teach you *anything?*"

At the sound of the name *Cecily*, the whole room fell silent. Chary's round eyes went impossibly wide.

"You just . . . how did . . . " Then Chary's entire body went taut. "Don't you *dare* act as if you understand. You have no idea—"

"What it's like to sacrifice a daughter?" Valerie yelled, her control breaking for a moment. Rawness saturated her voice and it raked across Chapel's heart. "Have I not done my part? Have I not torn my flesh in two to keep myself separated from her? So they wouldn't know what she is?"

Chary's eyes trailed to Chapel. "But she's alive."

"For now," Valerie said. "No thanks to *you.*"

Chary's lovely face twisted into a mask of rage. *"She killed my daughter,"* she screamed. "If not for her, Cess would *live.*"

"You cannot possibly mean that," Valerie said. She was slowly stepping backward, and Chapel followed her lead. Her vision was blurring and her head kept lolling to either side. She was close to passing out.

Tears slipped down Chary's round cheeks as she pressed a hand to her heart. "They promised me one year. One year with Gabriel, and Cess would be free from this life, this world."

"But they lied," Valerie said. "The Invisibles do that now. More than ever. That's what Michael has been trying to change. That's what—"

Chary screamed and it didn't sound human. "Don't act like you know how it feels. To hand over your child to be *murdered*. To be violated in the most gruesome way."

"Chary, Chapel did not kill Cess."

Chary's eyes found Chapel's now. They whipped across her like hot chains. *"They* wanted to change Gabriel's path. *They* wanted Gabriel to marry Cess. Not her. But she's such a *whore*. Such a *tease."*

"Wait a minute." Chapel looked back and forth between Valerie and Chary. "Does Gabe know this? About Cess?"

Chary turned out her bottom lip. "Of course not. He is a pawn. Just like I am. Just like you. In *their* game."

Valerie lifted both hands in front of her body. It looked like a peaceful gesture, but Chapel knew from training it was combative. Her mother was poised for attack. That meant Chapel needed to do the same.

"Why don't they want Gabriel to marry Chapel?" Valerie asked. Her voice was perfectly steady.

"They want her to marry Isaiah," Chary said. "They basically threw them together. Next-door neighbors? In the same class? Making Isaiah court her for his assignment? They're a *science* experiment," Chary said. "Or their children will be."

Chapel gagged in earnest, then. Her stomach heaving as if she'd held Tempus for half an hour. But there was nothing inside of her but confusion, anger, and fear.

Was Chary right? How much of her relationship with Zay was real? How much had been orchestrated? And the worst thought of all: *Did he know?*

"A Seer with Tempus who is unaffected by other energies," Valerie murmured. "That would be something to see."

"Exactly," Chary barked. "And Gabriel was the only one who could change that. And he loves *Chapel* now. Loves her in a way he never loved Cess. He didn't see Cess's death because all he saw was Chapel. All anyone sees is *Chapel!"*

"You're angry with the Invisibles, Chary," Valerie said. "Not with my daughter."

Chary leaned her head back and an animal-like growl crawled from between her clenched teeth. She reached into a pocket in her tunic and pulled out something silver. Chapel thought it was a gun.

"The girl," Valerie said, nodding toward Brandy who was running in the opposite direction. "She'll kill you if you don't kill her first." Her eyes found Chapel's. "I've seen it. If not today, another day."

Chapel thought nothing else could surprise her until Valerie vaulted in the air and did a front handspring that caught Chary right in the chest with her feet.

Chapel dragged energy from her center. It wasn't enough to Tempus, but it was enough to put more speed behind her movements. She was within a few steps from Brandy when the girl spun around, making Chapel stutter step and pull up short.

"They'll never stop coming for you," Brandy said, shaking her head at Chapel. "What you can do? Bellum and Thanatos will ruin themselves fighting for you. *That's* why I want you dead. Not because I hate you."

Chapel whipped a ribbon of stray hair from her cheek. She was sweaty and breathing far heavier than normal. "Gee, thanks." She adjusted the knife in her hand, drawing Brandy's attention.

"Come on," Brandy said. "You might be able to shoot me, but you're not going to *stab* me."

Chapel shuffled her feet. The knife felt heavy in her hand.

"You're right," Chapel said. "I'm not going to stab you. But I've learned something about scars." She tugged her tank top down, revealing the ugly lines that Hunter had left over her heart. "They serve their purpose."

Then she dredged up every ounce of strength she had left and threw her shoulders toward the ground in an aerial. It wasn't pretty when her legs snapped back down, but Brandy hadn't moved.

Chapel was behind her now, and she brought the blade of the knife against Brandy's back. Her other hand snaked around Brandy's neck in the exact way Zay had taught her, constricting her airway and paralyzing her.

She sawed through the shirt Brandy wore until it fell away from her back.

"You are spineless," Chapel said, pressing the knife into Brandy's skin just over the bone. It nauseated her, to pierce human flesh, but Brandy was right. She couldn't stab her and she couldn't kill her. But she could remind her.

Chapel brought the knife around in curve—a perfect *C*.

"I hope every time you see this scar," Chapel hissed in her ear, "you remember that there's someone out there who knows exactly what you are *inside*. And is brave enough to let you walk away."

Chapel pushed the girl to her knees.

"Because killing you would be the easy way out, Brandy. Murder is for cowards."

It might have been from the pain, or it might have been from the chokehold, but when Chapel released Brandy, the girl's eyes were rolled in the back of her head. She slumped to the floor, passed out.

Chapel picked the knife back up and staggered down the hallway. She used the cool sheetrock as support, her energy perfectly spent.

Then, like glass shattering in the dead of night, a sickening crack tore through the silence. At first Chapel couldn't place the sound. But her brain replayed it automatically, sending her stomach to her knees.

A gunshot.

Chapel's feet moved faster, tangling in themselves as she came back into the room. It seemed darker than before, or maybe it was just her eyes. Chary stood in the center of the room, the gun raised straight out from her chest and pointed at Valerie. Both women had bloodied noses and ripped clothes.

A creak overhead drew Chapel's attention. A light fixture swung perilously from side to side. They must have struggled over the gun and shot it.

"Now, I have no *need* to kill you, Valerie," Chary said, running her arm beneath her nose. She swung suddenly toward Chapel, the gun leveled to aim right at her heart. "But, you? Well, the Invisibles want you more than ever." She clicked a bullet into the chamber. "They took from me the most important thing in my life. Now I will do the same to them. A daughter for a daughter," she said quietly. "It's only fair."

Chapel didn't close her eyes. She stared at the deliverer of her death with wide eyes, pulse aching at the base of her neck, mouth completely dry. It was not a beautiful moment. It was not a life-flashing-before-her-eyes moment. It was terrifying, and so unbearably *real* that Chapel physically felt time falling away, ticking off precious seconds with each flick of her heart.

Movement to her left made Chapel flinch. An office chair rolled in front of her, circling and coming to a jerky stop. Chary must have been as distracted as Chapel, because she moved too, firing at the black leather, making it explode just to Chapel's right.

Chapel looked up in time to see Chary's determined expression as she re-steadied her aim, pulled the trigger back, and fired. Right at her.

She closed her eyes this time, waiting for the impact, for the splintering of her bones and spilling of her blood. But what she felt instead were two arms coming around her from the front, drawing her into an embrace. Chapel's eyes shot open.

"Mom?"

Valerie jerked once, twice, three times. A clicking noise told her Chary's gun was out of bullets.

It hit her with a terrible sickness. It was empty because the rest of them were imbedded in her mother's back.

"What did you do?" Chapel asked.

Valerie slid to the floor, and Chapel went with her.

Across from them, Chary rocked to the ground as well. The silence that followed was a roar of grief and injustice.

Chapel turned to her mother, spread across her lap. Valerie's pale skin was already ashen. Blood trickled from her mouth.

"Let me apply pressure," Chapel said, snatching her flannel shirt and trying to lift Valerie to press it into her back. There was already so much blood that Chapel couldn't believe there was any left inside Valerie's slight frame. "Mom, hang on. They'll be here soon. Someone will be here soon."

"Cut . . . power to elevators," Valerie worked out. "Truck at other exit. No one . . . coming."

"No!" Chapel yelled, her shrill demand echoing back at her.

One single tear drifted down Valerie's cheek. "Pocket," she whispered. "My pocket."

Chapel shifted to draw out a folded envelope from Valerie's front pocket. *To My Daughter, My Love*, it read.

"What's this, Mom?" Chapel said, pushing the fly away hairs from Valerie's cheeks so Chapel could see her clear, green eyes. "This is not goodbye, Mom. This is not."

"Yes," Valerie said with a sad smile. "For now."

"Don't say that," Chapel said, a sob pushing out of her body and making her quake "I love you. I love you and I'm so sorry. I wish I—"

"Shhh, baby," Valerie whispered. "It's . . . okay." Then her eyes got round and unfocused. A breath got caught in her chest and Chapel shook her shoulders.

"Mom. *Mom!*"

Valerie's mouth opened and closed twice before a small smile stretched the stained edges of her lips. She coughed and it was an awful sound. Splatters of blood blew from between her teeth and stained her ivory chin and neck.

"My life . . . my gift to you," Valerie wheezed. "Together . . . on the other side." Her eyelids fluttered closed. "I've seen it," she whispered on her last breath.

Then she was gone.

CHAPTER THIRTY-FIVE

My Darling Daughter,

The first time I saw this scene, I was twenty years old and pregnant with you. I didn't understand it then—and have had many different versions of saving you from Bellum and Battacharya played in my dreams. But I always die and you always live.

And that's all I care about.

I have made many mistakes as a mother, but you have somehow managed to become a beautiful woman inside and out. I am so proud of you.

I have held myself away from you. For selfish and selfless reasons. But, in the end, it served you well. You must keep the fact that you are a Seer a secret as long as possible. Tell no one else.

Don't be sad for me, Chapel. In these last few weeks, God has given me many revelations in my dreams.

I have seen you as a happy bride.

I have seen you as a gentle mother.

I have seen you as a brave soldier.

I have seen you as a strong leader.

I have seen you love, fight, give, and live.

You are free to choose now. My ending is the beginning of your story. Write joy with the pen of your life. Write generosity. Write life.

I love you,
Mom.

* * * *

Valerie Taylor was buried on a warm May morning whose beauty was in direct contrast to the cold black grief that Chapel felt sitting dormant inside of her.

Zay stood behind her, a hand on her shoulder. When the casket lid thudded shut, she turned, pressing her face into his navy shirt.

"I'm here," Zay said. "I'm here."

Chapel pulled away, not bothering to wipe her nose or eyes. She wanted everyone to see the ache on her face.

After years of mother and daughter denying each other their emotions, it was time to stop pretending. To unstop the bottle of feelings that she had carefully staved off. She longed to pour them out, like the freshly dug Georgia clay in front of her.

The rest of the afternoon was a blur of too-sweet desserts and crumbled tissues. Chapel sat on the sofa in Todd's house, receiving faceless and nameless guests that her numb mind refused to compute.

Gone. Dead. The concept lost meaning in the wake of her pain.

It felt like Chapel had plummeted into a lake of frozen water, weighed down by chains of disbelief and anger that cut into her skin. She feared she might drown.

When they had finally moved the truck that blocked the loading dock, Zay was the first to find Chapel. She was laying with her face pressed against Valerie's chest, soaked in her blood.

They'd had to pry her off her mother's dead body. Since then she had barely slept or eaten.

Michael had taken one look at the scene and turned around and left. Chapel hadn't seen him since.

Todd and the twins had arrived that morning and Chapel had spent the day watching Disney movies with Charlotte and Shae, trying to field questions about death and pain to little girls who should only know goodness and safety.

She still believed in God. But she had some questions of her own for Him. Some questions that burned in her chest like wildfire.

"Want one of my pain pills?" Erica asked. She was sitting to Chapel's left, looking uncomfortable and sore.

Timmy, to her right, sighed. "Erica. Felony. You hate how you look in orange."

Chapel put her hand on her friend's knee. "I think what Timmy's trying to say is, thanks, Jersey, but I don't think turning you into a drug dealer is the answer."

Erica shrugged. "Suit yourself." She popped a chalky white oval into her mouth. "Elbow me if I start snoring."

They were calling Erica's shooting a random act of violence. Chapel and Timmy hadn't had time to discuss when or if they'd tell Erica the truth. Chapel wasn't sure what she wanted.

In all areas of her life.

As if on cue, Gabe appeared. He shuffled by the two guards at the front door, looking handsome and shy in his navy suit and tie. His eyes shifted around the room until they rested on her. The worried wrinkles at his temples contracted, and he tilted his head softly to the side.

Home, his expression seemed to say. And that thought plucked a chord in her that made her neck sweat.

"Hi," he mouthed, full lips turning down.

"Hi," she mouthed back.

She felt Zay's fingertips come down on her shoulder from behind. Gently. Possessively. It annoyed her.

She had never been annoyed with Zay before. Not like this.

Chapel scooted forward and stood. If she wanted to talk to Gabe at her mother's wake, she would talk to Gabe at her mother's wake.

She walked to where Gabe stood, just inside the foyer. He handed her a single white rose, eyes searching her face. "You haven't slept," he said.

She tried to turn her lips up into a smile, but it felt more like a grimace.

"Thank you," she said. Her voice sounded foreign in her own ears. Scratchy and exhausted like an old record. "How are you?"

She had told everyone the truth about Cess. That she was a plant to distract Gabe from his visions of Chapel. It had broken her heart to think about Gabe receiving the information. She hadn't been there when he heard it, but she saw the truth of his regret radiating from his expression.

Gabe lowered his red-rimmed eyes. "I'm fine, Chapel. Don't worry about me."

"I do," she said quietly. "Worry about you."

His eyes fell across her face and he shook his head slightly. She knew what he was thinking: *What if?*

But Chapel was learning that life wasn't defined by its what-ifs. Life was defined by choices and consequences to those choices. The desire to press rewind and make another decision was as old as time itself. But the desire was also a waste. It was a labyrinth of nostalgia that Chapel didn't want to get trapped in.

There were quiet footsteps behind her and Chapel smelled Zay's aftershave.

"Thanks for coming," she told Gabe.

His eyes didn't move from her face. "I wouldn't have missed it for anything. Anything," he repeated.

To her right, the front door swung open. The breeze from the action stirred the loose strings of hair that had fallen from her knotted bun, and Chapel turned its direction.

On the other side of the two guards stood Daniel.

"That's her," someone yelled from outside. "It's the daughter."

A string of shudders sounded as cameras began their flashing frenzy.

A senator's wife murdered—her killer on the loose. It had made national headlines. Though Chapel knew what Todd didn't: The Invisibles had been contacted and two men in black suits had shown up and injected Chary with something in the back of her neck.

Now, she awaited trial for the murder and attempted murder of a Genex. Two deeds which, the way Chapel understood it, were punishable by death.

"Did you see who shot your mother?" someone yelled.

"Did your mother really save your life?" shouted another.

Immediately, Zay shielded Chapel with his body, pulling her out of the way.

Over his shoulder, Chapel saw Daniel push through, closing the door behind him.

"I'm sorry," Daniel began. "The guards—"

"Get out," Zay interrupted. And though he said it softly, the words were razor sharp.

Daniel lifted a hand. "I'm not here to argue. I'm here to bring news." From his coat pocket, he pulled out his cell phone. After typing in his password, he handed it to Chapel. Daniel ran a hand down the side of his face. He looked exhausted. "It's a memo from the Invisibles."

Chapel held the cool rectangle in her hands.

To Whom It May Concern,

Donita Battacharya was found dead in her holding facility at 0700 this morning. Her trial has been removed from the docket, and her body disposed of. There will be no further investigation into the matter.

Chapel's eyes burned, though she didn't know why. Shouldn't she want her mother's murderer to die?

"Who did it?" she whispered.

Daniel lifted one stiff shoulder. "I don't know. It doesn't appear that the Invisibles care." His pale eyes traced the outline of the room.

Zay still stood beside her, but everyone else had shifted away from them.

Daniel returned his gaze to Chapel. "I just wanted to tell you in person how sorry I am for your loss. Family is . . . sacred," he said.

It sounded like he forced that last word out with effort.

"I appreciate it," Chapel said.

Daniel took his phone back and fidgeted with the rubber edge of its case. "There's more."

Chapel felt her eyebrows press down. "What?"

The front door opened again, and this time it was Jackson. His eyes looked wide and landed immediately on Zay.

Daniel glanced over his shoulder, then back at Chapel. "Is there somewhere the four of us can talk?"

Chapel led them to her bathroom where she turned on two faucets, the bathtub, and the shower to cover up the sound of their conversation. Zay knew that Todd had once bugged his own house during his election, but Jackson and Daniel didn't.

Neither acted surprised.

The four of them stood with heads close together. Daniel motioned for Jackson to begin.

"It appears change is on the horizon," he said. Chapel noticed he kept rising up and down on his heels. So very un-Jacksonlike.

"What is it?" Zay said.

"There's a hearing being held next weekend in D.C.," Jackson said. "A hearing that would call into question the divisions of Genex society."

Zay's head jerked back. Apparently, that wasn't what he was expecting. "What do you mean?"

Daniel leaned forward. "All Directors are being asked to submit their formal opinions on how we currently operate." His eyes held Chapel's. "There's talk of The Invisibles disbanding Bellum and Thanatos. Of bringing Genexes under one order."

"Just like my dad wanted to?" Chapel asked.

Jackson lifted both eyebrows. "Actually, *exactly* like that."

Zay ran a hand down his jaw. "This is huge."

"Yes," Jackson said. "Very."

Daniel tilted his head. "Your mother's murder must have swayed someone with influence."

Chapel shook her head. "My mom didn't know any Invisibles. I mean—I don't *think* she did. She hadn't had much contact with the Genex world since my dad left."

Chapel felt Zay's gaze linger on her face for a long moment. Just slightly, the edges of his eyes creased, and she knew he was thinking something specific. But she also knew that if he wanted to share, he would.

She let it go.

"Why are you telling us this?" she asked.

Daniel looked at her. "I wanted you to know that your mother's death was not in vain. That, . . . " He paused and licked his lips. "That even if our government doesn't change anything, that it's made them *think*."

Chapel looked to Jackson. What was his reason? His pale complexion and waxen skin told her: *Fear.*

And there it was.

Jackson was afraid. Afraid to lose his family. Afraid to lose his station. Afraid to lose Isaiah. And his side had been the one she'd battled to be on.

Chapel felt sick. She barely made it to the sink in time to empty her stomach, her body heaving until she saw black dots behind her tired eyes.

* * * *

Later that night, Chapel burrowed her face into her mother's pillow. Zay had brought it to her along with some of her clothes. She slept in the room in Jackson's house she always used—ever since the first night she found out what she was.

Genex.

Different.

Special.

Cursed.

Blessed.

It was all there. The good with the bad. Only lately, it felt like a lot of bad.

She tossed and turned in the tangled sheets, trying to find a position that felt comfortable. But she couldn't stay still. Her insides felt jumbled. She felt cramped and achy and restless.

So, she gave up.

Chapel dressed quietly, slipping on a sweatshirt and sneakers over her pajamas. She moved soundlessly through the house. Her hand was on the doorknob when Zay's voice came from the top of the stairs.

"Wait."

She turned and watched him walk down, anticipating a lecture, a warning, a pitying look. But like Zay often did, he gave her just what she needed: in one hand, the Shelby's keys, in the other, her Smith and Wesson.

She held up the keys. "Are you sure?" she whispered. "You just got her back yesterday."

He pulled her to him with a lazy hand at her hip. His lips, warm from sleep, brushed her jaw. "I took the safety off."

Then he kissed her on the mouth drowsily, ran his nose up and down the length of hers before turning and going upstairs.

It was like the car knew the way. Chapel drove with her head full of static, and when the headlights flashed over the yellow chipped siding, Chapel knew what she would find inside.

Her father sat on the floor of the kitchen with his back against the oven and his long legs sprawled out across the cracked linoleum. His strawberry-blonde hair was sticking up in the back, and Chapel noted that the black pants and shirt he wore were the same as the day Valerie died.

He hadn't showered.

There was a white-blonde smattering of hair on his chin and face—a face that looked suddenly slacker. Older. Like the last four days had shaved years off his life.

Michael didn't react when she walked into the room. He just took a long drink from the bottle in his right hand and used his arm to sop up the excess on his lips.

Chapel walked in and stood at his feet.

"Hey," she said.

He blinked a few more times than normal, but that was his only response.

Chapel slid down the fridge across from him and pulled her knees to her chest. She remained quiet for a length of time. Ten minutes. Maybe an hour. She wasn't sure.

She sat silently across from the man who helped give her life, and stared at his shell. She'd never seen someone so hollow. Except maybe Hunter, after he'd burned her last year.

Finally, in the silvery shadows of the shifting moonlight, her father's eyes found hers.

"I'm not . . . a . . . drunk," he said. His speech was deliberate. It sounded like every constant and vowel was forced through space not quite wide enough for their proper release.

Chapel nodded her head slowly. "Okay."

Michael pulled both cheeks into his mouth and bit. "My daughter hates me. My wife is dead. The boy I raised as if he were my own is rallying troops against me." He whipped his head back quickly and slammed it into the oven, rattling the wall and making Chapel jump. "I am nothing."

Chapel felt the painful prickle of tears rush to her eyes. It burned, and it spread from her sinuses into her throat and neck.

She clenched her teeth, opening her lips enough to spit out, "Don't do that."

Michael's light eyebrows tugged down briefly, but he lifted his top lip in a slight snarl.

"No." Chapel's voice was stronger now. She pushed from her position on the floor. A white-hot rage flashed through her trembling body. Chapel lifted her finger to point. "You don't get to sit in here and feel sorry for yourself."

Michael stared at her, face expressionless. Then his lips tightened over the lip of the bottle and he took a long swig.

Chapel's body snapped. She jerked the liquor from his hand and used the thin neck of the bottle to slam it against the lip of the countertop.

The glass shattered against the laminate, and the clear shards sprang in the air like raindrops. The amber liquid sloshed down her wrist and arm, dripping down the cabinets in streaks like dirty tears.

The angry *CRACK* echoed in the absence of all other sounds, splintering the false sense of calm, splintering her control.

"You *left* us!" she yelled, spinning back to him. "You left me. You left her. For a good cause, I get it. But you still *left!* And now you're sitting in *my* kitchen floor and all you can do is say *you* are nothing? What about me? What about my *sisters?* What about *Mom?*"

Michael used his left hand to try and push himself into a standing position. He misjudged his body weight once, twice, three times before he was able to drag himself upright.

Chapel waited on him to say something. Anything. But he didn't. He just hunched his shoulders and stared at her.

That only made her angrier.

"Well?" she demanded. "Say something. Anything."

"What . . . do you want me to say?" he asked lethargically. His eyelids looked heavy and he kept licking his lips nervously.

"That you're sorry?" Chapel fisted her hands at her sides.

"I'm sorry," he mumbled.

Chapel groaned. She took two steps forward and grabbed his shoulders. She meant to do it so he would look at her, but she ended up just pushing him instead. She wanted to hurt him, to *break* him like he'd broken her every day that he chose to stay away from her.

"I want you to say that you wish you had decided differently," she yelled, pushing him again. "That you would change it. That you missed *me*. That you want me. That you love me. That you—"

Michael's arm wrapped around her, flattening her fists against her sides. She thought he was restraining her at first, but then she felt him dip his head beside hers. He was hugging her.

She had never hugged her father before. Not that she remembered. It was such a shock that it was like water on the fire that had been burning inside of her. She didn't return the embrace, but she grew still and quiet.

He smelled like scotch and body odor and tobacco. The rough sides of his face caught in her hair and pulled at it. He was holding her too tightly.

But she didn't care.

Chapel felt the ropes of her control burning as they slipped through her hands. She let them go, with her cheek smashed painfully against Michael's chest, and she let herself fall apart.

He didn't say anything. He didn't brush a hand down her hair. He didn't even relax the grip he had on her. He just stood still, his stale breath at the top of her head, while she cried until she couldn't make any more tears.

When finally he stepped away, Chapel used the edge of her shirt to mop up her face. Michael just stood awkwardly in the middle of the kitchen, staring out the window over the sink.

"Where are you sleeping?" Chapel asked.

He shrugged. "I've been sleeping on the floor here."

"You should come to Jackson's," she said. "Or Gabe's. Or a hotel."

Michael shrugged. But then his eyes touched hers. "Would that make you feel better?"

It was her turn to shrug. "I don't want you choking on your own vomit and dying, too."

Michael pushed both hands through his hair. He paused, tilting his nose down to his armpit. "My God. I smell like cat urine."

Chapel wiped her arm beneath her nose. "You really do."

"Okay." He sighed. "I'll go to a hotel."

They looked at each other for a long, wary moment. Chapel wasn't sure what to do or say, but she was exhausted. She look a step toward the hallway that led to the foyer.

"Chapel?"

She paused at the sound of her name. His eyes studied his feet. She could tell he was trying to find the right words for whatever came next.

"I *am* sorry," he said. "But I don't wish I had chosen differently."

She swallowed the hurt that his words caused. He wasn't finished.

"I had a choice, yes," he said, nodding, looking at her now. "But it was an impossible one. It was a choice between honor and love. It's a choice you'll be asked to make, too."

Chapel tilted her head and studied her father. Dejected. Alone. Hard. Sad. "Then I'll choose love," she said. "Because look what honor gets you."

She got all the way to the front door before he spoke again.

"You won't," he said. "If you choose to be a leader, you will choose honor. You're too much like me. Too much like your mother."

A thought occurred to Chapel. "Daniel came by the wake today."

Michael shifted his weight from one foot to the other. "What did he say?"

Chapel relayed the quiet conversation she'd had just a few short hours ago. By the time she had finished, Michael's entire body had gone rigid.

"You're sure?" he asked.

She nodded.

"And he said the meeting was soon?"

"Next weekend. In D.C."

Michael nodded again. "Good," he said after a minute. "This is . . . " His eyes looked at hers. Something shimmered beneath them. Hope? "This is good," he said.

Chapel put her hand on the doorknob. "You're going, aren't you?" she asked. "To D.C."

"Yes." He answered without hesitation. "I have to be in that meeting."

Chapel lifted an eyebrow. "Seriously? You think The Invisibles are going to let you in their meeting?"

Michael dipped his chin to chest. "I have a contact who owes me a favor. Plus, I'm sure they've heard I'm back from the dead. And know what I've been up to."

"But you'll see them, right? The Invisibles?"

"Yes. But they hear testimonies from non-Invisibles all the time. They just slate their identities from attendees' minds."

Chapel nodded slowly. A meeting with the Invisibles? She needed to be there. She needed to go. Her love life had been tampered with. Maybe irrecoverably. Her best friend had been implicated in a world that put him in grave danger. Erica had been shot. Her mother had been murdered. All in the name of the factions—*who were supposedly on the same team.*

"I want to come, too," she said. "I'd like to try and speak to someone. Anyone."

"What about school?"

Now he wanted to be a father. "Next week is my last week," she sighed. "But I've already taken my finals. My teachers let me do them early after—" She hated to say it, *Mom died.* So she didn't.

"Okay," Michael said. "I'll take you with me."

"Okay, then," she repeated. At least she had a plan. She felt a little better.

Michael shook his head. "I can't believe you won over Daniel Sevawn. I hate to say it, but you got your charm from me."

Chapel took a moment to process that name. "Sevawn? As in . . . "

Michael nodded. "As in Dr. Sevawn. The psycho behind Project Exception. Yes, Daniel is his son."

Chapel shook her head. "Wow. That's so weird." She thought of his gray eyes, of his dark hair and cool demeanor. "Daniel reminds me of Zay for some reason."

Michael's chin jerked to the side. "Well, that's because he's Isaiah's brother, Chapel."

Everything. Stopped.

"Wait. What?"

Michael's eyes scrolled the length of her face. Apparently, her shock read like a phrase, because his complexion paled.

"You did know that," he said. "Right?"

Chapel's chest felt like a balloon about to burst. "No. I didn't."

"I see." Michael slipped his hands into his pockets. He pressed his lips together. "We all have secrets, Chapel."

The balloon tightened. "Yeah," she sighed. "Some more than others."

CHAPTER THIRTY-SIX

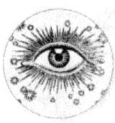

Chapel's last week of high school flew off the calendar like dandelions blown into the wind.

Erica returned to classes, and Timmy escorted her from door to door like her legs had been shot and not her back. She'd been lucky, they said. No permanent damage.

Chapel returned to work at Back Porch and tried not to let the lingering gazes of pity pierce her carefully constructed façade of *okay*-ness. That meant never looking Thomas in the eye, or many of her regulars, but she never broke down in public. In her car, in the shower, and once in the bathroom at school—that was all she allowed herself to grieve.

Chapel hadn't the emotional energy to bring up her conversation with her father to Zay. It hurt her, yes, to learn that he'd kept his father's identity a secret from her. One day, she'd confront him about it. Just not *today*.

Then, on a hot Thursday evening, Chapel and two hundred other students sat in hard plastic chairs in the center of the dusty Bennett Park fairgrounds and waited to graduate.

Chapel's heart clipped inside her chest when Timmy's name was called to give his speech as Valedictorian of their class.

She watched as his brown penny loafers crossed the stage and stopped in front of a podium draped in the purple, black, and white of the Bennett Park Jaguars.

He didn't look nervous. He didn't look pale or green or even ambivalent. He placed a single sheet of paper in front of him and paused a moment to sweep his eyes over the crowd.

When they rested, they were on her. He took a deep breath.

"I know I'm supposed to get up here and tell you what a great group of students we are, but I'm not going to do that," he said. The audience chuckled. So did Chapel. "Yes, our future is as bright as we make it. Yes, we all have potential. Yes, some of you sitting in front of me could be a president, or a rock star, or a scientist, or a pastor. But instead of looking too far forward, I want to take a moment to look back at the past."

Timmy placed one hand on the podium, and motioned to the audience with the other. He looked like a natural. He looked strong and composed. He looked like a man.

"I know what a lot of you are probably thinking. We've grown up hearing that we shouldn't dwell on the past. That we should try and forget our past. And, in a lot of cases, that we should run from our past. But honestly, I think that's a bunch of crap."

Chapel joined in the laughter that rose around her. Timmy continued.

"Here's what my past taught me. My past taught me that lying to your dad about who broke the kitchen window will get you grounded for a month. My past taught me that sushi from a gas station is never, never a good idea. My past taught me that cheat codes take the fun out of video games. Except when there's *no* way you'd beat said video game without them. Because my past also taught me that winning feels good, and losing feels bad."

Timmy paused, his gaze on Chapel, before going on.

"My past has taught me that *nothing* feels better than being known by someone. And not only being known by them, but being accepted by them. Nothing feels better than being given permission to be nothing but yourself."

His eyes left her face. She was glad, because she had started to cry.

"My past taught me that true friendship transcends social status. My past taught me that it's okay to take a chance on love, even if it could end badly. My past taught me to study hard, to pause and enjoy the good moments, and my past taught me to forgive."

Timmy stopped speaking, and Chapel watched as his Adam's apple rose and fell several times before he opened his mouth again. His voice came out sounding slightly strained.

"But the most important thing my past taught me is that our future isn't nearly as valuable as our *right now*. Because tomorrow isn't a promise to any of us. And I'm tired of living every day, wondering when my life will start."

Timmy touched the tassel at the side of head. "I'm tired of waiting," he said, moving the string across his face to the other side of his black cap. "I choose today. This hour. This minute. I bring my past with me, the good and the bad, and I don't look at it as baggage. I look at it as luggage. Luggage that contains every lesson, every memory, every lunch, every sunny day, every loss, every win, every laugh, every embarrassment, every challenge, every *thing* that has brought me to this glorious present."

A guy in the front—Logan, Chapel thought—let out a whistle.

"Heck yeah, Valentine," someone else shouted.

Timmy smiled, blushing for the first time, but his gaze remained on the audience.

"Class of 2013," he said, voice booming over the speakers, "it's been an honor sharing my past with you."

As Timmy walked off the stage, the crowd thundered with applause.

Surrounded by the faces she had watched shed baby fat and mature into near-adulthood, Chapel threw her cap in the air and let Logan pick her up and swing her around like he had on the football field after nearly every victory.

Before Zay had arrived, of course.

That was how Chapel's life was divided now. Before Zay and After Zay. He had changed everything. In every way. He had opened her heart and eyes and made her *feel* for the first time in her entire life.

She caught his eyes in the crowd and held them steadily. Timmy was right—her past was her past. His past was his past. But this moment? It was *theirs.* And she had to stop spending so much time in the innumerable possibilities of the future.

Had her mother's death taught her nothing about the transient quality of this life?

* * * *

The next night, Thomas opened Back Porch late for a graduation party for Chapel and Erica. Todd came, even though he'd only been back in D.C. for a few days. He spent most of the night in the corner on his cell phone.

For once, Chapel didn't judge him. With purple bags under his eyes, a rumpled suit, and waxen skin, he looked, if possible, worse than Michael had last week drunk and dirty on the kitchen floor.

Chapel spent most of the night playing with the twins— who were up way later than they should have been— watching Zay give them piggyback rides and soaking in every detail of their perfect faces and giggles.

He caught her staring at him once and winked at her. "Love you," he mouthed.

"Love you, too."

And she did.

The food was delicious; Motown wafted through the ceiling speakers, and Thomas even broke out a few bottles of wine with the adults. Everyone lingered. It was almost as if real life was suspended inside that clapboard cottage, and they were all allowed a brief respite from the blistering pain of the outside world.

It was after eleven when Chapel pulled away from the crowd. Her flight left early, and she wanted to wind down before they returned to Jackson's. She had been taking sleeping pills all week long to go to bed, and she was afraid she'd be too groggy the next day if she took one tonight.

Chapel slipped through the kitchen and out the back door to the pad of pavement where she and Erica used to take their breaks. She paused as the steel door clicked behind her, sensing she wasn't alone.

"It's just me," Gabe's accented voice said quietly. He pushed from the shadows of the brick retaining wall. "Sorry, I wasn't lurking. I was just trying to get the courage to come inside."

Chapel joined him in the darkness and slid to the ground. He lowered himself beside her.

"Why would you need courage?" she asked.

She could barely make out his features, but she felt him stir beside her. His hand came down over hers, and he tugged it to his heart. Beneath her fingers, it sped.

"Because of that," he said quietly.

She pulled her hand away gently, swallowing. "Gabe, I—"

"I know," he said. "I know. You love Zay. It's my fault, and I don't blame you." Gabe leaned forward, casting his face in the wan lamplight above them. He looked handsome. "But I also know," he said, "that we are supposed to be together."

Now Chapel's heart sped up. "In versions of our destinies," she corrected.

Gabe shook his head. "No." He tilted his head. "Have you not been dreaming, lately?"

"Sleeping pills," Chapel said. "They knock me out. No dreams."

Gabe touched his lips with his tongue. "I have," Gabe said. "I've been Seeing us again." He shifted, turning his body toward hers. "Chapel, they were keeping us apart for a reason."

"What do you know?" she asked. He seemed sure of something.

"Nothing for sure." His hand came up and brushed down her cheek. It was a loving gesture, and it made her shiver. "But I promise you—I will find out. And after I do, I'll win you back."

EPILOGUE

Rough hands ran along her sides, legs, and back. When the four guards surrounding her deemed her unarmed, Chapel was ushered through a set of double doors.

"Where's Michael Ryan?" she asked the man at her elbow. "He and I came here together. We were separated after the first round of tests."

Michael's contact had pulled through. He and Chapel had both been granted admittance to the Invisibles' meeting, based on the fact that both Michael and Victoria had given up their lives in the name of faction violence.

Valerie, literally, and Michael figuratively. And Chapel, as a result, was seen as a prime example of why the factions had to be dismantled. Not only were they given clearance to attend, but they were asked to prepare a three-minute talk about their experience.

Chapel's hands felt heavy and sticky.

"All Genex guests will enter at staggered intervals," the man answered her. "Your turn is soon."

Chapel figured it was a security measure. She'd already been through seven checkpoints since she'd arrived.

A few minutes later, the man punched in an elaborate code to a keypad, pressed his fingers to its center, and spoke her name into a microphone. The thick sheet of metal before her slid sideways.

"Whoa." Chapel couldn't suck the dumbfounded word back in her mouth.

The room she entered was a perfect circle. It was about the size of Bennett Park's lunchroom, with a raised stage in its center.

The perimeter of the stage was hugged by a shiny wooden high-top counter, with too many stools to count—probably fifty—spaced out among them. On each stool sat a man or woman.

The Invisibles, Chapel guessed by their position. And she was a little disappointed by how *normal* they all looked.

They ranged in age from early twenties to hunched over with wrinkles. They were dressed in clothes as casual as jeans, and one lady with pink hair wore a black cocktail dress with a ruched sleeve that had a bunch of rosettes at its center.

There was a pocket of sunken chairs at the head of the stage, and Chapel was ushered down into it. There were probably thirty people waiting. She was the last to join, and sat beside her father in a worn leather chair.

"You okay?" he asked.

She jerked her head. "Fine. You?"

"This isn't my first time here."

"What should I expect?" she asked.

He shrugged. "I don't know. They slate you before you even leave the pit."

Chapel wanted to probe more, but she was cut off by a female voice coming from the center of the stage.

"Now, now," she said. She sounded much younger than she looked, and she held up her hand while the room grew quiet. "I know we're all *anxious* to get these proceedings started."

Around her, the atmosphere grew still and expectant. Chapel soaked in every detail, knowing it would be washed from her brain before she went to sleep.

"For our guests," the lady said, addressing the pit, "My name is Monique Gumbel, and I am your hostess today. We will begin our meeting with a debrief of our current state of affairs. Then you will be given a turn to share as you are called upon." Monique lifted her shoulders back up and looked at her peers. "Would everyone in the room please rise as we welcome our leader, the President of the Invisibles. Mr. President? The floor is yours."

One by one, each Invisible slipped from their chair and stood, clapping their hands. They looked so *happy* at the mention of their leader. So excited.

Chapel craned her neck to see who was taking the stage, but all she saw was a gray pair of trousers and shiny back shoes. Until everyone sat down, she wouldn't be able to see the President of the Invisibles.

The applause was thunderous and ongoing. Chapel gave up at a certain point, letting her hands fall to her sides.

Seriously? she thought. *How great can the guy be?*

After two full minutes of cheering, the roar in the room subsided. Everyone around her bent back into their seats, and Chapel followed behind.

She was bending down to adjust her shoe when a familiar voice echoed through the auditorium.

"Hello," it said. And Chapel's heart stopped beating.

Her eyes lifted slowly, skeptically, and looked straight into the face of the man standing on stage.

"My name is Todd Taylor," he said. "And I am the President of The Invisibles."

ACKNOWLEDGEMENTS

Thank you,

-Heavenly Father. I stand in awe of your great love.

-Benny. You believe in me more than I deserve. Without your support, *Expertus* would be nothing but a page of notes (that make no sense) in my cellphone.

-Lilah and Esmae. You give me two reasons every day to chase my dreams. I pray one day you chase yours until you catch them.

-Jessica, Taylor, and Cole. No one can understand a person in the exact way a sibling can. Thank you for being people I'd choose to be around even if we weren't related.

-Mom, Brian, and Marc. From keeping my girls so I can work, to cooking for my family several nights a week … I'm pretty sure I owe you something significant. Like an organ or my next-born child. Will you settle for this Thank You and a gift card to Applebee's?

-The Crawshaws. How did I get so lucky with my in-laws? Thank you for loving me like I am yours. And thank you for your unending prayers and support.

-My friends. Thank you for knowing that I am weird, and loving me anyway.

-Browns Bridge Community Church. Your grace gives me a place to belong and improve.

1

-All my beta-readers! Natalie, Angela, Kristen, Kathy, and Echo, I can't thank you enough. Seriously—THANK YOU.

-Brenda. Your encouragement (not to mention the HUGE box of Sour Patch Kids you sent me) was sometimes the only fuel in my tank.

-Jennifer, my editor. Your thoughtful considerations sharpened this manuscript to the novel it is today!

-READERS! Every email, Facebook message, Tweet, and Instagram comment you have left has been screenshotted and put in a folder on my computer. I don't take you for granted, and I am so deeply humbled you choose to read one word I've written.

About the Author

Holly was born and raised in a small town in North Georgia. The third of four children, Holly grew up telling stories to get herself out of trouble. When she was eight years old, she penned her first publication: a newspaper called Sunny Dayz News. While she didn't sell any actual copies, her sympathetic grandmother did peruse the edition at least once.

When Holly isn't dreaming up new plot lines for her next book, she enjoys breakfasting at Picnic Café in Dahlonega, Georgia with her husband and their two daughters.

Email Holly your favorite scene or line from TEMPUS:

HollyLaurenWrites@gmail.com

Visit her blog for information on upcoming projects:

http://hollylaurenwrites.wordpress.com